AVRIL MARIA SERENE

SIX DEGREES FROM KILLING BRIAN

A DEBRA ANN WYNN MYSTERY

AMS MEDIA

AMS Media
1646 East North Street #1H
Springfield, Missouri 65803-4357

First printing, March 2025

https://AvrilMSerene.com

Printed in the United States of America

10 9 8 7 6 5 4 3 2 1

ISBN (paperback): 979-8-9928602-2-1

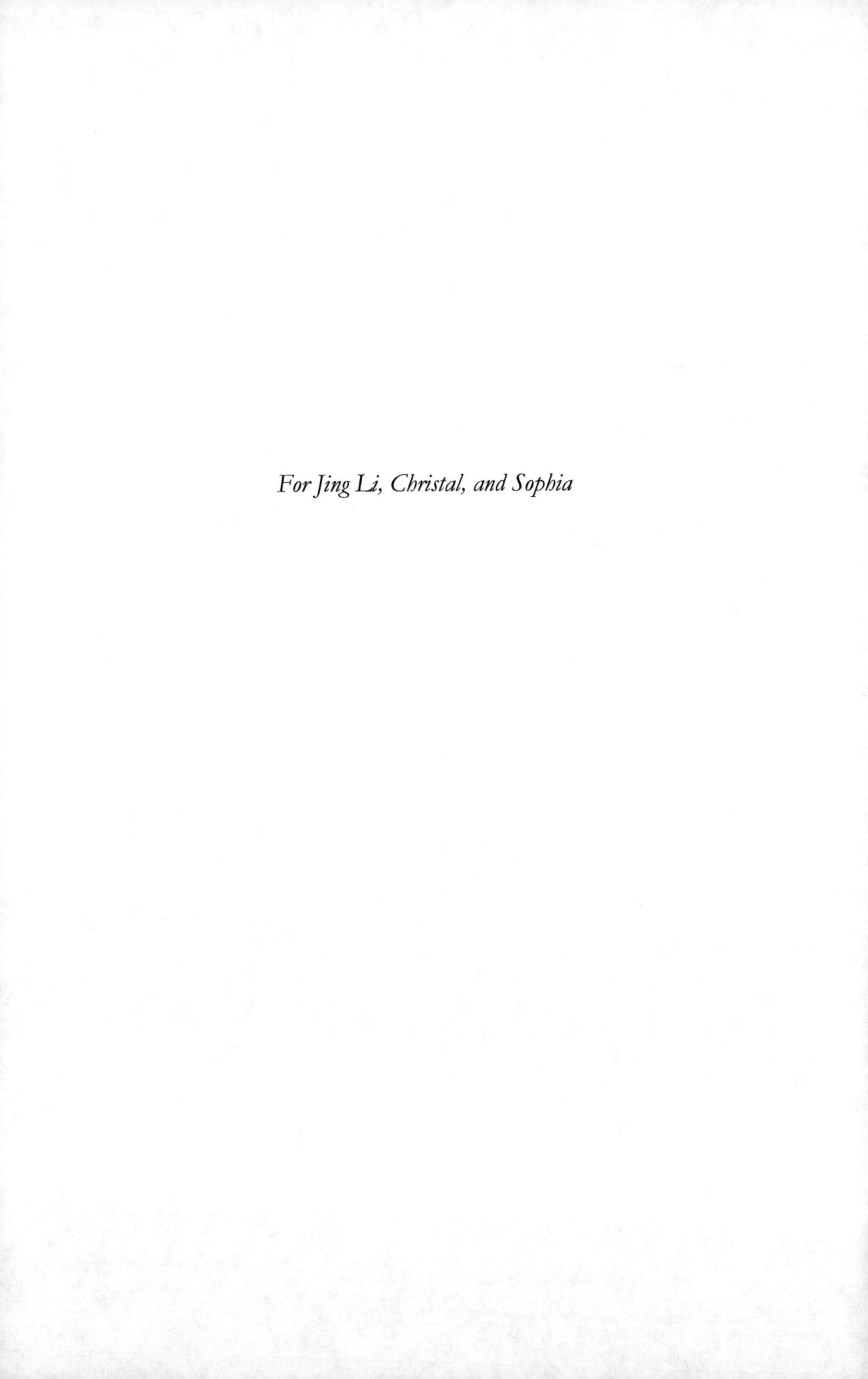

For Jing Li, Christal, and Sophia

I love quotations because it is a joy to find thoughts one might have, beautifully expressed with much authority by someone recognized wiser than oneself.
—Marlene Dietrich

PROLOGUE

NINE MONTHS AGO

The sunset slowly faded across the neighborhoods abutting the Navy base off San Diego Bay. As the sodium-vapor streetlamps flickered on, their amber glow projected wide, oval arcs onto the potholes and cracks in the asphalt. A nondescript gray Toyota Corolla slowly slinked along between the curbs of Dalbergia Street, littered with beer cans, broken liquor bottles, discarded fast-food wrappers, and the occasional used condom or needle. A white Valentine's Day teddy bear, sitting sideways on the car's dash, peered through its windshield, drawing raised eyebrows from onlookers. Creeping forward leisurely in a southeasterly direction toward the intersection with Vesta, the lone occupant randomly slowed for brief exchanges with female pedestrians along the roadway.

Dalbergia bisected a seedy mixed-industrial area defaced with gang graffiti, the occasional banger or pimp prowling the semidarkness. This strip of asphalt was well-known among sailors and locals as a place to pick up professionals plying the sex trade. The unhurried Corolla seemed obvious as it cruised for the working girl who could satisfy the driver's tastes. Still, it wasn't alone — several others on the street were doing the same.

The car slowed further, pulling to the curb in front of a silicone-enhanced, diminutive blonde. Attractive from a distance, she looked older than her competition when closer.

The shadowy figure behind the wheel, wearing reflective Ray-Bans and a ball cap, pressed the door switch to open the passenger-side window. As the hooker leaned in, her come-on smile relaxed when she saw her customer was a woman. "Sure, honey, I can do girl-on-girl. What kind of action are you looking for tonight?"

"It's for a threesome, nothing kinky, straight sex...," the driver replied.

"For how long?"

"Two hours."

"Me and you look the same; your man must like a certain type. Okay, five hundred. And the guy wears a condom."

"Done." The driver peeled five one-hundred-dollar notes from a roll she pulled out of her purse. As the hooker grabbed for the money through the window, the driver yanked back the sheaf of bills.

"No, sweetheart, that ain't happening. Get in, pull the door closed, and lock it. Once we're rolling, you get the five hundred."

"*Jesus!* I wouldn't rip you off," the working girl protested even as she complied.

Pulling away from the curb, the woman at the Corolla's wheel handed over the promised money. Her passenger didn't complain when the car cut onto a dark side street. The sedan swung into an alleyway beside an old brick building, rolling to a stop just past the last overflowing bin in a row of dumpsters at the backstreet's end. Next to the garbage bags and stacks of wooden pallets, rusting steel steps climbed the side of the building, leading to a battered, gray metal door lit by a naked bulb.

"We're going in there." The driver pointed toward the entrance as she exited the Corolla.

The prostitute opened her car door. Hesitating, she wrinkled her nose at the stench of urine, dead rats, and rotting food that drifted her way. As she gingerly stepped out into the alley, shadows cast by a stack of pallets blocked the light, obscuring her vision.

Suddenly, a fast-moving figure leaped from the darkness behind.

Startled by a flash impression of wraparound shades and a hoodie, she shrieked, twisting away as the car door swung closed.

Three feet of two-by-four swung like a baseball bat slammed into the back of her skull. Driven forward by the impact, her head ricocheted off the Toyota's roof, snapping her neck. Splintered wood and splattered blood stippled her attacker and the filth around them.

She collapsed to the ground with a groan, the sudden movement jerking her right foot sideways. A stiletto heel punched through the slat of a pallet protruding past the end of the garbage bin.

Her leg bent out from under her awkwardly as all her weight came crashing down. The echo chamber between the buildings amplified the sickening crack of breaking bone and the thud of her braincase on the pavement.

Then, silence.

Her assailant, an older man with thinning hair and a protruding gut, loomed over the lifeless body for a moment, resting the weapon on his shoulder. Seeing no movement, he flipped the board by its end into the dumpster behind, yanked off his sunglasses, and threw back his hood. Kneeling, he pincered his victim's wrist with forefinger and thumb to feel for a pulse.

"She's gone," he announced in the general direction of the woman in the ball cap, now leaning on the trunk of the Corolla. She'd recorded the assault on a digital minicam behind her purse, out of the killer's line of sight; she deftly slid it back into her bag as he stood up. If her partner saw the camera, he didn't acknowledge it.

"*Goddammit!*" he cursed. He was looking down at the jagged edge of the dead woman's shattered fibula. The broken bone jutted out from the side of her leg, and blood flowed freely in fading pulses. "That's going to be too fucking obvious. We'll be carrying her around by her feet and armpits. If we drop her, someone will notice."

He paused, pondering their next move.

"*Son of a bitch...* and she was perfect, too. The right height and weight. Shit. Doesn't matter now. We'll have to get another one."

The man grabbed the fallen working girl under her arms, dragging her toward the car's trunk.

"Can't we just leave her here?" The woman's voice didn't hide her irritation.

"If the street gets wind of a dead hooker, they'll all go inside for the night. It'll be harder to find her replacement. Grab the money and help me throw her in the trunk."

The man grabbed a crumpled sheet of plastic from the dumpster to wrap around the corpse. After they'd wrestled the body into the car's trunk, the man stared at it before slamming the lid closed.

"Let's try our luck on the other side of the Navy base. We need someone tonight, and we'll have to get moving. I gotta scope out the right place, away from any security cams."

Climbing into the driver's seat, he shook his head as he reassessed his priorities.

"I've got to be more careful how the new one falls when I do her."

A week had passed, and the desert air was cooling quickly as the torrid day slipped into a moonless night. Small lizards scurried to either side ahead of the advancing light sword that sliced and danced through the sparse bramble and darkness. Two men stumbled forward, struggling to carry the ends of what looked like a long sack of potatoes sagging in the middle.

"This'll be good enough," the older man at the front rasped. He unceremoniously dropped his end of the load, his gravelly voice broken up by panting gasps for air. Bending over at the waist with one hand on his knee, he used the back of the other to wipe the sweat from his forehead. Coughing and spitting, the old-timer tried to catch his breath.

The younger, shorter man at the rear laid his burden down carefully, then stepped over to a large rock a few feet away. Sitting on it, he pulled a penknife from his pocket. He began hacking away at the wire ties that suspended a folding camp shovel from a loop on his utility pouch.

The older man had tied the bulky battery-powered LED lantern to his waist. He unbuckled his leather belt and pulled it from his pants to free the lamp. Setting the flashlight to one side, the graybeard shined its beam alongside the bundle they'd brought. He traced a rough rectangle, a little larger than their lumpy package, in the rocky soil with the toe of his hiking boot.

Pulling a squashed pack of cigarettes from his soggy tee shirt pocket, the senior of the two motioned with his thumb for the shorter man to get up. Commandeering his partner's seat, he lit up as the evicted man trudged toward his assigned task with the shovel.

With only the occasional respite over the next forty-five minutes, a rhythmic *ka-chunk!* and *schwoosh* filled the still desert air. Over and over, the shovel blade bit into the hard ground, the sandy soil sliding off it onto the pile behind. As the digger labored, the faint but unmistakable odor of rotting flesh meandered through the immediate vicinity.

The younger man stood, leaning on the shovel handle to take a final break, a rough, shallow grave now carved into the desert floor. With a grunt, his comrade rose from his seat. Placing the heel of his boot in the middle of the bundle they'd lugged here, he gave it a hard push, rolling it into the hollowed-out depression. With each turn, the lantern's reflected light glinted off the duct tape at both ends. The package landed with a slight bounce, its wrappings releasing a *whoosh* of cadaverine strong enough to take the men's breath away momentarily. Holding the back of his hand up against his mouth with his head turned as far away as possible, the older man began kicking the excavated soil back over the top of the burial pit with the side of his boot. His companion scooped stones, dead leaves, and small branches he gathered from the surrounding area over the pile. Together, the two created a mound rising several inches above the ground.

"You sure the animals won't get to her?" the young man asked.

"Fuck her." The elder's voice was scornful, as if blaming her for his exertions. "She's long past giving a damn. Why should *we*?"

THE WRITINGS OF
AVRIL MARIA SERENE

CHAPTER 1

ONE MONTH AGO

My mood was one of quiet contemplation as I walked the grounds of the Crestview Memorial Gardens. I cradled a bouquet of mixed flowers for Mom, along with Eddie's favorite, a vivid yellow dandelion. Bright-red summer tanagers, mercurial and insistent, flitted about the treetops. Anna's hummingbirds and lesser goldfinches darted among the emerging leaves and beautiful blooms that lightly scented the air. It was the height of the mating season, another gorgeous spring day in late May. I was grateful for the weather, a reward that comes with living near the coast of San Diego.

As a freelance investigative journalist, I'd been working on two spec pieces with real potential for violence from sketchy characters. The brutality had spilled out from those stories to affect bystanders, including yours truly. Yesterday, I found a copy of an article slipped under my door in my secured apartment complex, with no note or other explanation. It described in detail the death of a respected acquaintance, Jeff German, who did the same sort of local investigation for the *Las Vegas Review-Journalist* that I do here. He'd been murdered two years ago by Robert Telles, a Clark County administrator Jeff had been digging into.

My challenge was that I hadn't discovered which of my two current projects had generated the not-so-subtle warning, if either. I've developed a philosophical attitude about such threats, seeing them as a badge of honor; they come with the territory if you do the job well. Still, I'd promised to shut all that out for the next twenty-four hours in deference to my emotional health. I needed to get away for a little break.

And so, this day would be a tranquil one for me. I was here because I missed my opportunity last weekend. To prevent a repeat, I'd set this breezy, early spring morning aside for personal reflection and to reminisce with my family.

After Mom and Dad adopted my younger brother, Eddie, and me twenty-nine years ago, they purchased the Wynn family plot. Dad used barter and his persuasive talents to get the tire-swing oak from my grandparents' farm moved to the head of our burial site. Uncharacteristically, Dad had rushed the work. *Had my parents known that Eddie was sick and adopted him despite the challenges?* That would have been like them. Just six months later, Eddie passed away from glioblastoma multiforme, becoming the first of our family interred here.

I needed to visit Mom and Dad today, partly to confront an unhealthy reserve of guilt and a general disappointment in myself. I'd begun skipping weekends here and there; my excuse was the extra freelance writing assignments I picked up to pay my bills. The shame came from knowing Eddie's memory required sustenance and that my parents had taught me better.

I kneeled before the marker, my fingertips gently tracing the inscriptions carved into the stone. A childhood remembrance leaped over the years, suddenly replaying the naïve confusion and fear I'd felt the first time I saw this monument. For Eddie's funeral, Dad had ordered the headstone pre-inscribed with the names and the dates known to him. A wide arch over the top bore our family name, and carved near the bottom were our first names in two columns of two rows each: Marianne, Alexander, Edward, ... A terrible thought came to me when I read "Debra Ann" beside my birth date. I yanked my father's sleeve and, sobbing in fits and starts, wailed, "Dad, does this mean I'm going to die soon?"

"No, honey." Dad lowered himself to his knees and wiped my tears softly with a tissue. "You're going to be fine and live a very long time. We wrote all our names so Eddie could look down from Heaven and know he wouldn't be alone."

"But Eddie doesn't know how to read," I worried.

"The good thing about Heaven, sweetheart," Dad replied with a reassuring smile, "is that he can do anything he wants."

And with his words, the terror subsided. The memory, however, had stuck with me all this time.

We'd buried Mom in the family plot almost four years ago. But the loving mother we once knew had left us a year before. Her Alzheimer's had progressed steadily. Each month, a little more slipped away until she no longer remembered who we were or what we meant to one another, a perverse installment plan for heartache. Mom developed a deep-seated paranoia that we — now unknown to her — were taking and misplacing her things, playing mean-spirited jokes. Her suspicions and frustrations exposed the cruelest of ironies; to us, she was no longer the person we'd once known. Six decades of warmth and familial togetherness ended with people alien to her respectfully attending a stranger's funeral. We'd lost more than our mother.

After Mom passed, my father religiously visited her every weekend and holiday. He never shirked despite the pressures of running his construction business. And when we both knew Dad's time was coming, I promised him solemnly that I'd stop by regularly.

The loss of my father hit me so much differently than that of my mother. His diagnosis was pancreatic cancer; we had only three months together after learning of his illness. Through the end, Dad was still sharp, his mind as keen as when we'd played chess when I was much younger. Had we enjoyed a game, I suspect he still could have beaten me, but I would have hoped he'd let me win, as was his habit during those long-ago days.

The hours we spent talking over those final weeks meant everything to me. But Dad was selling his business interests as a general contractor and builder, and I had the pressing demands of my career. So, though we often conversed by phone, we didn't get together those last two Saturdays or Sundays.

Then came that Tuesday, the abrupt seizure, his last breath drawn amid the organized chaos of the code blue. Before the harsh reality struck, I'd interpreted every colorful sundown as a heavenly promise of a shared sunrise to come. The self-deception came at a steep cost — I've wished *so* many times since then that he and I could reclaim those final weekends. There'd be no more opportunities.

Yet, though I'd shed tears over losing my father, I hadn't grieved the way I'd expected. I've felt as if my emotional being were hovering in a corner near the ceiling, silently watching, biding its time before getting involved. There've been moments when I thought the floodgates were about to burst open, overwhelming me into a sobbing heap of tears, hysteria, and release. But it didn't happen. I'd feel a catch in my diaphragm at some passing memory of him. Or I'd lose my thoughts for a moment, a sense of panic rising within me, but then it would subside into numbness. In the place of the soul-emptying sorrow that I felt Dad deserved from me, an overarching sadness lingered, taking away the peaks of any happiness that came my way.

Crouching down, I removed the dried-out and decaying petals and stems from the memorial vase and laid them on the ground. Unwinding the green floral tissue from around the bouquet I'd been holding, I tucked it under the old flowers.

Arranging the new blooms carefully in the vase, I placed Eddie's dandelion front and center. Just as I was standing to admire my artistry, a little gust came up and caught enough of the tissue paper to blow it several feet away. I walked over quickly and tried to pick it up, but the playful breeze carried the green paper sail several feet further from our tree. I felt foolish being teased along through the grass in my high heels by the impish impulses of the wind, but I wasn't about to desecrate the gardens with paper trash. Finally, I caught a corner of the vagabond tissue, wadding it into a ball so it couldn't escape again.

When I turned to go back, the heel of my right shoe became stuck in the soil. I'd crossed the edge of a mound of earth meant for the gravediggers to shovel in over the casket. Four orange cones at the corners marked off the open hole for the grave, and I could see the edge of a casket resting in it.

Tugging my foot to pull it away, I popped off my shoe. Suddenly, the thought flashed across my mind that something was holding me there, keeping me from leaving — I had no clue by whom or what. I immediately dismissed the silly idea and knelt. I balanced on one leg, trying to keep my shoeless foot out of the dirt and holding the ball of tissue against the top of the closest cone to steady myself. When I pulled my shoe out of the damp soil, it released with a slight sucking noise. That sound was familiar to me. I'd spent my last two summers of high school as Dad's helper in the Deep South when his construction business followed the hurricanes of those seasons. The high clay content of red soils acts like glue when moist.

I rose, still leaning over, to put my shoe back on. As I did, I raised my head to look at the monument at the front of the grave. The family name was Pierce. None of the three names on the stone, the last one recorded as having died a couple of years ago, was familiar to me. The engraver hadn't yet carved the new casket occupant's name or date of demise into the monument.

Now free and ambulatory, I nodded my respects, heading back to my family. Once under the protective umbrella provided by our tree, I bent over to finish adjusting my floral arrangement. Grabbing the remnants of the old flowers, I stood — it was time to go.

"Eddie, Mom, Dad, I love you. Take care, and I'll see you next week."

As I turned away, my ear caught the rustle of a gentle breath of wind through the leaves of our tree, and I looked up. In the three decades since its replanting, the oak had grown, spreading its shade magnificently, reminiscent of an Ansel Adams photo. As it matured, the groundskeeper scrambled to stay ahead of the plentiful acorns it dropped. Each time I heard that little *plink* on a stone or root or saw one bounce in the grass, it pleased me that Dad and his decisions still had a noticeable effect on the world where I lived.

But my father's influence was about to extend far beyond acorns falling from the old oak, and I'd be his willing agent.

THE WRITINGS OF
AVRIL MARIA SERENE

CHAPTER 2

PRESENT DAY

It had been two months since Dad passed. The movers were stacking the last boxes retrieved from his house into the corner of the spare bedroom I used for my home office. I wasn't anxious to move them again by myself. That thought had me helicoptering over the workers as they rolled in their dollies of cardboard boxes. As they arrived, I sorted the cartons by their labels into stacks that made sense to me.

I had the men set a few of them aside — those with names that didn't fit any of the categories I'd assigned to my stacks. One box stood out, marked with a Sharpie in Dad's distinctive handwriting, "CEMETERY LETTERS." Maybe records about buying the plot and planting the tree?

After the workers finished, I put everything I'd moved out of their way back where things belonged. Now sitting by its lonesome, that oddly labeled box drew my interest.

When I opened it, I discovered a dark brown, expanding legal file folder labeled "For Debra Ann." It had a big flap over the front opening secured by a cloth ribbon wrapped around the entire binder. Along with the folder was a carefully packed 24-inch fluorescent black light — old school, like the ones used in the seventies to give a Day-Glo effect to the printing on posters.

Also in the box were two handmade square forms about a foot wide and eighteen inches tall, made of PVC tubing used for plumbing. Dad had joined them at their shorter sides with two thinner sections of plastic pipe, in parallel, about three inches apart. I wasn't sure what he'd intended the framework to do.

I checked out the contents of the folder first. The front pouch contained a small audio tape, nothing else. The other pouches held letters, envelopes, and photocopies clipped together in zip-locked freezer bags. Dad must have recorded a message on that tape, inflaming my curiosity and adding anticipation to the mix. I longed to hear what I hoped were my father's last words for me.

The tape Dad made was a microcassette. I'd kept two recorders in the hall closet, relics from the days before fully digital voice recorders or cell phones. I wasn't sure what shape either was in. Not wanting to risk damaging Dad's original recording, I crossed my fingers and picked one, testing the rewind and playback functions using an old microcassette. Hoping it wouldn't eat the tape, I used a software app to convert the output from Dad's microcassette to a digital file, backing it up several times. I'd need only my laptop to hear Dad's words.

His voice was barely recognizable on the recording. Frail and quiet, it lacked his usual energy. "Hi, sweetheart. I hope all is well. I meant to call you. I wanted you to help me with some unfinished business if you can. But my sleep schedule is all screwed up. It seems I'm awake when the rest of the world is asleep and vice versa.

"I'm grateful for every day life gives me, and I don't mean to complain. But it's getting harder for me to do things. There's not much time left, so I thought I'd record this for you. Bill Hanniquet is working on securing your future after I'm gone. He tells me he'll finish this week. I've asked him to give you this tape and some letters that go with it."

My father didn't live long enough to deliver this. Mr. Hanniquet was our family lawyer, and he'd have brought it to me personally.

"You'll need some background so that the letters make sense. You know that until I got too sick to make the trip, I visited your mom every weekend since she left us. She's always been such a patient listener. Even when her mind and memory were going, she had moments where things were lucid, and she was one of the few people who *got* me. That's not something you'd give up once you've experienced it.

"Your career has blossomed, and you've become so busy, especially with the travel. But I've always appreciated that you went with me whenever you could. I know Mom welcomes your visits.

"It was while spending time with her that the letters started turning up. They're in the folder Bill will have for you. I noticed the first about four months ago, cartwheeling through the grass on its corners. It caught my eye — a square wheel rolling along in the breeze. I grabbed it, thinking someone meant it for a deceased loved one. They'd want me to return it. The sender didn't seal the letter — they just pushed the flap inside. Something had curled the envelope and its contents a little. The outside of it just said, 'Sis,' underlined. Inside were four pages of blank paper. I brought it home, promptly forgetting about it.

"But the next week, it was the same thing. This time, three empty pages with the same writing on the envelope, everything slightly bent. Now I'm starting to wonder. But again, I didn't give it another thought for the rest of that week. The third letter got me off my duff, and I went to the caretaker's office.

"His greenskeeper had another three he'd collected. He usually found them on a Monday or Tuesday — always the same story, unsealed, several blank pages, 'Sis' written on the outside. I've known the caretaker since your brother passed away, so I asked him for the three letters he had. I told him I'd track down the writer and let them know their messages were going astray. He'd posted notices about the envelopes at the main entrance and on the memorial wall, but they went unclaimed. He said, 'Sure, but check with me occasionally to see if someone asks for them. And let me know what you find out.' So, that was our deal.

"My time with your mother means everything to me. It helps me keep things on an even keel. Maybe the sender wanted to do the same through their letters. I wanted to pay things forward by letting the writer have a second chance to deliver their messages.

"Almost every week, I'd find another letter. The sender likely meant them for a headstone close to our plot. I found several monuments with a deceased female's name and made a list. I kept an eye out for anyone visiting those graves. Twice, I saw a man walking toward one of the markers. But when I approached, he said he knew nothing about the envelopes. He took off in a different direction when we parted. Several weeks later, I saw the same man and pressed him a little. After he brushed me off the second time, the letters stopped for two weeks. But they began showing up again.

"I wasn't sure how to proceed. Maybe find someone with access to a DNA lab or fingerprint database who could check out what was on the envelopes — perhaps a private investigator? But when I got serious about looking for a PI, I noticed that the blank pages in one letter had indentations. They were like a ballpoint pen would make, clearly visible when the light was just right.

"Discovering those reminded me that my brothers and I made a secret clubhouse under the basement stairs when I was a kid. We wrote notes in disappearing ink made with lemon juice and a fountain pen. To read what you'd written, you had to heat the backside of the paper with a candle. Of course, once you did that, the writing remained legible. We had a rule: you had to burn the message after you read it.

"Did secret messages mean something to the letter-writer and his sister? Perhaps from their childhood? Most adults would know there's nothing secure about disappearing ink. There must be some other significance, or maybe the writer was very young. I experimented with the letters to test my theory. I tried using heat from a dry steam iron and an incandescent bulb, but that didn't work. Then I looked at them under a black light — that got the job done.

"When I started reading, I intended to identify the writer so I could return their letters, nothing more. I wanted to do the minimum possible because it felt like I was eavesdropping on private things. How would Mom or I feel if someone was snooping on our talks? But there was no name or address in the writing — just enough specific information to tell me that the writer was a man named 'Bubba.'

"He wrote the first letter after his release from incarceration. His sister died in a car accident during his time in jail. The other content was profoundly personal. It wasn't something anyone would want random people reading and possibly disseminating, especially not at a time when personal data security is so important.

"So, I kept the letters and printouts of the pictures I took of their exposed images. I thought there might be a chance I'd run into their author one day and could return them.

"But last week, my nurse took me out to visit your mom. The caretaker gave me four letters he'd found since I went to the hospital. One of my guys in the office brought me a black light, and I soon learned that Bubba's life had changed, and not in a good way.

"In the last letter, Bubba says that he witnessed the coverup of a murder.

"If there's a capital crime involved, the contents of these envelopes need to be taken seriously. There'd be more at stake than the author's feelings or my playing the Good Samaritan. And if there's a killer behind this, telling the wrong person about a witness could jeopardize Bubba. That makes me uncomfortable casually sharing these letters with just anyone.

"I wrestled with what to do about the envelopes, the privacy thing against the potential harm to others. Maybe it was all just a tale Bubba was telling — something meant to entertain his sister. Or not, which meant the police should look into this because of all the potential consequences.

"Finally, I called the precinct here. It must have sounded pretty nuts when I told the story over the phone. I'm sure the officer took it as some wheezing old geezer calling from a hospital, possibly with dementia. Talking about secret writing describing the dumping of a body. And in letters that he found at a graveyard while he was grieving for his deceased wife, no less. They said they'd send someone out, but I sensed they were patronizing me. Of course, no one showed up. I called back two days later and didn't fare any better.

"The possibility of homicide raises the ante, and I know I'm almost out of time. Someone else needs to hear what's in those letters, so I'm passing them to you. Maybe no one can do anything. Perhaps the letters aren't what they seem. It might be too late to act, or their contents may not be helpful or relevant.

"Investigative journalists train for circumstances like these — your instincts and resources would be much better than mine. I can trust your judgment about the right thing to do. I'm asking you to check out these letters as a favor to me if you can find the opportunity.

"Enough about that. I don't know when or if I'll get to talk to you again. But I wanted you to know I love you and think of you always. If I can't be there in the flesh the next time you need me, trust that Mom and I are watching over you. You've made me so happy to have you in my life. Be as good as you can be, but give 'em hell when you have to. Take care of yourself, sweetheart."

I took the headphones and the laptop to the recliner. I played that recording at least a dozen times. His final spoken words had started the tears flowing, and they wouldn't stop. Dad sounded so infirm, his voice almost whispering, and I missed him. I deeply regretted that we weren't together when he made the tape, something that would bother me the rest of my life.

At almost eleven that night, I awoke after falling asleep in the recliner. I got up to put the notebook and headphones back on my desk in the den. I knew the heartache would be with me for a long time, but Dad had gifted me something I could do to help me through it. I'd commit myself to that task, beginning with learning the contents of those letters.

CHAPTER 3

D ad knew I'd leave no stone unturned following up on his request. He understood me better than anyone; he'd also have known this challenge would tease my journalistic instincts.

My father's intuitions were good when it came to people. That he'd kept those letters told me he'd felt a connection to them, perhaps a human interest story others would find relatable. That he'd made that recording, along with his worries about a potential homicide, suggested it could be much darker. But certainly, *something*.

It was time to dig into the other contents of that legal file folder. The second through fifth set of pouches contained the original letters Dad had retrieved. They were in order by date. My father had placed the pages of each letter together in a manila folder along with its corresponding envelope. Most of the writing was on lined white letter-sized paper. But scattered among them was the occasional card commemorating a birthday or holiday. These were most often blank except for their invisible ink contents.

The sixth through tenth pouches contained printed photos of the letters captured under black light, which explained the light fixture in the box. Also ordered by date, Dad had paper-clipped the page images of each letter together. In the margins were sporadic, sometimes lengthy, notes in my father's handwriting.

I didn't want to risk spoiling the originals until I knew what I was dealing with. I began by printing Dad's black-light photos of the letters. The prints would become my working copies. The author addressed each letter, "Dear Sis," followed by the month and date, nothing more. "I miss and luv you — Bubba," or similar sentiments, signed off every letter. The handwriting was distinctive. It randomly but regularly switched from readable cursive to block lettering and back. Pronounced shifts in style were evident whenever the writer tried to make a point or express an emotion. Several apologies started the series off:

I'm so sorry I screwed up Sis. My land lord was hassling me for the rent. The grab was sposed to be a quik in and out but I ran into that Ring home securety thing with the drones and doorbells taking picturs. I allways thought I was safe from alarms or some one being home if I cut the phone line. Guess the new sistems dont need telefone wires, they use the internets.

Its allways something. Maybe thats a messige. I shoud have listened. I'm trying to lern to make better choices. Thats how they talk about it in the sessons at the half—way house. So they want me to admit my B&E's were wrong even if I didn't get cauht. I still dont know what I was sposed to do to make the rent.

I guessed that Bubba deserved some credit for paying homage to the conditions of his parole. But he seemed a little lacking in the sincerity department, not even considering getting a job to discharge his debts. Still, he'd endured his fair share of bad news:

Thanks for coming to the trial and every thing. I know it was hard for you to travel with the new baby.

Hearing about your acident made me cry. I hoped youd come out of the coma ok. Or at least the docters woudnt pull the plug until the court releesed me. They woudnt let me spend time at the hospital with you. I coudnt get a pass in time to be at the funerel but Letti sent me some picturs. She says her and Joe are taking care of Mikey now. Thats good. She's a grate mom. The funerel picturs looked nice. Lots of flowers and people crying that you woudnt be here any more. All your freinds were there that made me feel a little beter.

But its sad to think I wont ever see you again. When I got out, it didnt seem real, and I kept looking for you to pop up in diferent places in the naberhood. Sometimes I cant help it. I wake up at night bawling my eyes out when I have a dream about you.

His mistakes and poor judgment drove many of his problems. His environment and associates caused others. The letters often referred to a hard-knock existence. One of his first read:

I don't know why I ever beleived Sheila was any thing exept a ball buster. You tryed to tell me. I thouht I was proving some thing by taking her away from Georgio. But later I found out she was bleeding him dry. She ran up $20,000 in credit card dett. The word on the street was that her leaving Georgio was the best thing that coud have hapened to him. I saw him at a rave and I was sure he would punch me out. Instead, he just nodded and said GOOD LUCK. And I think he ment it. Like he knew I woud need all the help I coud get.

She wont let me see Casey because Ime too far behind in the child support. I told her she coudnt do that. But she said she'd take me to court. Shel tell them I'm a bad influince because I keep getting arrested.

Like she does any thing to help me do better by Casey. She didnt even bother to show up at my last trial. Come on GET REAL. If I didnt have the money for a decent lawyer, how woud I have enuff to catch up on my child support? Money is all that bitch cares about.

I learned I'd rushed to judgment earlier about him not seeking employment — later letters described his situation:

I tryed to find a decent job Sis. I havnt been screwing around. The only things out there I can get are in the back of resturant's. Maybe day labor in construction. I can make money unloding trucks and taking temp jobs at the Home Depot parking lot. But my parole officer says its got to be a perminent full time positon. He doesn't care if its shoveling shit all day.

Please dont get mad at me, but when I need money, I deal some drugs. Mostly weed, but some times speed when I can get it fronted to me. But usualy, I have to break into houses. The last time they locked me up I was in with a guy named Stitch. He's a lejend doing 459s — that's what they call hitting up rich guy's homes.

They busted him for the stollen car he was driving. But they never get him for the burglarys. This guy is slick and knows all the tricks. He even uses drones for casing houses — flys them right up to the windows and looks inside. Can you beleive that shit?!? He tauht me some things. He gave me the names of some High End fence's, so Ill be ok. I promise Ill keep trying to find a beter job. Maybe one that pays enuff to go strait.

I got the impression of a small-time criminal who wasn't all bad. Bubba showed some intelligence and had moments of earnest introspection. He'd gotten off to an inauspicious start in life and made some abysmal choices. His emotional range seemed on par with most people's. Bubba wrote about bonding with a dog he'd cared for after someone accidentally hit it with a car. He flashed sincere anger when he described his landlord threatening to evict him if he didn't get rid of the pooch. His empathy extended beyond animals to include other people, especially his sister.

But Bubba exhibited mental health issues, too. There was his extreme dependency on his sister, of course. His use of invisible ink and writing style reinforced signs of a developmental disorder. It was almost as though he clung to a phase of childhood. I could see how hiding what he wrote might give him more confidence to share his private thoughts. But as Dad said, relying on invisible ink to protect a secret is juvenile. Grownups would know it's too easy to make readable.

And Bubba likely suffered from some form of social maladjustment. Snippets of his correspondence suggested he had genuine problems forming relationships, including friendships. Bubba kept referencing both the physical reality of being alone and the emotional feeling of loneliness. Perhaps those amplified his neediness and reliance on his sibling. It wouldn't have surprised me to learn he tended toward depression.

But something else was off. Most of Bubba's writing was rational, understandable, albeit barely, and occasionally insightful. But his logic had severe lapses. For example, at one point, he wrote,

"Im glad to see your geting my leters."

He'd kept returning to the gravesite and finding the previous week's message missing. Until I read that comment, I'd assumed he was writing for therapeutic reasons, like someone might keep a diary or a journal.

Did he genuinely believe at some level that there was a mail delivery service from the earthly plane to Heaven?

THE WRITINGS OF
AVRIL MARIA SERENE

CHAPTER 4

After taking a break to grab a quick bite and start the dishwasher, I returned to Bubba's letters.

I found it a little odd that Bubba never mentioned his mother. I guessed that "Sis" was an older sibling and possibly a parental substitute. Whatever his approach to other aspects of his life, he seemed open and honest with her, even verbose. Perhaps writing in invisible ink helped with that, maybe even gave him a sense of freedom. His signature, "Bubba," could have been his real name, but somehow I doubted it. It was more likely that it meant simply "brother," as Southerners often use it. Or it could be a nickname.

The last letter Dad collected gave me pause, just as it had him:

Sis — do you remember that naberhood you worked in back when you were doing the In Home care services? The last one before I left, that old man? Now, <u>that</u> guy had some $$$! I went there to check out the house three door's down from him on the corner lot. Its pretty nice and has a hiden ally in the back. I think for the garbaje trucks, so peeple won't see the trash bins on the street. The place looked good to me. Lots of ways to get in and out of there, probly some great stuff inside.

The sister's name would be engraved on the headstone if I could find the gravesite where Bubba dropped off these letters. I'd need to do some legwork at the memorial gardens to figure out Sis's name. He'd just told me she was a registered nurse and worked for a temp agency. I'd have to cold call the employers in the area to run down the last one she worked for. From them, I could get the address of her final client. I should be able to locate the house Bubba described. Some time spent on the phone should get me the rest of the information I wanted. The letter continued:

I woudnt have done it if you were still here — Id never let anything come back on you or Mikey. You know that right? But one nite I went to do the job. I'm figguring out what to take and I check out one of the side bedrooms upstares. It had a sweet computer set up. I was getting ready to grab it when I saw this lite flashing on the walls. Shit, somebody else was robing the place. At least, thats what I thouht.

They were amachurs. You cant just wave a regulr flashlight all over the place. It makes wierd light patterns cops can see from the street — maybe reelize what's hapening. Remember Ted the doochebag who used to date your freind Ellie? Thats how they busted him — a nose-y old lady down the street saw the lites and called 5-O.

If these idiots caught me in the house, that was 1 thing. More of them then me, so that was a problem. Other wise what woud they do, call the cops on me and get them selves busted? But what freaked me out the most was these rookey assholes would send us all to jail because they didnt know what they was doing. Id have to go back in to finish my parole time and do another nickel for this B&E. I woudnt have anyway to get my letters to you.

I was stuck in the farthest bedroom on the 2nd floor. They was rite in the midle of my escape rout. I just stayed in the closet to ride it out. Nothing better I could do then sit there lissening.

There was 3 of them, 2 men and a lady. They wasnt from our naberhood; I didnt know anyones voice. They was trying to keep quite but not doing a grate job. The lady kept geting upset and rasing her voice. I guy was getting angry at the other 2

I thought it mite be some insurence scam because the older guy kept talking about every thing like it was his stuff. He knew where to find what they needed in the house. I herd him call one guy Rickie. That was the I he sent to get the duck tape out of the kitchen closet.

Then I figgured out they was trying to move some thing wraped up in a oval rug. I'm pretty sure it was a dead body. They all kept calling it Her and they was worryed about leaving a trail.

Bubba's chosen profession had significant downsides. But I doubted anyone could have foreseen that situation: two sets of criminals sneaking around the same house in the dark of night. It didn't seem like it would turn out well. But Bubba *had* survived whatever happened long enough to write and deliver this letter. Fascinated, I continued reading:

I coud see the room I was in had a window. Maybe I could rase the bottom part and not make any sound — clime through

the opening onto the little stub roof then jump down and run
for it. The same way we used to sneak out as kids. If I made a
big enough racket geting away it woud draw atention to the
house. Those peeple woud be too bizzy covering their tracks
to worry about chasing me.

But what if they had guns? So I stayed put.

Now they was in the bedroom across from the I I was in. From
what they said and what I herd some body was already done
rolling a body into the rug. It was seeled up with the tape.
The 3 of them was trying to push and pull it out of that
room. Once they got it out they slid the whole thing down the
stares.

After-words, the woman vacumed the other bedroom hall and
steps. I spose they wanted to leave the same patern on the
carpet as the made left. That way it looked like they didn't
do any thing.

Once I knew they was all on the 1st floor I looked out the
window. I wached them carry the roll out the house thru the
back door going to the ally. I coud see the corner of a dark
van. I saw them yanking and shuving the roll in to the back of
it. I guy returned, and I herd him lock the rear door of the
place. He went back to the van, and the 2 guys took off. The
lady walked out to the sidewalk by the street, and I coudnt
see her anymore. I thouht it woud take them a while to bury a
body so I had some time.

After they was gone, I went into that master bedroom to see
what they did. I coudnt tell. But I saw diplommas and placks
on the wall, so I knew the house belonged to some docter. I
figgured screw him for making me wait. I took every thing I

could carry from the place. I was pretty sure they woudnt report a theft. They woudnt want the police looking at nothing that went on that nite.

But if they killed some one I didnt want them trying to pin it on me. They coud say See Somebody broke in and They must have killed that lady. You know how this goes Sis. No bodys going to beleive me over a rich docter and his freinds.

So before I left I took a scale and one of the throw rugs out the upstares bathroom. Used them to replace the drag marks from the master bedroom down the stares to the living room. I scouted out the utilety room off the kitchen to see if there was any power tools I coud take. There was some paint in airosol cans. I sprayed Doc killed a Woman and Hid her Body on the wall and the carpet in the livingroom. I went to my car and grabed my cell. I snuck back in and took some pictures.

That way I coud show I tried to set things rite if they pointed fingers at me.

"*Christ*, Bubba, why were you screwing around?" I asked out loud. "It's not a video game — you should have just gotten out of there and called the police." As if to answer my question, the letter continued:

I wanted to call 911 to report a prowler, but I allredy cut the phone wire when I broke in. I didnt have a burner phone in my car. The only phone I had was the one in my name. So I just blew it off. Maybe Doc woudnt be the 1st person to come back to the house. Or the painter or carpet guy he hired to cover up my messiges could report them. Even if the docter found what I tagged and got rid of it, at least he woud know some body else witnesed what he did. Maybe hed turn himself in. Or he mite get nervous and make a mistake that woud get him cauht without my help.

The thought again crossed my mind that perhaps Bubba hadn't fully matured into adulthood. I didn't know him, of course. Still, it disappointed me; his response to a likely homicide relied on hoping things might work out without him getting involved.

Just one step above the lowly "thoughts and prayers."

CHAPTER 5

I'd need to spend more time looking into the circumstances described in the letters to do justice to Dad's request. But I also needed to pay some bills, meaning this project would have to take a back seat until I caught up. I tried to clear another day between the freelance projects I'd committed to. After juggling my schedule for half an hour, I laid my head in exasperation on my forearms, crossed upon the tabletop.

Just then, the phone rang. The call was from the probate attorney's office manager. She wanted a meeting tomorrow to discuss the final distribution of my father's estate.

Maybe it was because I wasn't in the best of moods anyway. But after I'd hung up the phone and given it some thought, I found the forthcoming stamp of finality on everything unsettling. Dad had passed almost three months ago. While I was long over the initial sorrow, I hadn't entirely accepted that he was gone. Peace of mind wouldn't come from talking to an estate manager. Would a sympathetic conversation with an old friend help?

I'd known Lindsay Barnes since junior high, and we'd always been close. No matter how much time had passed since we'd last seen one another, we could always pick up where we left off.

Lindsay had that girl-next-door thing going on big time — she was pretty, but in a way boys found approachable. She liked to change things up. Even when we were younger, you never knew from day to day what color her hair would be. Short for her age, she'd always struggled with her weight — still, as a grownup, she was what our parents' generation would have called "shapely." And when she chose to let loose, she wasn't shy about voicing her opinion, especially when under the influence of adult beverages.

Lindsay and I made different career choices. When I went off to USC Annenberg, she came with me. However, Lindsay dropped out to attend cosmetology school before getting her public relations and advertising degree. That strengthened our friendship because talking with her meant escaping my world for a while. After graduation, she'd built a nice clientele in a chic La Jolla salon. I became one of her most loyal customers.

Lindsay found room for me on her appointment calendar with little notice. "Did you hear the awful news about Coach Cantor?" she asked as I settled into her salon chair in front of the mirror. She threw a smock around me and fastened it in the back.

Her question caught me by surprise.

"No, I haven't heard anything but good. I just saw Coach's picture on the church website. He was ladling chili at the homeless outreach. He wrote the nicest comment on Dad's memorial page. What happened?"

"It was Thursday night after you set your appointment. I heard about it on the evening news."

Keeping her voice low to avoid disturbing other stylists' patrons, Lindsay guided me to the shampoo bowl in the corner.

"Someone killed Coach in the middle of his living room."

"What? *Oh, my God*, no…." Stunned, I stopped, pulling Lindsay's shoulder to me.

Searching her eyes, I found no solace in her expression.

"Coach? *Are you sure, Lindsay?*"

She pursed her lips, bowing her head, eyes to the floor.

I stood silently, struggling to accept the news, then resigned myself to it.

"Oh, no…"

Julius Cantor was our girls' basketball coach at Torrey Pines High School, beloved in our little community. He'd taken the Falcons to the state finals in our senior year. I'd ridden the bench, but Lindsay was one of our stars, even with her height challenges. Coach knew how to get the best out of us. That was as true on the basketball court as in our Sunday school classes at Torrey Pines Church. There, he'd been an elder and our teacher.

Once we'd grown, we'd kid Coach that he had Danny Glover's face stuck on Usain Bolt's body. As he aged and eventually retired, he never seemed to gain an ounce. He was someone you could tell anything to and rely on for help when needed. There was a price he'd make you pay — if there was something you had to do, he'd keep on you until you did it. But I didn't know anyone who didn't love the man. That someone would murder him was unthinkable.

"How does that *happen?* In his living room!" Coach *couldn't* be dead if it didn't make any sense. "Did they say how he died?"

"The news said there were no signs of a struggle. They didn't take anything; none of the neighbors saw anything suspicious."

"Was anyone else hurt?"

"Coach was by himself in the house. You remember when the stroke took Celia — after that, the kids and grandkids scattered to the four winds. You'd hear him talking about rattling around that old house alone, just Celia's cats for company. Some of us in the church were trying to find him a girlfriend.

"Anyway, it seemed like he let somebody in that night. Whoever they were, they just shot him cold, looked like for no reason, and left."

Neither of us spoke as Lindsay massaged shampoo into my scalp; the rhythmic motions were comforting and seemed to help the reality sink in.

"Jesus… I don't get it," I said, still trying to make sense of the circumstances. "Coach wouldn't hurt a fly. If he *were* dating, he'd have taken it slow. He doesn't gamble or do drugs. I'm not even sure if Coach drinks. He's got some houses he rents out, but he's not rich. Maybe he got some money from Celia's insurance. But Coach is — *was* — a careful guy. It would have gone straight into the bank, maybe some in an investment account. Why the hell would anyone want to hurt Coach, much less kill him?"

"The TV reporter said the same thing," Lindsay replied. "Police think maybe mistaken identity. Or a home invasion where the thieves knew right away they had the wrong address. Maybe killed him because he'd seen their faces?" She toweled off my hair and led me back to the cutting station.

"In all my life," she continued, "I saw Coach drink just one beer. One. He loved his NFL football. He'd watch to see a team he hated lose. Or to see his favorite team win. Either way worked for him. And there weren't any NFL teams he didn't have strong feelings about. No game he'd miss if he could help it. My boyfriend and I went there one Sunday after church to say hi. Coach nursed that one can all game long." She began trimming the back and sides of my hair.

I couldn't turn back the clock, but I needed to do *something*. "Linds, I want to check into it and see what happened. Would the family mind if I did a little sleuthing on the side? I'd ask their permission first — some people might rather just let it go, leave it to the police...."

"You and Cassidy always got along. As his oldest, Cassidy would speak for the rest. She's married now, and her last name is Plame. She lives in San Francisco. I called her with my condolences, and she stopped in yesterday. Now that the police have released the crime scene, Cassidy's staying at Coach's house, taking care of the funeral and the estate. So tough on her. Her kids and her husband are tending to their business up north. But I'd ask her."

Lindsay pulled my bangs tight, working her magic with the texturizing shears.

"I know she'd love to see you again."

"Can you give me her number? I've got an old one — I haven't kept up with my phone contacts."

Lindsay wrote Cassidy's name and number on a business card and handed it to me.

"Thanks, Linds. I'll give her a call. I'll do anything I can to help find who did this."

Lindsay and I reminisced about the times we shared with Coach. We moved on to other things when the sadness became overwhelming, then fell silent while she blow-dried my hair. I wanted to let my natural red tresses grow out of the highlights Lindsay gave me in our last session, so there'd be no coloring today. After thanking her for making me look presentable again, we said our goodbyes.

Once I was back in my car, I found that my resolve had hardened. I knew there was no way in hell I could let what happened to Coach Cantor go.

Writers of the occasional cheesy novel want readers to believe things that just aren't true. One is that a clever and resourceful investigative journalist has carte blanche to investigate open murder cases. *Oh, what I'd give if only that were true!* Unfortunately, the powers that be do not share my enthusiasm for such access. In real life, the law prohibits news reporters from interfering with active homicide investigations. The police have exclusive first dibs on evidence and witnesses.

It's not a First Amendment issue; it has to do with obstruction of justice. Reporters can and should become aggressively involved if the police miss essential elements of an investigation. That's especially true when a case has gone cold or if there's strong evidence of police malfeasance. And quality reporting has helped more than one person wrongfully accused.

Even so, a journalist's investigative efforts wait for authorities to clear the crime scene and mustn't interfere with the active investigation. However, reporters can and often do immediately begin investigations of lesser or related aspects to a killing, especially those in the financial realm.

I urgently wanted to jump into Coach's murder. To do that, I needed to find something tangential to the crime that would let me help without getting in the way of detectives. Until I discovered that safe angle, I'd need a hall pass. For situations like this, I turned to Sgt. Marci Robbins

THE WRITINGS OF
AVRIL MARIA SERENE

CHAPTER 6

My relationship with Marci Robbins began when I was a newbie reporter, and she served as my first dependable San Diego police department source. Over time, she'd become a trusted friend and ally.

Marci had been on the force for twelve years, sober for the last three. Whenever she and I talked, somewhere in the early going, she'd tell me the number of days she'd been on the wagon. Marci had been a Vice undercover for a long time during her darker days before AA. She'd also been in a rocky marriage that ended with her surrendering primary custody of her two young boys. More recently, she'd survived breast cancer, now wearing a prosthesis on her left side.

Meeting her the first time, you'd suspect none of that. Tall and blonde, Marci was naturally beautiful and didn't fit the image most of us have of a recovering alcoholic and cancer survivor, much less a police officer. With a genuine smile and a self-effacing nature, she projected confidence and congeniality. I interviewed a friend of Marci's for the department morale piece — he told me that when she worked undercover, they had to do a lot to make Marci more commonplace. Being noticeable isn't healthy for a Vice officer.

But other currents ran under the surface. Marci had dealt with self-control challenges in her personal life. She'd often been in a position of projecting herself as something she wasn't, either to conceal her addiction or to earn a paycheck. Her covert role on the job was usually as trustworthy if somewhat ditzy arm candy with a transparently vulnerable side. She made a perfect moll, just the target to attract a manipulative and sadistic criminal. She busted offenders by the dozens in her work as an undercover, but avoiding seriously flawed characters in her personal life had been difficult. As part of her healing process, Marci developed a strong distaste for being pushed around or intimidated. The breadth of her understanding and the challenges she'd faced and overcome made her an invaluable friend. Her viewpoint and the advice she's shared have helped me through many of my issues, professional and otherwise.

The department's environment wasn't supportive when she wrestled with abuse, alcoholism, and family issues in private. But her superiors stepped up to the plate once everything was out in the open. To their credit, they pointed her to the help she needed.

And so, the department had finally made a home for her. Marci was primarily a desk officer now; her days on the street are over. Toughened by her experiences, she made for a natural mentor, especially for female officers. Still, though happy in her role, Marci occasionally found herself frustrated, wanting to fix all the problems she saw around her.

It was the last part that connected us. Marci had been a critical source for my piece several years ago on morale, management, and deployment issues within the San Diego Police Department. We'd clicked and became fast friends, although our long work hours when I was still at the *Union-Tribune* meant we didn't socialize much. Now that I was freelancing, we had begun seeing more of one another.

It was late afternoon, and I hoped I could reach her on the job.

"Hi, Marci. I apologize for calling you at work. I have a question I hope you can answer."

"No worries, Debra Ann. It's been a crazy day here. I'd rather talk to you than some people I've dealt with in the last hour or two. What's up?"

"I just found out my old basketball coach, Julius Cantor, was killed Thursday in his home. The news said there were no signs of forced entry, one to the head, one to the chest, cold-blooded, and that you don't have a motive yet.

"Coach was the nicest guy, and I can't get my head around any of that. I wanted to get the straight story from someone I trust."

"Oh, Debra Ann, I didn't realize the two of you were close." Marci's tone was softer now. "I would have called you myself and let you know. I knew Coach, too. Lots of people here did. It was a sad day when we got that call."

"Just so you know, I'm not calling as a reporter, Marci. I'm just trying to understand what happened to that poor man. He was a dear friend. If there's anything I can do to help, I'd like to be involved. But only if."

"I understand, I do," Marci said quietly. "Ordinarily, I'd give you that speech about everything I'm not allowed to tell you. But in this case, we don't have anything that falls into that category. Honestly, we don't have much. What we do know raises more questions than it answers."

"Can you give me a rundown?"

"That night, neighbors reported his porch light on. He was famous for pinching his pennies — people who know him say he only left it lit when expecting visitors. Right after halftime of the football game, a guest arrives. Our best descriptions are of a Caucasian male mid-forties, maybe five-ten or five-eleven. So, shorter than Cantor — average weight, say, one-eighty to one-ninety. Long black coat, gloves, old-style gangster hat, dressy clothes and shoes. He might have gray hair. And get this: it's dark by then, but he's wearing aviator sunglasses. He walked up to the house; no known vehicle. Cantor let him in. Ten minutes later, the visitor leaves — again, walking — porch light is out, and neighbors see and hear nothing amiss."

"That's it for witnesses?"

"Not quite — we have an older lady three doors down and across the street, the Neighborhood Watch captain. She saw a black van pull up about ten — no plates she could see.

"Two figures in head-to-toe dark coveralls and face coverings entered the residence with toolboxes. According to the witness, average everything — couldn't give us race, gender, or age. They walked straight in; there was no porch light or greetings at the door. They left about twenty minutes later. In the meantime, the neighbor tries to call Cantor but gets no answer. She phones 911 to report a burglary. When patrol officers arrive, the occupants and their transportation are gone."

"It sounds like whoever was in the van knew no one would be answering the door," I thought out loud. "And it doesn't sound like they broke in. Maybe the house was left unlocked for them by Coach's first guest. Cleanup crew of some kind?"

"The detectives think either that or Cantor was still alive when the first guy left, which means the two in the work vehicle did the killing. It might have been a hybrid deal, where the first guy incapacitated the man so the other two could gain access. When we got there, nothing was out of place. The crime scene was pristine. Cantor was laid out parallel to the couch with two .22 entry wounds. One to the head, one to the heart. No stippling or powder burns, so at least four to six feet away. With no reports of gunshots or loud noises, we have to assume a silencer. Hopefully, ballistics can tell us something good.

"But first impressions suggest a classic pro hit. The shooter was in and out, and there were no signs of a struggle, so we believe this was premeditated. One thing could be helpful. The arriving officers made note of two large Maine Coon tortoiseshells whining for their evening meal. We think that might be good for us because once we have a suspect, the trace evidence team could match up the cat hair."

"Any ideas as to motive?"

"We've been looking, but nothing's turned up yet. Cantor's finances are in good shape. I wouldn't say he was wealthy, but he did alright and managed his money well. Social Security, a good pension from the school district, and he had four houses he rented out. He has three kids and seven grandkids he got along with, all living out of the area now. We haven't turned up any problems with his tenants. No bad habits, addictions, personality issues, sketchy associations, or secret lives we've found. He wasn't romantically involved with anyone. It wasn't that long ago he lost his wife, and from what we know, he was devoted to her. Just a nice guy living out a good retirement, from what we know so far."

"Have there been any other violent crimes in the area, a pattern his killing could be a part of?" I'd hoped Marci would know of a motive, but she seemed as perplexed as I was.

"We're not seeing that, but we have looked into it. It's a peaceful neighborhood. We've had a rash of break-ins into unattended houses recently, but no confrontations or violence." Marci paused. "There is one bit of a coincidence. The closest thing to a potential person-on-person crime is next door to the Cantor residence. About a month ago, a young man filed a missing person report on his mother, a Theresa Seaver."

"Is there any tie to Coach?"

"Nothing obvious. Mrs. Seaver's relatives think her husband may have harmed her. He's claiming she ran off to Europe. Ordinarily, you'd roll your eyes and say, 'Yeah, sure.' But there's some history there. The detectives think he could be telling the truth.

"We considered the possibility Coach saw something he wasn't supposed to regarding her disappearance, but he wasn't one to mess around — he'd have reported anything immediately. We asked around, and there's no indication of obvious problems between the two neighbors."

"Thanks, Marci, for letting me know." I was disappointed, but understanding where things stood would help. "Sounds like the detectives are on it. Coach's family and mine were close; we went to school and church together. I plan on talking with his adult children. I'll get in touch if I hear anything helpful."

"The officers who knew him liked and respected Coach," Marci shared. "Their sons and daughters — the lives Coach affected the most — loved him. Everyone here involved with this is going after his killer like Coach was one of our own."

Coach deserved that much, and Marci's update left me some openings to help find his murderer.

THE WRITINGS OF
AVRIL MARIA SERENE

CHAPTER 7

Morning broke as a clammy, dismal, and drizzly day, more like what passes for winter here in San Diego than the middle of spring. Clouds hung low to the ground as the early fog rose into them. The air reeked of dank basement and earthworms. Stepping outside, I felt surrounded by the dreary gloom.

The weather might have irritated me any other day. But somehow, it seemed a perfectly appropriate setting for meeting with the probate attorney for Dad's estate.

I ran to my Uber at the curb, holding a newspaper over my head, and my ride took me downtown to an older, three-story, brick office building. While waiting in the anteroom, I tried to keep my thoughts from going to Dad. I didn't want to be upset or cry before meeting with the lawyer. So, I pondered the floor-to-ceiling dark walnut paneling and matching solid-wood trim. I considered the deep maroon, leather-upholstered chairs, indirect lighting, and copies of nineteenth-century oil paintings perfectly mated to the smell of an old library. I idly contemplated whether the attorneys had chosen the solemn, almost depressing décor on purpose to suit the somber nature of their business. Or perhaps they'd inherited these offices and had no opportunity to remodel. Was it verboten or considered in poor taste to cast a more positive vibe?

Meanwhile, I nibbled on a Ferrero Rocher hazelnut ball. A chocoholic as long as I could remember, I'd often wondered how I'd stayed so trim. That I was tall and used my gym membership fairly regularly probably helped. Still, by rights, I should weigh three hundred pounds. Jessica, my then-BFF in high school, once accused me of selling out my virginity for a Dove chocolate bar. She wasn't wholly wrong. I can only say in my defense that he was smoking hot, and it *was* Valentine's Day.

I had to cut my musings short when the administrative assistant defending the entrance to the attorney's office turned to me and said, "Ms. Wynn, Mr. Hanniquet can see you now."

William Hanniquet had been Dad's lawyer for many years, providing for his corporate legal needs. He was one of my father's most trusted associates in his construction enterprises. I'd visited here many times as a child when Dad had business with him. Hanniquet was an older, slender, white-haired gentleman with a mustache and goatee, wearing a quaint bowtie and a dark suit. Colonel Sanders would have been proud. He rose to his feet, stepping around the end of the desk to take my hand as I entered.

"Debra Ann, it is good to see you again. I'm sorry that it must be under these circumstances." Hanniquet motioned me to the chair in front of his mahogany desk. "Please, have a seat."

"Before the funeral, the last time I saw you was at my graduation from USC," I replied as I settled into the comfortable, tufted leather seat. "Your daughter and I both got our masters' that day. Mine was in journalism, and Jill's was in communications management, so we'd shared a lot of classes. I've always thought it was nice of you to stop by and share in our family's congratulations, Mr. Hanniquet. I heard Jill's with the governor's office now."

"Please, just call me Bill. Yes, she's doing quite well. I remember your father was so proud. I know it gave him great pleasure to tell others about your career. I still have the draft he gave me of your Fat Leonard piece. Great work."

"Thanks, Bill, that's good to hear." I had to smile at the compliment. "I thought it was one of my better articles. Still, you always secretly wonder what real people think."

"I was glad to learn you'd moved on from the paper after that. You wouldn't have been able to find and push the limits of your talents in that environment."

"I appreciate you saying that. The timing could have been better, something I probably should have considered when it happened." Raising an eyebrow, I gave him a sideways grin. "I hated to leave a situation that provided a weekly paycheck. But I needed to do other things. It was something that had been building for a while."

"I don't know how much Alex shared with you," Bill said, returning to his chair on the other side of the desk. "But that was exactly the situation your father wanted to address once he knew his time was short. He thought it important that you have the financial support you need to pursue your work without worrying about your day-to-day survival."

"I knew you were working on setting up a trust, but he didn't tell me the details. Money didn't seem important at the time. His illness came up so suddenly. Dad and I had been laughing — he was sitting on the edge of the gurney, telling jokes. Then the doctor came in, and you could see it in his nurse's face. I knew, we knew, something was wrong, horribly wrong."

"The last time he and I saw each other, he struggled. I must admit that I was concerned." Bill's voice was sympathetic.

"When the physician tells you it's cancer," I said, nodding slowly, "you get your hopes up a little because of everything the medical profession can do now. Then he said it was stage four pancreatic cancer. He explained what that meant, and I wanted to scream at him, 'There has to be a mistake!' I kept telling the doctor how healthy Dad was and how good he looked."

Bill listened patiently. As I thought about it later, he'd probably heard many such stories, each new to the teller but only too familiar to Bill. Still, he let me speak; no hint of anything but empathy showed on his face.

"But Dad knew. He hugged me tight and rocked me back and forth, saying, 'It will be alright, honey' as I bawled my eyes out. There wasn't any choice but to accept what was happening. And eventually, I stopped crying."

"He mentioned he was more concerned about how you were taking it than he was about himself." Bill's voice was sympathetic. "He seemed to have accepted his situation by that point."

"From that moment, with all he was going through, his worries were about me," I agreed. "I wish I hadn't caused the added burden for him."

Looking away, I wiped a teardrop from under my eye with a forefinger. Bill handed me a tissue as I collected myself.

"Come, now," he said gently, "you know your father was all about his responsibilities. I don't doubt he welcomed the familiarity of his role in caring for you. Being the subject of all the sympathy he was getting couldn't have been comfortable for him. It would have made him feel helpless, which he didn't need."

"You're probably right." The thought *was* comforting. "The nature of pancreatic cancer is that it didn't give us much time, and that's the part I regret most. We didn't want to dwell on a future we wouldn't share. So, our last conversations were about other things. Mostly Mom and Eddie, and our family memories of when they were still with us."

"I can only imagine. You know, of course, that your dad loved you dearly. You'll find that reflected in the will and the trust we'll discuss today." Bill turned to why we were here. "We've been busy with many complicated aspects of his estate, mostly dissolving the construction companies. I'm required to review the full will with you as part of the probate process. But let me summarize it now so we can address anything you didn't expect before we reach that point."

"Is there something I should have brought? If you require documents, I'm afraid I didn't come prepared."

"All we need from you today is your patience, understanding, and a few signatures. Once we've taken care of the legal necessities, you can go. I'll have everything arranged then, and we can close probate."

"Thanks for letting me know," I replied, grateful for his guidance.

"Some of this was in the letters we exchanged. You're the only heir mentioned in the will; no other claimants have come forward. As you're aware, following his wishes, they interred your dad next to your mom and brother. Your father provided a small set-aside trust to maintain the family memorial for the next hundred years."

"I was wondering how that would work...."

"There's another small set-aside fund. It will cover any post-sale legal expenses related to your father's construction entities and the family real estate. I understand you've elected not to live in your father's residence. Is that correct?"

I nodded.

"The trust has a regular income distribution schedule," he continued. "We'll set that up today to designate how you want to receive those funds."

"Do I need to set up a new bank account for that purpose?"

"No, any existing account will do. There are online forms if you need to change the designation."

I nodded again.

"A tax-favored, modified, income-producing, irrevocable third-party trust represents your inheritance. Word salad, I know, the bane of the legal profession." Bill was apologetic. He must have seen something in my expression that told him most of that was passing right over my head.

"Selling the construction companies, real estate, and your father's other assets funded the trust. The nominal value of the estate today is approximately fifty million dollars. Most of that will go to charities, endowments, and Alzheimer's research. The terms of the will set aside ten million for your trust."

"*Ten million?*" I couldn't have heard the man correctly.

"I know it sounds like a lot, but the goal of good money management is not to touch the principle. The trust contains revenue-generating assets, so it should provide substantial returns over your lifetime. Interest rates today are high and may not be sustainable in the long term. However, they'd produce five hundred thousand in annual income using the two-year treasury as a guide. With state and federal taxes of 35 percent, you're looking at twenty-seven thousand and change every month."

"Oh, my God!" My mouth hanging open, I'd glued my hands to both sides of my face in surprise.

"Disbursements will begin the month after we clear probate. You should start receiving checks by the time the holidays roll around." He paused. "Your father intended that you always have an ample income to sustain you. That should provide you as much creative freedom as possible in your career."

"I didn't realize Dad was that successful. I mean, I knew he did well, but…."

"Your father was an accomplished man. I know he wanted to be sure he covered all the bases. The trust has lending provisions for interest-free loans should you need a major outlay, such as for a home. Some clauses allow you to contribute to the trust, including assigning real property for tax deferral and reduction. Have you made any investments of your own?"

"I have a 401(k) that I rolled over from my work at the *Union-Tribune*," I replied.

"I'd like to look at it whenever you have the time — there's no hurry. You'll want to consider transferring any real estate that comes your way into the trust. That allows us to deduct maintenance and other costs for tax and accounting purposes. You may also want to protect assets you acquire by transferring them into the trust before engaging in a social contract, such as marriage. We can discuss all those things as necessary when and if they arise — be aware that those options exist. Do you have questions so far?"

"I'm struggling to absorb all of this," I answered, "but I can't think of anything to ask right now. I believe I understand most of it. As you said, I can consult you later about anything I've missed."

"I'm always available to you, Debra Ann. Let's proceed with the will reading and signing of the auditor's estate accounting. We'll have you sign the releases and approvals we need for the trust to get you out of here."

Once we concluded our business, I thanked Bill for his help and hard work. It wasn't until I had gotten into the back of another Uber to return home that a sudden wave of conflicting emotions hit me like a hard kick in the stomach. There was this incredible feeling of just how much Dad had loved me. Despite all his pain and suffering, especially at the end, he'd gone to great lengths not only to provide for me but to enable my dreams.

I'd barely processed that thought when an intense, soul-wrenching despondency overcame me. I realized I couldn't thank Dad with a hug or a kiss, now or ever. Even as he had immersed me in all the love he could muster, I needed to show that I loved him just as much. But he wasn't here. I desperately needed to wrap my arms around him one last time.

I could only hug the thick folder of legal papers on my lap. I softly cried the rest of the way back to my apartment.

THE WRITINGS OF
AVRIL MARIA SERENE

CHAPTER 8

My Uber slowly navigated the streets of downtown San Diego in midday traffic. When it pulled up in front of my apartment building, I needed a few moments to collect myself enough to open the door so the driver could go about the rest of his day. I apologized and thanked him for his kindness and patience.

"It's no problem," he said. "I hope your afternoon goes better for you."

I found his decency comforting, more so coming from a stranger.

Too exhausted to walk to the parking lot at the back of the building and use the tenants' entrance, I went to the visitors' door in the front. Entering my apartment and closing the door, I placed the folder of estate paperwork on the table. I took a moment to reflect on the old photo of Mom and Dad that had hung on that wall next to the door for years. The sorrow still lingered in me, but the thought that they were together now helped.

With a touch of my fingertip to Mom's lips, a nod to Dad, and an enormous sigh, I walked over to my desk and flipped on my notebook computer. The normalcy of that act and checking my e-mail started the process of refocusing on my regular routines.

While I suspected Dad's demise and my feelings of loss would make me sad for a long time, there *was* a bright spot. The project Dad had given me, something I'd taken as a small way to return his affections, sat waiting on my desk. I could put off my other assignments for one more day since I no longer depended on them to survive.

I'd need a reset back into work mode, so I grabbed a quick nap on the couch. The brief respite helped me gain some clarity.

My father's love for me had always been unconditional, even in his final wishes, expressed as absolute acceptance when I needed it most, counsel when I'd gone astray, and support that never wavered. And I hadn't made it easy for him — I'd never been Daddy's goody-two-shoes little girl. Nothing illustrated that quite like the last conversation I had with my editor at the *Union-Tribune*.

It occurred in late 2015, right after the *Los Angeles Times* bought the paper, then called "*U-T San Diego*." The new owners laid off almost a third of our staff and ended local printing of the paper. It would take another two years before the *Washington Post* would expose the most egregious military bribery scandal in the nation's history in November 2017. The name "Fat Leonard" had not yet exploded onto the national media landscape.

During the summer of 2015, I heard rumors of a Malaysian citizen living in San Diego. This man was funneling high-end prostitutes, rare whiskeys, Cuban cigars, and outright cash to those in power. The recipients included local active-duty and retired U.S. Navy officers and politicians. The more I wrote about his activities, the more I discovered. I couldn't find a good stopping point and had to reformat the work as the first of several pieces I intended to write about him.

Three months later, I'd submitted my lead Navy corruption article for publication. I was taking a celebratory run around the track in my head when Jerry Dark, my editor, called me into his office. I expected he'd want to turn my piece into a series. Though I hadn't yet discovered the bribery's true purpose or national scale, I'd exhaustively tracked the flow of illegal merchandise and services to local beneficiaries. I *had* established that Leonard

Glenn Francis, who'd eventually become famous as Fat Leonard, was behind all this activity and that this story had real legs.

"Take a seat, Wynn, and close the door." Dark didn't look away from his monitor. After a few moments, and in that how-dare-you-challenge-me tone of voice he liked to use when asserting his authority, he barked, "What is this supposed to be, Wynn?" He spun the monitor toward me. It displayed the print version of my article.

"That, Jerry, is a great example of the damn fine investigative reporting readers are proud to see coming from their local paper," I replied. "It hasn't been so long since my last piece that you should have forgotten what it looks like."

"Wynn, we've had this conversation before. You told me you would check out a source about a potential story. You don't get back to me, you're not picking up your other assignments, and then three months later, you turn in this crap. Three weeks before Christmas, no less. What the hell is the matter with you?"

Standing up with his finger shaking in anger, Dark pointed at a large blue area on the left side of a city wall map. "Do you even know what this big fucking swath here is, Wynn? It's the Navy base, and three-quarters of San Diegans depend directly or indirectly on the base for their jobs and businesses. You don't attack it willy-nilly just because you think a story lurks around it somewhere."

"Good eyes, Jerry! Yes, the Navy base is the biggest show in town." I wasn't willing to yield an inch. I felt the anger rising within me again, an old friend girded for battle. "And so, news flash: that's where all the corruption is when you search for it. And looking for it is what responsible investigative journalists and newspapers are supposed to do. It's our *job*. And if you are trying to say the entire Navy base will pick up and leave in a snit because honest reporters are doing their jobs, that's pure bullshit, and you know it."

Our voices had risen. I could feel in the back of my head the curious eyes of the other reporters and staff outside Dark's office window.

"I'm *saying* you can't attack the personal lives of every citizen in our fair city as they read the morning paper over their bowl of cereal." Dark had become louder. "They want nothing thrown in their face that could pose an existential or other threat to their employment as they prepare to punch the clock. You may not understand the link, but *they* do, and *I* do."

Dark noticed that our yelling at each other had attracted an audience. He got up from behind his desk to close the window blinds.

"Here's what I understand, Jerry," I fired back. I twisted my hips to follow him so he didn't miss a word. "I know you checked out my sources and the facts in my copy. And how did I discern this? Because if there were anything amiss there, you'd be reaming me for that with your self-satisfied 'got you now' grin. So, we both know my work is solid."

"Are you done?" Dark's tone was mocking.

"No, Jerry, I'm not. It's *never* about the quality of my writing." I jumped up out of my seat. "First, you buried my piece about the dumpster fire that the San Diego Police Department has become on page twelve. Then you gutted it into an opinion piece. You suggested the department could correct all those pervasive and endemic problems with a few tweaks in management here and there."

Dark was back behind his desk but had remained standing. As I was talking, he began rolling up his sleeves.

"That department is a one-stop shop for everything a rotting police unit can offer," I ranted. I was on a roll, pacing back and forth before Dark's desk.

"Morale in the low zeroes, training failures, racism, sexism, bias, abuse, and intimidation. Management attitudes, turnover, recruiting problems, incompetence, corruption. All the issues you've helped sweep under the rug since you've been here. The paper has published the same do-nothing pablum about the police and their problems for a hundred years. Not coincidentally, you crank out another round of insincere apologism every time there's another use of excessive force incident against a person of color or other minority."

"The police don't answer to you...," Dark began.

I wasn't having any of it.

"All that garbage is hiding something San Diegans have a right to know, and they look to this paper to tell them. A sizeable chunk of our taxes goes to the half-assed training of recruits and giving them one or two years of experience. Then they quit and move on to better, more lucrative jobs in our neighboring cities and counties."

Dark placed the knuckles of his balled-up fists on his desk, leaning forward and shifting his weight onto them.

"Well, Wynn, you're assuming that some part of that matters," Dark replied, denying nothing. "Your laundry list of complaints refers to things that you say happened then, but this is now. Going over all your past grievances won't help you this morning. They illustrate my point. You haven't got what it takes to deliver what I need. This newspaper is a business."

"It's an embarrassment...," I started, not hiding my disdain.

Dark deflected it, saying, "We depend on ad revenues for our existence. We must provide a stable, positive face for the community and its business leaders to attract money for your paycheck. That requires careful consideration of what we put out there. We have to be responsible — you struggle with that concept. I told you the last time we had this conversation that there are only three options. One, you toe the line; two, you resign; or three, we fire you. Now, we're down to…"

Not in the mood to back down, I placed the heels of my hands on the edge of the desktop on my side. I shoved my face forward until we were almost nose-to-nose. "Your past story decisions are very much part of the problem," I interrupted, pre-empting the threat I knew was coming next. "You castrated my article about the obscene water desalination cost overruns, which have now shifted to the taxpayer. Why? Because some of your advertisers were involved in the profiteering."

"You don't know that.…" Again, Dark didn't defend the accusation.

"You've clarified that being a paid shill for those advertisers is not only your number one priority but your *only* priority. I don't know why you don't just print an Oreo wrapper as the front page of every issue. The same basic principle is in play. People will subscribe because they have fond childhood memories of it. Never mind the fattening and cancerous, over-processed garbage inside; American capitalism at its finest."

"So, you think socialism is.…" Dark was about to invoke his same old, tired tropes about anything the least bit liberal, and I cut him off.

"When I got my master's and told people about your employment offer, they warned me. They said the *Union-Tribune* has a history of conservatism-slash-collusion and that whole no-such-thing-as-a-bad-profit schtick.

"But in 2006, the year before that — not coincidentally, a year before *you* got here — Marcus Stern and Jerry Kammer won a Pulitzer *and* a Polk. For what? For reporting a corrupt U.S. House member taking bribes. Public official. Bribes. Pulitzer. *Here*. I know — mind-boggling."

I don't think I could have been more sarcastic, and I wasn't about to stop. "With my student loans, earning that paycheck looked pretty good. I figured, 'How bad could this place be?' But now Marcus and Jerry aren't around anymore. All *you've* done is add more embarrassments to the 'Criticism' section of the paper's Wikipedia page."

"You know, Wynn, fuck you," Dark said as he stood up and jammed both hands into his front pants pockets. He seemed to be tired of arguing. "So, you think you're so talented that your crap doesn't stink? Then, genius, explain why no paper is surviving on your brand of trash-everything investigative reporting. Do you think it means *anything* for your friends in *my* newsroom to tell you how much they respect you? Not a damn one of them will lift a finger when security comes and cleans out your desk in your absence. Why? Because they're *grownups*— they know they don't get paid if we don't have revenue coming in.

"Resign this minute. Or I swear to God, I'll fire you and have you marched through every floor of this place in a perp walk for the ages."

"Please, go ahead, Jerry," I shot back, my face still projected over his desk. "But before you do, you'll want to talk to Legal. If the paper can't afford decent reporting, I doubt they can pay what making that last threat will cost them. So, screw you and your self-serving rationalizations for pumping waste out of every orifice, Jerry. I'll resign, but you *will* surrender the rights on the Fat Leonard piece to me since you won't put on big-boy pants and publish it."

Made in the heat of that moment, the decision to quit wasn't well-considered, but I was gambling. I hoped I could sell my Fat Leonard piece to compensate for any severance or unemployment I'd give up by resigning.

Getting fired would hurt the reputation I'd built, one I needed to attract quality freelance work.

"Done. But I want you out of here — *now*," Dark snapped. He'd finally enunciated the words I knew he wanted to tell me from the moment I walked into his office. "And no rabble-rousing in the newsroom on your way out!"

I headed to the ladies' room straight from Dark's office and took the stall at the far end. I began shaking uncontrollably, fighting back the urge to vomit. Quiet and withdrawn when I was young, I still avoided confrontation, though I could hold my own when I had no choice but to fight. It was afterward that my mind and body would eventually revolt. I sincerely appreciated all the guidance my parents, especially Dad, had given me in standing up for myself. But they'd never been able to show me how to deal with the aftermath.

Friends and relatives who know this about me have questioned why I chose this combative profession. The prevailing stereotype in investigative reporting is one of a grizzled and battle-hardened male. He's an antisocial type who compulsively and aggressively cross-examines everything and everyone, with no thought to reputation or feelings.

But those who ask why I do this don't see the other side to the work — the intellectual challenge of solving a puzzle or pulling the core truth out of a problematic situation. There's an intense satisfaction in yelling to the world the things the bad guys don't want anyone to know.

Those rewards have their price, though, and sitting on a toilet fighting to regain my composure was the tax I paid to do what I wanted with my life.

Once I pulled myself back together, I grabbed two flattened boxes from Shipping and walked to my cubicle. Apart from the reporters on the phones working stories, the bullpen was unusually somber and quiet as I began packing the things from my desk. The news of my demise had preceded me. Slowly, one by one, my co-workers, some of whom had become dear friends over the years, stopped by to hug, say goodbye, and wish me well in my next venture. We exchanged home numbers and personal e-mail addresses.

Saying goodbye to Doug Stein, with whom I'd shared so many bylines, was very emotional, though neither of us said a word. We held each other for several moments until he patted me twice on the back and turned away without making eye contact.

It wasn't until Dolly, our copy girl, wrapped her arms around me and laid the side of her head against my chest that tears returned to my eyes. Her disability was on the milder side of the autism spectrum, and she was very personable once she got to know you. But even then, she rarely expressed herself with any physical contact. Her hug reminded me of the good things about the newsroom that I would miss.

Scott, my intern for the previous six months, helped me carry boxes to my car. As we parted, I offered the only words of encouragement that came to mind. "You've got the talent, Scott. You work as hard as anyone. But build a blog around something you are really into. Keep up with it and learn how to promote it. Put out regular podcasts. My leaving is as much about my personal choices as anything else, but we both know print news is a dinosaur. Make sure you have a solid backup plan."

And just that quickly, I was no longer the lead investigative journalist at the *San Diego Union-Tribune*.

CHAPTER 9

JANUARY 2016

That episode pushed me into the second week of 2016, listing but not rudderless. After several days of cleaning up loose ends left over from leaving the paper, I began picking up freelance work from Internet free-agent websites. I sold my Fat Leonard piece to Gannett, and it would eventually appear in *USA Today*. However, the *Washington Post's* national military bribery story would break before my article was published, and the timing diminished the effect of my work. To the casual observer, what would, and *should*, have been a seminal exposé appeared instead to be leveraging the national scandal to ride its coattails.

Six weeks after the fateful day I exited the *Union-Tribune*, I visited a trusted friend of many years. Lindsay stood behind me, a hand on each shoulder as I considered my options in her chair at the salon.

"I want something different today," I said as we peered into the mirror at her station. "The gods seem to favor change, and I shall give it to them."

"Okay, I see you're in a strange mood today. But I'm here to serve milady," Lindsay said. She cocked her head and sized up the possibilities, her creative wheels spinning. "How far do you want to go? I have weaves. I can do extensions, and I can always cut and color…." She began positioning the laptop camera for use with her hairstyle visualization software.

"I don't want to go *too* crazy," I wavered. "Maybe try a different color and a more modern style. Something easier to care for; maybe not so long?"

"How about a tousled look with some highlights?" Lindsay leaned back and regarded me in the mirror. "I can do a textured, short bob. How about deepening your natural color to more of an auburn for the base? I could layer over some ginger and strawberry blonde shine…."

"Oh, that sounds great." I was intrigued by the possibilities. "Can you show me a what-if?"

As the 3D rotating image of my head popped up on the screen, I had to admit I liked the look — with a qualifier. "Can we make the base color a tad darker?"

Lindsay changed one of the app's settings and glanced back at me to see my reaction.

"Perfect." I was excited over the fresh look. "Let's do *that!*"

"So, what's motivating the 'new you'?" Lindsay began prepping her station for her task, her voice sliding into a tease. "Is there a romantic development I *must* hear about in your life?"

"Oh, no, nothing like that. I quit the *Union-Tribune,* and I'm going to freelance for a while." The news dropped like a bomb.

Though the surprise on her face was apparent, Lindsay absorbed the hit without saying a word as she began sectioning my hair for coloring. She quickly settled into acceptance. "To be honest," she said, fastening clips to separate my hair into sections, "I never understood why you went to work for such a stick-in-the-mud paper anyway. Then, after you'd been there so long, I didn't think you'd ever leave."

I relayed the basic story of my departure from the newsroom, reflecting aloud on why I'd left. "Linds, I think I inflict some of these challenges upon myself. Maybe it's genetic or just inherent to my nature. I've been called 'incorrigible' occasionally by those who love me," I added wryly.

"Oh, *no!* Say it isn't so!" Lindsay cooed in falsetto. She stopped her work to laugh without pulling out any of my hair.

"Hey, it's not so much that I *can't* change. It's more that I have to do it at my pace." I mounted a weak defense. "Still, I know much of it's on me. I have this hardheaded idea about not compromising my core beliefs. Or shortchanging certain reporting standards. I like to think it's my brand of professionalism."

Lindsay vouched for the idea as she began placing towels to do the color. "It's worked pretty well for you. Come on, you're respected, and I've read some excellent stories you wrote."

"Thanks. You are *so* discerning, Lindsay," I said with faux arrogance before getting serious again. "But I can't quite get to that next level. The mark of a true professional in this business is making the sacrifices necessary to get the story out. I knew that going in. I haven't picked my battles well. I get into situations where worthwhile outcomes suffer in the quest for perfection."

"Your Fat Leonard piece was great. Is that what bothers you? That it didn't turn into something bigger?" The acrid smell of the chemicals she was mixing filled my nostrils.

"That's part of it," I admitted. "But I tried too hard at the beginning of my career to fit in. I've gone out for drinks more than a few times, thinking I was 'one of the boys,' only to find out later that I wasn't. Letting your hair down among those you believe you can trust only works if the trust is there. And people have thrown things back in my face that I never meant to be fodder for a public discussion."

"That's why I like what I do," Lindsay offered. "I could never deal with that whole 'glass ceiling' thing. You need to lighten up on yourself — it's not all on you, right?"

"Thanks, Linds…. That's true. The industry itself is the root cause of many of its failings. Those problems have become legion, familiar to everyone. The sordid groveling and selling of publishers' souls for ad revenues as they try to compensate for shrinking circulations and newsrooms. Weak organizations buying out the weaker — which wipes out the local competition that drives investigative reporting."

Lindsay nodded. "Wasn't the original purpose of the ads to support the newsgathering? Now, they tailor the news to promote the advertising. Turning all the Coke cans so the labels face the camera — just before the TV reporter narrates the home invasion that killed five people," she said disdainfully. "Soon, your family's death won't get reported at all if they didn't buy enough Coke to show the viewers."

"There's no money in regional markets for in-depth reporting," I added. "So, talent and resources flow to national conglomerates owned by billionaires. In their minds, it's their money to do with as they please. They feel they bought the right to impose their slant on the news. That attitude trickles down to or gets forced upon the editorial boards and only worsens from there. That's the situation at the *Union-Tribune.*"

"All that has to affect the quality of the reporters they can hire," Lindsay offered. "Who'd accept a situation like that? Maybe someone fresh out of college?"

"Your 'glass ceiling,'" I agreed. "Staff diversity and seniority are among the first casualties. I know it's directly affected my career, especially as a woman." We fell silent momentarily while Lindsay began to apply color to my hair.

"Do you plan to freelance permanently? Or is that just to fill in until you find something better?"

"I'm not sure," I answered. "My portfolio shows I have the chops to compete for a slot with one of the big online media organizations. Maybe CNN. But those outlets are tightening their belts, too. The competition would be stiff. The result wouldn't differ much from what I had before."

"At least you'd be on the national stage instead of stuck in a local market…."

"True." I thought about it. "Maybe a meatier selection of stories to chase. But the reporting would still take a back seat to profits."

"It's always about the money, right?"

"Greed," I granted, then gave a big sigh. Our talk turned to world peace, as was our wont when Lindsay did my hair. My future employment options would go unresolved.

Still, the conversation proved a healthy one for me. My mood had improved, and I liked the change in my appearance. I took some time to reflect on the outcome of my Fat Leonard work. Even though I wasn't the one who got to tell the bigger story, its impact proved I still had the instincts for a great news piece. Now, I was free and hungry to report that breakthrough magnum opus I could call my own.

But I'd be hungrier than was good for me if I couldn't pay my bills.

THE WRITINGS OF
AVRIL MARIA SERENE

CHAPTER 10

PRESENT DAY

Since leaving the *Union-Tribune*, I'd sought out unique narratives for my readers — pieces that would set me apart from other freelance reporters. Almost overnight, circumstances had granted me the freedom and funding to choose the articles I wanted to write. Just as suddenly, not one but two deeply personal stories had come my way.

Now, the challenge would be splitting my time while giving both the attention they deserve. In my mind, I heard Mom saying, "Be careful what you wish for, Debra Ann."

Coach's murder seemed the most urgent. The requirement not to interfere with the authorities in an active police investigation limited how far I could go. There'd likely be downtime I could devote to Dad's letters.

I called Cassidy Plame née Cantor to express my condolences and to ask her permission to investigate what had happened to her father. We'd remained friends over the years, although since she'd moved to San

Francisco, we hadn't seen much of each other. Still, we'd talked when opportunities arose, and she'd followed my career.

She welcomed my help now. While she had confidence that the police would do what they could, she knew they were working from very few clues.

It was seven p.m. when I got to Coach's house. He and Celia had purchased it long after I'd grown up, and I hadn't been here often. The yellow-bulbed porch light cast a warm, inviting glow over the entrance, contrasting with the heavy feeling in my heart. I rang the lighted doorbell, disappointed that it didn't have a video camera to help unravel the mystery — likely a reflection of Coach's frugality.

As I waited for Cassidy to answer, I scanned the front of the home. It was a large, older frame house in the Craftsman style, painted a cream color, with a river stone façade halfway up the exterior walls. Completing the front of the house was a wrap-around porch in dark green enamel flooring, with an oak swing that faced the street. The home's residents and visitors had used the swing often; the finish was wearing away from the seat's arms and the front and back slats. Frequent sitters had squashed the sun-faded cushions nearly flat.

The door opened with a slight creaking.

"Hi, Cassidy, it's good to see you again. I'm *so* sorry this has happened to your family," I said as we hugged. Whereas Coach had been tall and slender, Cassidy took after her mother, her physique shorter, rounder, and softer. I knew from past conversations that she struggled to lose the baby weight after Shannon was born, and she'd since given up the fight. Crying had rimmed her eyes in red, and she held a crumpled tissue in her right hand.

"You're looking well, Debra Ann. Thanks for coming over." Cassidy swept her left arm toward the living room to invite me in. "Father was always proud of the girls he coached and taught. I know he was pleased with how well you've done for yourself. He's said as much. He would have been grateful that you'd want to help."

"I was devastated when I heard the news. I still can't believe it. Lindsay told me when she was doing my hair. Such an incredible shame, and for the life of me, I can't understand why anyone would do this, especially to *Coach*, of all people."

"Lindsay called me after it happened." Cassidy dabbed at her eyes with the tissue. "She was as upset as I was. No one has any idea what could have led to this. The police were all over the place, looking for evidence, anything at all. They haven't found anything that tells them why.

"They say it looks like Father let the murderer in. Maybe he knew them. They traced their footsteps to the La-Z-Boy and the couch, but Father was shot twice without any sign that either of them sat down. The killer must have worn gloves; nothing says they went anywhere else in the house." She sounded defeated.

I glanced over the area around us. The home's furnishings, though not luxurious, were comfortable, of good quality, and well-treated. An overstuffed, brown leather sofa with accent stitching complemented a matching recliner. They bordered a round, hand-braided rug with fringed edges. A large, irregular brownish stain remained near one end where someone had attempted to clean up Coach's blood.

Centered on that rug was an oval coffee table. Its top had a striking framed honeycomb pattern of various complementary woods. An end table with the same design took up the area between the recliner and the nearest arm of the sofa. Two table lamps and three ceiling fan globes illuminated the living room. The lights in the rest of the house were off, though a dim glow came from what I assumed was the kitchen area. The outlines of a darkened dining table and chairs were visible in the next room.

"I put Mom's cats in the bedroom – I couldn't remember if you were allergic."

"Oh, Cass, that was so thoughtful, especially at a time like this, but no, I'm fine — let them have their freedom."

"They'll be OK for a while longer. I've just started packing some of Father's belongings from his office. It's hard. I keep coming across things I remember, and they make me cry."

"I got to spend some time with my dad before he passed," I said, my heart aching for her, "so it's not the same as someone you love being taken from you suddenly, especially with such violence. Still, when I had to go through my father's things, there were several days I didn't think I would make it. But the guilt from not seeing it through would be worse. It's so lonely because no one else wants to be around to do that part. They just can't deal with it. I think I understand a little of what you must be feeling."

"You'd know as well as anyone. I'm sad for anybody who has to do this. But I'm glad you're here. I know you want to help; I wouldn't have any idea where you'd start."

"I don't want to add to your pain," I said after thinking a moment, "but honestly, Coach's office might be a good place to begin."

"It'll be easier with you here. Father's desk is back here."

She turned to go down the hall on the left side of the living room, flipping on the lights as I followed.

In a little alcove, I saw a half-filled cardboard box with the ears folded down, sitting on a padded, black vinyl office chair. The second drawer down on the left side of the dark-oak desk was open. I assumed Cassidy was working with its contents when my arrival interrupted her.

"May I?" I asked before peering into the box.

"Please, if you need to see anything, feel free."

I first noticed a jumbled pile of inch-and-a-half-square yellow Post-it notepads.

"What did Coach use all these sticky notes for?" I was puzzled.

"Oh, *those*," Cassidy said, and for the first time today, I saw a little smile cross her face. "For all the people Father enjoyed, and for everyone who liked him, he was famously horrible at remembering names. So, Father developed this habit, something of a memory trick. When he heard the name of someone new to him, he'd write it down somewhere. It was the first thing he'd do once he got the chance; he preferred that no one see him.

"That's why he has these little Post-it notepads everywhere. Trying to remember a name long enough to write it down helped him recall it later. He didn't need whatever he wrote down after that, so he'd eventually throw it away. If you looked at his play sheets at our games, you'd see it wasn't just basketball notes. He'd fill them with names of opposing players, coaches, and the fans who came up to convey their congratulations or sympathies."

"*That's* interesting and maybe helpful…. Where did he throw away his trash?"

"Here's the little one he uses in here." She reached over and handed me a wire mesh wastebasket.

The basket was full of crumpled sticky notes and other papers. Near the top was one that read "David" in quotes. None of the other discarded paper looked promising.

"Is this where Coach took all his messages?"

"When he wasn't cooking, out in the yard, or watching TV, yes," Cassidy replied. "He did most of his business from this desk."

"Can we gather the other trash cans from the house?"

"Sure, no problem. Give me a few minutes."

"I'll come with," I offered. We brought the five wastebaskets we found into Coach's office. Cassidy checked outside, but the garbage and the recyclables bins were empty.

"Is there space somewhere we can go through these?" While walking through the house, I noticed that furniture took up most of the rooms.

"Father's bed is king-sized — we could cover it with a shower curtain or plastic garbage bags and dump these out on that. There's not much in most of them," Cassidy said.

"That sounds great — let's do that."

"I'll put the cats upstairs. They're too nosey, won't leave us alone."

We worked together for an hour, looking for anything that struck us as meaningful. There were several notes where we weren't sure what Coach meant and three that had promise.

Cassidy identified one of the three as a prescription. That left two: the "David" note and another from the kitchen that read, "Carmel mtn C/L - Barnwell 7 Th."

The little yellow squares were undated, so we didn't know their order or how recently they'd been written. We speculated what that last note could mean.

"Can you think of anything Coach had going on in Carmel Mountain?"

Cassidy wrinkled her brow in concentration. "Father has a house over there that he rents out, off the Rancho Bernardo exit on I-15.... The rental houses were Mother's hobby, but he still has them." She wasn't ready to use the past tense — still, having something we could do seemed to help both of us.

"Does he have tenants in the house?"

"Yes, but the renter's name is Tisdale. I don't know of any 'Barnwell' or even 'David' among his tenants. But now that you mention it, Father told me the Tisdales are on a month-to-month agreement because he put the place up for sale. He said it was too much work keeping up with the rental houses."

"I don't suppose he listed it on Craigslist?" A lightbulb had gone off as to what "C/L" might represent.

"He wasn't in a hurry to sell." There was curiosity in Cassidy's voice. "And he wasn't about to pay six percent for the MLS realtor commissions. So, yes — he wanted to save some money. It completely skipped my mind."

"Okay. For the sake of argument, let's say somebody named 'Barnwell' — maybe 'David Barnwell' — expressed interest in that Carmel Mountain property. Let's assume that '7 Th' doesn't mean 'the seventh;' it means 'seven o'clock Thursday.' So, the note *could* refer to around halftime of the football game on the same night they killed him.

"Do you have Coach's cell phone or his laptop? Maybe he left us something useful."

"No, the police took both as evidence," Cassidy replied. "They needed their computer forensics expert to see what was on them. I didn't have Father's password."

"Let me try googling different combinations of keywords from these two notes." I pulled out my cell phone and let my fingers do some walking.

A half-hour later, nothing interesting had jumped from the screen. I made a mental note to call Marci when I got back home. I didn't want Cassidy to overhear any information that might upset her.

Cassidy's comment about her father watching TV had put another thought in my head.

"Can we go back to the living room? I want to check something."

I spotted the smart TV remote sitting on the end table by the La-Z-Boy.

"Do you know if the TV was on when the police officers first arrived?"

"No, I remember the detective asking the patrol officers that, and they said it wasn't on."

"Have you used the TV since you've been here?"

"No, trust me, watching a TV show was the last thing on my mind."

I hit the remote's On and OK buttons to see what Coach had last watched. The flatscreen displayed CBS News 8. Something wasn't right. As the daughter of another rabid American football fan, I knew that Thursday Night Football aired on Amazon Prime, beginning at 5:15. There was no way Coach would have missed it unless he had something else more important going on. That suggested not only did Coach know his first visitor that night, but he was expecting them. It wasn't a social meeting because they would've watched football. And whatever the meeting was about meant enough to Coach that he'd forego the game.

"Cass, can I have your permission to canvass some of your neighbors? I need to understand better what they may have seen or heard."

Cassidy nodded.

"It's too late for that tonight, so I'll start in the morning,"

"Do you want me to go along?" Cassidy seemed nervous about the prospect.

"No. Thanks for the offer, but not this time. I don't want to intimidate anyone who happens to be alone with a two-on-one situation at their front door. Homicides in a neighborhood like this tend to freak people out anyway."

In work mode now, I realized too late I'd used the wrong word for her father's death. I winced inside as I saw I'd upset her again.

"I'll let you know what I find out," I said lamely, unable to think of anything I could say to help her feel better. I could only hope that once we solved Coach's murder, the lesser hurts would fade with time.

THE WRITINGS OF
AVRIL MARIA SERENE

CHAPTER 11

Returning to Coach's neighborhood the following morning, I began canvassing around ten a.m.

I didn't fare well with the first three neighbors I visited.

James Seaver, the next-door resident Marci had described as a possible suspect in the disappearance of his wife, was the first neighbor to answer my knock. He was in his mid-fifties, balding, his remaining hair almost entirely gray. The blue polo shirt and shorts he wore emphasized a prominent beer gut.

Close to six feet tall, Seaver had a sallow complexion and wore a full gray beard cut to moderate length, with noticeably untrimmed nose, ear, and eyebrow hair. A prominent snout, large ears, and what seemed like a permanent frown etched in creases dominated his face. The leathery wrinkles on what I could see of his skin suggested he'd been a lifetime cigarette smoker — I could smell it in his clothes even across the several feet between us.

He was carrying a tiny dachshund with pronounced graying around its muzzle. The little dog was hoarsely yipping as if it couldn't manage a full-throated bark. Seaver, who at first impression hadn't struck me as capable of much affection, kissed the pooch on the top of its head. "It's OK, Bubbles, daddy's got this," Seaver whispered into the back of the animal's neck as he stroked it gently between its ears with his nose. The little dog raised his muzzle in response, and I glimpsed a bright red bowtie fastened to its collar. Without lifting his face, Seaver raised his eyes to peer at me from behind Bubbles's head.

The effect was so creepy it sent a shiver running down my spine. But for all the man's sentiments toward the dog, his response to my questions was notably curt. He'd only say that he hadn't been home at the time of the homicide. He closed the door before listening to my response or further questions.

The neighbors across the street from Coach and beside Seaver said they'd been watching the game. They hadn't heard or seen anything unusual, and what they knew of the homicide came from newscasts and the local rumor mill.

Then I hit paydirt with Jess Nessbaum, the Neighborhood Watch captain across from the Seaver residence. In her late sixties or early seventies, with white hair and hearing aids, she came off as someone who'd been a strict taskmaster back in her day — my first thought was that she might have been a Catholic nun. Still, she was friendly once she opened up. A retired schoolteacher, she'd worked with Coach for several years. She liked to gossip and felt it was her duty to keep a vigilant eye on the neighborhood.

Much of what she told me early on was a repeat of what she'd said to the police. When we got to the part about the first visitor that night leaving, I almost missed it.

"It was only ten or twelve minutes, and then the man left," Jess said.

"Was there anything different in the man's appearance from when he first arrived?"

"I don't think so, but I couldn't tell because Coach had turned out the porch light."

"What about as he headed out Coach's door?" I thought her first answer described the man as he was walking further down the street.

"That's what I said — the light was out, and I couldn't see very well," Jess repeated, believing I hadn't heard her.

"Wait — the porch light was off *before* the man left and walked down the front steps?" I wanted to make sure I hadn't misunderstood.

"Yes, like I told you … is that important?"

"Let's just say it could be helpful, and I appreciate your attention to detail." I smiled.

Coach might have been diligent about saving electricity; still, he was too considerate to make a visitor navigate his front steps in darkness upon leaving. That told me Coach was either incapacitated or already dead when the first visitor left the premises. The turned-off TV and the Post-it notes suggested this was a planned meeting between two people who had communicated with one another beforehand. That ruled out Coach or his address as mistaken targets and meant the van's occupants were the cleanup crew.

Marci had listed for me several of the detectives' questions. In my mind, I now had answers for three of those.

"Is there anything else you can tell me?" I asked, ready to wrap up the interview.

"When the guy walked in front of my house, he seemed to be walking gingerly, like maybe he had blisters on his heels," Jess added.

She'd just said she couldn't see him well, so I wondered how she picked up on a nuance in his walk.

Catching the look of confusion on my face, she quickly explained. "See that streetlamp?" She pointed through her front window. "He had to walk underneath it. I wasn't paying much attention when he came, but I *was* looking when he left and passed by."

"Ah, I see. Thanks, that makes perfect sense. So, this man had something wrong with his feet?"

"He was sideways to me, and I couldn't see his front, but he was limping, that's for sure."

The quick in-and-out, placement of his shots, and probable silencer meant he was a pro. *Does an otherwise well-dressed professional killer walk to a planned murder wearing ill-fitting shoes?* That didn't wash. Did he have a physical impairment? Maybe he was injured while in the house? The scene didn't suggest any struggle, though with a crew cleaning up, it would be hard to tell.

I knew of another possibility from having dated a short man once who had a complex about his height. If you place lifts in standard men's dress shoes, it changes where the back seam around the top of the shoe opening rides the heel. Walking any distance that way can cause blisters very quickly. Was our killer trying to disguise his height or perhaps intentionally altering his gait?

I would need to add some new possibilities to our killer's description.

"One final question, Jess, and I promise I'll leave you be," I said with a smile. "What made you call Coach to see if he was okay after that van arrived?"

"I wasn't going to, originally," she replied. "It wasn't all that late yet, and they weren't breaking in. But as they entered that house, the second man turned back and looked around — like he was trying to see if anyone was watching.

"And then I thought: *Why didn't Coach turn on the light for them if they were supposed to be there?*"

CHAPTER 12

s soon as I returned home from interviewing Jess Nessbaum, I called Marci to share with her what I'd found and learned. The department's investigators hadn't written any connection to a "David Barnwell" or similar name into their notes. But Marci promised to pass the information along to the detectives working Coach's murder.

Marci was grateful for the clue about the porch light and the first visitor's limp. Investigators had already interviewed Coach's tenants and checked out the real estate angle, though it hadn't produced any leads. We agreed to keep each other in the loop.

That left me, at least for the moment, without anything further to pursue on my own that wouldn't entangle me in the investigator's work.

So, I returned to Dad's graveside letters. As I considered Bubba's dilemma over other people moving a dead body while he was stealing from the home, I also understood Dad's concerns about the possible commission of a homicide. His original simple intention to identify the author and return the letters might not cut it.

My father's attempts to turn the letters over to the police and not being taken seriously must have been humiliating. It could have been worse. They could have accepted the letters to humor Dad, then sat on their hands and done nothing.

A side effect of writing an in-depth article about the department's many problems was that I'd learned too much. I could never trust them again like an ordinary citizen might if they were ignorant of those issues. There were exceptions, but for too many officers, wait-and-see had become the San Diego Police Department's unofficial standard policy for anything out of the ordinary.

Sadly, the problem of quality policing was country-wide in scope. Several years after my piece on the San Diego department, the FBI reported that the national homicide clearance rate had dropped to 54 percent. When a murder happens anywhere in the U.S. today, it's a coin flip as to whether the courts will ever punish anyone for it. In an article entitled "Six Reasons the Murder Clearance Rate Is at an All-Time Low," published by *The Atlantic*, the subtitle stated the issue succinctly: "For the past 60 years, U.S. detectives have gotten worse at one of the most basic jobs of law enforcement."

San Diego officials claimed to solve homicides at a rate higher than the national average. But there's a dirty little secret underlying the numbers. Many homicides begin as missing-person reports. But only a percentage of the missing in San Diego are ever reported, which keeps the reported murder rate artificially low. If you're not looking for them, it's less likely you'll discover a homicide. Not wanting to look explained why Dad's reports went uninvestigated.

It started with the homeless. SDPD didn't mind hearing that homeless people were missing — not at all, so long as no one expected them to *do* anything about them. Then, there was the unholy alliance with the Navy base. Most of the unreported missing in that area were sex workers. Their murders tended to get reported sometime after their killer had dumped the body —that's an issue in San Diego, where their final resting place could be far out in the Pacific Ocean. Proactively monitoring that at-risk community to identify the missing would embarrass the base and incarcerate more of its sailors — and, in all likelihood, officers as well. So, those missing went ignored, along with any homicides among them. Even with those undiscovered murders, San Diego still added about a quarter of their unsolved homicides every year to the hundreds of cold cases in their files.

But as things worked out, circumstances had rendered giving Dad's letters to the police moot anyway. Nearly three months passed between his recording of that microcassette and my hearing it. Any benefit to immediately turning them over to investigators had vanished. I still didn't know who originally wrote the letters or anything about who he'd written them to. I couldn't even be sure if the events described in the correspondence had happened or could have.

Still, I thought there might be a story here. And if that story had taken a criminal turn, I'd agree with Dad that the police should be involved.

I'd need more facts than I had in hand for law enforcement to take the story, these letters, and the situation seriously. Finding the letter writer was still the first part of the task, but I also had to learn more about the circumstances he described. One challenge I faced was that I might not have everything Bubba wrote. We buried Dad two and a half months ago. The last time he'd have been well enough, even attended by a nurse, to go to Mom's gravesite was two weeks before that. I was missing around twelve weeks of letters if the pattern had continued.

Hopefully, the caretaker at the memorial gardens kept collecting them in Dad's stead. I'd been wanting to visit my parents. If I timed it right, I should be able to chat with the caretaker during his work hours.

It was pleasantly cool and sunny as I approached the caretaker's tiny office. It was situated next to the walkthrough mausoleum, where two rows of above-ground memorial crypts awaited visitors. A note on a whiteboard suctioned-cupped to the office's door glass said that the caretaker had gone to the utility shed — he'd return in thirty minutes. It was a perfect day for some exercise, and I knew where they kept the mowers and garden equipment in the back corner of the grounds, so I walked to the storage building.

Behind a stack of bags of fertilizer stood a short, portly man with a ruddy complexion, a ready smile, and a friendly disposition. The name tag on his uniform shirt identified him as Gary "Gravy" Gilbert. He certainly wasn't the stereotypical superintendent of a cemetery I was expecting — I may have watched *Army of Darkness* one too many times as a teenager.

"Hi, Mr. Gilbert. I'm sorry to interrupt what you're doing. I'm Debra Ann Wynn. You helped my dad, Alex, with a little mystery he was trying to solve around some letters found on the grounds. He asked me to take up the challenge."

"Ms. Wynn, it's nice to meet you. But I'm not sure what you mean," Gilbert replied.

"Oh, I apologize. Let me start from the beginning," I said. "The Wynn family — *W-y-n-n* — has one of the large plots in the Gardens. We interred my mother, Marianne, and my brother, Eddie, here. My father recently passed away and is now buried in our plot…."

"I knew Alex, and I'm truly sorry for your loss," Gilbert interrupted. "I worked with him many years ago when he had the oak tree replanted. But he should have turned them over to me if he had found letters belonging to someone else on the grounds. I haven't spoken with him."

Gilbert was not a good liar, but something had made him uncooperative, and I needed his help.

"Look, Mr. Gilbert, I'm not trying to get anyone into trouble, but those letters…." Gilbert interrupted again before I got any further, showing me he was nervous about something.

"Ms. Wynn, we have strict policies here in the Gardens about property belonging to the loved ones and visitors of the deceased."

He began parroting the sign on the back wall of the caretaker's office: "We hold everything someone turns in for six months in the name of the deceased party. After that, we're not responsible, and we dispose of the property or donate it to charity, as management deems appropriate."

"Mr. Gilbert, will you *please* listen to me? The letters my father discovered were in unsealed envelopes with blank pages. They were next to our headstone, but the writer didn't address them to us. My father had taken it upon himself to find out who they *did* belong to."

Gilbert looked at me for several moments, finally responding, "Ms. Wynn, you must understand. We've had an uptick in complaints about missing and damaged items. We've had to let some people go recently. Do you hear what I am saying to you? I've been here twenty-two years, and I like my job."

"All I'm trying to do is finish something Dad started." I was treading carefully. "Something he asked me in his last wishes, and I need your help. That's it. The one thing I don't want is for you or anyone else to lose their employment over anything."

Rocking back and looking down at his shoes, he gave in. "I can only talk hypothetically." His speech slowed, his enunciation precise. "Your father and I *might* have worked out an arrangement where he'd try to find out who those letters belonged to. And theoretically, I *might* have given him a few our groundskeeper found."

Gilbert paused, still sizing me up. He seemed to debate with himself if he wanted to continue the conversation. After a moment of silence, he spoke again.

"You know, Alex warned me about you. He mentioned several times that his daughter was an attractive redhead. Alex used the word 'pretty' because fathers never consider their daughters grown up. He said you could be persistent, sometimes even stubborn." He flashed a quick grin. "I don't like misleading anyone, but it's been rough around here lately. What say we start over?"

"I'm game," I replied, returning his smile, relieved he'd decided in my favor. And even though I knew he meant the backhanded compliment on my looks to cover for his earlier recalcitrance, he *had* flattered me. The closer I edged toward forty, the happier I was with any positive comments that came my way. I couldn't help but smile a little at my vanity.

"Well, Debra Ann, I'm Gary, and it is so nice to meet you. I always enjoyed talking with your father during his weekly visits." He extended his hand, and we shook.

"The two of you spoke often?"

"He was such a decent man. Most visitors want me to chase down flowers that have gone missing. Or they'll complain about how the groundskeeper trimmed the grass around a marker. Sometimes, the bereaved are just looking for an outlet to express the anger and frustration that can accompany a loss. Your father wasn't like that. He always seemed to appreciate what little help I could offer."

"Dad preferred to look at it as though this place was caring for Mom and Eddie. He would have wanted everything around them to be peaceful and positive."

"That came across in our conversations; it truly did," Gary acknowledged. "We talked about other things, too. Your father shared stories about you and your mother, and we discussed world events. I always enjoyed our exchanges. I was so sorry when I got the internment request. I didn't realize he'd been ill."

"It was pancreatic cancer," I explained. "Dad didn't have any symptoms he recognized until it had already spread. He didn't have long after the doctor's diagnosis."

"I'll miss him." Gary sighed. "It's been the best part of six months since he and I last spoke. I imagine you're here to pick up the final batch of the letters he was trying to figure out?"

"Yes. It's my duty now to pursue the mystery to its conclusion." I gave him a purposeful smile. "You said 'final.' What told you there won't be more?"

"I honestly don't know that for a fact." He frowned. "But it's been around a month since we've seen any new envelopes. It's good to know you're following up with them. I'm curious myself where it all goes."

"I'm just glad you kept saving them."

Gary nodded as he closed and locked the shed door.

"Your timing is great. No one else has expressed any interest in the envelopes. Since the greenskeeper hasn't turned up any others, I was about to discard what we have. I'd just gathered everything together to dispose of them. Follow me; they're back at the office."

As we walked, curiosity got the best of me. "You probably get this question constantly, but I *must* know how you got the nickname 'Gravy'...." I waved at his name tag.

"Oh, *that*." He laughed. "I consider my work here my second job. After my wife, naturally, my next great love is smoking and barbecuing. So, when you mix barbequing with being the caretaker of a memorial garden, it comes out 'Gravy' — a terrible pun, but it just kind of stuck."

"Ahhh, that explains it." I had to grin.

"In my glory days, before I came out to California, I was a pitmaster champion. I competed with the likes of Myron Mixon before he became famous. I still pick up ribbons from time to time. My wife and I have a dually rig with a whole-hog smoker in the bed and a trailer with a spit, grill, and braising setup."

"You're serious about it, then. That's quite an investment!" I exclaimed. I remember vehicles like that being expensive when Dad would buy them for his construction business. "I take it you travel a lot doing this...."

"Not like we used to, but we attend local meets and competitions every few weeks. We can usually get into four national competitions a year."

"Now, *that* sounds like an awesome life." I meant every word of it.

We'd come to the office, and Gary let us in. After rummaging behind the counter, he produced a thick bundle of letters and cards bound with postal twine. "Did your father tell you about our deal?"

"Return the letters if anyone asks for them, and let you know what I find out?" I answered quizzically.

"And the lady gets an 'A plus.' I hope this helps and that some good comes from it for someone."

I thumbed through the corners of the letters in the packet. A few looked like the sprinkler system, or perhaps rain, had gotten to them before the greenskeeper recovered them. "Gary, you've been great. I hope you have a wonderful day, and I'll stay in touch," I said, then left to return to my car. Once there, I took the flower arrangement out of the cooler and carried it back to the gravesite to spend a moment with Mom, Dad, and Eddie. I wanted them to know I was on the trail and would check back in a week. After saying my goodbyes, I turned to go back to my car.

But on a whim, I decided instead to try finding the headstone where Bubba was leaving his letters. There weren't any notes from Dad in the folder he'd left me besides those he'd scribbled in the margins. I'd hoped to find something about the headstones he'd checked out surrounding our plot. Absent his guidance, I decided to map out the other markers around ours. As I did, I'd assess them as candidates for Bubba's intended letter recipient. I stuck a moistened finger in the air. The prevailing breezes were from the west, so I plotted out a rough spiral centered on my parents' headstone, favoring that side.

The circumference of each circle I walked outward from our monument was becoming much longer. I hadn't thought it through beforehand and was still in my heels. My feet were killing me, pun unintended. With early evening approaching, clouds of biting gnats rose from the grass. I was reaching the point of exhaustion and getting ready to call it a day by the time I approached the fourteenth headstone. I'd found a few possibilities up to that point, but none very encouraging.

A more prominent monument, this headstone fronted a family plot for parents with two children. The family name was "Pierce," and one grave appeared freshly dug. This gravesite was all too familiar to me. I couldn't explain why, but I vividly recalled the odd sensation of being held here when I'd gotten my heel stuck chasing down that tissue three weeks ago. Since then, the engraver added the headstone's last name and date. A daughter, Bridget Erin Pierce-Coleman, passed nearly two years ago at age thirty-four. The son, Brian James Pierce, had died early last month at thirty-two. That would have been right about when Gary Gilbert said the greenskeeper had stopped turning in more letters. Doing the math in my head told me Brian's father passed when he was just two and his mother when he was only four. Bridget would have been eight when they interred her mother.

There was a memorial vase holder on the right side of the Pierce family monument, a thick iron ring welded to a steel stake driven into the ground. The vase was missing; the diameter of the iron circle was about eight inches. Now I had an idea how those letters began their trip. I could picture Brian curling the envelopes to fit in the ring. Friction would no doubt hold the letter for a while, but it wouldn't be enough to withstand the breezes and the gentle showers of the nightly sprinklers for very long.

The Pierce marker was three large family plots west and one row north of my family's. The pathway between their headstone and the base of our oak tree was broad and unobstructed.

The chances that Brian Pierce was the author of these letters were hard to dismiss. That would mean he, too, had come to a premature demise. My immediate concern was his passing meant I couldn't keep my promise to

Dad. If this monument was the intended destination of those letters, I couldn't return them with the entire family now gone.

I'd have a lot of research to do on the Internet this evening to confirm my suspicions. Still, if I was right, Brian's death at a young age and its proximity in both time and space to the capital crime he'd written about was no coincidence. That was troubling to me.

Had someone killed Brian Pierce because of what he'd seen that night? Or because he'd told the wrong person the same story he'd written for his sister?

THE WRITINGS OF
AVRIL MARIA SERENE

CHAPTER 13

With my growing confidence that Brian Pierce could be the author of the letters, I had some work ahead of me. I wanted to google Brian and his family to find out anything I could learn about his situation. I needed to treat the task as I would research for a piece — follow every lead and rabbit trail to its ultimate resolution, which could take several days

But I was also eager to read the letters Bubba had left since the last one Dad had seen. The Internet could wait. Reading the letters would be a better fit for the time I had remaining today and might tell me what led to Bubba's death — if, indeed, he was Brian, the newest piece to the puzzle. I headed back to my place and the collection of odds and ends I'd gathered from my father's home after he'd passed.

I retrieved Dad's 24-inch fluorescent black light from the box he'd marked "CEMETERY LETTERS." It hummed and flickered a moment after I plugged it in before settling into a steady, purplish glow. I had no clue what the PVC framework Dad had made was for, but I grabbed it anyway.

He'd included it in that box, so I assumed it had *something* to do with reading those letters.

Since the last letter Dad decoded referenced a crime, I needed to make working copies of the new batch. I wanted to read them but not disturb any trace evidence still left on the originals. Setting up a production line, I scrubbed the top of the kitchen table clean. Putting on some latex gloves. I laid each page next to the other. The original idea was to darken the dining room and turn off the cell phone camera's flash. I'd hold the black light in one hand and take photos with the other. That proved cumbersome, and the focus and size of the results were uneven.

I suddenly realized what Dad designed the PVC framework to do. The homemade stand held the black light perfectly for evenly illuminating the page, allowing my camera to center and focus on the entire sheet of paper. I set the black light on the parallel tubes. By placing the camera next to the nearest cross-member when I snapped the photo, I could quickly shuffle the pages in and out between the legs of the frame. The process produced perfectly uniform images. Once I'd captured the pages digitally, I shared them to my computer as e-mail attachments. I'd print each one off as needed, making the letters easy to read while sitting crossways in my recliner enjoying a cup of coffee.

The last two letters were the most relevant. I was now assuming that Bubba was Brian. The next-to-last letter described the repercussions that Bubba was experiencing from spray painting the wall and rug of Doc's home. He'd intended to call out the presumed murderers, but things had gone awry:

> The popo arent doing a damn thing about Doc or his dead wife. I finaly called in a tip on my burner, and they still havnt arested him. Maybe they thouht I wasnt serius because I used a voice changer.

I had to empathize with that, at least a little, because of Dad's experiences trying to get the police to listen.

There was a one-week gap between Brian's letters. The one that should have been next in the series was missing. I'd have to check with Gary to see if anyone might have turned in another letter since I last saw him.

The letter following reflected Brian's increasing paranoia, probably appropriate under the circumstances:

Doc must have some jiuce or a lot of money. Theres a bunch of faces in the old naberhood who dont belong, and there asking a lot of questions. No body you or I know. These guys look like hired goons — mostly x-military, with shaved heads, buzzcuts, and army tattoos. They arent too bright, and there not being quite about it. Thugs mussleing every body around. They kept throwing Bennie against the brickwall outside the strip club until they nocked him out cold. They said he better snitch on any one who talked about seeing a murder or someone hiding a body but he woudnt.

I dont know how they figgured out someone from <u>our</u> naberhood saw them move the dead lady. Coud have spotted my car leeving the block where they killed her, maybe followed me part way home but I dont think so. Maybe they tracked some goods back to my fence — I shoudnt have used my regular guy. He always dumps the stuff that isnt worth much at a pawnshop where people can see it. I should have thouht about that.

There flashing badges — the ones I saw looked like they came out of a cereal box. No way they are real cops, not undercover anyways. There calling themselves detectives but the sheilds they show are tin not gold. Two goons rented your old place, where you lived when Mikey was born.

3 turned up at Johnny Roccos without an invite and then asked for a menu. If you have any bisness being in Roccos, you

shoud know exactly what Johnny serves. Cannoli — pizza — lasagna, thats the deal. If they dont know you and specialy if they dont like you — you take a pretty good chance of getting your stomack pumped. And unless your a made man, you dont walk into Roccos without an appointmint. You forsure dont ask questions of peeple you dont know. And thretening them?!?

That would help pin down the general location where Brian lived — though it wasn't familiar to me, Johnny Rocco's shouldn't be too hard to find.

No, these wasnt locals. They damn sure wasnt cops — didnt have a clue about the naberhood. You know half the regulrs at Roccos are Confedential Informints for legit feds or local cops. They feed informaton to their handlers to get rid of their competetion. The other half are paying off the cops to protect their varius activeties. And we allways know which is which and who is who and they have some style, like Letti says, Panashe. These new guys dont know who they are messing with and have no class. If they keep it up then Frankies crew will have to explain the lay of the land to these clowns. I want to be a fly on the wall when that goes down — the last time something like this hapened they puled body parts out of the tumble dryers at the landromat for a week.

But until there gone, Ime shut down, cant do nothing, cant have a life. Your the only person Ive told about the docter and his people moving that body. But now I cant go out for a joint or a drink with my buddies — Im scared Ill let down my gard and say some thing mite get back to those ass wipes.

And now there asking who speshallizes in B&E's in the naberhood. They want to know who got poped for vandalising houses. Ive got one on my sheet from when I was a stupid kid. I did that Helter Skelter thing spraying serial killer shit on the walls with red paint. Remember? You got so mad at me when I told you I was the one who did it.

Brian's fear and sense of entrapment were palpable and came through in his writing. The loneliness must have been incredibly intense if he had to pen all this to his dead sister just to feel heard. I, too, was beginning to share his apprehension and immediately moved on to his last letter. It was dated three days before the engraving on his headstone said that he died:

Sis, Ive got to fix this. The cops arent checking out nothing about the dead lady. They woudnt beleive me if I told them — if I did, Ime back inside for the braking and entering. I cant go back to prison. This shit has made me too paronoid, and Ime not on my game any more when I go out. I'm afraid Ill make some idiot mistake and get busted.

And Ime not safe in the naberhood no more. These mercenarie ass clowns look like they arent here to spred a messige — there here to kill some body. I need to get these hired goons out of the pictur. Dammit I shoudnt have painted that message on the docters wall — live and lern I guess.

My only way out is to set things up to put them away for good. Maybe the cops wont do any thing about the lady getting killed. But if an other body shows up tyed to those same peeple, that shoud get the atention of the police — speshialy if its 1 of the 3 that was there that night. Sis you know Ime no killer, but the stakes are geting too hi. If I dont get them first, theyll get me. I can hear you telling me not to, but Ime seriusly out of optons here.

"Awww, Brian," I said out loud, "couldn't you have found someone else to tell and get *them* to talk to the cops?" I guessed he didn't feel he had anyone he could trust not to give him up to the goons. I had the clarity of hindsight on my side, of course, but if he'd written just one of those letters to law enforcement, just *maybe*…

But with Bubba likely Brian and Brian dead, we were long past anything that *maybe* could fix.

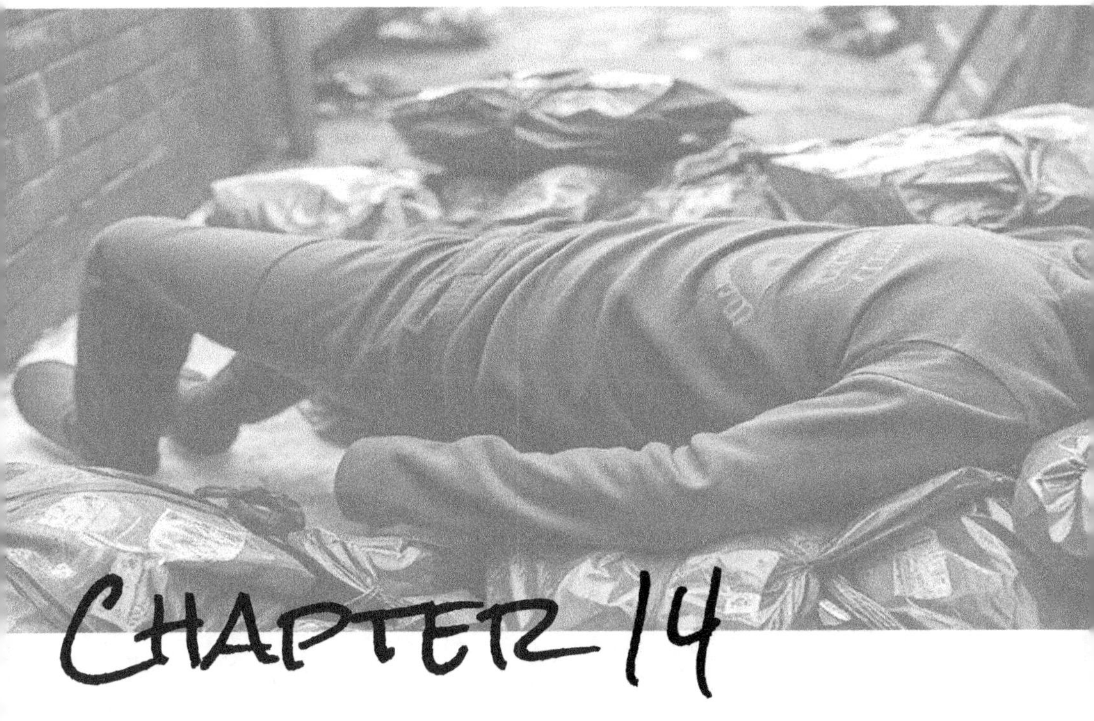

CHAPTER 14

I took thirty minutes to get a snack and think of other things. Still, a real uneasiness lingered in my mind about Brian becoming more aggressive. Though I could almost feel his desperation, his view of a "body" in the abstract as a bargaining chip was disconcerting. Brian's last missive continued:

Decided my best bet was to take it to there turf, where they woudnt expect me. I was doing driveby's of Docs house. One day I saw Doc & his girlfreind and another man leaving Docs place. I followed the smaler guy — it was hard to tell from a distanse but his voice sounded like the Rickie I heard that night. Hes shorter than me going bald, maybe 30 something — you can never realy know — they look older when they loose there hair. I folowed him for a while, not too close because I didn't want to get caught. He landed in this older kind of crumy-looking naberhood, mostly houses.

When Rickie puled up to a set of rail-road tracks, the crosing arms came down lites flashing. Rickie scooted around and thru them but I had to hang back so he woudnt get suspicius I was folowing him. Figgured Id lost the guy. But after the train was gone I saw he parked his car 2 doors down on the R side of the street. As I past by I scoped out the place. The house was small and rundown — 2-bedrooms on an ittybitty lot. No obvius securety I could see. No trees no dogs or other animals outside — he probly rents it. Theres a chainlink fence around the back and sides but nothing cross the front.

Good, I thought, more information I could use to find Rickie's house. Brian's correspondence continued:

So I pull over to the curb a few doors away and wait to see what was hapening. About 15 mins later Rickie left the house carrying a jim bag. He locked the deadbolt with his keys. That told me he lived there and hed be gone a while. After his car left I grabed my lock picks and a big screw driver — snuck around to the back side of the house and tried the sliding door. There was a broom stick handle on the inside track so it woudnt open. So I found an unlocked kichen window above the sink and got in that way.

This Rickie is a slob — lives alone — just Mens Clothes in the closet, Mens stuff in the bathroom — no pets. Hes into working out. Theres jim equipment and swet clothes all over the place but cant say Ime impressed with the results.

Took the broomstick handle Rickie was using to block the patio door but didnt take any thing else today. I got an idea tho, and Ill come back — I'm putting together a plan. If that goes the way I want Ill take Rickie's computor TV sound bar &

subwoofer – I shoud get some thing for doing all this work.

I was reminded just how differently professional thieves arranged their priorities from how I ordered mine. But even between criminals, I could see glaring differences: A wealthy, white-collar con artist like Fat Leonard wouldn't do anything if it didn't result in maximal gain for minimal risk. Yet someone like Bubba, fighting daily for his very existence, would take extreme chances based on emotion alone, giving very little consideration to either the investment or the rewards. The letter carried on:

Before I folowed Rickie, I thouht about killing a home–less dude with some poison hooch. Id hide the body in Docs house and call the cops. Theyd think it was him did it. But when I tried to pick some body I got sick. Looking some one in the face and killing thems one thing – draging an innosent person into all this is even wors. And without some thing to tye them together the docter might wiggle out of that 1 too.

But now I plan to go back to that little house one night – get rid of this Rickie and pin _that_ on the docter. Rickies smaller than me and hes a bad guy. Therell be less links to me if I dont use a gun. Ill catch him on a nite hes wasted – do it while hes sleeping — he wont feel a thing. No gilt no mess.

Sis I got it all figured out. 1st Ill print out a note and leeve it by Rickies computor. Say how hes trying to blackmail Doc for what they did with that ladys body. I still have some of the stuff I took from the docter's house that dosnt have my prints so I can leeve litle things around Rickies place for the police to put the 2 of them together.

Then Ill grab some things from Rickies and plant them at the docter's house. use a burner to call 911. The cops will have to at leest think about the docter getting revenje aganst Rickie for the blackmail.

But theyll have to get more serius about finding that mising girl. All the heat this spreds around shoud chase the out of town goons away from our naberhood. The note I made up to leeve at Rickies is awesome and shoud do the trick — it gos like this:

> Doc,
>
> I decided the $10,000 isnt enuff — I need more. You and your girlfreind will make big money from that lady you killed. I need $50,000 by this weekend or else I tell the police where we hid the body and what we did to it.
>
> — Rickie.

What do you think — pretty cool, huh? See how I turned it arond on them? I've been watching Rickies place. He goes out drinking Friday nites and comes back pretty hamered. Thats tomorow night, so Ill do it then — let you know how it goes. Maybe theyll finally do something about the docter and all this will help make up for the things I messed up. I coud acomplish some good in the world — Karma ha

I hope your doing ok wherever your at — thanks for lissening.

I miss you and love you —
Bubba

Aww, Jesus, Brian, what have you done? I thought to myself.

I'd begun to identify with Bubba and maybe even relate to his situation. Perhaps I shouldn't have been surprised, but the sudden turn to violence as a solution to his problems disheartened me. Whatever he'd done after that letter likely played a part in ending him. The day he wrote this last message preceded the date on his tombstone by just forty-eight hours.

Brian's situation reminded me of something Marci firmly believed. "That's the thing with life on the streets. The choices they see, and therefore, the ones they make, differ greatly from yours or mine. We say, 'Get an education!' and expect them to do that living in crime-ridden neighborhoods with a single parent going to crappy schools overrun by gangs — with no legal way to support themselves in the meantime. 'Mortgage the future you've never had for school loans!' For a lucky very few, guarantees from the federal government; for the rest, two words: 'credit score.' Meanwhile, we bombard them with peer-pressure ads demanding they spend what little money they have on the latest material fad.

"We then marvel at why they sell drugs or hang their dreams on athletic scholarships one out of a thousand might get, insinuating they have character flaws we don't share. But their world is one where the only access to good choices is through having power and resources, most of which we give, or surrender, to the already empowered and rich. That doesn't leave much to the poor or disadvantaged. We keep disregarding the disparities, but they're growing; eventually, we won't be able to ignore them any longer."

Marci might be the right person to ask for help verifying Brian's letters. But before I enlisted her, I needed to get on the Internet and track down what I could.

It didn't take long to nail down the basics. An article in the electronic edition of the *Union-Tribune* confirmed that Bridget Coleman née Pierce was in a head-on collision two years ago. A drunk driving the wrong way on I-5 struck her vehicle while she took her son, Michael, to school. She was in a coma for over two months. According to her obituary, the hospital pulled the plug after doctors diagnosed her as brain dead. Michael survived with minimal physical harm, and Bridget's aunt had been caring for him.

There wasn't much on Brian Pierce, but I found a revealing entry in an archive of Bridget's old MySpace account. At the time of her posting, Brian would have been sixteen. In her text, Bridget asked for prayers for her brother. Brian had severely injured himself in an off-road motorcycle accident when not wearing a helmet. Her sibling was undergoing life-threatening surgery for the frontal lobe injuries he'd sustained. Using Google Images, I found a photo of Brian in his mid-twenties. It showed significant scarring on his forehead, nose, and chin. It was clear why Brian might have had some of the social, emotional, and mental challenges I picked up from his letters.

Two brief articles referenced the same badly beaten body found dumped in an alleyway downtown the day after Brian's death. Both appealed to the public for more information. The mutilation was too severe for immediate identification at the scene, and police matched the victim through DNA — Brian was in the system for past crimes.

My heart sank, though the adult in me should have known it was coming — I'd stood over the man's grave. For all his flaws and failings, and perhaps because of them, I could relate to Brian at some level. An irrational part of me had been rooting for his story to have a happy ending, giving Dad some peace. That couldn't happen if we left things as they were.

The question that started me on this journey needed re-phrasing: *What good can we make from those letters so Dad can rest easily?*

⁂

I'd been looking for an excuse to see Marci again anyway, so I texted her, "Can't believe how long it's been since we've done lunch! My treat if you have the time 😊 — I want to catch up, and there's a good story I've been researching. You might have answers to some questions I have…."

A few moments later, my phone buzzed in my pocket. "Perfect timing," Marci texted back. "Taking the day off tomorrow — does 11:30 at Born and Raised work for you?"

"Great choice; see you then!" I finished.

I made an extra copy of the black-light versions of Brian's letters I could share with her or anyone else. Out of printer paper and needing a few things for the kitchen, I headed to Von's. After finding what I wanted, I turned the corner into the bread aisle and was surprised to see Gary Gilbert. He was standing with a plump woman in a flowered print dress. "Gary, I didn't know you lived in the area," I said, sidling up to him from behind.

"Oh, hi…." He was struggling to remember my name.

"Debra Ann Wynn, the lost letters…?" I offered.

"Oh, yes, Debra Ann. I'm sorry, but I've gotten so bad with names lately. It's nice to see you. We've been here for about fourteen years, right, honey?"

The woman he turned to had a round, reddened face, and she used all of it when she smiled.

Gary introduced her. "Debra Ann, this is Barbara, my wife of twenty-two years. Honey, this is Debra Ann, Alex Wynn's daughter."

Gary's description of his spouse reminded me of Dad's care in acknowledging Mom's territorial rights. He'd mention how he felt about Mom whenever an attractive woman, especially one my mother didn't know, would introduce herself as having any prior relationship with him. He explained why when I, a teenager then, called him on it.

"It's not that I'd have anything to answer for," Dad explained, "or that Mom is so insecure that she'd feel threatened. It's a little thing that doesn't cost anything; you do it out of respect for the person you love. Something to pre-empt any misunderstandings not just with her but also with the other person."

Seeing Barbara's smile linger, I knew where he was coming from.

"It's so nice to meet you, Debra Ann," Barbara said. She exuded warmth, and I could sense that she had grandkids thrilled to see her when she came around.

"Alex was the man I told you about who found the blank letters out in the Gardens," Gary continued, "and he was trying to find who they belonged to. Since Alex passed away, Debra Ann has been trying to solve the puzzle. She was a journalist with the *Union-Tribune* and now works on projects she chooses.

"Oh, Debra Ann, that reminds me: one of our visitors turned in another of those letters. She'd hung onto it for a while; she wasn't sure what to do with it."

"Wow, thanks. Will you hold it for me?" I asked. "I've got some things going on for the next few days, but I'll be out soon to pick it up."

I turned my attention to Barbara, who was resting her purse on the shopping cart handle.

"Gary tells me you do the pulled pork and the sides when you go out on the road barbequing — everyone knows those are the best parts," I said with a little laugh. "I'm looking forward to going to one of your competitions."

"We'd be pleased to see you there. Have you had any luck tracking down the letter writer?"

"Yes, I think I have the answer," I replied. "Believe it or not, the author wrote them in invisible ink, so they have actual contents you can read once you know how."

"Invisible ink! Seriously?"

I nodded. "Brian, the youngest of the family, left them at the Pierce family plot near Mom and Dad. He wrote the letters to his sister Bridget. Sadly, though, I won't be able to return the letters after all."

"Doesn't the brother want the letters back?" Barbara was puzzled.

"Unfortunately, Brian was just laid to rest in the memorial gardens. It looks like he was the victim of foul play, and the authorities are trying to figure it all out. I'm still investigating because what happened to him might have something to do with the contents of his letters."

"Aw, that's too bad." Gary frowned. "I expected a happier ending out of all of this."

"Me, too." I tried to put a positive spin on it. "I'm hoping to find something that brings a better resolution. Even if that only means getting justice for Brian and learning the truth about what happened. I've got to run, but it was so nice to see you again, Gary, and to meet you, Barbara. Best of luck at your next barbecue event!"

"Thanks, Debra Ann — keep us posted, and I hope you find the answers you're looking for," Gary called after me as we parted company.

From your mouth to God's ear, I thought to myself. I knew that with Brian's murder, the list of questions I had in hand was only growing and becoming more serious.

As things would turn out, I should have added to my request, *"and only God's ear."*

CHAPTER 15

The lunchtime crowd was building at the Born and Raised Steakhouse as office workers from the surrounding businesses filtered in on their breaks. Marci beat me there and took a table in the back. As I joined her, I couldn't help but notice she had a new emerald ring. The way she was displaying her hand made it hard to miss.

"Oh, Marci, I see you've been holding out on me…. Care to share?" I sat down, taking the extended fingers of her right hand into mine to admire the stone.

"I thought you'd *never* ask!" Marci raised her nose, an affected high-society inflection in her voice.

We both laughed, and I said, "Nice rock! So, who's the new love interest in your life? Or is the jewelry on your finger something you saw in a store window that you couldn't resist?"

"I've kept it a secret until now, but I met Danny at AA. I'd seen him at several meetings — he just got his five-year recovery medallion. Four months ago, we left a meeting at the same time and played a round of 'Whose

Uber is it, anyway?' He asked me out for coffee, and things took off from there."

"I can tell you're happier than I've seen you in quite a while," I said, thrilled for her. "Okay, out with the goods — what's Danny like?"

"He's a lieutenant at the Balboa Park fire station. He has a nice little place not too far off the beach. His sister dates my cousin, and we learned we have much in common. We've had some pretty deep conversations, some of them difficult. He's good at accepting me as I am, warts and all."

She broke off into introspection for an instant, then brightened again.

"So, he surprised the heck out of me last Wednesday when he popped up with this. He calls it a friendship ring, but I think it's a little more than that for both of us. Day by day, right? We'll enjoy the journey until we get to the destination, wherever it is."

"I am so *happy* for you, and it's good you found someone who feels right."

"What's going on in *your* romantic life?" Marci asked. "Not to be nosey, but Ray Costello in Major Case has a thing for you. If I don't ask, he'll keep bugging me."

I raised my eyebrows. "We saw each other at the Warnake crime scene; I guess it was … three months ago? I *thought* he was acting pretty friendly to be working a kidnapping," I said with a snicker. "He's a nice enough guy, but I don't think having a cop in the family would work too well for my career. No offense intended."

"None taken. Any other prospects I should know about?" Marci asked, batting her eyelashes.

"No, I've not been in the mood since Dad died. And I've set myself a pretty high bar. I had a great relationship with a college ROTC cadet, Paul Castro. Everyone knew him as 'PJ' before the Navy commissioned him as an officer, and he had to use his given name. Gotta love a man in uniform, and I did. He was my first experience with anything real, one of those things that snuck up on me. You don't realize how great it was until worse things come along. I still think about him now and then…."

"What broke the two of you up?"

"PJ had to serve out his Navy obligations. He ended up in Annapolis. When I graduated, I landed a good job here. You know how it goes — you promise to keep in touch, but…"

"That was it? Nobody else came along?"

"When Mom got sick, I was thirty-one and feeling that biological clock ticking. The relationship I was in was horrible, but I talked myself into making do. I'm ashamed I didn't leave the first time he hit me. But the second did the trick."

"Having been through that myself, I'm sorry it happened to you." Marci's smile had left her face.

"Dad would never admit it, but he had some muscle from one of his construction crews visit the guy afterward. Once my ex left the hospital, we never heard from him again. Two years of my life wasted. I just wasn't prepared for the depression and feelings of complete worthlessness that followed. People like that plant things in your head — you don't realize that so much of it has taken root. I soured on relationships once I got some semblance of myself back. Lately, I've had too many other things going on."

"You've not shared that before, but it explains why we connect like we do," Marci's voice had softened as she slowly nodded.

"Compared to all the challenges you've had to overcome, mine were so trivial. I was surrounded by people who loved me. They'd witnessed the situation unfold before them — I didn't need to explain myself or what happened. They'd seen me change even as I refused to acknowledge what was happening. Without them, it could have been a lot worse."

"That last part is so important," Marci acknowledged. "I didn't have it. No one was there to keep me from spiraling down. I've come to appreciate my friendships and relationships more, my safety net."

"I've never said this to anyone, and I hate to admit I'm so selfish. But that thought has terrified me at times since I learned I was going to lose Dad, not having someone who loved me, who'd be my anchor and protector when things get to me.

"Still, I'm not the same person I was ten years ago. No one can compete doing what I do unless they're willing to seek out the ugly in the world and go after it. Even so, I don't know if anyone but you would understand how hard I work to keep the bad from reaching the 'me' inside."

Marci's eyes were on the fork she was turning between her fingers, her lips pursed. Her expression told me she understood, though she said nothing.

"It helps me to know that you get it. Sometimes, people who don't know me see the façade I put up to deal with my work and accuse me of being naïve or idealistic. When they do, I hear instead, 'Good job, kid, you've held off becoming a cynical burnout for one more day.' I talk it over with my mirror every morning before I take on the world again."

"I've not heard it put that way, but it fits perfectly...." Marci took a moment to reflect. "Ever think about looking PJ up again?"

"Now and then, yes, but I've never followed up. Trying to reconnect gets more awkward as time passes without a good excuse. I used to fantasize we'd hook up again, maybe at a school reunion, but we had different alma maters." A warm memory came to mind. "You know, PJ never lost his cool. We got a puppy, a little white poodle, from the shelter. We spoiled her — she was our baby. I kept Darla when PJ left; she was with me until three years ago when I had to put her down.

"But when we got her, paying a pet deposit on our apartment didn't occur to either of us. One day, we came home, and the landlord was in our room, bent over next to the bed, furiously whacking underneath it with a broomstick at Darla. She was whimpering and scared to death, trying to hide. PJ's expression turned as hard as I'd ever seen, and other men would have killed that guy. I truly thought Paul might, and I'm not sure I'd have held it against him."

"Oh, God, what did he do to the landlord?" Marci's eyes had widened.

"I didn't learn how angry he was until he told me later when we were alone. PJ yanked him off the floor by the back of his belt. But that's as far as PJ went; he just stood there, listening with a clenched jaw to that jackass. The landlord was bitching about the dog, claiming she disturbed the neighbors with her whining whenever we were out. PJ didn't move a muscle when the man made a stink about us not paying that damned deposit. PJ just promised we'd keep the puppy quiet and wrote the landlord a check. It might have seemed like no big deal to people who didn't know PJ and the situation. But I learned so much about PJ that day. An officer and a gentleman to the core.

Much better than me. I'm no fighter, but I wanted to kick the bully in his fat ass when he was bent over."

"PJ's the one who got away...."

"Yup. But hope springs eternal." I gave Marci a sly smile. "I interviewed a man named Sven Nielssen for the Fat Leonard case. He imports fine wines and liqueurs. Tall, blonde, Swiss, gorgeous hair, built like a wrestler...."

"Hubba, hubba!" Marci grinned at my enthusiasm.

"Sadly, he's married. But if *that* guy had a brother, and he was available, I'd be back on the market in a heartbeat."

Marci shook her head at my over-the-top wink.

"I hope that works out for you, Debra Ann; I truly do. But this is a family restaurant — anything more would be *too* much information," Marci smirked, then intentionally changed the subject. "I meant to phone you so we could meet up and I could show you the ring. But you called me first. So, what's on your mind?"

The waitress appeared before I could answer, and we ordered. Marci knew, of course, about Dad's passing. She'd been a stalwart friend to me as I'd worked through the initial anger, frustration, and acceptance in their turn. But I hadn't told her yet about the trust or anything that happened after Dad's estate had settled. I opened up about some of my struggles in the years between quitting the paper and Dad providing for me in his will and the emotional roller coaster I'd been on the past few weeks.

"But the good part is that I'm paying for your lunch now that I'm financially secure. I can't stop saying 'trust fund baby' in the mirror — it makes me feel so ... *young!*" I said with a laugh.

THE WRITINGS OF
AVRIL MARIA SERENE

CHAPTER 16

Our server brought our entrees, asked if we wanted anything more, and left us to continue our conversation.

Dad had failed twice to generate any response from the police based on Brian's letters. So, I wanted to approach Marci from a different perspective. If Brian's correspondence proved truthful, it described links between his murder and another. But I had nothing else to confirm the other homicide — likely the wife, but I'd need to know for sure.

Brian's letters told an exciting and emotionally appealing story, even if it turned out the crimes he described didn't happen exactly as he said. Any unreliability on his part was understandable as symptoms of his mental health issues, key elements of who he was as a person. It made sense to separate Brian's and the wife's murders in my questions for Marci —I could later reconnect the two if warranted.

"Now that I'm free to manage my career and am no longer paycheck-to-paycheck, I want to do a story on spec. Something where I can go deeper without worrying about editorial or commercial restrictions."

"Our butterfly spreads its wings...." Marci was digging through the woven basket the waitress left on our table.

"Something like that," I replied with a laugh. "I'm looking at two different story angles. One of them is a human-interest story about a man by the name of Brian Pierce. A month ago, someone beat him to death and left his body in an alleyway downtown."

"Unfortunately, that happens more than it should. What makes Pierce's situation unique?" Marci asked as she nibbled a warm breadstick.

"His family's grave is close to Mom's and Dad's. I have a series of private letters that Dad found where Pierce was writing to his sister, describing his decisions and behaviors. Some of those things could have been pretty dicey if they were factual or if he acted on them. For example, he claims to have witnessed three people moving a body."

"Yeah, *that's* a little different — might have something to do with why someone killed him," Marci mused.

"What he wrote about was bad enough that Dad called the police here twice about the letters. But the duty officers weren't interested in them."

"Your father wasn't one to waste the department's time." Marci's voice showed concern. "And that doesn't sound like something they should have blown off. I'm sorry they didn't take him seriously."

"To be fair, he didn't have much for them to go on. Maybe there's nothing there, but it would've been nice if they'd at least looked into it. Pierce's story intrigues me because he's badly flawed yet seems like a good guy in many ways. One of those stories that never gets told but should."

"Why do you think that is?" Marci picked at her salad.

"Ivory-tower elites rarely dip their toes into the real lives most of us experience. Yet they've imposed upon society this idea that to qualify as a victim, someone must be pure and innocent. They prefer a child or a young, beautiful, blonde woman with ample breasts."

"We see that with how much interest the media expresses in certain of our cases," Marci agreed.

"That means justice gets meted out in individual situations only to the same degree that the sufferer makes for a perfect victim. That's also true of which page in the newspaper they choose to print your story. Very few of us are perfect. So, only a tiny percentage get front-page attention or the justice to which the Constitution entitles us, at least theoretically."

"I dated a lawyer for a while," Marci offered, "and that attitude gets slammed home during negotiations for civil case settlements. The lawyers openly debate how sympathetic a litigant comes across as a strength-of-case matter."

"I want to tell Pierce's story and contrast it with what might have been without trying to paint him as perfect. Instead, show him as a regular, defective human being stuck in an environment where there wasn't any way to completely avoid the truly evil set of characters he got tangled up with. Maybe revisit our definitions of victimhood by applying them to someone more like ourselves."

"I can see where you might go with the human-interest aspect…" Marci said. "Even as a police officer, I could relate."

"There's been nothing in the news with any details about how the Pierce case is going. How I'll write the story depends on the likely outcome. I wanted to know if the detectives are actively pursuing it. If so, do they have enough yet to charge anyone?"

"I don't know myself, but that's easy to check. I'd be happy to find out; it shouldn't take long. Is that all you need?"

"That'll help a lot with my first story." I felt a brief twinge of guilt that I hadn't shared more with Marci about Brian's letters or told her how they might relate to my next ask. Still, I had to look at it from Marci's professional viewpoint. She'd have to consider those letters and the connection as evidence and motive. She'd be required to tell her superiors about them. While I trusted Marci to do her part, I knew she had no authority to push anything forward within the department once anyone down the line dropped the ball.

Dad had on two occasions offered those envelopes and their contents, and the police had both times turned them down. Their refusals led directly to my investing effort and time in them. I wasn't ready to give up the letters just yet. As a professional journalist protected by the shield law, my situation differed from my father's. I certainly didn't want to make the information in them the subject of another conversation with anyone in law enforcement, even a close friend, until I had enough that they couldn't refuse for a third time to do their jobs.

"The other story stems from a rumor on the street about a doctor who killed his wife, but no one can find her dead or alive. I don't know if there's any basis for it, but I wanted to check it out. I googled what I had but got back too many hits, and I couldn't filter out all the movie, book, and social media references."

"Hmmm, a doctor being investigated for possibly killing his wife? That's one you'd think would draw some interest." Marci cocked her head. "Should have made for conversation around the water cooler."

"I thought there might be an ongoing investigation, maybe one that isn't solid enough yet to give the media. I need to find out if anyone has reported a doctor's wife missing or found murdered. Or simply that the wife died and the circumstances were suspicious, or someone manipulated the situation somehow. Anything that might have resulted in a body someone would want to hide."

"'Doctor' could mean many things," Marci pointed out. "A medical doctor, a dentist, a PhD in some other field, or just somebody's nickname. An egotistical blood bank phlebotomist lying in his Match.com profile? Maybe he's just a guy working in a machine shop who someone thinks is smarter than the rest of the employees."

"Now that you put it that way," I admitted, "it might be a taller order than I thought. But my information says he has a degree of some kind."

"As I think about it, that *does* ring a bell." Marci furrowed her brow. "But I can't put my finger on exactly why. I'll ask around."

"Thanks, Marci, I'll owe you one. The problem with freelancing and not answering to a boss is there's *too* much freedom. Hard to know the best place to spend your time on a story so that you end up with something to show for it."

With that, we turned away from business and to our meals, sharing rumors and opinions about people, places, and news items. As I paid and Marci was leaving the tip, she said, "I'll call you as soon as I have something, and we can get together then."

"I'm looking forward to that," I said as we parted ways. I didn't tell Marci I'd be waiting with bated breath for her call. Unnecessarily pressuring your friends won't make you very popular.

But everything I wanted to do with these stories depended on what she turned up.

CHAPTER 17

arci's phone call early the next afternoon was a welcome surprise. After the usual pleasantries, she said, "It didn't take long to get answers to your questions. But Danny's taking me to lunch tomorrow. I wasn't sure how soon you needed the information. No sense in making you wait until our calendars synced up again for a meal."

"That's very kind of you — I'll give you a rain check. What did you find out?"

"First, as to Brian Pierce: I think you know we collect both prints and DNA at crime scenes if they're available. Prints are quickly and cheaply processable and can be matched immediately to nationwide information online. Law enforcement has kept and stored them since before anyone alive was born. DNA, on the other hand, hasn't been reliably collected into databases nearly as long. And, unlike a print, DNA is easily transferred, even unintentionally, from one person or thing to another. So, it's not the uber-reliable evidence that people think it is. It also takes time and money to process — some of our rape kits have taken months, even years.

"In this case, we were lucky and have both. Two sets of viable DNA and prints, palm and finger, were taken from the body. We've also got fibers and hairs that we could likely match to environments or subjects once we have candidates."

"Sounds like a good beginning…."

"Not sure yet," Marci replied. "I mentioned all that because despite gleaning everything we'd normally ask from a body dump, nothing matches anything currently in the AFIS or CODIS databases. That's odd because, in a beating severe enough to kill someone, you'd think at least one of the two perps would have a record. Not finding a match could mean one or more of several things. Chances are good that our killers haven't served in the military since '92. They probably don't have professional licenses. The perps likely hadn't spent time in prison recently or not in a place or at a time when they collected DNA for the national databases. They haven't been suspects in a major crime. If they were, it was in a jurisdiction which doesn't submit investigative candidate samples for non-convicts."

"The detectives still have a lot of work left to do."

"Exactly," Marci acknowledged. "The one thing we don't have yet is the crime scene, which would help us identify persons of interest. Victimology isn't helping because the decedent was a petty criminal with shady associates who kept his activities under the radar. The good news is that once we have matching suspects for either of the two assailants, we'll be able to prosecute them for Brian Pierce's murder."

"That tells me exactly what I needed to know." I hoped my gratitude came across over the phone. If I could figure out the people involved with the crimes mentioned in Brian's letters, I should have at least a few candidates for suspects.

"But there's something a little odd that we haven't released to the public," Marci added, sounding hesitant. "I'm assuming this is all off the record, and you won't be sharing it. Do I have your word on that, Debra Ann?"

"You have my word, Marci," I assured her. "I'm not taking notes, and anything you tell me will remain confidential between us."

"I could lose my badge if this gets out." Marci lowered her voice slightly. "But it could be important for identifying the doer. When they found the body, there were traces of ink on his fingertips and thumbs. Because the victim's record is for small-time stuff, we thought maybe someone in the department had picked Pierce up, then booked and released him in short order. In that scenario, the offender killed Pierce after he left the station before washing his hands or the ink rubbed off. But the forensic tech was on her toes. She tested the ink because she didn't think it looked right."

"What did she find?"

"It wasn't the same ink used for fingerprinting," Marci answered. "It was the cheap bulk ink for notary public stamps and fountain pens."

"Somebody who wasn't a law enforcement professional took Brian's prints around the same time he died? Does that mean what I think it means? That whoever killed him didn't know him beforehand?"

"We have no booking record, and nothing else suggests law enforcement was involved," Marci replied. "We'd know if a registered user of the AFIS system made a fingerprint check that produced a match. It would take anyone else considerable time to get the results. Assuming they killed him *after* learning who he was, the ink should have been long gone. That it was still there when we found him suggests someone took the prints after his death. So, yes, they likely killed him without knowing who he was and *then* checked his identity. If so, that removes an advantage we thought we had. Normally, beatings that savage — overkill — suggest a strong connection between attacker and victim that we can trace. Stranger murders are that much tougher to solve."

That adds a whole new wrinkle to all of this, I thought.

"Which brings me to the other thing you asked me to look into. There are two missing women we know of in relationships with doctors. First, we have an invalid husband reporting an 83-year-old woman, known to be suffering from dementia, as missing. Next, an adult son asked for a welfare check on his mother. She's the 42-year-old wife of a suspended doctor, and officers haven't found her. I assume it is the second one you're curious about?"

"Fits what I'm looking for, yes."

"Just so you'll know what you're stepping into, this one's an open sore in the department. You'll recall that I said this rang a bell. There was an internal memo circulated department-wide. It stated that all investigators must get approval from their unit commanders to work any part of this case. But I'm getting ahead of myself."

"*Department-wide?* Somebody's got some juice...," I mused.

"The lady in question is Theresa Seaver, married to Dr. James Seaver. Her son Terrence reported her missing almost three months ago."

"Coach's neighbor!" I exclaimed. "I talked to him briefly to ask if he'd seen anything the night Coach was killed. Sorry to mix metaphors, but he comes off as a cold fish *and* an odd duck."

"That's the guy. Theresa Seaver was married twice, the first time to Darrell Woodson. If *that* name sounds familiar, he's a local self-made multimillionaire. He owns several restaurants and nightclubs around town."

"Money always makes things more interesting...," I observed.

"Those are the only undisputed facts. We've gathered other information, but sorting rumors from reality is tough. James Seaver is involved in so much dishonesty. Until we investigate further — and that's another can of worms — I don't know how reliable anything we have is for him. I'll stick to the parts we're pretty sure of."

"If I need them to make the story more interesting, I might hit you up for some of the other pieces," I said half-seriously.

"I don't think that's going to be a problem," Marci responded. "This James Seaver character is one nasty piece of work. For starters, it's a stretch to call him a doctor. The medical board stripped him of his license three years ago for writing and selling OxyContin scripts. Other than that, the guy's been Teflon-coated."

"You've not been able to hang anything on him?"

"Nothing more than slaps on the wrist. I read through the witness interviews for several cases involving Seaver. This guy's a real wheeler-dealer who's never seen a scam he didn't like. The bunco squad and Major Case have gotten close to him in several shady deals — online gambling, MLM Ponzi schemes, and telemarketing fraud. It's almost like he's trying to collect enough felonies that he, too, can someday become President. But they haven't been able to close the loop and put him away."

"I assume James Seaver is a suspect in his wife's disappearance?"

"Our disgraced doctor has plenty of motive," Marci replied. "His history and nature say he'd want access to his wife's accounts without her being in the way. Theresa has all the looks and the legitimate money in the marriage. She's an attractive blonde with a decent figure, even before all the plastic surgery. In her early forties, petite — the 'trophy wife' type."

"Where did her money come from? Her previous marriage to Woodson?"

"Her father was super-wealthy. She inherited a pretty good chunk of his estate when he died, enough that the Court didn't see fit to award her anything from her ex in their divorce."

"The doctor must have an alibi…?"

"More like a cover story, and that's where things get hinky. The doctor insists his wife ran off and is running around Europe under another name. Supposedly to embarrass him and see him sweat — in other words, that version of the story is all about him. Of course, Seaver doesn't know what that other name might be. He claims the wife hasn't been in touch with him or anyone he knows." Marci's tone of disbelief was exaggerated. "Sounds way too convenient, unbelievable, even … right?"

"I wouldn't buy it for a minute," I agreed.

"Me neither. Except for one *teensy-weensy* problem," Marci had raised the pitch of her voice. "Before Theresa's divorce, she did *exactly* that to her first husband."

"No way!"

"Yes, way, unfortunately," Marci continued. "It put Darrell Woodson under the microscope for a month. The allegations were that he had something to do with his then-wife's disappearance. All that, only to have authorities find her after seven weeks, alive and well. She'd been hiding in Copenhagen with a passport under an assumed name. Both Woodson and her son Terrence confirmed the story when investigators of the later disappearance interviewed them."

"I assume James Seaver is saying her being gone now is the same situation?" I tried to keep my disappointment from showing in my voice. The unexpected muddying of the waters was frustrating, even irritating. It further complicated the article I'd wanted to write once I knew that parts of Brian's story checked out. As things stood now, only Brian's letters supported my hunch that Theresa was dead, making them even more critical if she genuinely was. Still, I felt I had to verify some things before sharing more of what I knew or suspected with Marci.

"Yes, the doctor claims that, while there was a minor argument with Theresa, it was over her much bigger legal disagreement with her ex-husband. He says Theresa truly left to escape the court case. The problem with the ex was related to the property division after their divorce. That also squares with what Woodson confirmed to our detectives — she was due in court on criminal charges the week after she disappeared."

"Marital property? But that's civil, not criminal, right?" I was confused.

"The DA is prosecuting her for a fraudulent property purchase using marital assets belonging to Woodson. She hid her ownership when it came time to divide those assets in their already-adjudicated divorce proceedings."

"So, the wife takes after the new husband regarding character issues?"

"It would seem so," Marci replied. "The son says the doctor and his wife have other issues, and there's been some violence. But neither husband nor wife nor anyone else has reported a physical altercation to the authorities."

"And since the son's not objective, his statements alone aren't enough to justify any official action. So, you're stuck until you have a body or something else definitive...," I surmised.

"Exactly. We're not buying James Seaver's story about Theresa leaving. Still, it's plausible enough that we'd have to prove any contention otherwise. Seaver and his attorneys have sent us cease-and-desist letters and threats to sue, claiming we're harassing him to support an unfounded belief he's harmed his wife. We can't specify *how* or even show *that* it happened. They've manipulated the situation to keep us from pursuing the missing-person complaint and hampered our investigations of his other crimes."

"This guy's pretty slippery, then...."

"I'm telling you, this so-called doctor has a set of brass balls. About a month ago, his lawyers sent us a letter claiming somebody broke into his house and sprayed graffiti on the walls. Whoever tagged it wrote that James Seaver killed his wife and hid her body."

Holy crap, then Brian was telling the truth, I thought. Brian *was* there and saw what he claimed. Which raised the likelihood his other statements were factual, in turn suggesting *somebody's* dead — Theresa if that body was hers. The situation was changing right in front of me. *How, and how much, do I tell Marci?* I needed time to think.

"Earth calling Debra Ann...," Marci said playfully.

"Sorry, off on a tangent," I fibbed.

"The lawyers included a photo but won't let us investigate. They're alleging we put someone up to it as further harassment and intimidation of Seaver. And they don't want us in his home again after having been there twice already – they're throwing around accusations of 'planting evidence,' leveraging what happened with the O.J. Simpson case."

"Did they mention anything taken during the break-in?" I asked, looking for another link to what Brian had written. "You'd think someone going to that much trouble would steal what they could once they're in the house." I wanted as much corroboration as possible, even as I wrestled with how much I should tell Marci.

"If the intruder stole anything, Seaver's attorneys aren't sharing the details. They don't act like they want anything solved...." Marci's voice had a touch of sarcasm.

I'll bet.

"... They seem more interested in jerking our chain, putting their spin on things. For all we know, Seaver or one of his accomplices might have tagged his place themselves just for the camera. So, when your instincts tell you that there's a story here, they're right. Still, I don't have enough to know myself what that story might be."

"So, the investigation is active but stalled," I summarized.

"That's a fair assessment. For now, we, as a department, have no choice but to tread water with Theresa's current husband, which prevents us from learning more."

Okay. The situation's stabilized, so I've got a little time. Seaver's lawyers had the police tied up. But I was free as a bird. Maybe I could do some real good here and dig up the information the detectives couldn't.

"Wow, Marci, this background helps me out a lot," I said, ready to sign off. "Let me know when you can do lunch or want to get together on the weekend, and I'll make good on the rain check."

"I'll hold you to it," Marci warned. "And keep me apprised of any fresh developments from your end."

Once I'd made that commitment, we said our goodbyes and hung up. My stomach had become unsettled, something my body does to express doubts about my decisions. Knowing I'd not wholly confided in my friend tore at my insides. I promised myself I'd make it all up by seeking the answers the department couldn't get for themselves.

But my pledge wasn't as comforting as I'd hoped.

CHAPTER 18

My friend and once-fellow reporter at the *Union-Tribune,* Doug Stein, called in the middle of the afternoon to keep in touch. He was bored and irritated by the atmosphere around his office. We usually spoke every few weeks, but we'd both been busy and hadn't talked for a while.

Doug wasn't someone who rants, but he was upset.

"So, I found a new angle, and I've got our congressman dead to rights on a political corruption story, funny money in the election coffers, insider trading around bills he was working on — you know the drill."

"Patterson, right?" I guessed. "That guy's a mutant snail; he can't go anywhere without leaving a trail of sleaze behind him. He just made the news complaining about reverse discrimination, that there weren't enough old white guys doing the same things he does."

"You got it," Doug replied. "Patterson's sleeping with a powerful lawyer's wife. Our sleazy politician uses her as a conduit for information and to push around his influence. The lawyer in question is a partner in McQuade and Morrison, one of the paper's advertisers."

"Oh, crap, I've seen this movie before...," I said, grimacing.

"I make the deadline." Doug's voice was growing more agitated. "But before it goes to press, that idiot Dark cuts any reference to the lawyer or his wife out of the piece to 'protect' them. He waters down the whole damned story. Good reporting means less to him than ensuring advertising revenues stay where they were. I'm so mad I could spit nails."

"I'm sorry, Doug," I said, scrambling to say something helpful. "It's just not right. But I don't know what you can do. I should have some answer or suggestion for you, but I couldn't come up with any for myself when it happened to me."

"I know. I just wanted to share what's going on with someone who would understand how I'm feeling right now. That *somebody* gets it helps more than you know. I should have quit when you did, but it's not an option with my oldest at Stanford."

"Just between you and me," I offered, "I was sweating bullets after I quit — there are a lot of quality stories out there begging someone to tell them, but few organizations will foot the bill. If Dad hadn't had my back, I don't know what I'd be doing now."

"Okay, my whining session is over," Doug relented, his voice brightening, "for this day, anyway. So, what have you been doing? We both went radio silent, and with you, that usually means you're on to something."

Unlike Marci, with whom I often had to parse my words because she was a law enforcement officer, I could trust Doug with anything. With Dad's passing, I didn't have anyone else to share all the gory details with and get good advice in return.

So, I let loose with what I had on Brian and the Seavers, albeit the abbreviated version, out of respect for Doug's time. That took me to my conversation earlier today with Marci.

"Because I'd held out on her," I told Doug, "Marci didn't know how right she was that there was a story here, one much bigger than she might have guessed, and I was sitting on it. Not only are things pointing to the murder of Theresa Seaver and the moving of her body, but Brian's letters tie it all together."

"You should have told her about the letters." Doug chided me for knowing better.

"I know, Doug," I tried to plead my case, "but I didn't realize what I might have until she told me about the graffiti on the wall way into our conversation. And I don't have any confirmation yet on the rest of what Brian wrote, just conjecture."

"I get it. But let's see if I was paying attention. We'll assume Theresa is dead. You know who Brian was, and you have an idea of the neighborhood where he lived because of the reference to Rocco's. In case you didn't know, that's where Frankie Ventana's crew hangs out.

"So, there are two threats we know about to Brian, and both tie back to James Seaver. We have the thugs in Brian's neighborhood asking a lot of questions. Then there's this 'Rickie' that Brian wants to go after and set up for Theresa Seaver's murder."

"That sums up pretty well what I know so far," I confirmed. "I have Rickie's name to go on, Brian's threatened violence against him, and only three days elapsed between Brian's threat and the dumping of his body. I'm inclined to chase that lead first."

"Makes sense," Doug agreed. "If that doesn't work out for you, maybe Marci can hook you up with a CI that frequents Rocco's. Cold-calling the cannoli crowd wouldn't be productive and might not be safe. They're not going to talk to you. But they'd probably be happy to tell someone they trust what they know about foreign muscle on their turf. If the CI route isn't productive, I might know some people in that area who would whisper in your ear — for a price."

"One of those options should get me a lot closer to who did both murders." I paused a moment to think.

"You know, I'm not convinced of James Seaver's presumed motive that he would have killed Theresa to get at the inheritance from her father. The erstwhile doctor reads as a cagey con artist and master manipulator. He would surely know that the authorities would heavily scrutinize her account activity as soon as Theresa went missing. That would include her past, present, and future financial behaviors. And importantly, any sudden pause in the transactions in those accounts."

Doug picked up from where I left off, just as he did when we worked on stories together. "Theresa not making timely court appearances would only delay the litigation that was keeping the focus on her finances, thereby tying her hands. His claim that she was be-bopping around the world logging flight miles on a fake ID doesn't seem reasonable. It's not easy, given how much countries have strengthened international security protocols, which were already strict. It will only worsen in the face of terrorism, wars, and pandemics. And then there's the growing immigration and tourist resentment in some countries."

"If he killed this woman," I added, "and any doubts I had are shrinking with every passing hour, there had to be another angle he was working. You'd think it would be better for him to have the body turn up sooner rather than later. Did he seriously intend to twiddle his thumbs for seven or more years before having her declared legally dead?"

"A con artist like Seaver," Doug speculated, "would have gotten life insurance for a spouse he intended to kill, multiple policies with obscenely inflated payouts based on the size of her inheritance. It makes no sense he'd want to wait to get his hands on those. And he'd know life insurance companies don't write checks if there's any suspicion around a death."

"I'm curious about something else," I continued. "Two different husbands in consecutive marriages have now made the 'my wife ran off to Europe' allegation after incidents of marital strife. The first was truthful, and the second most likely not. It would be fair to ask if the two men cooperated in the second instance."

"Now *that* idea raises a few questions." Doug was leaning into this. "Was Theresa's taste in men consistent, meaning Darrell Woodson was also a sleaze? Could the first husband have fed James Seaver the idea of repurposing what Theresa had done to Woodson? Maybe a hybrid deal — the doctor using repeat history to exact Woodson's revenge against Theresa while satisfying the doctor's desire to kill her."

"Yeah, it might be a stretch," I said as I thought about the situation. "James Seaver could have leveraged the story after hearing it from someone other than Woodson — but it *is* possible the two colluded."

"Where do you want to go next with this?"

"I need to talk to Woodson. I'll approach him to seek additional information and background on the divorce and property fraud. I'll ask him more if he proves cooperative and amenable to a broader conversation."

"I gotta hand it to you, Debra Ann … that's quite a story!" Doug exclaimed as we ended the call, his approval apparent in his voice. "A damned shame you can't tell it to anyone just yet.…"

AVRIL MARIA SERENE

CHAPTER 19

Brian's letters and Marci's work convinced me that Theresa Seaver's current husband had been evil coming out of the womb. Yet Theresa had considered James Seaver enough of an upgrade to jump ship on her previous marriage, so the ex must have been even worse.

But the Darrell Woodson I phoned was accommodating, moving his other obligations around so we could meet at his home. As I crested a hill in a nice La Jolla neighborhood, I saw their large, dark-red brick Tudor. It had a cone-roofed tower at one end, generous curving walkways, and a wide drive leading to a three-bay garage. A collection of boys' and girls' bikes, football pads, and a radio-controlled model P-38 Lightning were visible in one of the open bays. They suggested several children. Or maybe the Woodsons were just the cool parents in the neighborhood.

Darrell met me at the front door and invited me inside. He was very tall and handsome — enough that I reflexively looked for his wedding ring and saw he'd remarried. In his early forties, his fading Aussie accent was more pronounced than it had sounded over the phone. Despite his apparent business success, he came across in small talk as self-effacing. Still, I sensed he was wary of my presence.

As Darrell took my coat in the vestibule, his spouse joined us from the dining room. She was a short, curvy brunette with a beautiful face worthy of an Estée Lauder model. Darrell's wife gave me her full attention when I spoke and made me feel immediately comfortable, as though I'd known her from childhood. Her dimples highlighted an open, genuine smile, and she didn't hesitate to show me that it was her nature to hug people.

"I'm Emma, and it is a delight to meet you," she announced. "We used to follow your stories in the *Union-Tribune*. It's disappointing that it's been so long since your articles were featured there. I understand that you moved on several years ago."

"Yes, it's been a while now, but I always appreciate a reader wherever my stories end up," I said with a grin. "And especially one who is so gracious."

Emma accepted the compliment with a smile and an over-the-top curtsey straight out of an old movie, followed by a quick laugh. "Would you like anything to drink? Coffee, perhaps?" she asked.

"No, I'm good, thank you."

"The kids are in school, and I've put away the pets, so nothing should disturb us."

"How many do you have?" I asked out of politeness.

"Two boys in elementary school, one in junior high, a girl in preschool, two dogs, two cats, and a turtle," Emma inventoried as we adjourned to their living room.

Spacious with a recessed floor and a sculptured ceiling, the décor showed noticeable taste from a talented decorator. The base was primarily a pristine white. Bold red and black accents were placed randomly throughout, with the occasional dot of bright yellow. The photos of their family and friends on the walls and the mementos on the shelves reflected the happiness of the Woodsons' marriage.

Emma offered me the overstuffed wingback chair. She and her husband took the adjacent couch, sitting side-by-side and holding hands. The seat was so plush that I struggled a little to lean forward. So, I sat back in the comfy chair, looking through all the notes I brought. I thanked them for their hospitality and then launched into the reason for my visit.

"When I spoke to Darrell on the phone, I mentioned I work independently, primarily freelance and on-spec projects. A story opportunity came my way as a missing-person report, someone you know very well — your ex-wife Theresa, now married to James Seaver."

Darrell's demeanor stiffened noticeably at the mention of James Seaver's name, and he immediately took command of the conversation.

"You and I've never met and certainly haven't worked together, so you'd have every right to think I'm paranoid. But you don't know how many con artists I've dealt with since James Seaver came into our lives." Darrell's tone was firm and businesslike.

"I've talked to quite a few people." I tried to assuage his concerns. "I do understand some of what he put you through…."

"Trust me, you don't have a clue," Darrell retorted. "I get that you used to be an investigative reporter with the paper here — 'used to be' as the operative phrase. It's tough in that business and rougher still for stringers. You're in our home under the pretext of discussing my missing ex-wife. That's one thing. But if this is more about her asshole present husband, that's a different matter. How are we to know Seaver isn't paying you on the side to do some reconnoitering on his behalf?"

"I'd rather have the frank conversation than suspicions we don't discuss," I said carefully, aware there was an open wound. "I understand your concerns are legitimate, given what I'm learning about Seaver. And you're right; I have a hidden agenda, but it's not what you're worried about. I'm here to find out who murdered a young man who *may*, emphasis on 'may,' have seen at least a part of Seaver hiding a woman's body. I think it might have been Theresa's."

A brief but noticeable silence ensued as the Woodsons considered my words and glanced at one another.

"You know that we have a hand in tangling Seaver up in lawsuits, and investigators of Theresa's disappearance have interviewed us, right?" Darrell asked, relaxing slightly.

I nodded.

"And as far as the latter goes, I've been a person of interest myself. Even a suspect at some points, off and on. I should have an attorney here before I say too much of anything."

"And that's perfectly within your rights," I replied. "I'd be happy to reschedule and talk to you once you have representation. I understand your need to protect your and your family's interests. I didn't intend to threaten those, but it wouldn't hurt to have a referee watching the boundaries."

Emma turned and whispered into her husband's ear for a moment.

"Would you mind if Darrell and I stepped into the kitchen for a minute or two?" Emma asked. "We won't be long."

I nodded, and true to her word, Emma and Darrell returned after a few moments. It was apparent that Darrell's attitude had softened.

"Emma's people skills are better than mine. Having her on my side has always been a big help to me," Darrell explained as Emma smiled and glanced down at the carpet. "She thinks we can assist each other since you seem to have the better information. She pointed out that if someone's murdered Theresa, the sooner we can get the details out there, the better for everyone. We can have a conversation without the attorney. I'll keep faith that you'll let us know if we get anywhere near the line."

"Thank you for your trust in me. I won't abuse it, I promise. If it helps, you should know my financial situation is very secure, and Seaver wouldn't get anywhere trying to buy me off." I grinned, my gratitude sincere.

I went on, "I need your permission to record this. My sources are privileged, and the recording is for my use only. It ensures I don't misquote anyone and allows me to confirm information between multiple sources later. It'll save us from constant interruptions in our conversation for verification. If you want something off the record, please say so, and I'll respect that. If that's not enough to make you feel comfortable, I can turn the recorder off until we get through that part. Does that work for you?"

Darrell looked at Emma, and she back at him.

"We're okay with that," Darrell said.

With a nod and a smile of thanks, I pulled out my digital recorder and flicked it on.

"Let's go to the beginning of what I know. So, Theresa is Seaver's wife when that missing person report gets filed...."

"Before I say anything else, let me tell you right up front," Darrell interrupted. "I'm not much of a hater, but I detest that son-of-a-bitch. While I'll tell you anything you want to know that might nail the prick, don't expect me to apologize for any biases I harbor towards Seaver."

"Understood." I welcomed the honesty.

"Hopefully, after you've heard our story, you'll understand how I feel," Darrell said. "But yes, the police interviewed me right after Terrence filed the report."

"Terrence is her son from an out-of-wedlock relationship she was in before Darrell married her," Emma added. "He lived with us occasionally after Theresa remarried, a good kid. We all got along."

"Do you know how I can reach Terrence? He's someone I'd like to talk to."

"I honestly don't," Darrell answered. "He phoned us looking for Theresa before he called the police, and I haven't seen him since. I know he and Seaver didn't like each other, and he's old enough now to be on his own."

"We offered to help him pay for college," Emma said, "but he was into music with his friends and didn't seem interested. He should still be in San Diego."

"I'll let you know if I find him," I offered. "Do you have a recent photo of Terrence that you can share?"

"I can text you a couple of pictures we took the last time he was here," Emma said as I gave her my phone number. "I'll include the cell number we have for him. He won't answer if he doesn't recognize the Caller ID. You'll want to text him first and explain who you are. Let him know you're trying to help his mother."

"I'm sorry I don't know more about Seaver's and your ex-wife's activities," I apologized. "That's why I'm here — to learn whatever you want to share. Parts of the story have come to me from someone who claims to know how Theresa disappeared. I'm trying to establish the validity of their account. If it bears out, it may help law enforcement and other individuals who've gotten themselves caught up in the events. If it sounds like I'm trying to be coy, that's not my intention. I'm unsure of my footing yet and don't want to spread rumors or innuendo."

"I get it," Darrell replied, "but I have to ask for some quid pro quo here to support our litigation against Seaver and Theresa."

"That's fair. I need to understand better how Theresa's disappearance, this disgraced doctor and his scams, and what my witness had to say all fit together," I replied. "When I do, I'll happily share."

"Darrell and I talked to the police about what we know," Emma explained. "But they tell us James Seaver has used his lawyers to tie them up in knots, to the point they can't do anything until Theresa surfaces, dead or alive."

"His attorneys have threatened us as well," Darrell added, "trying to confuse Seaver's role and visibility in this. The DA filed a criminal complaint against Theresa on my behalf. Her husband claims that filing drove her to run off this time."

"Okay, good, then you're both aware of Seaver's lawyers hamstringing the authorities. That helps because it frees me from walking around on eggshells. Seaver isn't aware that I'm looking into this, and until he is, I've got a little more freedom to poke around than the other actors. I'm trying to stay under his radar as long as possible."

"You have our word he'll not learn anything about your interest from us," Emma said.

I took a deep breath, calculated the risks, and continued. "Everybody has an agenda, fundamental human nature, and I have mine. So that you'll know where I'm coming from, I'm interpreting my witness's claims to mean Theresa Seaver is no longer alive. I hate to put it out there like that. Especially to someone once married to her, for whom there is an understandable emotional impact. I'd rather not express anything I can't yet prove is true. But I don't know of any way we can have an honest and open conversation between us if I do not share at least that much."

"I've prepared myself for that," Darrell replied. "I know what James Seaver is, and the minute Theresa went silent, I was certain something bad had happened to her."

"Exes not talking wouldn't be that unusual. What told you there was something seriously wrong?"

"She'd been bickering with me night and day almost from the moment we married," Darrell replied. "The quiet, when it started, felt foreign and uncomfortable because I'd gotten used to the noise for so long. A little taste of how Stockholm syndrome must work."

The *Ding! Ding!* of a kitchen timer rang through the living quarters. "I've got some baked goods in the oven for the kids, so if you'll excuse me for a moment," Emma said as she got up and headed off to the kitchen.

"You know," Darrell continued, "even when Theresa disappeared the first time, we never spoke or had contact directly while she was away. But she'd do things to irritate me."

"Like what?"

"She'd use my credit cards to buy erectile dysfunction meds online — in bulk. Signing me up for dozens of gay magazine subscriptions was one of her ideas. She'd use burner phones to text me child pornography website addresses and have salespeople call on me for all kinds of crap."

I could think of at least one potential reason for that behavior. "I know there were allegations of abuse between Theresa and Seaver," I said, taking advantage of the fact Emma was in another room. "It's hard to phrase politely, but were there any incidents when the two of you were married?"

"No, and thank God, she never tried to accuse me of anything," Darrell responded. "But she did try to set me up ahead of her clandestine trip to Europe before our divorce. Theresa sent texts, messages, and letters to all her drama queen friends and relatives. She said the authorities should blame me if anything ever happened to her. Once my then-wife turned up in Denmark, everyone understood that was just part of her staging things. My reputation didn't suffer any long-term damage."

Emma returned quietly to her seat in the living room, obviously not wanting to interrupt.

"That she couldn't leave you alone is an important detail," I reasoned. "It helps distinguish the doctor's claim that she ran off this last time from that previous runaway. He's not mentioned her harassing him during the most recent time she's supposedly been away. I suspect you know many little things that might help answer some questions. I want to back up to before your divorce — I'm looking for anything you know that contributed to the first time she took off."

A cell phone sitting on the end table vibrated. Glancing at the Caller ID, Darrell apologized, "I'm sorry, I have to take this."

"Perhaps now would be a good time to take a break," Emma offered. "Would you like to reconsider coffee, tea, or juice? Maybe a cruller to go with it?"

As Emma spoke, Darrell left the room to continue his phone conversation. "You've been so gracious with your time," I told her. "Already, this has been helpful. I hate to abuse my welcome, but coffee does sound great."

"Come with me to the kitchen," Emma invited, "and see if we have anything you'd like to nibble with your coffee. It sounds like you may be here for a while — we could talk about so many interesting things. And you know, nothing goes better with tales of evil and intrigue than a cup of java and a warm Danish."

She thought for a moment, her expression seeming to turn serious.

"Well, okay, maybe S'mores," she corrected herself. "But since that last itty-bitty incident, Darrell won't let me build open campfires in the kitchen…."

The laughter that burst from her was genuine and infectious.

Chapter 20

We idly chatted while Emma poured coffee. I teased through the warm bakery goodies in a wicker hamper on the kitchen's center island. After a few moments, we returned to the living room with our hot caffeine and an éclair that looked too good for me to pass up. Darrell had already returned, scanning the e-mail on his phone.

"Honey, would you like a cup of coffee?" Emma asked.

"No, sweetheart, I'm good. We've set the grand opening of the new restaurant for the tenth. Remind me to ask you, Debra Ann, what your schedule is like — it would be great if you could join us," Darrell said, glancing over his phone at me.

Laying the cell on the end table, he returned to the relevant subject. "I think you last asked what led to Theresa leaving the country the first time?"

I nodded. "Yes, that would be great; perhaps help set the context."

"Knowing now what I didn't know then, it began with Theresa's and James Seaver's affair right after her father died. The old man was loaded, and Seaver must have targeted her the minute his death hit the papers."

"I assume there were changes in your relationship...," I said, treading softly.

"In the beginning, I had no clue. I was busy adding new restaurants and a new club downtown. But I started noticing issues with our personal finances — credit card charges for things that didn't track. Theresa wasn't working or volunteering anywhere, yet she was always gone from the house. Terrence was staying with us, almost sixteen then, not driving yet. She'd forget to pick him up from school, or she'd be way late to his events, so I was fielding a lot more calls from him."

"At what point did you think she might be cheating?" I asked as I finished my éclair.

"I suspected for a while before I did anything about it. Little things, mostly. It came to a head when Theresa became desperate to get money from her father's estate. He had complicated business interests, and probate had gone on for almost three years — claimants trying to break his will. She insisted she needed a sizeable chunk of money for 'the opportunity of a lifetime.'"

"She wouldn't have been the primary breadwinner for the family, right?" I asked, wanting to understand their financial arrangement.

"Not at all. By then, I was providing us with a pretty good living. Theresa had no business training or experience. She wasn't returning to school or looking for a job, and we could get any real estate through my company. It seemed odd."

"Did she give you any idea what the opportunity was about?"

"She wouldn't tell me. She played that 'if you truly loved me, you'd want me to grow my wings' card. So, I figured it was *her* inheritance; she could do with it what she wanted. I loaned her two million dollars through my business against her eventual probate settlement. She didn't completely take me in, though. My attorney wrote an ironclad agreement guaranteeing I'd get my money back, mainly to protect my business."

"But now Theresa's got two million dollars to do with as she wishes," I concluded. "What happened to the money?"

"My question, too, and a couple of other things. Once Theresa deposited the check into a separate account, she was increasingly gone from the house for entire nights. She'd show up at ten the next morning with horseshit excuses. So, I hired a private investigator, one of the best in town. That's when I learned about her cheating with James Seaver."

"And what did your detective tell you about him?"

"That he's been a player in many questionable or flat-out illegal activities over the years. Everything he does seems to have a manipulative twist to it. He started as a straight-up con man and pimp, albeit brilliantly, if the standard is not getting caught. Seaver loaded up on student loan debt in college while partying and running a string of prostitutes out of the frat house. He ducked out of the pimping charges by joining the Navy. He conned the recruiter into picking up his college loan obligations, a program your government started in 1990."

"I didn't know you could even *do* that — heck, *I* would have joined if it meant I could have retired my student loans...." I grinned.

"The medical school accepted Seaver on the Navy's dime, but he got out of any essential service to the country. His field of choice to make that happen? He trained as a gynecologist. I assume that was because military personnel wouldn't require those skills on any battlefield. All the services banned women from active combat back then."

"Wait, the U.S. Navy trains *ex-pimps*, and *males* to boot, to provide intimate services only women would use?" I exclaimed, putting myself in a patient's shoes. "I assume they didn't do any psychological testing for his suitability, given that Seaver doesn't seem to demonstrate much empathy."

"Hey, listen, you're preaching to the choir." A wry smile crossed Darrell's face. "I served in the Royal Australian Air Force before I came here. By the time my tour ended, nothing anyone did in the military surprised me anymore."

"My father served, and he'd often say the same thing. I didn't realize it was international," I said with a touch of sarcasm.

Darrell gave me a crooked grin and a nod as he continued, "So, James Seaver gets out of the Navy and needs money. He did the only thing you would expect a greedy, manipulative, military-trained gynecologist to do. The doctor offered discreet, high-end abortion services to the rich and powerful. Or more accurately, to their outside-the-marriage girlfriends."

"Could he get any sleazier?" I didn't expect an answer — but that didn't stop Darrell from providing one.

"I'm not sure I'd want to challenge him on that score. For one thing, he'd get you any pharmaceuticals you want or need for a price. Rumors say Seaver would sell fetal tissue or an organ here and there into the black market. Eventually, the medical review board busted him. They stripped him of his medical license for writing and selling OxyContin scripts. But by this time, he's accumulated hard drives full of blackmail material he can use against politicians and wealthy businesspeople."

"*That's* enlightening." One of my missing puzzle pieces had fallen into place. "I knew Seaver had a couple of arrests for writing illegal prescriptions. And that the vice squad had looked at him for fraud, embezzlement, and running a gaming establishment without a license. I hear he's gotten nothing more than probation or a small fine for any of those things. The blackmail probably played a part."

"His schtick is that he can find the bad in everybody he's up against," Darrell said. "He leverages their weaknesses to his advantage. Judges, investigators, prosecutors, jurors — it doesn't matter; he figures out how to get to them."

"We got a personal taste of that when Darrell asked the prosecutor to file charges on the mall property fraud." Emma chimed in with a look of disgust on her face. "I had a rough go of things in college and did some modeling to make extra money. The shoots included some unsuitable-for-work stills for a skin magazine. I made several decisions that life hadn't yet equipped me to handle back then. I'd also been in a disastrous relationship where I got an abortion."

"Did Seaver perform the abortion?"

"No, he didn't," Emma replied, "but he found out somehow. He sent copies of the photos and the clinic receipt to Darrell. He threatened to destroy Darrell's image for the family-friendly restaurants he owns."

"That had to impact your marriage...," I surmised.

"Fortunately for us, Darrell and I had talked about those things when we were dating." Ema and Darrell looked at one another with terse smiles. "Darrell stood up for me and told Seaver to go screw himself. If there was an effect, it was that James Seaver strengthened our marriage."

"Blackmail is bad enough, but brute force like that? That's especially cold and cowardly." Darrell and Emma were filling in the outline of Seaver I had in my head. "One of my friends is a good cop who fought through some personal problems. I'd hate to think how it would have hurt her career if someone had exposed them before she got help."

"I'm sorry to interrupt the flow," Emma said, "but how do you feel about cats and dogs? Any allergies?"

"I like animals, and they usually like me…," I replied.

"We've had the dogs penned up in the bedroom for quite a while, and they're used to having the run of the house. Can't release the dogs without letting the cats have their freedom, too." She laughed. "If you don't mind, I need to let them out. Don't worry; they're pretty well-behaved."

Turning back to the conversation with Darrell as Emma headed towards the rear of the house, I reviewed my notes.

"Emma mentioned 'mall property fraud?'"

"The doctor found a corrupt bankruptcy trustee who sold him an insolvent mall developer's holdings for pennies on the dollar," Darrell responded. "That's why he needed the advance on Theresa's inheritance. The city zoned the property C34 multi-use, which made it quite valuable at that location. Better yet, it was on the tax rolls as undeveloped, even though construction work had already started. James Seaver somehow got the property reassessed, so the taxes were minimal — based on what he'd paid rather than its actual value. Those things are all greasy and unethical, possibly bribery, but not fraud."

"So, where does the fraud come in?" I asked.

"The doctor sold the property back and forth between several shell companies he controlled," Darrell explained. "He'd get investors to pay increasingly higher prices for the same property. It was a hybrid Ponzi-slash-pump-and-dump scheme. The purchasers in each new round pay off the previous round's investors. He'd double the property price each round, give each selling investor a quick 10 percent profit, and pocket the balance."

"So, the investors who made money in the early rounds, I guess every round but the last one, would make passionate suckers for his next scam. How did he convince investors of the increased value for each round?" I asked.

"Feeding frenzy, mostly. Seaver used the activity generated for a previous round to pique curiosity. Then, he'd seed rumors among the new investors. He arranged with a construction equipment rental company to park heavy machinery on that land. They'd have people move dirt from pile to pile. I assume that was to convince investors that work was progressing."

Before I could ask my next question, fur-bearing beasts suddenly attacked us. The two dogs bounded into the living room, with a tan-on-white Burmese following at a more casual trot. A blue-point Siamese came far behind at a slow walk, appropriately aloof and disdainful, tail straight up except for a curl at the tip. The black-haired Schnauzer went straight for Darrell. The dog bounced up and down like he was on a spring, tapping Darrell's knees with its front paws at the top of every jump.

The snickerdoodle was *so* cute, and she knew how to work it. She instantly decided I was her new best friend, standing up on her hind feet and begging with both paws held together. Emma handed me a treat over my shoulder to give the little poodle mix, saying softly, "Her name is Dipsy, short for Dipsy Doodle." With that, I belonged to the dog. She bounded into my lap and settled in like it was her bed, now and then licking my hand between the thumb and forefinger.

The calico circled at the foot of the chair, waiting for Emma. Once Emma sat down, the cat gracefully leaped up to lie on the arm and began cleaning herself as Emma petted her. The Siamese hopped up on the end table and then to the top of the seatback of my chair. He sauntered to the highest point of the curved part, laid on his tummy, and then dropped one paw down to play with the hair at the nape of my neck.

As he played, he flicked the end of his tail past my right ear. The tickling made me half-laugh, half-yelp. Darrell and Emma were watching and grinning, enjoying the show.

"He does that to everyone sitting in that chair the first time he sees them," Emma said with a wide smile.

"And before you ask — yes, he knows what he's doing and does it on purpose."

CHAPTER 21

Once everyone had enjoyed a good laugh and I'd recovered what I could of my dignity, I returned to my interview.

"Your dogs remind me of a question bugging me. It's completely irrelevant to anything, just one of those things I can't let go. What's up with Seaver and his dachshund? I think he calls it 'Bubbles?' When I met Seaver at his front door, their interaction was so weird I wondered if I should call somebody to ensure the poor thing was OK…."

"After they were married, Theresa complained about his relationship with that little dog," Darrell answered. "She told me the story. Seaver had been out drinking and was urinating in an alley. The dachshund was a stray that kept hanging around. It was bothering him, so he tried to pee on it. But the poor thing is paralyzed in its hind end — has to hop and drag its back feet along, couldn't get away."

"My friend Marci has two boys, and their first dog was a dachshund," I offered with a nod. "Once they reach a certain age, they can simply jump down from something, say a couch, and rupture or slip a disk. It's a congenital thing common to the breed."

"For whatever reason, Seaver felt sorry for the dog and brought it home. As far as we know, Bubbles is the only true friend he has. Carries the little thing everywhere he goes."

"Carries it?" I asked. "It still can't walk? I know that with surgery and therapy, they usually recover. Didn't Seaver have that done?"

"Not that we know of," Darrell replied. "Sad, sad situation. I have a theory about that. Seaver's gotten away with so many things because the guy doesn't trust anyone. He's so afraid somebody's going to turn on him. Paranoia makes him careful and hard to catch. As small and crippled as it is, I think that dog is the one living thing in his world that could never pose any threat to him. It's the only creature to whom he can express affection that he wouldn't eventually regret. But that's true just so long as the little guy can't defend himself or escape."

"Wow, that *is* sad." I sighed. "Sick on a whole different level."

The room, full of pets and animal lovers, went silent for an uncomfortable moment before I returned to the original topic.

"So, what did Seaver finally get out of gaming his investors?"

"The net effect? Promoting the nominal value of that land to an obscene level. Almost a hundred million dollars," Darrell answered disgustedly, rubbing the belly of the Schnauzer now lying on his back in the restauranteur's lap. "The last transaction transferred ownership into a shell corporation. Its filings show Theresa having 51 percent control. Because he'd destroyed *his* reputation, James Seaver wanted the cachet of the Woodson name. I've paid my dues to be known around here for being business-savvy and legitimate, or I've certainly tried my best."

"So, Seaver *has* to marry Theresa to gain control over her if he's allowed her sway over negotiable assets...," I mused.

"As a practical matter, yes," Darrell replied. "The doctor created a BS story around this shell company. He claimed a secret deal with General Dynamics to research hypersonic weapons. He explained the urgency by claiming the U.S. was way behind the Russians and the Chinese in developing the technology. Why San Diego? Because the Navy base was right here for operational testing on its ships. The secrecy? Of course, everything had to be hush-hush, else foreign agents would sabotage the facility or the work."

"An answer for everything. So, what was James Seaver's end game in all of this?" I asked.

"The idea was to max out loans anywhere he could get them, securing them with the real estate's inflated value. Seaver would take in a final round of investor money. Then, he'd cash out with a fire sale of the company's unleveraged assets, leaving Theresa holding the bag." Darrell motioned as if to dust off his hands. "Pretty simple once he got the land value up where he wanted it."

"Hmmm … obviously, something didn't work out because James Seaver hasn't yet flown the coop." I frowned.

"Exactly. In California, family law courts don't consider an inheritance part of the marital estate if it goes to just one party in the marriage. In other words, the inheritance remains the property of the inheriting person; ordinarily, I'd have no claim on what her father left her during Theresa's and my marriage. But that's true only so long as the parties keep everything related to the inheritance separate from marital property."

"So, once James Seaver had his hooks into Theresa, game over. You couldn't stop her from giving her father's money to Seaver if you'd wanted to, right?" I asked.

"You'd think," Darrell replied. "But when they got impatient and borrowed money from marital assets against her inheritance, that broke the separation. Now, the inheritance becomes community property. Had she not had an affair, and I not filed for divorce, I wouldn't have known or cared about going after what her father left her. It's not like I needed the money." Darrell spread his hands palms upward and looked around the room.

"At that point, I assume her affair with the doctor is driving everything she's doing — him using her," I said.

"Yes. Seaver kept Theresa focused on the perceived slights she saw coming from me, though it was Seaver's mistakes creating her problems. Theresa was furious to learn during the divorce that her inheritance was now joint property. With plenty of the doctor's help, she did everything she could to hide assets and destroy paper trails."

"Wait — your loan to her gets him the land, but not the funds he needs for the rest of the con?"

"Precisely. I hired a private investigator once I suspected Theresa of cheating. His report led to the divorce. That, in turn, mucked with Seaver's plans, tying up his assets," Darrell said. "Purely by coincidence, she'd gotten her father's inheritance settlement before I filed for the divorce. She had to repay the loan from the inheritance proceeds."

Darrell stopped to let down the restless Schnauzer.

"Those transactions fell into the ninety-day window that made them part of the divorce proceedings. The remaining portion of the inheritance became community property for the court to divide between us. That was Seaver's first major setback. He wouldn't get his hands on nearly as much of that endowment as he'd expected."

"But there was enough left that the crooked doctor was still interested...," I guessed.

"I think that's why she took off for Copenhagen, to buy time. They had to devise a scheme to keep the court from dividing that inheritance. It wasn't fancy; she didn't come home one evening and got on a plane under a different name, leaving her passport. I assume putting me under suspicion of murder was just dumb luck, accidental icing on the cake."

"How long was she gone?"

"She only stayed away for a month and a half — she never enjoyed traveling. Taking off like that was our discredited doctor's idea. Theresa has some intelligence, but she's never been what I'd call 'devious.'"

"Seems James Seaver's trademark is that somebody else does any suffering his plots require," I said.

"Absolutely. But Seaver's plan wasn't well-considered. My divorce wasn't final; he couldn't marry Theresa beforehand and couldn't benefit from her presumed demise. He had no access to that inheritance without Theresa's witnessed signature and the court's approval. Even with her power of attorney, nothing he could do would pass muster with the court."

"None of this shows any forethought."

"I think he was spit-balling it, making it up as he went," Darrell agreed. "Ultimately, the authorities found Theresa. Her father's estate repaid my company the two million with interest. The court split the inheritance.

As far as I was concerned, that was that. Her infidelity with the doctor upset me more than I wanted anyone to know. I was eager to divorce her and move on. I wasn't thinking about anything else. Emma and I met shortly after the divorce; she helped me to a much better place."

"I'm glad for both of you." I nodded to Emma and got a big smile back.

"But Theresa and the doctor are like fruit flies around an old banana. Can't seem to get rid of them," Darrell continued. "My private investigator tripped over the property fraud during the divorce proceedings. The scam showed up as tied to James Seaver, not Theresa. It wasn't until Theresa married the doctor that her role became apparent. The doctor was the puppeteer, but Theresa would take the fall if anything went wrong — he'd just cut her loose."

"How did your investigator come to learn all of this?"

"Incorporation filings listed Theresa Woodson as the primary stockholder in the shell company. It now owned what had become a very pricey property. The paperwork still showed my last name, and she hadn't filed a change of address, so the legal and tax notices came here."

"Pretty careless."

"Details weren't Theresa's thing," Darrell went on, "and the doctor would lose track of his various ruses, so these mistakes happened. I had Harry, my investigator, look deeper. By then, the Seavers had committed half a dozen crimes around that property. Theresa was right at the front of it. She hid her stake in the shell company from the divorce court, getting one of her attorneys censured for the deception."

"The court's involvement ended Seaver's games, right?"

"*Au contraire.* James Seaver had transferred the mall property from the shell company Theresa controlled into another. After the divorce was final, Theresa reacquired the same property at fifty times its original value. The corporate veil protected her as the majority owner of the shell company, even one with enormous assets and no history. I asked the DA to look at it, and he filed a criminal case, tying up her interest in the property again."

"You needed the DA's help to put some distance between the Woodson brand and Seaver's shenanigans?"

"Exactly. Now, James Seaver must remove her claim to the land so he can clear the title, or he can't get more loans against it. And Theresa says 'no' to him for once, but she couldn't have picked a worse time. It can only go to him now if she's out of the picture. He has to inherit it as her surviving husband — or, in her documented absence, proxies and powers of attorney — to regain control of the property."

"Strong motive for a homicide case. You almost feel sorry for Theresa, though she can't claim innocence."

"She was in *so* far over her head," Darrell replied. "Once the DA knew what was going on, it was simple to get indictments against both Theresa and the dishonored doctor."

"It's oddly funny — given their personalities, I'm surprised he didn't kill her simply because she nags incessantly," Emma put in.

"'Once a woman has forgiven a man, she must not reheat his sins for breakfast,'" I quoted. When Darrell looked at me quizzically, I explained, "Something Marlene Dietrich once said."

"Oh? You seem too young to have been a fan…," Emma said.

"My grandfather was, and I loved him dearly. So, by extension, I became one, too." I turned to Darrell. "You said Theresa was hard to live with — that wasn't exclusive to your relationship with her?"

"Oh, no, not at all," Darrell replied. "Trust me on this; it takes a patient and forgetful man, any man, to deal with her day after day. James Seaver's not that kind of person. I'm ordinarily tolerant, but some days took every bit I had to give. The Lord knows that more than once, even *I* thought about putting her out of my misery." Darrell's look was apologetic.

I couldn't help but smile at the candor, though I left his comment out of my notes.

Emma gave her husband a concerned glance, then turned to me. "I'm so sorry to interrupt a fascinating conversation. But the kids will be home soon for lunch and like to ask nosey questions…."

"Oh, no, my bad, Emma, honestly," I apologized. "I knew I was intruding on your schedule and meant to be watching the time more carefully."

"This has been a great discussion," Darrell said graciously. "Therapeutic in some ways, at least for me, and I know there's much more we need to discuss."

"I did mean to ask you if you knew any of the people my witness mentioned...."

"Listen, we have independent auditors coming into the office tomorrow morning at eight," Darrell replied. "I've got to let them in and ensure they have all the access they need, but other than that, they won't require my services. If you don't mind going downtown a little early, we could grab a conference room, and you'd have my full attention for a couple of hours. Say around 8:30?"

"I can do that," I agreed. "You've both been so wonderful; you truly have."

"Here's the address, though I don't think you could miss it," Emma said. "Just look for 'The Nocturnary.' It's one of Darrell's clubs, and his offices are on the third floor above it."

With that, we said our goodbyes. But my departure didn't thrill everyone.

Dipsy tilted her head and pushed my guilt button for leaving her, and it worked.

THE WRITINGS OF
AVRIL MARIA SERENE

CHAPTER 22

I'd spent most of the evening on the Internet verifying the information the Woodsons had provided me. My Dun & Bradstreet account proved valuable running down the business entities, including Darrell's. What I found there and through my browser generally backed up Darrell's rendition of events. The discrepancies had more to do with the timeliness and completeness of the data recorded online than with inconsistencies.

The morning traffic rush into downtown wasn't as bad as I anticipated. It was a Friday, and the weather was beautiful, which may have helped. I got there a little early, and as I stood at the bank of elevators to go to the third floor, I idly perused the building directory. I saw that half a dozen of the business names listed had "Woodson" somewhere in their titles. It seemed likely Darrell also owned the building. Having this many entities paying someone else rent wouldn't make sense.

The Woodson Group corporate offices were open and spacious, finished in glass and chrome, broken up by the occasional fabric-covered wall. Hidden spotlights illuminated modern art in the nooks and crannies.

The ambiance wasn't that of the typical cubicle farm. The walls stood at odd angles, and groupings of couches and chairs, intermixed with small bar-height dining sets, furnished the spaces. Ceiling lights recessed into dark walnut panels augmented stand-alone fixtures to provide plenty of light. The atmosphere was more comfortable and laid-back than most offices I'd experienced.

Darrell came to the receptionist's desk to meet me, and I followed him into a small, glass-walled conference room. It featured a fully stocked coffee bar, and I took advantage. We sat catty-corner from each other at the long oak-trimmed Formica table. I began by thanking Darrell again for the hospitality he and his wife had extended me the day before.

"I'm learning a lot, and I can't tell you how much I appreciate this information."

"It flows both ways — the conversation helps us, too," Darrell replied. "I'm happy that you've taken an interest in this. Whatever there was between Theresa and me, she didn't deserve what we believe happened to her. Certainly, somebody needs to bring James Seaver to justice."

"Cross your fingers that Seaver doesn't see me coming, and I can gather enough to help put him away without hurting anyone else."

"Given how he's hamstrung the police and stalled the criminal cases around his fraud, you may be the only one still standing who can nail the defrocked doctor."

"Even so, I don't think Seaver can hold everyone at bay forever. Eventually, the authorities *will* catch up with him, but I think I can break down his defenses faster. You've supplied a lot of missing pieces that fit the story my witness told. I say 'told' in the past tense because at least two people beat that witness to death and left him in an alley downtown."

"You think James Seaver had something to do with that?"

I nodded. "I'm not sure *how*, but I *am* sure the doctor was involved."

"Beaten to death, wow," Darrell murmured. "That someone would lose their life in such a brutal way... It takes this out of the realm of speculation."

Darrell paused for a moment to reflect.

"I suppose all Seaver cares about is that there's one less person to testify against him. What a horrible measure of a human life. But with all due respect to the victim, he's probably right. Losing a witness doesn't seem like something that helps us."

"On the surface, you'd think not. But as unfortunate as it is, that witness's death could help resolve all of this. Before his murder a little over a month ago, he wrote several letters. In those letters, he described events that coincided with Terrence reporting his mother was missing. They make a decent outline for telling that part of the story. By filling in the missing details, we can make the case that Seaver killed Theresa pretty solid."

I told Darrell what Brian had witnessed the man he called "Doc," Doc's presumed girlfriend, and "Rickie" doing that night.

"The girlfriend *could* have been Theresa, and the body, someone else entirely," I allowed. "But we've heard nothing from Theresa in the almost four months since. From what you told me yesterday, the doctor had many motivations to kill her. I have to go with the body being Theresa's. Otherwise, she *is* on the run, and she's gotten very good at it this time, which doesn't track with her history. If the woman helping move the corpse at the house wasn't Theresa, would you know who Seaver's outside-his-marriage girlfriend might be?"

"Harry looked into several people, but his reports don't mention a person with a relationship like that to Seaver."

"What about this 'Rickie?' Of the people you know tied to the doctor, is there anyone he'd trust enough to ask for help moving a body?"

Darrel tapped a pen on the table.

"That's probably Richard Ainsworth, James Seaver's right-hand henchman. Rumors say he has underworld connections and does a lot of the strong-arming and dirty work for the doctor, or has it done. Ainsworth would be Frank Nitti to the doctor's Al Capone. He gets almost as many mentions in Harry's reports as James Seaver."

"Do you know where Ainsworth lives or anything about his home?"

"No, I'm sorry, I don't."

"Sorry to keep peppering you with questions — I appreciate your patience. I've got two more: Would you describe Ainsworth as 'short' or 'small,' and do you know if he works out?"

"I've not met the man, but Ainsworth *is* a few inches shorter than the doctor in photos I've seen. And I'm taller than Seaver, so depending on the viewer's perspective, you could say Ainsworth is on the short side. He looks to be in good physical shape. If he's Seaver's muscle, you'd think lifting weights would go with the job."

"Well, that's it for now. Between my witness's letters and what you've told me today, we may have enough that the authorities can break the gridlock or get someone to talk. Once again, thank you for your time; it's been a pleasure. Please give my regards to Emma. I'll get out of your hair now, but I'll keep you posted as things develop."

"I've enjoyed our conversations," Darrell said. "Feel free to call or stop by if there is anything else we can do to help."

Returning to my car, I was giddy with how the interview had gone. I still needed to check out a few more things, but I felt like I'd won the trifecta with my first on-spec self-assignment. Having Richard Ainsworth's name could close the loop on a great story. The information I gathered would help the authorities nail the bad guys in at least two murders. And I would have fulfilled my commitment to Dad to follow up with Brian's letters.

Once the idiot in the green Mustang behind me quit riding my bumper, I could return home content with the day's start.

I couldn't wait to get up close and personal with my Internet browser.

⁂

I launched Chrome and typed "Richard Ainsworth San Diego" into the search bar. Not much turned up for the Ainsworth I was looking for. The police arrested him ten years ago for beating a man to collect a loansharking debt. Court records showed Ainsworth indicted for running a neighborhood protection racket. He'd then hooked up with James Seaver. The authorities had charged him, along with Seaver, for Medicare fraud and the selling of OxyContin scripts.

A photo featured them together for a perp walk into the San Diego County jail booking room. Ainsworth was indeed shorter than Seaver but a little thicker. "Smaller guy" wasn't a phrase that came immediately to my mind as a 5' 9" woman, but I could see how a bigger man might describe him that way. He was undoubtedly muscular. A video of Ainsworth running interference against a reporter trying to question Seaver showed he had an enforcer's demeanor and body language.

After serving ninety days and paying restitution for the medical fraud and drug charges, Ainsworth stuck with white-collar crime. Investigators arrested him for a Bitcoin Ponzi scheme, though a jury acquitted him. Ainsworth settled out-of-court with a business partner who had accused him of embezzlement. He'd avoided further criminal complaints. Seaver's Teflon umbrella seemed to protect Ainsworth as well.

The *Union-Tribune's* sports page carried a lengthy piece about a sports memorabilia counterfeiting scheme. It mentioned Ainsworth as a principal in the fraud. Still, I couldn't find anything that showed authorities had ever charged him. Ainsworth was currently the subject of at least one protective order resulting from a domestic violence incident.

Using Google Maps and Streetview, I tracked down each address connected to the Ainsworth name in the general San Diego area. None of them matched the description Brian had given in his letters. That didn't necessarily eliminate Ainsworth as the "Rickie" Brian mentioned. The house Brian had staked out could have been a safe house owned by anyone. Or it may have been held or rented in the name of a friend or romantic interest. Without a specific address, I couldn't backtrack for a connection to Ainsworth.

I shifted to another task. I wanted to contact Theresa's son, Terrence. Following Emma's advice, I texted Terrence at the number she'd given me, telling him I was a reporter looking into his mom's disappearance. I intended to wait a few hours before trying again if he didn't respond. In the meantime, I googled around. There wasn't much online about Terrence, but I did learn he used his mother's maiden name, Martin, as his surname.

According to his Facebook page, he was a fill-in guitarist for a local band called *The Frenetic*, which had played several clubs in the area and had a following. Their latest booking was at The Casbah, which told me they must be at least halfway decent. The venue held about two hundred people, and acts like Alanis Morissette, The Breeders, Ben Harper, The Cult, Blink-182, and Dinosaur Jr. had all played there in their careers — bands I knew from my formative years in the nineties and at the beginning of the millennium.

I hadn't been online long before my phone rang, and Terrence's name appeared on Caller ID.

"You said you wanted to help find my mother," Terrence said after introducing himself.

"I'm trying to understand what happened to her," I replied. "The police haven't been able to learn anything. After hearing she was missing, I wanted to see what I could do. I talked to Darrell and Emma, so I know some of it. Still, I'd like to hear what you know."

"It's not like it's a secret or anything — everybody knows that asshole so-called doctor killed her," Terrence blurted out angrily. "But the police won't arrest him."

"That's what I want to talk to you about. My job is to find out what I can and, if there is a story there, to tell it. Sometimes the publicity helps."

"That's all I want — somebody to say what's real. I don't have time to talk now — I have to work, and tonight we've got a gig. I just called to see if you wanted to come during our break. It's slow on weeknights, and I can talk to you then."

"You're playing at The Casbah tonight?"

"Yes — our first set ends at eleven-thirty."

"Okay, I'll be there."

"I can get the manager to reserve you a table off to the side. Just give the bouncer at the rope your name — you won't need a ticket."

We signed off with my plans for the evening set.

After the brief interruption, I stepped back to review the story elements. Going through my notes and Brian's letters one last time reminded me that Gary Gilbert was still holding one. If I hurried, I could get out to the cemetery, collect the final letter, and see what it could add to the evidence I'd collected.

I called the friendly caretaker and caught him in a free moment. He still had the letter and would be there until at least five.

He was looking forward to catching up with my story.

CHAPTER 23

Traffic was heavy, and I arrived at the memorial gardens later than I'd wanted. Gary was locking up as I got to his office door. While he was polite, it was clear that he was anxious to get home. Telling him of my latest adventures would have to wait. Still, he'd kept that last letter under the counter for me as promised. Moments later, I thanked Gary and wished him and his wife well, a letter-sized manila envelope firmly in my hand.

Gary had put shipping tape over the metal clasp after he'd sealed it, probably to keep the contents safe from further damage. Once I'd gotten back inside my car, I used my keys to tear it open, concerned the letter inside might not be one of those from Brian. The outside of the standard white envelope was a little worse for wear, and it had been wet at some point. But when I flipped it over, there it was — "Sis" written on the front, nothing more.

The trip home was against traffic. It wasn't long before I'd scanned and photographed the letter under black light on my kitchen table. As I read it, I realized it filled the gap immediately after Brian's complaint that the police hadn't taken his anonymous tip seriously. Brian had written this letter before becoming paranoid about "goons" strange to him rousting his neighborhood's residents.

One paragraph made my jaw drop:

You remembr Donnie the hacker who lived above us in the old apartment? He got Docs number for me from the house adress. I texted Doc from my burner and told him Id rat him out if he didnt turn himself in. One day I was casing another house on the same block. They were taking the naber out on a gurney. The peeple on the street waching said a profesional had shot him dead. He took one to the head and one to the hart in his living room during the football game. The doc probly killed him or got some one else to do it cause he thought the naber sent my text. Why dos this keep hapening Sis? When ever I try to fix some thing — the wrong peeple get hurt.

Could it be? He's talking about Coach's murder! My emotions around Coach's death clouded my judgment, and the first time I read Brian's words, I skipped over the "probly" in his most important sentence. I had to reread it to realize that Brian didn't know any of this for a fact — it was simply a guess by association.

But it shook me that the two events — Brian's tagging of Seaver's wall and Coach's murder — could be related; worse, that the possible linkage hadn't occurred to me. Still, I'd had no way of knowing until now that Brian had tried to blackmail Seaver, apart from trying to set the doctor up for Rickie's intended murder. The blackmail would have been the event that likely set things in motion.

Still, could this have caused Coach's murder? Holy crap…

I checked the date on Brian's letter. Sure enough, it was written three days after Coach's death. So many thoughts were racing through my head that I couldn't focus. I had to leave my chair and began pacing back and forth.

Seaver kills his wife, and Brian catches him in the process of hiding the body. Brian tags the place, so Seaver knows that there's a witness. Seaver has something against his neighbor anyway, maybe racism? Either way, he thinks seventy-year-old Coach sprayed paint on his walls and texted that blackmail message. Seaver has an alibi; he doesn't match the witness description for Coach's first visitor that night. But Richard Ainsworth might. As a neighbor, Seaver's too close and subject to suspicion, so say he has Ainsworth kill Coach. Ainsworth's underworld connections clean up the mess. Then Brian tries to take on Ainsworth in his own home, getting himself killed for his trouble.

It's not the first scenario you'd think of, but it's plausible and possible. And Brian's letters tied all of it together. *Okay, Debra Ann, concentrate. First question: does Ainsworth make sense for Coach's homicide?*

Ainsworth's Medicare fraud perp walk photo showed he fit Jess Nessbaum's general description. At a little under five-ten, the lifts-in-his-shoes theory worked. Between the Internet and what Darrell Woodson said, I knew there was a strong connection and known history between Seaver and Ainsworth.

But all I had to tie Coach and Ainsworth was the leap of logic Brian made in the letter. It was speculative, based on the timing and proximity of events. I had nothing else to connect Coach and Ainsworth. Coach's only known relationship with Seaver was as the next-door neighbor, which wouldn't necessarily extend to Seaver's associates. *Unless....* I did have a hunch, but I'd need Marci's help.

As far as Brian Pierce's and Theresa Seaver's murder investigations went, I was satisfied with what I would present to Marci. I could provide plenty of information that would help the police. It should get them past any barriers Seaver had erected to keep them from continuing their investigations. Anything I learned from Terrence tonight would supply the finishing touches. The police could tie Brian's death to Ainsworth with DNA and prints. They could then link the other participants, including James Seaver, with the letter contents. That would resolve the murders of two of the victims, Brian and Theresa. Flipping Ainsworth or diving deeply into Ainsworth's activities and associates would strengthen their cases.

I knew there was more I could do to investigate Brian's writings. But I'd been flying without a net for several years now — I didn't have the resources of the paper backing me. Without those, I couldn't take on these likely killers alone. I certainly didn't want to defend myself against both Seaver and Ainsworth and whomever else might be involved with them.

It was time to text Marci, set up a meeting, and turn over Brian's letters. My notes contained basic facts the police would want. But they also included creative snippets to spin those facts into entertaining material for my readers. I'd have to retype my notes into a new document file. I'd carefully separate the artistic nuggets I wanted to use in my article. Then, I'd have a version of my notes that I could give Marci.

Excited to be this close to the end of the story, I texted her: "I have something for you that will make your day. Want to solve at least two homicides, maybe three, and put away some nasty people? Let's get together. I have some things to give you (please bring your laptop). Let me know when and where. I owe you another lunch!"

Now was the time to put my hunch about Ainsworth and Coach to the test.

"Meanwhile, would you check to see if the detectives have a connection between Julius Cantor and a 'Richard Ainsworth?' Would also be helpful to know if David Barnwell, or a David or Barnwell, is in department databases as an alias for Richard Ainsworth or James Seaver. Or maybe as a known associate of either of them. I'll explain when I see you…."

The feelings washing over me ran the gamut. On the one hand, there was a joyless sense of fulfillment, answering the call of duty in helping solve Coach's murder. The feeling did nothing to mitigate the tragedy of losing Coach that way. Resolving the return of Brian's letters also turned out sadly because Brian was murdered, and there was no one left to give them to. That sensation of loss was more abstract; I didn't know Brian. And I did feel some satisfaction in accomplishing the last thing Dad had asked me to do.

But I'd be lying if I didn't confess that I was drooling over the hero's welcome I was expecting from the San Diego Police Department. That wasn't too much to ask for removing the shackles James Seaver had clamped on them. With my help, they could claim credit for solving two murders and a third if I was right about Ainsworth killing Coach. They'd also garner all the positive publicity from the articles I'd be writing around these events.

I gathered the freezer bags containing Brian's original letters and envelopes and placed them in a new expandable file folder. Then I copied the digital black light images of Brian's letters that I'd captured with my cell phone onto a thumb drive. I would later add a copy of my newly edited notes to the flash drive. The images of Brian's letters I'd already printed out had several of my handwritten comments. Those I'd keep for myself. I'd also retain duplicates of all the digital image files. I copied photos of the uncrumpled "David" and "Carmel mtn C/L - Barnwell 7 Th" sticky notes to the thumb drive.

Sure enough, as soon as I finished, I got a text from Marci. "You had me at free lunch, but I *am* curious about whatever trouble you've made for yourself. BTW, I did some digging, and I earned my lunch. Turns out Richard Ainsworth used the name 'David Barnwell' as the CFO of the shell company he created while working his Bitcoin Ponzi scheme.

"Busy tomorrow, but how about the day after, Greenfinch in La Jolla, maybe 1 pm?"

Got you, you son of a bitch!

Not Marci, of course, but Coach's likely killer, Richard Ainsworth. I'd need to call Cassidy and tell her, but I wanted to get Marci's reaction first. Once Marci told me what to expect from the department in Coach's case, I could pass that to Cassidy along with the news that we'd identified her father's murderer.

"Works for me 😊" I typed. "If you get there first, ask for a big table — see you there!"

I began editing the new version of my notes, a rendition I could give Marci and still leave myself with a good and, importantly, *exclusive* story to tell.

THE WRITINGS OF
AVRIL MARIA SERENE

CHAPTER 24

My mind and body are no longer what they were in my twenties. Visiting a bar after eleven on a weeknight now requires preparation. I was all set after napping for a few hours and taking in some carbs with leftover lasagna.

It was about ten as I readied myself to head out to The Casbah, using tonight's little adventure as an excuse to play dress-up. I picked out some distressed black jeans, a tight, charcoal V-neck sweater, a cropped and studded leather bolero, and black stilettos. As I walked to my car in the apartment parking lot for tenants, I practiced my runway strut. A dark-colored Dodge in the row behind my Toyota started its engine and turned on its headlights, catching me by surprise. I instinctively raised my left hand to block out the high beams the Dodge flashed in my eyes. The driver lowered his lights, but the experience irritated me more than it should have. I wasn't sure why — it was just a little thing, with no reason to believe it was intentional.

The Casbah has a definite vibe that fits its history — a "real rockers play here, posers go home!" feel. It was easy to see why every up-and-coming musician wanted to perform on their stage. That would be especially true for one not yet old enough to drink legally.

The bouncer directed me to the small round top Terrence had reserved, and I ordered a Scotch and soda. I listened to the band play for the half-hour before the break. I had to admit, their music was pretty good, certainly better than the alcohol the establishment served. The band's energy would make a good introduction for my first face-to-face conversation with Terrence.

Terrence unslung his guitar a few minutes after eleven-thirty and headed my way. He was around nineteen, slender and dark-complected with curly black hair, and no taller than me.

"This is a sweet venue for a local band — how did you land this gig?" I asked as Terrence took the seat across from me.

"*The Frenetic* have played here before. I auditioned for them a while ago and played with them at a private party when their lead guitar went to jail for a DUI. Now he's sick with COVID. He's still fighting it after three months. The band liked my sound, remembered me, and asked me to help again. Don't tell anybody my age; I'm supposed to be twenty-one to play here."

"You have my word," I said with a soft grin. "So, your mom's husband says she's in Europe having fun, but everybody else thinks she's in trouble, maybe worse. On the phone, you said he killed her. What makes you think that?"

"That douchenozzle doctor hates animals, except for his wiener dog," Terrence replied. "I'm pretty sure he tortured them back in elementary school." Terrence's face became dark red when upset, enough that I wondered if he had an underlying medical condition.

"So, when I got my new apartment with two of my friends, Mom gave me Bentley to keep. Bentley is Mom's Pekingese mix, and she loves him — a lot. She used to come over every other day to play with him. She'd take him for walks or to the park, and they'd run through the water at the beach."

As soon as Terrence calmed down, his face returned to its healthy color. The deep red seemed a reaction to specific triggers; in our conversation, that meant almost anything to do with James Seaver.

"So, I take it she hasn't been around to see Bentley?"

"It's been almost six months since I've seen her. She wouldn't go away like that. She just wouldn't. My mom's not perfect, but she cares about Bentley and me. And Mom doesn't like change that much. Traveling isn't her thing."

The last part confirmed something Darrell had said. "What was your mom's relationship with James Seaver like?"

"He used to con Mom all the time. But he knew I liked Darrell and Emma, so he didn't even try to fool me. When Mom wasn't listening, that cracker would call me her 'colored boy' to make me mad and act out. He tried to make it look like it was *my* fault we didn't get along."

Terrence's face had turned red again.

"After Mom and Darrell split up, she kept saying how hard it was for someone her age to find a good man. She said she needed to be happy with what she had. Mom kept saying her father had looked out for us, and things would improve once the court was through with PawPaw's estate."

"Do you think she was just waiting for the right opportunity to get free of the doctor?"

"Maybe. I don't know what Mom wanted. If she even knew, it would have surprised me. I co-wrote one of our songs called 'Simpering Dog.' Mom was like that when she was around him. But that wasn't who she was, not really. She wanted him to acknowledge that he cared about *her*, not just her money. Before they married, he'd play that game like it was her fault for misunderstanding him. But he didn't give a rat's ass how she felt after they said their vows. They always fought, mostly about money, and he didn't like her friends or Bentley. Or me."

"You know that the doctor claims she's doing the same thing she did right before Darrell divorced her?"

"That was different." Terrence's voice was insistent. "Mom and I would exchange notes on my Facebook page when she left the first time. She asked me not to tell anyone, so I didn't. I tried to let Darrell know she was okay without saying anything, and I think he knew."

"When did you last hear from your mother this time?"

"It was a little more than five months ago. You can tell from when Mom last updated her Facebook page. I know she's dead because she always added things to her timeline when she was alive."

"For your sake, I can only hope you are wrong about that. I wish I could offer something to prove your mother is still with us, but I can't. I can only imagine what it must be like not to know."

Terrence's eyes were tearing up as he fought to maintain control. "Just please, please tell me as soon as you hear something, whichever way it goes," he begged. "You're right; the hardest part is not knowing. I need to keep the faith for her sake. But it's hard to shut out that Mom's not been around."

We could both see his bandmates taking their positions back on stage. Terrence apologized for not having more time as we said our goodbyes. After the break, I kept my seat through their first song. I reflected on how Theresa's going missing might have affected Terrence. I experienced a pang of guilt about not giving the young man more thought before meeting him. I realized I hadn't considered Terrence an audience member when I mapped out how to write this story.

Terrence had indirectly confirmed the racism I suspected Seaver might have felt toward Coach. But our conversation hadn't revealed anything about his mother's disappearance. Still, our exchange would positively affect how I would tell her part in all of this. I owed him that.

The likelihood was that Theresa was dead and James Seaver had murdered her, or at least was heavily involved. And sadly, like Brian, Theresa, too, would make for an imperfect victim.

I pondered Theresa's circumstances as I headed across the poorly lit club lot to go home. Then, from several car lengths away, I saw something out of the corner of my eye that made me do a double-take. Wasn't that the same Dodge two-door sedan I saw back at my apartment? *Oh, come on, Debra Ann.* I shook my head at my silliness — there must be tens of thousands of those things in San Diego.

And that was precisely the type of vehicle someone might own if The Casbah was one of their hangouts. *Still....*

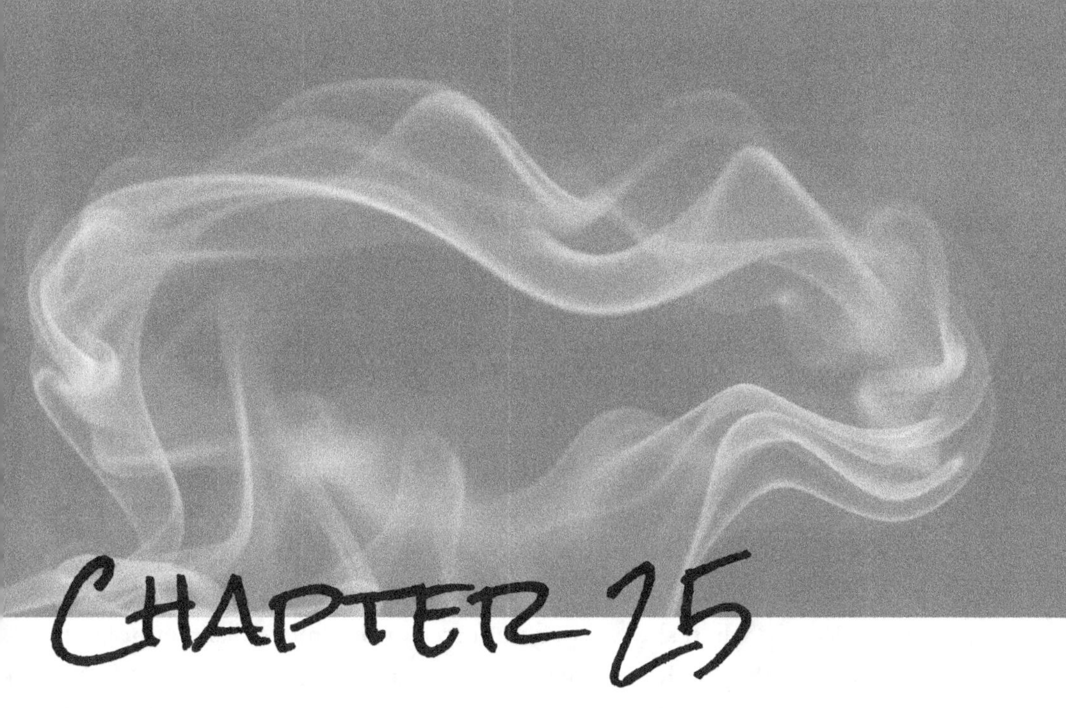

CHAPTER 25

I'd had little to drink, yet I was dragging as I got around the following morning. It was approaching nine o'clock when I had my second cup of coffee. With a bowl of Rice Krispies and sliced bananas to one side, I began checking my e-mails.

The *Bang! Bang! Bang!* at the front door startled me into dropping my half-full cup onto the table. Warm coffee splashed across its surface and onto my robe, then dribbled to the floor. I never got unexpected visitors, and the pounding generated a panic within me as it reverberated through my small apartment. I took a deep breath and snatched the hand towel hanging from the oven door handle. Dabbing at my robe, I hurried to the peephole at the front door and peered out.

Two fit, tall, youngish men in dark suits and mirrored sunglasses stood side-by-side in the hall. Standing a foot in front of them was a shorter man I recognized, at least two decades older.

Why in God's name would he *be here?*

"What do you want?" I asked through the closed door.

"My name is Dr. James Seaver, and I hear you've been asking about me, Ms. Wynn," the older man replied. "I was in your neighborhood. I thought I'd drop by to clarify some things for you. It would be easier to talk if you'd open the door."

My heart was pounding, but I needed to show that I wasn't afraid of him. I fastened the security chain and opened the door the four inches permitted, making it clear Seaver and his cohorts weren't welcome inside. Seaver wore a camel sports coat with black slacks—his checked blue shirt didn't hide the pronounced paunch I remembered from our first meeting. With the door partially open, I saw he'd brought Bubbles, again cradling the dachshund, now sporting a yellow bowtie, in his arms.

The two bodyguards were large and muscular, each with a five-day growth of stubble, their hands crossed in front of them and their feet apart. They were each a half-foot taller than Seaver, making him seem short by comparison. I could see that the escort to Seaver's right had an earbud. Both had the telltale bulges of firearms in their suit jackets. I knew from Marci's wardrobe selection when she worked undercover that more discreet holsters were available — they'd chosen these to send a message.

To make a point of my own, I grabbed my cell phone. As obviously as possible, I videoed the three men through the door's opening. Stepping back to show more of my apartment for context, I returned the focus to my visitors.

"Mr. Seaver, I...."

"That's *Doctor* Seaver, Ms. Wynn. It's rude not to acknowledge your betters," Seaver interrupted, wanting to control the conversation.

"No, *Mr.* Seaver, politeness has nothing to do with it." I chose to confront him. "But facts do. The medical board stripped you of your title because you broke the law — not just once, but several times."

Seaver gave out an over-the-top sigh. With purposeful deliberation, he placed his hands under Bubbles's front legs, holding the dog out with its belly toward me, and passed it to the bodyguard on his right. As if the situation weren't already edgy enough, as he did, I saw the pooch had an erection — I wasn't about to speculate why. Because of his reflective lenses, I couldn't see into the armed man's eyes. Still, his body language suggested he didn't want anything to do with the little guy. Rather than pulling Bubbles into his arms, he stood there, holding the dog out and away from his suit.

With a theatrical flourish, Seaver reached into his inner coat pocket and pulled out a pack of smokes. He removed one, put the package back in his pocket, and lit the cigarette.

"This is a no-smoking building — please put that out." I made it more of a demand than a request. The door opening was wide enough that I briefly considered using the kitchen fire extinguisher if necessary.

Seaver squinted his eyes closed as he inhaled deeply in transparently feigned enjoyment without saying a word. Then, opening his eyes and keeping them on me throughout, he slowly exhaled the smoke, blowing a ring at the end. With grand ceremony, Seaver removed the cigarette from his mouth with one finger and a thumb. Extending his arm to its full length straight out in front of him, he let the lit cigarette drop onto the hallway carpet. Pausing to flash me a wide, clownish smile, he forcefully ground the butt into the fibers of the floor covering with the toe of his shoe.

What a classless prick.

"There, you see how cooperative I can be? Ms. Wynn, we can debate your misinformation all day long if you want to, but wouldn't it be better to have the conversation inside?" Seaver's request came off as disingenuous. "Your neighbors don't need to know your business."

"That's the one thing you may be right about, Mr. Seaver." I made a move to close the door but reconsidered. "They don't. And you wouldn't be comfortable inside — the landlord sprays for roaches regularly. You should leave. *Now.*"

"C'mon, be reasonable. What kind of attitude is that for a professional reporter, Ms. Wynn? You *are* a professional, are you not? Oh, wait, they fired you from your last actual job. So sad. Well, here's a news flash, lady. Responsible reporters interview people before accusing them of anything. I am presenting myself for that interview."

"You are again mistaken — responsible reporters take statements from reliable witnesses, and you don't qualify, Mr. Seaver. When and if I expose you publicly for who you are and what you've done, we can discuss whether you have any right to an interview. I haven't, and you don't. But I'll assume your request for a recorded statement serves as your tacit approval of the video I'm capturing of your visit here today."

"You're not understanding how this works." Seaver's jaw muscles were tense, and his struggle to control his anger was evident. "I'm a private citizen, not a public figure. You have no right to stalk me, harass me, or interfere with my life. I was trying to do this peaceably, but if you prefer me to go the cease-and-desist route, I can do that. Ask your friends on the force how that's working out for them."

"I don't think it's as quiet on that front as you'd like to believe," I retorted. "It's just a matter of time before you go to prison for the murder of your wife and your part in the killings of two other human beings. I intend to be one of many people helping make that happen." Challenging him might not have been my brightest move, but I wasn't about to let this SOB run all over me.

"For someone who claims she relies on facts, you need to get yours straight." Seaver's voice was steady but controlled. "I was a person of interest in just one disappearance, where the subject ran off of her own volition. And they only looked at me because I was her husband. Ask your friend Darrell Woodson how that goes."

"Are you through, Mr. Seaver, or will I have to call the police to remove you from my doorway?" I asked as firmly as I could, trying to keep my voice from quivering.

"Publicly making ridiculous claims is slander." Seaver glowered at me. "Libeling people is one of several ways you might never work again. Crawling around in the muck and the mire trying to make something stick that never happened is risky business. There are consequences. People have accidents. Sometimes consequences and accidents can end careers."

"So, your 'tell' is making gangster threats," I said matter-of-factly. "I find it fascinating that you went to all this trouble to intimidate little ole me. I've been doing this a long time, and that says to me we're getting close, and you're running scared. Is your little house of cards collapsing in on you, Jimmie?"

I could tell that hit the mark. Seaver didn't seem to like dealing with strong women in the first place, and one had just called him out in front of his henchmen. I saw his face redden, and for a split second, I thought I'd overplayed a weak hand, that he'd rush the door in uncontrolled rage. The thought terrified me, even as I tried not to show it.

Instead, he pursed his lips and glanced down at his shoes, raising his eyes to glare at me with a menacing look. "As you wish, Ms. Wynn. We'll be on our way — *for now*. I have a feeling we'll be taking up this discussion again. Sooner than you might think. After all, it's not like we don't know where you live. Oh, and you *do* work from home, do you not?"

Keeping his eyes fixed on mine, Seaver held his hands out and off to one side to receive Bubbles from the bodyguard. Then, turning on his heels, he walked casually down the hall, the two suited hoods trailing closely.

I closed the door softly so that I wouldn't let Seaver have the satisfaction of knowing he'd gotten to me. Fastening the deadbolt, I had to admit he'd achieved his desired effect — I was shaking like a leaf in a windstorm, a mixture of fear, helplessness, and anger swirling in my head.

James Seaver couldn't take all the credit for how I felt. Seaver's behaviors betrayed him as the doppelgänger of my great-uncle Leo, whose ghost had to shoulder some of the blame.

THE WRITINGS OF
AVRIL MARIA SERENE

CHAPTER 26

It was several years ago, and my arm was still in a cast when I last talked to anyone about Leo Hartley Wynn. I'd suffered a spiral fracture, a parting gift from Dennis, my second boyfriend. Dennis was finishing his first month of a three-month stint in the hospital, an old-school goodbye present from a couple of guys on Dad's construction crew. Lindsay had just opened her new salon, and I was among her first clients.

As Lindsay worked her magic, we conversed about jerks in general, migrating to specific examples from our pasts, the topic inspired by the plaster adorning my wrist and forearm.

"In our family, it was Leo the Loser," I related. "As a child, you wouldn't dare call him that to his face. Rumors said that kids he caught mouthing off ended up in a freezer in his basement, and even adults were afraid to tell on him."

"It's easy to scare someone littler than you," Lindsay observed.

"Despite being an embarrassment to the Wynn family name, Leo's had a pretty strong influence over me, even though he's gone now. He became a permanent part of my psyche when he set his sights on me for a week of sheer terror one summer. I've not forgotten one moment, and I doubt I ever will."

"Wait — your mom and dad are awesome. What's Leo's connection to your family?"

"Leo was my great-uncle on Dad's side. He was a throwback stuck in the fifties and sixties. As Dad explained it, in those days, otherwise unworthy individuals could claim manhood by the number of babies they made with submissive wives."

"Neanderthals with clubs, then…," Lindsay mused.

"That was a big part of it. Leo had five children. He ruled with an iron fist, and he believed in two things: keep the wife barefoot and pregnant, and children were to be seen but not heard. He left all the non-disciplinary parenting duties to his second spouse."

"What was she like?" Lindsay asked as she clipped away with her scissors.

"Her name was Donna," I answered. "She was petite, mousy, eight years his junior. She was a full-time housewife who took part-time jobs when they needed money. The two things that stood out about her were that she worked hard and wouldn't talk back."

"Classic enabler, I'm guessing?"

I nodded my head.

"Leo owned a collection agency in a small rural town, Spencer, Iowa," I continued, "during a time when those businesses were largely unregulated.

"I have to give the man his props. It was through him I became intimately familiar with intimidation techniques. Now I can recognize them when I have to interview bullies."

"Are we talking busting kneecaps, that kind of thing?" Lindsay's only familiarity with thuggery would have come from old mobster movies.

"I'm sure he'd go there if it achieved his ends, but I never saw that part. Most of what he did was one step below that — planting threats and scary thoughts in people's heads. I didn't see Leo break any legs, poison any dogs, or deflower anyone's underage children. But I did see him go to extreme lengths to make someone think he might."

"Got it ... what they call 'mental abuse.'"

"Exactly. Leo would do anything to harass debtors. Things like taking Social Security, tax refunds, and other checks from roadside mailboxes. He'd hold onto them for ransom until he got payment on the debt he was collecting."

"Stealing mail — that's a federal crime, right?"

"Maybe, but that was outside the jurisdiction of the local police, hardly something they'd call the FBI about. Things were *so* different back then. The state capital was a hundred and ninety miles away. It was long before the Internet, and the only way to report him was through the mail — which he'd made unreliable. Or several weeks of exchanging long-distance telephone calls, which were expensive in those days."

Lindsay frowned. "Surely *someone* would get mad enough to turn him in, even with the hassle...?"

"I suppose, *if* they could get past the embarrassment of admitting a bill collector was hounding them. That was a bigger deal back then than today – there was a real stigma to being labeled a deadbeat. Either way, the result was always the same. The missing mail would mysteriously reappear back in the mailbox with no proof Leo had held onto it. Then he'd repeat the cycle the next month if he had to.

"That wasn't the only way Leo would abuse the mail. He would send a blank piece of paper by registered mail instead of any formal notice he was required to give. When the debtor claimed they'd never been told something, he'd show the registration receipt and assert the recipient was lying. Once word got out that he'd do these things, people would start paying up out of fear."

"*Jesus* ... and my parents used to call those the 'good old days.'" Lindsay gave me a wry smile.

"Selective memory, I suppose, or they were lucky enough that the bad things didn't happen to them. But Leo *was* worse than most. He had no real limits. The bully regularly boasted about locking a debtor in the poor man's outhouse. He thought the farmer went there to hide from him. So, he wrapped the little building with a chain he found and padlocked it. Then he drove away with the key in his pocket."

"Such a class act," Lindsay murmured.

"In the early days of Leo's business, the weather was good, and the crops came in. To most of the county's residents, Leo was no more than an irritant who preyed on the less-well-to-do farmers. But then the rains didn't come one season. Everyone in the community was affected. The local banks used Leo's services to demand money farmers didn't have. Leo quickly became the most despised man in Clay County as he went door-to-door threatening people to collect debts."

"Who would want to be like that?"

"When things got better later, it didn't cure anyone's hatred for Leo. The towns were small, the memories long. Very few people who've been detested that much ever regain respect. Still, Leo had no shame. He reveled in being hated. He'd go armed everywhere he went. He seemed to enjoy skulking in the dark every evening to accost debtors he accused of trying to avoid payment."

"Sounds like a total asshole," Lindsay said.

"And a hypocrite, to boot. There were lots of whispers. For someone so worried about what people owed, Leo didn't mind taking free handouts for himself. He claimed a hip injury from when he was in his twenties. He said it happened when his first wife died in a Jeep he was driving. Those who knew him best insisted it was no accident."

"So, do you think he murdered her?"

"It wouldn't surprise me. Leo collected seventy-five thousand dollars for her death. That was an astronomical amount of money for a rural area during those days. He used it to buy the debt collection business. Leo would milk any sympathy he could get for his alleged injury all the rest of his life. He even sued for Social Security disability after his collection agency failed."

"So, we, as taxpayers, subsidized this waste of oxygen?" Lindsay shook her head.

"Oh, yeah. Leo lived off Donna's earnings and those benefits for fifty years until he was ninety. That was thirty-five years more than he ever worked at anything even vaguely honest."

Lindsay stopped brushing color into my hair and looked at me with an arched eyebrow.

"It gets worse. Leo was too arrogant and uncaring to realize the effects of what he was doing on his wife and kids. They lived in the same small town where he was regularly collecting debts. The loathing he inspired reflected upon his family. Fellow students beat one or more of his sons nearly daily at the schools they attended. His daughter was the victim of vicious pranks, and townspeople shunned his wife wherever she went."

"How the heck did you get involved with this scumbag? I mean, personally...," Lindsay asked.

"Shortly after I turned eleven, his business partner accused Leo of embezzlement when the business went bankrupt. Leo and his family stayed with Mom and Dad for three months between jail stints. Later that summer, Dad had to go out of town on business for a week. My mother remarked that she wanted to make a romantic getaway of their trip. Somehow, Leo convinced Mom that he and Donna could look after me while they were gone."

"You gotta be kidding me....." Lindsay's eyes were like saucers as her mouth hung open.

"Mom and Dad had barely left the driveway when it started. To Leo, I was nothing more than a spoiled brat and coddled only child. He was constantly reminding me that I was adopted. He said I didn't have the birthright to my new parents' love or my living situation. Between me and our family dogs, I honestly don't know who Leo hated more. As for his kids, they welcomed me. I was a new, easy target for Leo's abuse, meaning they were out of the direct line of fire for the moment."

"*I'll bet!*" Lindsay snorted as she resumed her work.

"Leo habitually practiced a kind of emotional violence some people want to pretend doesn't exist. Or they believe it doesn't have any real meaning or impact. We've all seen examples of it. That mother in the mall's main hall towering over her four-year-old, going off on a raging rant because the tiny tyke lost his stuffed toy again. We might whisper, 'Wow, she must be having a bad day!' but then we avert our eyes and move on. I know I used to. But no one ever does anything about it. When a mother believes screaming at a little kid for any reason is appropriate, especially in a public situation, *she's likely doing it all the time*. We don't want to think about that."

"When you put it that way, yeah, I've been guilty of not saying anything when I should have," Lindsay admitted.

"But nobody did emotional violence quite like Leo. I didn't have to wait long for my rude awakening — literally. Mom and Dad left at four a.m. to catch an early flight. They came into my room for hugs, kisses, and goodbyes after they'd loaded the car and were ready to hit the road. I fell back into a deep sleep.

"The next thing I knew, my entire bed was being shaken from side to side. I was *so* frightened when I woke up. I thought we were having an earthquake. I'd never been in one, but I'd heard how terrible the damage could be. I was deathly frightened that the house would fall in on me."

Lindsay kept working, listening intently.

"*Get your lazy ass out of bed!* Leo was bellowing at me. 'It's eight in the morning. Decent people are up and out making their way in the world.'

"'You think you're so special. The little princess who gets everything she wants. Bitching and bawling anytime you break a fingernail. Well, guess what? It's time to come to Jesus! You have no right thinking you're better than the rest of us.'"

"My God ... you were *eleven?*"

"Oh, he ranted on for half an hour. Your real mother's a crack-house slut with a needle in her arm, too fucking lazy to work. She's lying around some ghetto flophouse right now screwing every Tom, Dick, or Harry who'll toss her a quarter to buy drugs. Making babies for the welfare checks. But she took one look at you and said, 'I'm not spending my money to feed this ugly thing.' And out on the street you go.'

"' She's sitting in some single-wide dump of a trailer right now doing some drunk — laughing her ass off because she stuck honest, hardworking folks with putting a roof over your head. And you're just like her, taking advantage of the kindness of strangers who aren't your blood. You sit around here all day long playing with Barbies you don't deserve. You get to sleep on a soft mattress and down pillows at night. You don't appreciate all the sacrifices people like me have to make so you can live in the lap of luxury.'"

"That's *so* ugly and mean — do you know why he went off on you like that?"

"One year, they were out of Tickle Me Elmo stock everywhere," I explained, "but Dad chased one down and gave it to me for my tenth birthday. His daughter found it and asked Leo why he'd never given her one. Dad told me later that set Leo off.

"Leo got the idea he'd make me work for him. 'You don't do a damn thing to pay your way around here. Well, by God, today you're going to earn your fucking keep. You're going to do *what* I tell you *when* I tell you and *the way* I tell you. And you'll keep your damned mouth shut.

"When I say 'jump,' you jump, and the only thing I want to hear out of that prissy little mouth of yours is, 'How high?' And you will follow that with a 'sir.' Do you understand me? There's only one right answer to that question, missy, and it's 'Yes, sir.' Or so help me, God, I'll tan your hide until next Tuesday. Now get your damned clothes on; there's work that needs to be done."

Lindsay was standing in place, not moving.

"*Wow*. I thought I'd known some abusers, but... just wow...."

"His Iowa business was in receivership, and California wouldn't license him. However, Leo picked up spending money by collecting debts on commission for companies in San Diego. All during that week, Leo made me knock on doors. The residents would open up for me, so that's how he'd gain entry to debtors' homes. Something I'm sure he used *his* children to do. After he'd reduced some debtor's wife to tears with his threats, he'd turn to me and leer, 'See what happens when they don't pay up.' He'd say it like an oracle come down from a mountain to teach me one of life's great lessons."

"Did he ever try to hurt you physically?" Lindsay asked.

"Just the one time. When Leo came back from a collection attempt empty-handed, I'd be quaking in fear. I'd never been cursed at before or had an adult scream at me six inches away from my nose. And I'd never done anything that resulted in a spanking, much less with a leather belt. But I was so nervous around him that I knocked over the pancake syrup one morning. In his eyes, I deserved corporal punishment for that.

"He dealt out pain the way a psychopath would 'train' a dog. He'd *slow*-ly remove his leather belt and fold it in half. He'd grab the buckle in one fist and the fold in the other. Then he'd jerk his fists apart so the belt would snap, like the cracking of a whip. You don't forget *that* sound.

"Worse than the spanking was how he and Donna tried to gaslight me the day before Mom and Dad came home. They half convinced me that

I deserved what happened. Leo said telling on him would only worsen things for me because my parents would side with the adults.

"After Mom and Dad returned from their vacation, Mom saw my backside, and neither Leo nor Donna was ever seen in our house again. But Leo didn't leave empty-handed.

"He took my piggy bank. It had the money I'd saved from my allowance and walking the neighbors' dogs to buy a new bike."

* * *

All that had come back to me in the aftermath of my encounter with Seaver, and I had no doubt why he'd come to my door himself. People who've never experienced that kind of bully might expect the Leos and Seavers of the world to delegate their dirty work to hired thugs. But abusers like that don't trust anyone. Immersed in their narcissism, they genuinely believe they are the only ones who can do things "right." They must be directly involved in anything important that needs doing. Seaver's nature left him no choice but to confront me personally — just as Leo collected his largest accounts himself.

So, after Seaver left, I leaned back against the door and breathed in as deeply as possible, exhaling slowly to regain control of my nervous system. It would take a dozen repetitions of the same exercise, the time spent cleaning up the coffee spilled earlier, and some chamomile tea — oh, and k. d. lang's *Juno Awards* rendition of Leonard Cohen's "Hallelujah" — to reduce my heart rate to its regular rhythm over the next twenty minutes.

James Seaver was a scary guy, no question. The good news was, he'd poorly timed his implied threats and tipped his hand. In our brief, heated conversation, Seaver had not mentioned Brian or the letters. He'd want to discuss them if he knew of their existence.

Still, the disgraced doctor's visit had put the exclamation point on the need to button up my journalistic examination of these things. I'd already gathered the critical information I needed. Marci would get the men in blue on the same page once she had the letters and my edited notes. I could write the rest of my story as the police department's work on the murder cases progressed. The events no longer needed me to push them along, and this seemed as good a place as any to stop while I was still ahead.

It was time to put things to bed and practice taking my bows.

THE WRITINGS OF
AVRIL MARIA SERENE

CHAPTER 27

I pulled into the lot at the Greenfinch Restaurant and Bar the next afternoon and parked two rows away from the entrance. As I walked to the eatery's front door, the green Mustang that had followed me gunned its engine. It brushed my coat as it passed me at too high a speed for a parking lot. Racing, I supposed, to grab one of the few remaining slots. I thought I'd seen the nose of a similar Mustang behind me a few days ago, but I wasn't sure. Still, I made a note to keep an eye out for any other green Mustangs that popped up. Two sightings might be a coincidence, but given my recent experience with Seaver and his bodyguards, three would be a problem.

I arrived a few minutes early and got us a four-top so Marci and I would have room to work. I was on pins and needles waiting to see her, but Marci wasn't far behind. To my surprise, she showed up in a cast and on crutches.

"Oh, Marci, what happened to you?" I asked, genuinely concerned.

"I met Liz Frank out on the dance floor," Marci replied, no expression on her face.

"What did she do, shoot your foot?" I still wasn't comprehending.

"I'm just messing with you. Lisfranc is a kind of bone fracture in the foot. That's where a bone, or maybe several, in the middle of your foot, the ones above your arch, get broken."

Seeing my blank face, she explained. "I'd never heard of one either, but I have to say, you go down like a falling rock when it happens. Want to take somebody out painfully and quickly without killing them? That's how you'd do it."

"This happened at work, an in-the-line-of-duty thing?" I was scrambling to understand.

"I only wish. Danny and I like country-western dancing at a nightspot where many AA members go. You can order club sodas all night, and they won't blink an eye. But it *is* a public bar, so you get people drinking. We were on the dance floor to a slow set, and some guy was pawing a girl beside us. Finally, she'd had enough and belted him. He came crashing into us — he must have weighed two-fifty or better — and the heel of one of his cowboy boots nailed me right on top of my foot. Danny caught me so my head didn't bounce off the floor. But by then, the damage to my hoof had been done."

I reached out and touched her arm. "Do they have you on sick leave?"

"No, I'm milking all the sympathy I can get and working it out. I figure I'll have some great leverage in the future if I need some paid time away. 'Hey, Captain, remember when…?'"

Marci chuckled – she seemed in good spirits for the pain she must be experiencing.

"Still, it looks and sounds painful — I wouldn't want it to happen to me." Suddenly, I felt an empathy twinge in my right foot.

"Other than childbirth, that was as much pain as I've ever felt in one go," Marci said ruefully. "But as long as I don't put any weight on it and take my meds, it's okay during the day. At night, it throbs, but I've gotten used to it enough that I can get some sleep now."

Even though we were a party of just two and the place was getting crowded, the hostess moved us to a bigger corner booth. That kindness let Marci rest her cast on the cushioned seat. Marci and I agreed we'd order before I got into why I'd asked her to come. "That's enough about me,"

Marci said with a grin once our server had taken our drink and food orders. "Put up or shut up. What in the world have you gotten us into that has you so excited?"

"Excited? How could you tell?"

"You used an exclamation point in your last text, and you *never* do that. Plus, I have a professional obligation to pay attention when someone mentions multiple homicides in the same sentence."

"Remember the last time we had lunch together? I asked you for help with two different situations and then texted you later about a third. There was the Brian Pierce beating death downtown and the presumed killing of Dr. James Seaver's wife, where no corpse has yet turned up. And we've talked a couple of times about Coach Cantor's execution-style murder in his living room."

"Of course. We had very little on either of the first two, but I got you what I could."

"And just what I needed, as usual." I leaned toward her across the table. "I couldn't tell you then, Marci, because I had no way to fact-check anything myself and didn't want to send anyone off on a wild goose chase. But I have reason to believe the three cases might connect. Fire up your laptop, and you can follow along with the story."

I handed Marci the flash drive I'd made containing the black-light images of Brian's letters from my cell phone.

"Here, the drive is yours to keep, but I need your promise I'll get the exclusive when it comes out."

"You know I don't have the authority, but if it is what you think it is, I can pass the request up the line."

"Fair enough." I began telling Marci the detailed history of the envelopes tumbling along in the turf at the Memorial Gardens and how my father had taken it upon himself to find the author. As I told the tale, I placed the expanding file folder with the original letters on the table. "These are the letters and envelopes as I got them."

I summarized Brian's story of catching three people moving a dead body while he was robbing a house. Then I laid out Brian's identification of the participants as 'Doc,' a woman he thought was Doc's girlfriend, and another guy he knew as 'Rickie.' I described Brian's tagging of the wall and carpet in the home. "James Seaver's complaint to your detectives about the vandalism indirectly confirmed the graffiti. The circumstances explain why Seaver can't let the police in to investigate. He has no idea where the tagger might have been in his house or what they may have touched to leave prints or DNA. As it happens, he's involved in the deaths of two people he suspected of the graffiti at different times."

Marci had gone quiet as she read along. "Okay, that tracks for me. Is moving the body the first mention of anyone committing new crimes in these letters? That is, any that would be unknown to the department?"

"Everything to that point had been about Brian's history," I answered, "or spoke to the time he spent with his deceased sister. The most relevant letter following is BriansLetter39.jpg. In it, he mentions his suspicions about the murder of James Seaver's neighbor, who we know is, or was, Coach.

"Oh, and just so you know, these didn't come to me in sequential order — I just retrieved this one yesterday — or else I would have told you about the tie to Coach sooner."

She nodded solemnly, her features conveying understanding.

"Brian goes on about strange faces in his neighborhood throwing their weight around, trying to find out who witnessed the removal of the woman's body. He feels trapped, and he's worried these thugs will find out it's him."

"Yeah, we know Johnny Rocco's and the crew that works out of there. I'll give your Brian some credit; he's got that neighborhood down cold."

"The last letter describes how he plans to address the situation head-on, laying out his plan to go after Rickie. He wants to stage a faked extortion attempt by Rickie against the doctor. Whatever Brian did to follow up on that thought probably got him killed. The filename is BriansLetter40.jpg."

"Got it." Marci's eyes zig-zagged side-to-side as she read along.

"I also included a copy of my field notes for the interview with Theresa Seaver's ex, Darrell Woodson. He had his private detective dig into James Seaver and Richard Ainsworth. I believe Ainsworth is the 'Rickie' in Brian's letters. Woodson lays out the motive for killing Theresa pretty well. If things went as I imagined when Brian entered Ainsworth's home that night, Ainsworth is Brian's killer. His prints and DNA should match one of the two sets your forensics team pulled off Brian's body in that alley."

"Okay… What are these two Post-it notes about?"

"Those Cassidy and I found in Coach's wastebaskets. They tie Coach's homicide to David Barnwell — Cassidy has the originals sealed in baggies. That's the name you discovered Ainsworth used as an alias in one of his corrupt businesses. When you decode them, the notes say that on Thursday at seven p.m., a man calling himself David Barnwell met with Coach in response to a Craigslist ad. Coach posted it for a property he was selling on Carmel Mountain. Brian's letter suggests a motive for Seaver killing Coach. Seaver may have assumed Coach graffitied the doctor's living room with the accusation that Seaver killed his wife. We know Ainsworth does Seaver's dirty work, and Ainsworth fits the description given by the Neighborhood Watch lady."

Our server appeared beside our table, patiently waiting for a pause in our conversation. The young woman announced she'd be going on break and another server would take care of us, then asked if we wanted anything. As Marci declined for both of us, I realized Marci wasn't her usual exuberant self. What she'd had to say in response to these revelations was brief, even terse.

It must be the pain medications she's taking, I thought.

THE WRITINGS OF
AVRIL MARIA SERENE

CHAPTER 28

Marci remained quiet as our server left us. She continued scrolling silently through the images displayed on the laptop screen as she read. Occasionally, she'd return to a previous photo to re-read a section. Finally, Marci sat back in the booth, repositioning her cast on the seat and not saying a word for several moments. Her eyes were closed, her hands pressed together almost as if in prayer, her middle fingers touching the underside of the tip of her nose, thumbs under her chin. Instead of showing surprise and excitement, as I'd expected, her countenance had become stern. With her brows knitted together, she'd pursed her lips in concern.

She opened her eyes and sat forward, looking at me like I was one of her older children who'd done something seriously wrong. Her expression showed apparent frustration mixed with genuine care. Her tone was one of compassionate authority.

"Debra Ann, you know I love you, and our friendship means a lot to me. What I have to say isn't about that; it's about the work.

"I think I understand what you meant to accomplish here. I can see how you might perceive what you've done as a good thing. In some ways, it is. We didn't have the connection between the Cantor homicide and Ainsworth until you gave it to us, and I appreciate that.

"Still, you're a journalist. People handle these things differently in your world than in mine. You've been very good at what you do for a long time, and you should know where the boundaries are."

"I don't understand; I thought you'd be thrilled...," I began.

"Debra Ann, please, hear me out. We both know you've had issues coloring between the lines at different times. There are some rules you've broken here that you should have understood and followed. I get your father's situation. He didn't know about any criminal behavior described in those letters until he read the last one he would ever see. By that time, his illness trumped other considerations. Had he survived with his mind clear and able to process what that last letter told him, I know he would have engaged law enforcement sooner rather than later."

Marci's words completely blindsided me. *Why was she attacking me and my work?* And why was she insinuating that my father had done anything other than everything he could?

Yes, Marci was my friend; she had every right to take issue with something she thought *I'd* done. After all, I was sitting right here with the opportunity to defend myself. But suggesting Dad could have done more when she didn't have the complete story was out of bounds.

"Dad *did* engage law enforcement, Marci." I was indignant. "He called twice from what would end up being his deathbed, trying to get someone on the force to take these letters seriously. The department wouldn't even show him the decency to take his statement, much less the letters, for either report." The old anger was rising within me; I needed to keep it at bay. I'd lost too many relationships and didn't want to lose this one.

Marci pursed her lips again. "I'm sorry, but I see evidence critical to three murder investigations. If it had been presented to me a few months ago when it could have done some real good...," Marci began her apology, but as an introduction to further complaints. Seeing the expression on my face, she realized that wasn't the way to go and tried to correct course.

"Okay, look, I forgot your father called it in. I should've remembered he'd have acted immediately. The department didn't follow…."

But I wasn't interested in hearing excuses.

"And why do you think that was?" I interrupted. "That last letter Dad read and tried to tell them about says nothing specific about what Brian saw. The letter only says that he witnessed, primarily just heard, three people he thinks were hiding a body in the darkness. There's a 'when,' but no 'where.' There's no definitive ID of anything or anyone.

"Heaven *forbid* that a citizen should call the San Diego Police Department about a *potential* homicide. Especially one that might mean more work for an investigator." My voice was icy with sarcasm.

"And how *dare* that citizen notify the police of such a murder when it's not been all wrapped up for them with a pretty red bow." That part came out more snarkily than I'd intended. Still peeved at how the department had handled Dad's pleas for help, I wasn't in the mood to let anyone off the hook.

"Spoken like a true investigative reporter," Marci replied evenly, ignoring my jab at the department and its transgressions. "But that wasn't your primary role once you knew of evidence strongly suggesting moving a body and, by extension, murder. It would have been better for us to have examined those letters four months ago — their writing and everything else. Our detectives would have looked at any trace evidence of DNA or prints. They could have investigated where the writer purchased the paper and the envelope. They should have tested the ink's chemical makeup and the pen's manufacture and sale, all those things."

My eyes went wide. "That could only have happened *if* you'd sent an officer in response to Dad's requests. Even with that information, you don't know that you could have identified Brian Pierce or anything about him…," I objected. I could see where she was coming from. Still, she was basing her assumptions on perfect-world conjecture, not the realities of Dad's and my situation in real time.

"That may or may not be true, but certainly, we could have done what you did after you got the letters from your father. He may have been in no condition to argue with the desk sergeant about sending an officer, but when have *you* ever taken 'no' for an answer? Once you had them, you could have pushed forward and gotten the department to at least look at them. Months later, sure, but still…"

"Come on, let's say they got the letters," I interrupted again. "It's still the same department with the same attitudes. Rather than blow Dad or me off to our faces, they patronize us, accept the letters, and sit on them. So, how does that help anyone?"

"I hear you, and you know I can't speak honestly about that. But what if you were wrong? Or, more likely, say they *did* try to ignore them, but you and your vibrant personality kept their feet to the fire using the power of the press. Our people could have collected the newer letters and walked through the Memorial Gardens for gravestones that fit what we learned from the contents. And with our more significant resources and workforce, more quickly than you could. You let your relationship with your father and what you saw as a promise to him blur the lines. It was natural for you to inject your reporter's agenda into handling these letters and what they led you to believe, but…."

"Marci," I protested, "Dad asked me to put my training and skills to the task only *after* he gave your people a chance to do it *their* way…."

"But you had no right to do that where other people's lives and deaths were paramount," Marci fired back. "In the real world that the rest of us live in, the story is *not* the priority — the brutal termination of human lives is. Debra Ann, these are *murder* cases. It's not up to you to ask for exclusivity as barter for evidence. Evidence you should have turned over the minute it fell into your hands. That makes you look, at best, terribly self-interested in the eyes of law enforcement, not to mention the victims' families. At worst, it's obstruction of justice. That's *not* how these things are supposed to work."

I fell silent, frustrated that my friend wasn't hearing me. My choices had been turning the letters over to an unreceptive department, in which case — minus the evidence — I'd be powerless to investigate. Or, hang onto them until I made enough connections that the department couldn't ignore them — the only right choice left to me.

"Look, I know you didn't mean any harm," Marci began again, more reasonably. "But now there is no chain of custody for the letters, which means they won't stand up to any competent defense attorney's cross-examination. They've been through several hands and the elements. That a journalist with an agenda to publish had them in her unsupervised possession for weeks…"

My face reddened as I became overtly defensive. I had been inordinately careful with the letters, handling them with gloves only long enough to make copies under the black light before sealing them in individual freezer bags. I told Marci as much.

"You're missing the point here, Debra Ann. The letters aren't valuable as evidence without a known and managed provenance. As you said, they don't contain definitive identifications of people or places — just generic descriptions and first names or nicknames. However, with a formal chain of custody, those letters would have been sufficient probable cause to counter Seaver's attorneys. Think about this: Once we'd gained access to Seaver's home again, we'd have found any DNA or prints Brian left there and made the link to his beaten body. Hearing that we could have addressed the probable cause issue weeks ago isn't going to thrill anyone in the department."

"So sorry the department's happiness wasn't the first thought on my mind," I retorted.

"Maybe it *should* have been." Marci was calm. "Your piece on the department's morale, management, and training issues didn't win you any friends among the brass."

How perfectly odd, I thought, realizing that today, Marci was playing the role of the adult in the room, a reversal of how we'd started our friendship. Back then, I was the grownup, writing the article she'd just referenced as she flailed, trying to defend a department she'd known was indefensible in many ways.

"They put me in the position of having to do a job they refused." There was more than a trace of ridicule in my voice. "Are you saying *that's* the excuse they would use to come after me?"

Marci just looked at me, then seemed to give in. "Okay. You've given us what we need to take a deeper look at Richard Ainsworth as this 'Rickie.' That gets us around any cease-and-desist restrictions that concern our lawyers. Let's say we run him to ground quickly, and his prints and DNA match. We'll have positive progress to report on two homicides and a motive for a third. Let's leave it at that. We'll have to hope the department will forget about any issues around collecting these letters."

To maintain our relationship, I matched Marci's acquiescence by keeping my further thoughts to myself. But she was mistaken. She'd made it sound like law enforcement was entitled to what came to me as a credentialed journalist. That couldn't be further from the truth. Several judges have explained to the department and the DA that the California journalist shield law grants prosecutors zero access to journalists' notes, sources, or research. I didn't *have* to do anything here to help the department. But believing that I'd uncovered crucial evidence in several ongoing criminal cases, I'd shared it voluntarily through my most reliable contact in SDPD — *after* I'd done my journalistic best to verify it. I did my job and much more.

My conscience was clean, and my disappointment in my reception warranted. But winning the argument wasn't worth losing a friend.

Chapter 29

Our new server had been hanging back, waiting for a break in a conversation that she could see had become intense. She asked again if we needed anything, and after we both passed, she refilled our water, moving on to other customers.

Having silently agreed to disagree, Marci and I regrouped. I still thought giving her what I knew about the crimes was the shortest distance between them and justice. And she knew she couldn't just walk away — no pun intended.

Marci rearranged her bum leg on the cushion, her facial expression softening. "Our friendship is important to me, Debra Ann, and I'm willing to go out on a limb here because of it."

Her echoing of my unspoken feelings struck a chord, and much of my tension dissipated.

"But I need you to understand this is my *job* at stake," Marci continued. "If my superiors perceive anything I say or do as deliberately dishonest, that's it. End of my career. And if they wanted to push it, they could charge *me* with impeding an investigation."

Again, I flushed, conflicted. While I felt bad about my friend being in a difficult situation, I wasn't the one who put her there – that fell on members of her department not doing their jobs. I was still a little upset she didn't see it the same way.

Marci paused for a moment. "Here's my proposal: When I present these letters to my bosses, I'll tell them that your freelancing opportunities kept you busy. You didn't get to read through what you'd gathered until just recently. As soon as you realized what you had, you contacted me. You spent the time between texting me and this lunch researching Ainsworth and Seaver. Are you comfortable with that?"

I understood that stretching the truth could put her employment at risk. It meant a lot that she would do that for me, even as I sought to satisfy the needs of my own profession.

"Thanks, Marci. I appreciate it. That should work for everyone." Going out of my way to help smooth things between us, I offered her a get-out-of-jail-free card. "And if anyone has a problem with that version, I'll 'fess up and say you were repeating to them what I told you."

That idea got a nod and a small smile from her. "Cross your fingers that Ainsworth confesses to the Cantor and Pierce killings and then flips on the former doctor and his girlfriend. That would render all this moot, anyway. The detectives still haven't located Ainsworth for questioning about the Cantor homicide, but we'll get him.

"I'm glad you came to me before you took it any further, Debra Ann. Seaver, Ainsworth, and their crew are real rat bastards, worst of the worst. They wouldn't hesitate to kill someone else with the stakes in the millions of dollars. For your safety, please — stay away from this until we get these people put away. Let us do our thing until there's something solid you can print. I promise I'll keep you posted on whatever transpires from this point."

"I understand. I'll be a good girl — that'll be *my* promise."

Something told me not to share my little encounter with Seaver and his henchmen just now. My credibility was already on the line, and Marci might not find my yanking Seaver's chain a smart move. I'd feel better if she and I parted on good terms.

Once outside the restaurant, I walked Marci to her unmarked, and we hugged around her crutches as best we could. She agreed to contact me in the next few days to give me a progress report.

When I got to my car, I discovered a black Transit delivery vehicle had parked too close to my driver's side door. Squishing myself into my seat took more than a few unladylike words, and I made no effort to keep my keys from scratching the van's paint. Still, after rearranging my clothes and pulling out of the lot, one thought made me smile broadly. The day was coming soon when the entire world would see that sneer wiped off James Seaver's face.

The imagery alone was worth getting chewed out a little over lunch. I could hardly wait for events to unfold over the next few days.

THE WRITINGS OF
AVRIL MARIA SERENE

CHAPTER 30

It was time to write the first article based on the most recent events of Brian Pierce's life. I'd envisioned the story as having multiple parts, with the first setting the stage for those that followed. I'd thought about what I would write for so long that the piece was almost creating itself. After several hours of writing, I felt I had a good start; I wanted to take a break and escape the apartment for a while.

Emma Woodson and I had exchanged numbers when we first met; since then, we'd talked several times. Our friendship blossomed quickly; in her, I found a confidante with whom I could share things without having an agenda. She was an excellent cook, always looking for an excuse to try a new recipe, so it didn't surprise me when she invited me back for lunch.

Heading to my car in the apartment's lot, I couldn't help but notice the dark blue Dodge. It was in the same spot behind my Toyota that it had been the night I'd gone to The Casbah. Though it was late in the morning, its lights were on. I saw the auto's designers had trimmed the parking light and turn signal modules on each front fender with thin white LEDs. I couldn't see the face of the shadowed figure in the driver's seat or recognize the sedan as belonging to any tenants I knew. But then again, I couldn't claim to know them all or what cars they drove.

Still... *Why would this vehicle be following me? Is it related to that Mustang?*

And even if my suspicions were well-founded, what could I do? Parking an unstickered car in a lot marked "Tenants only" might be frowned upon, but it wasn't a felony. No one has accosted anyone. I could approach the Dodge and ask what they were doing, but for what reason? That they were *looking at me*? For being caught too often in the same spot? I would look foolish, even paranoid, if they were here legitimately. I didn't want to be setting myself up as the girl who cried "wolf." If they *had* harmful intentions, bad guys would lie about them anyway. Worse, they could create serious problems for me and others if armed and aggressive.

There was but one practical step I could take. Walking to a spot as visible as possible from their windshield, I pulled out my cell phone. Lowering myself, I took photos of the car's license plate and grillwork. Then I snapped another that showed a view of its side. Finally, I leaned over the hood and captured an image of the driver through the windshield, though he covered his face with his forearms before I could get a good shot. I stood there with my arms crossed, camera app poised at the ready, staring at the driver for several moments until he finally put the car in reverse and backed out of the slot.

I'd e-mail the photos to building management, complaining the vehicle had no parking permit and that I suspected it was stalking someone. But there'd be no one to act on my complaint other than the contracted security company guards who rolled through the lot once an hour.

Marci had been right; I couldn't take my safety for granted anymore. There was, however, little I could do unless the situation worsened.

Once I arrived at Emma's lovely home, we chitchatted about nothing world-shaking. The conversation turned to a personal question I'd wanted to ask the first time we met.

"You and Darrell go together so well; you genuinely care about each other. How did you meet?"

Emma smiled, tilting her head as she looked off into space.

"I had an appointment with a client at the Pendry Hotel. I arrived early and was going through my presentation materials in the lobby — I'm an interior designer."

And a good one, I thought, letting my eyes wander through the house.

"I put one of my folders on the arm of a sofa in the waiting area, and once the client arrived, I missed it as I gathered my things to move. When we got to the conference room, Darrell came up behind me and said, 'Ma'am, I think you left this in the lobby.' He was very polite, nothing forward. But of course, you couldn't miss his sexy Australian accent. And I *was* grateful to have the folder back."

"How did you find out he was interested in more than just returning the folder?"

"When I opened it during my presentation, inside was his business card with a note, 'Would you care to share lunch?' Very smooth — I appreciated that he'd asked me in a way that didn't put me on the spot for an immediate answer. I texted him, and we went to lunch the next day.

"Four hours, and I didn't want it to end, even then."

I was happy for her and to hear her tell the tale. A story like that brightens your day because it reminds you that good things can happen unexpectedly with one's own prospects.

"The two of you seem to have it all, and from what I know so far, you had to go through rough patches to get here. I can only imagine what it must have been like in a new marriage, with the ex-wife constantly injecting herself into the mix."

"I think we grew closer because of it. Darrell was always very open whenever Theresa would pull some stunt; he included me in all the conversations he could. He never tried to hide or 'protect' me from anything," Emma said, making air quotes. "Darrell could have innocently tried to keep her out of our lives with secrecy, and I'd have understood why a new husband might. But he never went that route, and I'm so glad he didn't.

"Speaking of Theresa and all that, you said in our last phone conversation you're excited about getting the story down on paper. How's that going?"

I shared with Emma the gist of my last meeting with Marci and how badly I'd misread the room.

"It took me a few days to settle down from that misstep. But now, I view it as a learning opportunity. Murder investigations could become very difficult if reporters regularly glommed onto evidence for research."

"You're right; that doesn't sound kosher." Emma furrowed her brow. "*You're* trying to do the right thing, but what if somebody dishonest did that to extort someone or profit from the information they dug up?"

"Exactly. I should have turned the letters over immediately and followed up with law enforcement every chance I had to ensure they were doing the work. If the police saw me as helpful and I'd asked politely, they'd have given me story exclusivity. But to keep the two issues separate, I should've made my request *after* turning over the evidence in the three homicide investigations. I could have written the investigations' progress as a real-time series — maybe scored a ride-along for the crucial interviews."

"Seeing things after the dust has settled is much easier."

"Hindsight is *such* a wonderful thing," I agreed with a wry smile. "But to be fair to myself, I'd have needed far more faith in the San Diego Police Department than I have. Not to mention the psychic vision needed to see where these cases might have been going. Those things together set the bar too high for me to get over. I can't unlearn what I know about the department's dirty laundry. And I'm certainly no Nostradamus."

"Some of what you've turned up in these cases is too weird, frankly, for anyone to have seen it coming." Emma's tone was sympathetic.

"Oh, Emma, before I forget, I turned over what I gathered on Seaver and Ainsworth, including some of what Darrell told me, to the detectives. I never reveal my sources, but they'll make the connection because of Theresa and the litigation with James Seaver. The police will want to talk to Darrell again if they haven't already."

Emma nodded. "I'll make sure he knows. You worked things out with Marci, and it doesn't seem like any harm came from your talk. Are you happy with how the story's turning out?"

"Truthfully, I am. Of course, it's too soon to pat myself on the back — there's lots more work to do, depending on what SDPD finds out. You'll be the first to hear how it all ends."

While investigators may develop a higher tolerance over time, the details of murders and other crimes aren't appetizing to anyone. We steered our lunch conversation to lighter things that Emma and I shared from our life experiences. My time with her made for a wonderful reprieve from my work. I left her home feeling rejuvenated, eager to write more.

The words nearly flew from my fingertips as I sat before my laptop screen, pushing the story along as far as possible with what I knew. It needed only the ending, and then I could finish and publish the first tranche.

As I awaited Marci's next call, I busied myself with a ghostwriting gig from a freelancing website. At night, I'd scan the Internet for events that might make for good stories. I also set up a routine for calling friends, acquaintances, and old work partners. I wanted to catch up on anything they might have experienced or heard that would point me toward my next big article.

As promised, Marci called four days after our lunch meeting. "Hi, Debra Ann, I'm glad I caught you — I wanted to let you know where we're at with the Theresa Seaver missing-person case."

"Good morning, Marci; thanks for calling. I've been curious to hear what's going on. Nothing's shown up on local news yet."

"Sorry to be the bearer of bad tidings, but there's nothing there for them to televise. We interviewed Richard Ainsworth, and we can't make him as Brian's killer. He has a solid alibi. His DNA and prints were already in the system and didn't match. To be sure, we asked him for new samples, and he complied. We checked out every piece of real estate we could link to him, and nothing fits the descriptions in Brian Pierce's letters."

"*Dammit.* I was sure it had to be Ainsworth," I groused, dismayed by the outcome. Worse, I knew I'd let confirmation bias get in my way – I *so* wanted it to be him.

"Absent that connection, we've got nothing to tie him to anything that happened in the Seaver household. I wish I could say it was a dead end and leave it at that. However, during the interview, we had to make him aware that we had a witness and circumstantial evidence to justify our interest in him. We did not provide any details or names, of course. But he — and we assume, by extension, Seaver — is now aware that someone out there sees a link between the Brian Pierce killing and the missing wife. Worse, we went at Ainsworth too hard on the Cantor killing; he lawyered up. We've got him on a forty-eight-hour hold, but we'll have to release him unless something pops by tonight. Seaver will know we've put it together but can't charge him yet."

"Which means he's going to feel like he can go after people…." I suddenly felt sick to my stomach.

Marci didn't acknowledge my comment or deviate from what I knew to be her official tone of voice. "Unfortunately, we've now made an explicit accusation as to the Pierce homicide that's provably false, as far as Ainsworth is concerned. That gave Seaver and Ainsworth another opening to paint themselves as victims of a smear campaign. We got a second round of cease-and-desist letters from Seaver's attorneys before they'll sue. They're alleging harassment and seeking an injunction.

"Now I'm in a position where I have no choice but to tell you to stay away from this thing, Debra Ann. That's not a request; it's an order and not coming from me. It's directly from the captain of the homicide unit. I'm conveying this to you simply as a courtesy. As a friend, I have to tell you, they mean it. They've clarified they won't hesitate to charge you with obstruction of justice if you don't back off. I'm sorry, dear. This case means so much to you, I know, because of your father, but you must let it go."

"I understand, Marci," I said, my tone contrite. "Thank you for letting me know. I hope you realize I was trying to help, and I am truly sorry things didn't work out. I'll pray you nail those sons-of-bitches. Until you do, I hope we'll still be able to do lunch now and then."

She agreed, and with that, I tapped the touchscreen to close the connection and then held down the button on the side to turn the cell phone off. I needed some uninterrupted time to myself.

For the next twenty minutes, I sat on the edge of my couch, head in my hands, pondering my disappointment and thinking through everything that had happened. Then I panicked. Suddenly, James Seaver's implied threats from the hallway of my apartment building were far more frightening. Not having an immediate counter from law enforcement had left me exposed. There were at least two murderous thugs I knew of and one girlfriend I didn't, likely just waiting for the first opportunity to come after me.

I'd been naïve, coming to a game where homicides were the trump cards, holding only Brian's letters and a few clues in my hand. Impressed with what they'd dealt me, I didn't think I needed anything up my sleeve. Of all people, I should've known better — when the stakes are that serious, cheaters don't play fair. I write about the bad outcomes every day.

It shouldn't have surprised me that they weren't *about* to fold. They'd stay at the table until they flipped that final card — even then, the game wouldn't be over until the last person standing had left the room alive. As a teenager, I'd often spent weekday afternoons at Dad's construction trailer once my classes were over. With all the games I'd watched my father's crew play as they waited for the rain to clear, I'd witnessed it too often — when you're all in, what choice do you have but to see it through? But no matter, *I* certainly was done — I'd shown my hand by turning those letters over to the police and had no cards left.

The only smart thing to do now was to get out of the game, lay as low as possible, and wait for these killers to forget me. Or at least hope they'd embroil themselves in enough other problems that I was no longer their priority. As for the story, I'd take Paul McCartney's musical advice and let it be — at least for now.

And maybe I should practice coloring inside the lines for my next great adventure, something I'd do well to consider, though admittedly, it would be a stretch.

But where'd I ever get the idea *I'd* be making any of these decisions?

THE WRITINGS OF
AVRIL MARIA SERENE

CHAPTER 31

T he human mind is a fantastic thing. One of its underrated talents is the ability to record subtle oddities subliminally and nag its host with discomfort as the collection grows.

A few days had passed after the enormous letdown that Richard Ainsworth wasn't Brian Pierce's killer. I'd been aware that someone was watching me. Still, I'd ignored the significance, pushing it off to circumstances I couldn't control. I didn't need to add to all the negative emotions I'd recently felt around the Pierce and Seaver cases. And I was no longer actively investigating the discredited doctor or his cronies. Any side effects from poking my nose where someone thought it didn't belong should have gone away.

Today, while walking to my car in my building's parking lot, I spotted a dark green Mustang several cars away from mine. *I've seen that car before, too often for it to be a coincidence.* This time, the sense of déjà vu wasn't going away.

I knew what to do to get rid of it.

Backing out of my assigned space, I stayed in reverse, turning to my right with my foot on the gas until I was perpendicular to the rear of the Mustang.

Once I had a good view through my passenger-side window, I took a photo of the plate with my cell phone.

As I did, I saw the vehicle's brake lights brighten, forewarning me that the driver was about to do something.

When I ran from my Toyota toward the Mustang's door, it suddenly pulled forward with a roar, a puff of blue smoke, and a chirp from its rear tires.

The front tires' sidewalls squealed as the car lurched from side to side, snaking out of the lot.

I'd first seen that car behind me returning from Darrell Woodson's place. It wasn't a random predator stalking me; this had something to do with Seaver or his cohorts. I wasn't pleased about being followed, but something I'd done had hit a nerve — to a journalist, that's like X marking the spot on a treasure map as the place to dig deeper.

A few hours later, I had the same realization about a navy blue Dodge Charger idling without a placard in a handicapped spot at Von's supermarket. It looked identical to the one parked behind my car in my apartment's lot the day I visited Emma. I checked the plates against the photo I'd taken then, and they matched. The driver inside quickly averted his gaze when I looked directly at him.

And now, I noticed the too-familiar onyx Transit van with blacked-out side windows sitting on the curb of an access road inside the Memorial Gardens' gates. I'd had to squeeze past it to get into my car at the Greenfinch — the scratches I'd left were unmistakable. The strong sense that I'd seen it other times lingered. Still, I'd lost the memory among all the similar Amazon vehicles I'd seen dropping off packages. And yet again, an immediate reaction from the driver once I focused my eyes intently upon him — the van started up and moved off slowly.

Walking toward the family plot for my weekly visit with Mom, Dad, and Eddie, I felt genuinely anxious and threatened. If Seaver was having me followed, *why*? Only Dad and I, and now the police through Marci, knew of

Seaver's link to Brian's letters or their existence. I didn't have any other information concerning Seaver that I hadn't already given authorities.

But a half-hour of sharing with my family re-centered my worldview. It helped me see that someone following me was more upsetting than harmful so long as I knew of their presence. I *would* need to be more careful about who I might lead my pursuers to and any danger to them that could result.

While at the cemetery, I wanted to pay my respects to Brian and his family and apologize for not having found his killer. While gathering my thoughts on the stroll over to Brian's family plot, without warning, everything coalesced in my head.

I'd been confident that only the police knew of my connection to Brian's letters and wouldn't reveal how they'd obtained them to other parties. But a sudden, sickening feeling came over me — as though someone had punched me below the beltline. Fear coursed through every fiber of my being. *Dammit*, there *was* one way someone could tie me to Brian Pierce's murder as an investigator. *Please, please, let me be wrong.*

I abruptly changed course, making a beeline for the caretaker's office. As I entered, I saw Gary Gilbert bent over, sweeping a small pile of dirt into a dustpan at the side of the counter. He smiled when he looked up at me.

"Hi, Debra Ann; it's good to see you." Then, Gary's tone changed to one of concern. "Are you okay? You look like you've seen a ghost…." Given where we were, I would have smiled at the irony in ordinary circumstances. But this was not a normal situation.

"Hi, Gary. Yes, I've had a rough couple of weeks, but I'm alright, thanks. I stopped by our plot to see my family. While I was here, I wanted to ask if you've had any other visitors asking about Brian Pierce or his family. Since you and I last spoke, that is."

"Now that you mention it, yes, I have." His expression was questioning, almost as if asking whether he'd done something wrong.

"They didn't say I couldn't tell you…. Two guys from the FBI. They looked more like dock workers or bouncers but said they were undercover.

"They asked if Mr. Pierce had visitors lately — maybe someone who wasn't a relative — and if anything unusual had happened lately at his resting place. I told them about your father and my greenskeeper finding all those blank letters, but that your dad had passed away and we'd interred him here. They wanted to know where his gravesite was and if anyone else had seen those letters.

"I told them you had them, that you were a reporter and would know what to do with them. They inquired about you and wanted me to set up a meeting."

I gripped the counter and doubled over so my forehead was resting on the backs of my hands. *Goddammit!*

"Debra Ann, what's wrong?" Gary asked, obviously worried at my reaction. "Here, sit down; use my chair. Can I get you something? Water? Or a soda?"

Head still down and resting on my hands, I mumbled. "No, thanks, I'll be fine; give me a moment or two."

I looked at him, trying to hide the emotions coursing through me.

"Gary, there was no way for you to know, but those weren't FBI agents. You knew that two men beat Brian Pierce to death, right?"

"Yes, I read about it in the papers. And the mortician mentioned he wasn't recognizable when they brought him in."

Gary's face turned ashen as he realized the implications.

"Are you saying *those two* did it?" He'd raised his voice in surprise.

"We don't know for sure." I straightened, palms still on the counter. "But in Brian's next-to-last letter, he talked about strangers flashing badges in his neighborhood. They were looking for him because of something he saw.

"Same descriptions as the one you just gave me."

"Oh, no. Debra Ann, I'm so sorry. I didn't know — I just took them at their word."

Gary seemed crestfallen and unprepared for this turn of events. Except for his reticence when I first met him, I knew from our interactions that Gary likely trusted everyone he met until they gave him a reason not to.

"I know; it's not your fault. I've had the feeling someone's following me for several days. When I drove in through your gate, I saw a black Transit van again as it passed through the grounds. I've seen it hanging around several places I've been. I came in today because I thought my pursuers might have tried to get to me through you."

Gary shook his head.

"I don't know of any reason a commercial vehicle like that would be on the grounds. The cemetery doesn't own any vans, just hearses. Our purveyors are mostly in construction or landscaping — they drive pickup trucks. And our deliveries go to the mortuary."

"I think I know why they're following me. After I deciphered Brian's last letters, I researched what he had to say and then turned over those letters and my notes to the police. The authorities interviewed the people we think were behind all of this. When they did, the investigators let it slip that they had a witness and new information without revealing their source or the witness's name.

"But they'd killed Brian, so they knew he was here. That's why the bad guys visited you. They're worried about what I know now that they're aware of me. I've already surrendered what I had to law enforcement. The only reason they'd care now would be to corrupt or eliminate me as a witness."

The word "eliminate" hung in the air.

"I never should have told them about you." Gary had guilt written all over his face.

"I don't want to alarm you unnecessarily, Gary, but I'm more worried about you. If you've got any vacation time squirreled away, now might be a good time to use it. It wouldn't hurt to be somewhere other than here for a few weeks. Lie low for a while, maybe hit the barbecue circuit?

"I don't know who all the bad guys are exactly, but I know they aren't messing around. At least three people are dead, likely because of them. If they get to me, you'll become the loose end that ties those letters to Brian Pierce and back to his killers. Listen, here's the name of a friend of mine at the San Diego Police Department. She knows what's going on."

I scratched out Marci's name and number on the back of my business card and handed it to Gary. He was standing there motionless, seeming a little shell-shocked.

I looked him in the eyes to ensure he was paying attention.

"Tell her everything you told me about the men posing as FBI agents. I'm sorry to leave you with any thought of danger to you or your loved ones, but I've got things I need to do. Are you going to be okay?"

He shook his head quickly to snap himself out of it.

"I'll be fine, thanks; coming that suddenly, it's a lot to take in. I'll follow up with your police officer friend. I'm sure they'll handle everything."

"Be careful; I'll check in with you soon."

After I closed the door behind me, I heard Gary lock the deadbolt. I hurried back to my Toyota. No other vehicles were around, but I started the car in case I needed to become mobile quickly.

And then I just sat there.

It was probably the safest place I could be at that moment. Even if Seaver's crew were watching, they wouldn't likely try anything in public during the day. I tried to wrap my head around what I'd just learned and the danger I might face.

My biggest problem for now was not knowing what his goons wanted from me. Or worse, to do to me. So far, I'd seen no signs of outright aggression — no overt threats, no evidence of bullet holes in any of my windows or cut brake lines on my car.

With that thought, I pumped the brake pedal and tested my emergency brake for reassurance.

They knew I'd already told what I could to the police. Perhaps they were making sure I wasn't actively investigating anything further. And since I wasn't, maybe all I needed to do was stand pat until Seaver's thugs lost interest.

I thought about calling Marci for protection. But she'd already told me clearly to butt out. Gary Gilbert had become a witness as soon as I turned those letters over; I wasn't sure she'd be happy with me talking to him. One more chat with me about staying out of the investigation might be our last. I'd have to rely on Marci to connect the dots with what Gilbert told her. I hoped she could keep everyone, including me, out of harm's way.

And law enforcement was, for the moment, again stymied. Surely Seaver and Ainsworth wouldn't want to screw that up with the attention another murder would bring — more so if the body belonged to a witness.

Then again, was Seaver someone we could expect to behave rationally?

CHAPTER 32

When I entered or left a building or public area, I'd repeatedly seen those three vehicles — the Transit van, the Dodge, and the Mustang. Someone was spending significant time and effort watching me, and it was becoming apparent that I was supposed to know they were there.

Driving from my apartment to see my old friend and colleague, Doug Stein, I'd catch fleeting, sometimes partial, glimpses of the same dark-colored Dodge sedan in my side and rearview mirrors.

To confirm my suspicions, I circled entirely around the block in downtown traffic.

The dark-colored Dodge Charger hung close, a thin line of white LEDs trimming the parking light and turn-signal clusters on each side of the grille.

That vehicle seemed an odd choice for tailing someone. Marci owned one, so I knew Chargers came from the factory with that distinctive lighting configuration. I suspected they'd selected the car for its performance, not what it looked like with its parking lights on. Or perhaps their purpose was intimidation — again, wanting me to know they were there.

Don't panic, I thought to myself. *Whoever these people are, they're hanging back, just following me. That's much better than the more aggressive "out to get me."*

Still, my heart was beating faster, and my nervous system was on high alert.

I had a little time because I was running early for our lunch meeting. Doug had called me on Tuesday to let me know he'd compiled a list of good stories with legs that the paper wasn't pursuing. He thought those might serve as great writing projects for me.

I headed for the high-end leather goods shop where I'd bought my last purse — its location was in the middle of the block on Eighth Avenue. The one-way downtown street, about five miles from my apartment, had angle parking at the front of the store and, importantly for my purposes, a rear exit to the back alley.

I assumed my tailer was one of the Neanderthals Brian had described as looking for him. If so, he'd stand out shopping for women's accessories, making him less likely to follow me into the boutique on foot.

Turning onto Eighth, I parked in front of the retail outlet. I then cut through it and out to the alley.

As the clandestine nature of what I was doing hit me, I felt an adrenaline rush. I'd been in situations like this before during my investigative career, though as the pursuer, not the pursued.

The difference was visceral and chilling.

Circling back, I walked up Eighth and stopped half a block behind where I'd parked. Hidden among the cluster of people waiting for the light to change, I scanned the street for that Dodge.

And there it was, parallel-parked across the street from where I'd left my Toyota.

Halfway between me and my car, the Dodge's engine was still running with its brake lights lit, meaning the driver was inside. I ducked into a store entrance and snapped a shot of the Dodge's license plate with my cell phone, using the brick in the storefront to steady my shaking hands.

Then, turning to walk in the opposite direction, I checked to ensure no one was following. A few blocks away, I requested an Uber through the app and called Doug to tell him I'd be ten minutes late.

When my ride arrived, I tensed, realizing I couldn't know if the Uber driver was playing for the other team. The line between worry and paranoia was blurring. I'd need more trustworthy transportation in the future. For now, I calmed myself with the thought that Uber records transactions in the cloud. If anything happened to me, the police could track down the driver.

That the world would still turn on its axis after my demise wasn't all that comforting a thought.

As the Uber dropped me off at the Mystic Grill on Balboa, I spotted Doug sitting at a table in the front, a welcome, familiar, and friendly face. But at the same time, I suddenly felt exhausted, like the letdown from a sugar high. I tried to shake it off and put a smile back on my face as I walked toward Doug's table.

"Hey, stranger, don't I know you from somewhere?" Doug winked, putting down his cell phone and standing to hug me.

"Talking on the phone isn't the same as face-to-face. It seems like only yesterday that we were working together every day."

"It's good to see you, kid. Half the newsroom wanted me to say 'hi' and let you know they were thinking of you; the other half wanted your written reference for when the paper sends them packing. From what you told me on the phone, I gather you've been having interesting times?"

"I could write a book if they'd let me, but the men in blue have put me into time-out. I'll tell you the entire story if you want to hear it. But before I do, I need to ask a favor…."

Pulling out my cell phone, I texted Doug the Dodge and Mustang photos.

"Can you run these for me? I don't want to use my sources in SDPD. If those plates come back to someone involved in the events I'm about to describe — and I think they will — I don't want my name attached to the request. I could lose access to my department contacts for good."

"Sure, Debra Ann. Always glad to help. I'll text you what I come up with later this afternoon. Now, you owe me a full account of what you've been up to. Don't skip any of the juicy parts. Oh, but first, here's that list of story ideas the *Union-Tribune* dropped."

"Perfect — the best part for me is knowing you've vetted these; I can't ask more than that!" I eagerly took the printout from him. "Since when does the paper turn down decent leads?"

"It's getting *so* hard to stomach that place," Doug confessed. "Journalistically, those stories are all sound, but they offend the sensibilities of one or more advertisers running the joint. I highlighted a couple I think are pretty good. If you want to pursue the one I circled, I'm all in for a collaboration. I've got some leads I started working on before they pulled the plug on it."

I perused the list and the notes he'd included.

"Working with a friend is great and everything." I grinned. "But this is why I miss sharing bylines with you. You've got such a good eye for stories. It's too bad there isn't a reputable paper surviving in the area that could use your services. Especially as an editor."

"I've thought about moving on, but Beth and the kids are happy here, and with the way the whole industry is heading, I might as well ride it out where I'm at. But I'm going to finish my MBA, and I'm keeping an eye out. Okay, enough of the chitchat — spill!" Doug gave me his wide-eyed and innocent look.

I caught him up on everything happening with my Pierce and Seaver stories since we'd last talked, and we shared our sadness over Coach's murder. I started with the fallout from not being forthright with Marci and finished with someone following me on the way here. He was sympathetic but concerned. Still, this was what we did, and we both understood what we'd signed on for.

We switched gears to talk about a story Doug was working.

"Not that it's a competition or anything," Doug said with a sly smile, "but I've got one that rivals your graveyard letters."

"Okay, I'll bite — what you got?" I used my best "doubting Thomas" voice.

"There've been several murders in the city where the victims were unpaying tenants who'd delayed their evictions for years. Those pauses resulted from rules and laws enacted during the COVID-19 pandemic.

Making them worse was a massive dump of eviction cases filed with the courts as they transitioned into post-pandemic operations. In the meantime, our governor and his staff issued a series of contradictory proclamations, and there was the aftermath from those."

"I know from reading opinion pieces that all the landowners are up in arms."

"The net effect has been some tenants living effectively rent-free for years. Worse, they've built up enormous debts to their landlords that they'll never pay, even if they could.

"Quite a few of those tenants have suddenly begun turning up dead."

"You'd expect a couple, I suppose — tough times for everyone — but not a bunch of them...."

"That's what got my attention. At first, the homicides looked random and unrelated. But it caught my eye that the means and the methods of the murders were very similar. The guy gains access to the victim's residence without breaking in, holding them at bay with a handgun as he ties them up. Then he beats them to death with a club, baseball bat, or tire iron, which he leaves at the scene."

"So, serial killer, then?"

"That's where I started, yeah," Doug answered. "But if you assume a common financial motivation, that's unusual for serial murders; you'd expect strong emotions, maybe a sexual component, or killings for the thrill of them — not back-due rent.

"I looked at property ownership records; one guy was always in the mix. Partnerships or real estate investment firms owned most properties. When I dug deeper, his name kept appearing as a part-owner or investor. Very wealthy, powerful, backed two of the current members of the city council."

"Sounds pretty straightforward," I surmised. "The biggest problem would be to out this guy, what with all the roadblocks he can throw your way."

"As it stood at first, that's how I saw it, too. But then I noticed the murders were getting more frequent, and they didn't fit my assumptions. The same MO, but this guy wasn't turning up as involved in the property ownership where the tenant was squatting. So, I started watching the money trail in my suspect's accounts. Bottom line: Following every murder, cash that didn't match any invoices would eventually arrive at his doorstep."

"He's making money from killing nonpaying tenants he has nothing against? How?"

"This homicidal jackass just couldn't suppress his entrepreneurial instincts." Doug gave me a droll smile. "He was profiting from performing this service for other landlords. Then, he sets his sights on expanding his clientele and improving productivity. I noticed that the murder reports got to a point where they were holding steady. But there was this tremendous spike in missing-person reports — even entire families. I assume too many bodies were piling up, so he no longer left them in the rental units."

"What was he doing with the bodies?"

"That had me stumped for a while." I could see the excitement in Doug's eyes. "Then I realized that an investor my suspect partnered with in several properties had once owned a crematorium that went bankrupt. I ran him down and put the fear of Jesus in him. I just got him on tape — electrifying stuff — laying out the entire scheme, ending with his incineration of the remains."

"You're ready to put it to bed, then? I must admit, it's a great story!"

"By my count, thirteen known murders and eleven suspicious missing persons, all somewhere in the eviction process," Doug said. "San Diego County reports around what, seventy or eighty murders in a normal year? So, that's one perpetrator responsible for almost a third of those! And the police weren't seriously investigating any of these homicides."

"Congratulations, Doug. I need to take you out for a beer to celebrate."

"Cross your fingers." Doug's smile became cynical. "With how the damned *Union-Tribune* is going, it will turn out the killer is an advertiser, and they'll refuse to print my story."

Unfortunately, we had to end on that note — we could have talked for hours. But Doug still had story deadlines to answer. With some regret, we promised to get together and continue our discussion later.

"I'll let you know who those plates come back to when I get to the shop," Doug called out from behind me as I headed to my Uber.

His reminder brought me back to the real world. Getting back home would be much more interesting than it should have been.

CHAPTER 33

As I got into the back of the Uber, I briefly eyed the driver for suspicious intentions; upon reflection, I realized my other options could be worse. I had the rideshare drop me a block from where I'd left my car. As I approached my Toyota, I carefully scrutinized the cars and trucks on both sides of the street. There was no sign of the Dodge or the other two vehicles I'd caught watching me before. I walked around my car, looking for bystanders who were perhaps too close.

Then, as I reached for the door handle, I suddenly froze. *Could someone have planted a bomb?* Stooping down with my purse cushioning my knee, I peered under my car to see if anything was amiss. Then I realized I wouldn't recognize a bomb unless they left a prominent red LED timer on it, as they do in low-rent action movies. I got up off the pavement, feeling slightly foolish but still worried. Anyone following me would more likely have attached a GPS tracker — something else I wouldn't recognize — than a bomb. And they could have done that back at the apartment.

Still, I squeezed my eyes tightly closed and gritted my teeth, first as I opened the driver's door and again as I pushed the Toyota's Start button. The engine cranked and hummed to life; nothing exploded. I backed up slowly, testing the brakes a dozen times, then tried them again with several taps as I slowly pulled forward, increasing my speed.

As I headed home, I checked my mirrors frequently for a tail. I made a hard left turn from the far-right lane when I saw an opportunity that wouldn't get anyone killed or injured. Making a few random trips around the block, I saw no clear signs anyone was following me. But as my apartment complex's parking lot was coming into view, I noticed that black Transit van with my keyscratch artwork. It had parked in a slot assigned to a fellow tenant I knew well; he drove a gray Nissan Sentra and wouldn't be home late afternoons. The rest of the lot was almost empty, with a few vehicles scattered here and there.

Dammit, this will not turn out well.

Driving past my apartments, I continued for two blocks and turned left, parking on a side street. Head down, I casually strolled the far side of the street to the sidewalk passing in front of my complex, checking for any observers on the footpaths or occupied vehicles on either curb. I snuck into my building from the visitor's entrance on the opposite side of the structure from the parking lot.

When I entered my apartment, I didn't turn on the lights immediately. Instead, I closed the doors to the bedroom and bathroom, which had windows opening to the parking lot side. That would prevent the Transit van from seeing any light from the rest of my apartment. The other side of the flat was a windowless wall to a hallway between neighboring apartments, so that wouldn't be a problem. Once it was dark, I'd need to turn off all the lights in the apartment, close the blinds in both rooms on the parking side, and pull the drapes fully closed. Then I could open those doors again and turn the lights back on. No one from the parking lot could track my comings and goings.

I checked my messages — Doug had called while I was driving, and I'd let it go to voicemail. "Debra Ann, that plate comes back to Strike Response. Call me as soon as you get this message."

I typed "Strike Response" into the search bar of my browser. The company's home page was heavy on armed security; they advertised their specialty services as "defensive and preventive investigations," though the ad language hinted more at retaliation — hence the name, I presume. Among the reasons the contents gave for clients wanting their services were divorces, labor disputes, oppo research, background checks, internal theft, insurance, undercover, and investigating the investigators and business competitors. Riddled with Trumpie racist and gender-biased dog whistles, the text described, and all the photos featured, angry-looking white males, most of them armed to the teeth, in forearm-crossed poses backed by American-made muscle cars. Strike Response was purveying testosterone-fueled thuggery.

Hearing the urgency in Doug's voice on the message, I dialed his number, and he picked up immediately.

"Hi, Doug, I got your message, and it seemed urgent…."

"Debra Ann, I'm glad you called back." Doug sounded more tense than usual. "Strike Response Security and Investigations owns both vehicles tailing you. They claim to be a one-stop shop for security and private investigation services. If you've never encountered them, you must know they are serious trouble, as disreputable as they come."

That didn't turn up in my Google search, I thought. But I rarely rely on Google for that reason. With SEO manipulation of search results, reputation repair services, planted reviews, and carpet bombing with connected links, any business with adequate resources can squelch online negativity.

"I read about their services online. What parts are they not sharing?" I wasn't sure I truly wanted to know.

"There are two components to Strike Response. One is a security service that provides basic body and property protection, and they *will* intimidate people for the right price. They can cause serious problems for ordinary people, but they're hired muscle, dumb as rocks."

I relaxed a little, not seeing "Paul Blart, Mall Cop" characters as all that fearsome. "And the other component?"

"The other side of the house is *much* more dangerous. The rep on the street is that they're fixers. They'll do anything if the price is right; rumors say they'll do wet work. Ex-CIA and ex-military primarily, some are retired spooks and ghosts from the clandestine services of several countries. Debra Ann, I can't stress this enough — those people pose grave threats to anyone who gets in their way."

"How would I find out who hired them?"

"As a private citizen? No easy way comes to mind. But you should know that some of the worst people employ these guys. As I understand it, the client stays on the hook once they've engaged Strike Response. The company won't hesitate to use the services they've performed in the past as extortion to keep a customer's business — nasty stuff. My instincts say that what you told me about James Seaver makes him the perfect client. If he hired Strike Response, he couldn't get rid of them now, even if he wanted to. But whoever their client might be, you need to get into a safe situation now; you truly do."

I can't seem to catch a break, I thought.

"Thanks, Doug, for the heads up. I owe you one. Don't be surprised if I check in again soon once I'm somewhere safer. I might need to tap into your resources to get out of whatever I've stepped into."

"You know I'll help in any way I can," Doug promised as we said our goodbyes and hung up.

I thought about calling Marci, but investigative reporters know the problem only too well. To begin with, someone following you is not necessarily, by itself, a crime. Proving any future ill intent towards the person followed can be next to impossible. Following someone is part of what I do as a reporter when chasing a story, so there would be significant hypocrisy in my complaint. And then I'd have to reveal that I didn't tell her about my hallway encounter with Seaver or previous sightings of these vehicles.

I wasn't a victim of anything illegal or a material witness of significant value. Even if I could persuade the department to give me a protective detail, it wouldn't be for long. Worse, the bodyguard itself would render my movements visible. Given my belief that someone was following me to see who I was talking to, being more obvious wouldn't help my cause. However, the worst problem for reporters is that their witnesses and sources can be very reluctant to speak in the presence of a law officer.

Finally, Marci's help would come at a steep price. I'd promised to stay out of the Seaver investigations. An assigned police detail would allow her to monitor and enforce that agreement.

And that was going to be a problem.

My anger was poking at my insides to remind me of something Dad often said: "They didn't cast you to play the victim in this life, kid." I could feel my blood becoming heated, the same sensation I had fighting with Jerry Dark as I left the *Union-Tribune*. I know the feeling well — that outrage rising within me again, replacing the strange doubts and fears surrounding me. The anger was so much more familiar — comfortable, like a well-worn pair of jeans. It had been with me since childhood, usually lurking deep under the surface. Its clumsy appearances were often not welcome. But today, I celebrated its arrival with open arms, like an old friend coming to my rescue.

It was screaming at me the reason for its awakening: *"You're a law-abiding grown woman in a free country, cowering in your apartment, afraid someone might see you? Are you fucking kidding me?"*

And it had a point. Today, I'd learned who was doing this to me, an entity I could go after. The anger had come to push me toward what I'd wanted to do all along. It was time to fight back, but on my terms, not theirs.

Sorry, Marci, I tried to be a good girl; I honestly did. I want to keep my promise, and I would if I could. But somebody else is deciding for me. I can't live my life in fear of bullies. As an investigative reporter, I was a damned good one. I needed to put those strengths to work and nail these monsters so they couldn't intimidate or murder anyone else.

My first order of business was to add industrial-strength paint stripper and latex balloons to my shopping list, along with a turkey baster to fill the balloons. Maybe I couldn't stop them from following me, but it would cost them a paint job if they did. If a smokey, gas-guzzling noisemaker wrapped in polished tin makes the man, let's kick 'em right in the shiny A gooey mess bubbling away on their hood and eating away at the enamel should take the sneaky and intimidating crap down a notch.

The second item on my new to-do list: Get the plate number from that Transit van in the parking lot. I took my cell phone and snapped photos of the vehicle at different zoom levels through the narrow window on the side of the tenants' entry door. I quickly texted the best image to Doug Stein with a simple question: "This one, too? Thanks!"

Now to the meat of this thing. The contents of Brian's letters had tracked true through all of this. There *had* to be another "Rickie" in the mix, someone other than Ainsworth. One person I'd talked to seemed to know the players better than anyone. That was Darrell Woodson. I texted him: "Hello, Darrell, this is Debra Ann Wynn. I've got some follow-up questions; I'll need maybe 15 minutes. When's the best time to call?"

My next priority was ditching the surveillance at my apartment and stopping them from following me when I traveled.

Finally, I'd need to move somewhere safer. It wouldn't matter how much I wanted to fight back if I wasn't alive to do it.

CHAPTER 34

Dusk had surrendered to the darkness of evening. The glare of headlights would hide a vehicle's features, especially when seen in a rearview mirror. I'd use the night to organize and gather the belongings I'd need, but I'd move to a motel room during the next day's light. There'd be a better chance of seeing when someone was following me and, if necessary, escaping a pursuer.

My decision to fight back had seriously raised my adrenaline level. After taking a long breath to settle my heart rate, I sorted out the clothing and shoes I wanted to take and prepared a go bag for the morning. Once I'd finished, I did some DuckGoGo searches over VPN. I needed to find a motel with a low traffic volume where I could forego using a credit card and monitor the comings and goings of other vehicles. The trick with the kind of places that deal in cash is finding one without bedbugs. To deal with that problem, I'd bring a queen-sized air mattress with an electric inflation pump as a workaround. I knew there was no way to avoid the risk altogether because I'd have to change motels frequently for a while.

Strike Response had abundant resources, and I assumed they could tap into my credit card expenditures and bank accounts. I'd have to rely on Uber drivers since the people threatening me knew my car, and I'd have to pay cash for everything else. I signed up for a different Gmail address and used that to set up new Lyft and Uber accounts on my burner phone. I made a note to stop off at the 7-Eleven and get refillable debit cards for those situations where I had to pay with plastic. I'd link them to my new rideshare accounts.

The real challenge would be getting a good night's sleep so I'd be sharp for tomorrow.

But before that became an issue, I received two texts. The first was from Doug Stein about the Transit van plate request, and it read, "Same — Strike Response. They're assigning serious time and resources to watch/follow you. PLEASE be careful!" The second was Darrell Woodson returning my text and letting me know he was available for a phone conversation. I immediately called him back.

"Good evening, Darrell, and thank you for taking the time to help with this. I don't know how much the police have told you, but Ainsworth's prints and DNA didn't match either set the killers left on Brian's body. I hoped Richard Ainsworth was the 'Rickie' that Brian Pierce identified before his death. Unfortunately, that wasn't the case."

"Yes, I know," Darrell replied. "The police came to our home and re-interviewed me yesterday. When they visited before, they made it obvious they looked at me as a potential suspect. They were much more cordial this time and stayed mostly on the same topics you and I discussed. I share your disappointment that they aren't considering Ainsworth a suspect in Theresa's killing. Too much to hope for, I suppose."

"And that's why I'm calling you tonight. The police have told me to stay away from it, but since then, the official investigation's gone back to treading water. And someone from a private security agency is following me. That's why I wanted to talk on the phone rather than meet. I'm sending you photos of two Strike Response vehicles following me."

"'Strike Response' doesn't ring a bell…"

"I understand sketchy people hire them mainly as muscle and fixers. I'm guessing they work for James Seaver, but I haven't confirmed that. They have other vehicles in their pool; one's a dark green Mustang — oh, here's that photo; let me send you it as well. But if you see any of these hanging around, be aware they're surveilling you."

"I understand perfectly and appreciate your consideration and concerns regarding my safety. My PI caught someone tailing me several months ago, but we haven't seen them since and assumed they lost interest. I'll keep an eye out.

"Since Ainsworth isn't 'Rickie,' I need to find another candidate using that name, even if they are only peripherally associated with any of this. You seem to know the players best, so I wanted to check with you."

"I've thought about it," Darrell said after a brief pause. "Honestly, I can't think of anyone. But there *is* somebody who'd likely know better than I would. When Harry, my private investigator, writes his reports for me, he edits them to include only the salient points. Until now, those have covered just the criminal fraud cases against Seaver and my ex-wife. Harry has his issues — I wouldn't take any fashion advice from him if I were you — but he is very thorough. Harry would probably know if there's another 'Rickie' in this thing. Any associates Seaver dealt with regularly should turn up in either Harry's or one of his agent's field notes."

"Would it be okay for me to talk to Harry?"

"It's alright by me. I'll give you Harry's contact information and call him so he knows you have my blessing and full support. But there's a condition — everything you learn about Harry and his investigations must remain confidential. There are certain aspects to what Harry does that need to be free of police officers lurking about; I'm sure you understand. And I'd rather we keep Harry's private contact information between ourselves."

"To a decent reporter, protecting confidential sources overrides any other consideration. The hallmark of the profession. You have my word that I'll keep this conversation and any information you provide me off the record."

"Good enough — I just texted you Harry's e-mail address, physical address, and a phone number that he'll always answer. I'll make sure he knows you are collaborating with us. But you'll probably want to wait until tomorrow to contact him. He does most of his work in the evenings. A cell phone ringing or interrupting him while he's on a stakeout or following someone wouldn't be good, so he usually turns off any phones the public can access. He'll meet during regular office hours, nine to five."

After I'd spoken with Darrell, I considered my options for transportation. I certainly couldn't use my car. I didn't feel a hundred percent confident that Uber and Lyft drivers or their ride-sharing software were safe. Could Strike Response corrupt or replace a driver or hack a ride request? I thought about getting a rental, but that still put my face at the wheel, and once they had its tags, I'd be right back to the same problem I had with my vehicle.

Thinking it through reminded me of someone I hadn't seen in a long time. Cathy Andreesen was a veteran reporter who'd taken me under her wing when I started my job at the *Union-Tribune*. Cathy was well-traveled and bore an uncanny resemblance to Andrea Mitchell in appearance and personality. She'd since retired from a stellar career. She lived a few blocks from me, at the end of a quiet cul-de-sac in a residential neighborhood. After retirement, Cathy used to drive for Uber to make a little side money. I might get her to chauffer me if she still owned her Prius with the Uber markings. The vehicle type would be ubiquitous enough that Strike Response might ignore the car's specific details. It should take them a while to figure out it was the same Uber picking me up every time.

I still had her number among my contacts. I phoned her, and it went to voicemail. I left her a message that I had an opportunity for her if she'd like to earn some extra money.

As I returned to putting together my go bag, Cathy called me back. She was still driving for Uber to supplement her retirement, so I told her about my situation.

"I'm tracking a new story now, and the subjects know my car and may be dangerous. I don't know how safe or trustworthy a regular Uber or Lyft might be. But I could move around securely, hiding in plain sight, if I traveled in a nondescript vehicle with Uber markings driven by someone I knew. Not everyone's cup of tea, but I thought I'd ask you if you wanted to spice things up in your life. I would make it well worth your while...."

Cathy was receptive.

"I could use a little spice in my life, and the money helps ... How often are you going to need my services?"

"I'm guessing a dozen round trips a week for a month, maybe a little longer. I'd give you a generous retainer up front, yours to keep, and add more as we burn through it."

"I'm willing to try it; see how things work out. It would be good to share old times during our travels."

We agreed to meet at a minimart off Lexington the following morning at eight-thirty.

"Oh, this will be like the old days — I'll see you tomorrow." Cathy sounded excited as we signed off.

I thanked her and sighed in relief. "See you there. I'll have your retainer with me — I hope you don't mind cash."

<hr>

I slept fitfully through the night and wee hours. When I couldn't sleep any longer, I caught up on my e-mails and the local news, waiting for the cover of morning rush-hour traffic. Too restless to remain in bed, I made a generous breakfast of French toast, eggs over easy, and a slice of smoked deli ham.

It was time to take personal protection more seriously. I'm not a fan of guns, but I inherited an old snub-nosed .38 revolver. Dad had kept it hidden in his construction trailer for his safety and that of his crew. I took the locked case from one of the cardboard boxes of his things that I kept in the spare bedroom, along with a tray of ammunition and his gun-cleaning kit. Dad taught me how to care for this weapon when I was twelve. As I cleaned and oiled the revolver, I began feeling more secure, a sense growing in me that I was regaining some control over my situation.

Tucking the firearm into my purse, I realized I'd have to be careful until I could obtain a carry permit. I'd have to find time to fit in a gun course at a local shooting range to get one.

At eight-fifteen, I exited my apartment building through the front visitor's door, hidden from anyone in the parking lot at the rear. I walked a circuitous route to the Stop'N'Go to ensure no one had followed me. Cathy was good to her word and waiting for me. I jumped in, and we began catching up as she took off. She looked just as she had the last time I'd seen her, although I couldn't help but notice the two Albuterol inhalers she kept in the dashboard cubby.

My first stop was at a Walmart to purchase a TracPhone without a GPS receiver. I pulled out the SIM card from the cell I usually carry and hid it in the Samsung phone's case so I wouldn't use it unless I had to. That step would force me to depend on the untraceable burner phone instead.

Once I landed at the motel, Cathy and I said our goodbyes. I scouted out the room and its surroundings, and my choice satisfied my needs. It was downscale, to be sure, but it felt safe. Though a local family independently owned the motel, the furnishings and décor were reminiscent of a Motel 6 from the eighties. It reminded me of those portrayed in the old *Rockford Files* TV series that Dad and I used to watch together on DVD. I knew I'd find no gel-topped memory foam mattresses at this establishment. But as I tested the queen-sized bed, I found places on it that were reasonably comfortable.

The 42-inch flatscreen bolted to the top of the dark walnut chest of drawers looked like it might have been one of the first of its type, definitely pre-smart. However, other than not having a USB port for my Chromecast so I could display my cellphone screen, the TV was functional for my purposes. The management provided decent Wi-Fi services, and the room's mini-Keurig coffee bar was well stocked.

Dark wallpaper and furnishings made the room look smaller, but one feature was perfect — the drapes were heavy, stiff, blackout curtains. Once they were closed, no one could see into the room, even with the lights on.

I had a clear view of most of the parking area. The motel rooms sat on either side of a long, common outdoor hallway. Perpendicular to that hallway in the middle of the rows was a shorter exterior corridor with ice and vending machines. From behind the ice machine in the outside hall, I could see most of the rear area without being seen myself. That was where the trash bins were and where employees parked their cars. Few people were staying at the motel, which also helped because any new vehicles added to the mix stood out.

My first task in my new digs was to set up an appointment with Harry Sanderson, Darrell Woodson's private investigator. The receptionist took my call. She sounded like an older woman with a terse, business-like phone manner. She told me Mr. Sanderson was in a meeting but that he'd instructed her to set an appointment for us. We agreed on five o'clock, the last available time slot today.

Once I settled into my new room, I still had several hours left before meeting Harry. I called Cathy on my burner for another ride to a boutique for more clothes. When leaving my apartment, I'd packed only those items from home that I could carry in a bag and a backpack and still walk comfortably.

Once I'd dropped my new wardrobe off in my room, I invited Cathy to a late lunch. From the restaurant, she drove me to the detective agency. Our idle chatter as we rode together was relaxing, even as I mentally reviewed what I'd ask Harry about stressful topics. So far, the general plan seemed to be working. Though I'd diligently kept a careful eye on our surroundings, there was no sign that we were being watched or followed.

"Thanks, Cathy. I might be here awhile," I said as we pulled up to the address Darrell had given me, "so I'll just call you when I'm ready to leave."

"Oh, I'm so sorry; I should have mentioned this earlier. A friend is coming over for dinner at seven, and I probably won't be available."

It seemed for now that I was in the clear. It didn't look like anyone had followed us. Even if Strike Response could compromise Uber ride requests, they wouldn't have time to arrange anything untoward on such short notice.

"Oh, no problem, I can get another Uber," I told her. "I'll miss our conversation, but it probably doesn't hurt to mix things up a little. Drive safely!"

I didn't know it yet, but in the coming weeks, I'd often contemplate how that brief snippet of conversation with Cathy saved my friend's life.

THE WRITINGS OF
AVRIL MARIA SERENE

CHAPTER 35

Harry's second-floor office south of downtown was up a staircase sandwiched between two brown brick storefronts. A simple sign on the door read "Harry Sanderson and Don Manchusen, Private Investigations."

The office manager was in her early fifties, pleasant but curt, likely the same woman I spoke to on the phone. "Mr. Sanderson knows you're here and will be with you shortly."

I couldn't blame her for not wasting time on amenities. Her in-basket was overflowing, and there were myriad piles of folders, notebooks, and papers on her oak desk and the dark cherry credenza behind it. I didn't envy her workload.

Potted flowers hanging in the narrow anteroom's only window drooped sadly, nearly dead. The toxins in the atmosphere might explain why — the place reeked of Raid Ant and Roach Killer. A sooty ceiling fan with dark walnut blades twisted lazily overhead, wobbling with every turn. Two dim, flickering sconces provided light above a row of wooden chairs with black padded vinyl seats lining the wall.

At this late hour, no one else was in the waiting area. I thumbed through a three-year-old Family Circle magazine from the chrome and black end table that split the row of chairs. I could hear the commotion of conversation and activity through restaurant-style swinging doors directly across from me.

The desk phone beeped softly, and shortly, the receptionist announced from behind one of her piles, "Ms. Wynn, Mr. Sanderson asked me to send you back. His office is on the rear wall past the cubicles."

I nodded my thanks and pushed through the doors. In the middle of a large open area were a dozen workstations, six on each side, most occupied. Nearly all the employees were on their phones — some looked up and smiled, and a few turned their backs for privacy as I passed. The place reminded me of what Dad called his "boiler room," where phone solicitors drummed up business for his construction company. Sometimes, he'd let me play in an unused cubicle when he had to work a weekend. I felt a warm kinship with Harry's environs.

His office door was open. As I entered and our eyes met, he seemed familiar, evoking a flash memory of Granddad's beloved reels of old film noir classics. Harry's face resembled Morley Safer's toward the end of his *60 Minutes* career. A large sign, dingy with tobacco smoke, was posted prominently on the wall behind him. It read: "California banned smoking in offices in 1995. The maximum fine is $100.00. You can file a complaint on your way to the unemployment office." Hanging next to it was an unframed 1950s-era black-and-white photo of Anita Ekberg, cigarette holder in hand, her countenance stern as she looked directly into the camera.

Harry's space reeked of cigarettes. Two filled ashtrays, a butt smoldering in each, told me Harry was a chain smoker. He wore suspenders, with his tie loosened and the top two buttons of his white shirt unfastened — sweat stains were visible on the inside of his collar. He'd distributed his thinning hair in a not-very-convincing comb-over. His large abdomen was keeping him from getting too close to his desk.

As I walked in, I heard the tail end of his phone conversation, his sign-off given in the gruff voice you'd expect from all that nicotine over the years. He waved me into his office with two fingers as he finished his call and hung up, immediately giving me his attention.

"Hello, Mr. Sanderson…"

Harry interrupted before I got any further.

"Please, Mr. Sanderson was my father. Me, I'm just Harry."

He wore a puckish smile and seemed to be sizing up my reaction.

"OK… Harry… I'm Debra Ann Wynn. Darrell Woodson suggested I reach out to you."

"Ah, yes, the famous former *Union-Tribune* investigative reporter." Harry gave his pronouncement a bit of flair. "I've read you for years — great stuff — and meeting the person is a pleasure."

"'I am not a myth,'" I chuckled, resorting to one of my grandfather's favorite Marlene Dietrich quotes.

Harry stood up, his midsection shifting downward. Putting his hands flat on both sides of his belly, he pondered it, saying, "'It's either the candy or the hooch. I must say, I wish it was your chili I was gettin' fat on.'"

I couldn't help but laugh out loud at the reply.

"My granddad was a Dietrich fan," I said, reaching out to take his hand, "and I must have seen *Touch of Evil* a dozen times as a kid. Otherwise, I'd be turning around and headed out the door about now!"

"Touché," Harry said with a grin. Sitting, he rearranged the open folders on his desk. "Darrell's told me something about your story and your present situation. I've looked into recent developments since I last worked the Seaver and Ainsworth matters. If I understand correctly, you need background on two minor players. Darrell mentioned a 'Rickie' somebody and Seaver's outside-the-marriage girlfriend. Is that right?"

"Yes, in a nutshell."

"The mistress I can tell you about upfront. *That* ditzy tart pulled a cheap little .25 automatic and threatened Claire, one of my best operatives — big mistake. Claire has a concealed weapon permit for a .40-caliber Glock 22, and she's as good with it as they come. Claire kept her head — the only reason the girlfriend was left breathing. Still, we filed a complaint because the woman didn't have a license for her gun."

I felt a twinge of guilt at the revolver in my bag.

"How did the two come to be in the same place at the same time?"

"Claire was doing the legwork on Seaver and Ainsworth, questioning a man the girlfriend was with. The mistress goes by Sheryl Jansen now, but she's been married four times and uses half a dozen aliases. Besides Jansen, you might try Campbell, Clarke, Dearman, Garson, Samuels, Simpson, White, or Whitman, in alphabetical order." He paused as I scrambled for my notebook and pen. "As a first name, try Sharon, Sherrell — that's S-H-E, double R, E, double L — or Shirley. When she's dancing at men's clubs for tips, it's always 'Cherry Something-or-other.' Our last employment on her was as a nail tech at Color My World Beauty Salon, off Genesee."

"How did she connect with Seaver?"

"She used to be a doll, but when you see her teeth, you can tell she was into crystal meth pretty heavily at some point. She and Seaver have been an item going back fifteen years, even though both have been married to other people at the same time. I think it's more having a similar criminal worldview than anything romantic, but who knows? I can have Claire send you her workup."

"That'd be wonderful," I said, grateful for the help.

"I understand that you have letters written by a murder victim that show his killer may have been this 'Rickie' person. I read about someone beating your victim to death in an alley several blocks from here. Darrell told me what you'd explained to him, but if you don't mind, I'd like to hear it from you. Sometimes details can get lost in translation that would otherwise point to an answer."

"Where would you like me to start?" I asked.

"Let's begin with your father finding that first letter at your family's gravesite. And no need to hurry; we've got all the time you need."

He guided me with an occasional question. I didn't hold back, sharing everything, including details I hadn't told Woodson or Marci. We didn't talk for long before I realized Harry wasn't what he seemed. The tough-guy behaviors and attitudes you'd expect of an old-school, from-the-streets private eye were a facade. His words, facial expressions, and vocal inflections were those of an educated and contemplative man. At first, I found the contrast startling, and then, as we spoke, enlightening and enjoyable. I quickly figured out that he liked to play against type and used that to measure people, occasionally messing with their heads.

My quote collection began and ended with Dietrich. But the lineup of passages Harry could draw on spontaneously from memory was genuinely awe-inspiring. He was a walking, talking version of Bartlett's Familiar Quotations. Harry liked to throw quips from *Casablanca* and other film noir classics into the conversation — even a few from TV shows like *Columbo*.

"I collect quotes from past celebrities as a hobby," he somewhat sheepishly explained when I complimented his faculties.

It seemed he used them to probe the listener's awareness. That he did so put me at ease, something we had in common. Though I employed different methods, I often did the same in my interviews. And by introducing these clichés into the experience, he showed his individuality in counterpoint. For all his outwardly playing to stereotypes, this was an intelligent and complex man. As a result, I felt I could trust him in my present circumstances.

I took him through everything, concluding with the warning from Doug Stein about Strike Response and their hoods. I told him the steps I had been taking to protect myself, including my planned scarlet lettering of the several vehicles following me with paint remover. I paused to e-mail him the photos of the Dodge, the black van, and the Mustang that had been stalking me.

When Harry saw the images, he held up an index finger to request my momentary silence, tapping the intercom button on his desk phone with the other.

"Hey, Fred, I'm sending three pictures a client took to your cell phone. Whenever you finish what you're doing, I need you to hang GPS trackers on these."

"Got 'em," the voice responded after a moment. "Hey, boss, I know who drives that Dodge. Remember Barry Donnelly, the guy we fired two years ago for hitting on a client? I don't know how, but he got a job with Strike Response."

"Hmmm, fits. I didn't think that agency's standards were all that high," Harry replied.

Fred told us the ex-employee was down and out and couldn't get a vehicle in his name, so he drove the company car home every night.

"Tag it," Harry offered, "and I'll buy you and Valerie barbecue plates at Dickey's tomorrow."

"Okay, boss, we're gonna hold you to that — gotta run!" With that, Fred was gone.

"Thanks, Harry." I was surprised how quickly he'd acted. "I wasn't expecting that, but having somebody on my side watching him means one less person for me to worry about."

Turning back to me, Harry smiled. "Well, I wish I could say I was being kind and generous, but Darrell's picking up the tab for everything. And I know Doug well — we used to hang out together just to drive down the neighbors' property values. Say 'hi' for me when you see him."

The smile ran away from Harry's face.

"But take seriously what he told you about Strike Response. They have a long history. We've crossed paths with Strike Response PIs as they tried to dig up dirt on people in Darrell's fraud cases."

"Why haven't I heard about them before?"

"When bodies turn up around their ops, the individuals who did the deed get charged if caught, but Strike Response keeps their business name out of it. But make no mistake, they're dangerous. Our operatives sometimes run into them, and it's never pleasant. Nothing that's come to violence beyond somebody drawing a weapon, but the threat of worse is always there."

"Is that kind of behavior a regular thing?" The prospect of having a gun pulled on me made me nervous.

"We've spotted them around this area harassing our clients, but don't worry; we can handle them. We've had some practice. Quite a few people come to us for help after Strike Response targets them. The good thing for us is that subtlety isn't that agency's specialty, and we don't have any problem identifying them and calling them out.

"How *much* practice?"

"You wouldn't know it from looking at our offices, but we probably have three times the number of clients those goons do. We put our money into hiring the best people, not the décor."

I couldn't help grinning at his comment.

"Most of our clients come to us by word of mouth. They value discretion and a deft touch. They're used to a certain level of sophistication in personal and business matters. Those elements convey intelligence and finesse, and that's where Strike Response comes up short."

"Your agency and theirs are at opposite ends of the spectrum, then...."

"We like to think so."

Harry leaned forward, his expression showing concern. "You'll need an answer if they come at you with deadly force — do you have a gun?"

"Yes, I have my dad's .38. Which reminds me — how hard is it to get a concealed carry permit?"

"Thanks to the Supreme Court, there's not much to it. In California, you've got to take a reputable gun course and pass the live-fire handling test. The law requires them to give you the permit if you have no convictions or mental health issues. We can get you the training and expedite the process for you — we're set up for that to accommodate new hires.

"Regarding this 'Rickie' character, we may have something in the field notes. Claire should be back from dinner soon. She can tell you if there's a Rickie that she knows about."

Harry called out through the open door, "Claire, are you there?"

A husky female voice not far down the hall sang out, "Yes, Harry, loving every minute."

Harry followed up. "Can you join us for a moment? And bring your field notes for the Seaver case if you don't mind?"

"Oh, I mind, Harry, but I'll do it anyway just to save my spot on the company softball team," Claire replied.

Harry rolled his eyes at me, but I couldn't help a smile coming to my face. Her attitude was ... *interesting*. Now, I was curious to meet her.

THE WRITINGS OF
AVRIL MARIA SERENE

CHAPTER 36

An unusually tall but drop-dead gorgeous blonde appeared at the door to Harry's office. Although her appearance and mannerisms were feminine in every way imaginable, my intuition told me she hadn't always been a woman. But I doubted that, unless specifically informed, any man would have known — or cared.

She was carrying a thick stack of file folders under each arm. Dropping into the seat next to me, she plopped the folders on Harry's desktop, reaching across her body for a handshake.

Harry introduced us.

"Claire makes this place go. She was a decorated member of New York City's finest for eleven years. Some of Claire's personal choices weren't compatible with the working environment there, so she came out here. I'm glad we got her before anyone else did. Claire's been with us for almost ten years now. She does much of the heavy lifting to support our boots-on-the-ground fieldwork."

He turned to her. "Claire, meet Debra Ann Wynn. She's well-known in these parts as an accomplished investigative reporter. Debra Ann is working with Darrell Woodson to track down two players in the Seaver investigation. The guy goes by 'Rickie,' and we've ruled out Ainsworth. Debra Ann, tell her what you know about this Rickie character."

I pulled out my copy of Brian's letter describing Rickie and handed it to Claire. Several moments passed as she read, chewing on the inside of her lower lip.

"I might have something on this guy — hang tight for a minute." She tossed aside the top five folders on the right-hand stack, grabbing the next two. Flipping through the first folder, she threw it back onto the pile and opened the one remaining on her lap.

"Hmmm, here's an entry that might work for you. One of our operatives was waiting for Seaver's group to leave a restaurant. Seaver sent one of his minions to tell her to stop following him. The guy was five feet, six inches, maybe weighed one-sixty-five or one-seventy, and balding. She says, 'George Costanza's body with a ferret-face stuck on top, like Frank Burns's from *M*A*S*H*.'

"Not the type of guy you'd ordinarily think of as intimidating. The operative guessed it was probably some flunky who volunteered as a messenger to get into Seaver's good graces."

"That perfectly fits what Brian said about him." I could sense my prospects improving.

"We're always looking for supporting cast in the know, low-level players we can leverage later for information. So, after this guy accosted her, our agent exchanged vehicles for another one in our pool and returned to the restaurant. Seaver and his crew were still there, and when they left, she followed the short guy."

"Do you have an address for him?" My excitement was growing, and I wanted to jump ahead.

"Here we go; the operative wrote Rickie's address in the margin." Claire didn't seem offended by my enthusiasm. "It's 13482 Elm Bluff. Once she had his address, she did a reverse lookup and checked him out online. From that, she learned he was a tough-guy wannabe named Ricky Mason.

That's 'Ricky' with a *y*. Before the franchise went bankrupt, he was Seaver's trainer at Gold's Gym."

"That squares with what Brian found when he broke into the residence of this 'Rickie.'" I was becoming convinced Claire had found one of my missing killers.

"A short little dude with a Napoleon complex who tries to give the impression he's connected," Claire said. "But purely a hangaround aspiring to become Seaver's Mini Me. He tried to join the Marines during the latter stages of Operation Iraqi Freedom, but they wouldn't have him. Two years ago, your Ricky became Seaver's part-time gopher. The doctor lets him do odd jobs to earn spending money. He's a gym rat. I'm sure he's trying to compensate for his size. The detective's notes say he goes to that 24-Hour Fitness over on Valspar. He drives a twelve-year-old blue Honda Civic with a Trump 2016 campaign sticker on the bumper."

"A height-challenged 4F poser driving an old, underpowered Civic — that paints me a picture." I didn't hide my sarcasm. "Do you know if this guy has a wingman, somebody who would participate in a major crime?"

"I'm not seeing anything else here," Claire answered, flipping back and forth quickly through the folder. "It didn't seem to the operative that this Ricky was in a position where he could tell us much — likely unreliable, anyway. So that's where she left it — that's all we have on Mason. We concentrated on the doctor and his scams, focusing on Richard Ainsworth because he was a player in that world. We dropped Mason once we'd checked him out enough to see he wasn't useful to us."

"One too many 'Rickies' in the mix," I murmured.

"If it makes you feel any better," Claire added, "you're not the first to get confused about the nickname. There's a note here that when our operative asked around, she had to clarify which one she meant when asking about Ricky. Most people assume the interest is in Ainsworth."

"Well, you've pinpointed the guy I'm looking for." I held my cell's screen toward her. "I just entered the address you gave me into Google Maps. There it is, with the railroad tracks Brian described, right where he said they'd be."

"Mason doesn't strike me as someone who'd have what it takes to orchestrate a murder himself," Harry said. "He might kill in the heat of anger, but he'd have no plan. On the other hand, he sounds like the perfect patsy to help hide a body or anything Seaver wanted him to do. Someone Seaver could easily control."

Claire stood up. "I hate to leave a wonderful party, but I have some things I need to do. Debra Ann, it was great to meet you, and I hope you can resolve your situation."

"Oh, Claire, before you go, I promised Debra Ann we'd send her whatever we have on Seaver's girlfriend, Sheryl Jansen. I just texted you Debra Ann's e-mail address."

"No problem, Harry — I can't wait to see the bonus you give me *this* year!" Claire winked at me.

"It was nice meeting you, Claire." I turned back to Harry. "I can't thank you enough for the information. And I want to take advantage of your expedited firearms training program to get a concealed carry permit. What do I have to do to sign up for that?"

"If you call me next week, we'll get you going."

"Perfect. As long as I'm in this situation, I might as well do everything by the numbers."

CHAPTER 37

Southern California was entering its fall season, and while I'd been inside Harry's offices, dusk had yielded to complete darkness. Shop windows and front yards sported the ghostly apparitions, skeletons, and inflatable pumpkins of Hallowe'en, and holiday display lights were flickering to life as I opened the door to my Uber. Climbing into the Prius, I smelled lemons — the cardboard air freshener hanging from the rearview mirror must be brand new. I chatted up the driver to test his demeanor; he was friendly and talkative.

Antara was in his 40s; light-skinned with black wavy hair cut short, his face was slender and clean-shaven. Born in Morocco, he'd lived in the States since he was four — he had no trace of an accent. Antara showed me photos of his wife and four children. He'd taken the pictures at a birthday party for one of his kids, and they all looked genuinely happy. Driving for Uber was his second job — his regular employment was as a mover for a local "three men and a truck" moving company. He was trying to earn extra money for a larger home to relocate *his* family.

Comforted that I was safe, I put my time to good use as I rode back to my motel room. My burner phone was in my front pantsuit pocket, and I had to unfasten my seatbelt to reach it. I turned on the Prius's dome light to input a few speed dial numbers from my original cell phone into the burner phone, adding my essential contact information. A wholesale copy of the data wouldn't do — if I lost the burner phone, I didn't want to give up too much that was personal.

Antara stopped at the light, waiting for the green. I barely caught the old GMC heavy-duty stake-bed truck bearing down on us from the corner of my eye. The vehicle wasn't out of place in the heavily industrial area we were passing through — assuming it would turn and wheel in behind us, I dismissed it.

Antara was tap-tap-tapping on his dash-mounted touchscreen, checking his Uber app for new ride requests. I doubt he ever saw the approaching truck. I was squinting at the burner phone screen, trying to get my fingertips to activate the display's tiny icons.

Suddenly, there was a tremendous *BAMM!* as the window beside me exploded.

My phone shot into the air as I felt an enormous jolt. My head jerked to the side, and my hands flew up.

Instantly, everything around me was spinning and tumbling and bouncing in surreal slow motion — tiny crystals of shattered glass glittered in the air.

Blinding spears of light stabbed into the abrupt darkness. The nose of the truck had obliterated the warm yellow glow of the streetlamp. In its place, a shaft of white-hot glare from a single headlight cut through the Prius' interior.

My seat and the floor beneath me tilted at a crazy angle. I slammed against the inside door panel on the opposite end of the seat cushion, then flopped like a rag doll on top of the door handle.

The harsh, bright light disappeared as I tumbled, morphing the appearance of all I could see into dark shades of gray.

I instinctively curled into a fetal position.

Our vehicle was rocking on its passenger doors, popping out and smashing the glass in the windows, the sheet metal and glass granules grinding on the asphalt as the car finally settled.

The world became deathly silent for just a moment.

Then, total blackness.

And there I was, with Mom, Dad, and Eddie, sitting cross-legged on the top of our headstone. Not long after we'd interred Mom here, I discovered it was best to come just before dawn. If you caught a day right before the mowers came, the just-beginning-to-curl tips of the grass blades glistened in the walkways' indirect lighting. Sprinklers running during the night would bedew the entire area. The sparkling surface lay undisturbed by anyone else's footprints for more than an acre surrounding you.

And then, you'd wait for that first glow of daylight sneaking up over the trees on the horizon as the morning breezes began their stirring. You could jump up and sit on Dad's side of the marker as you swung your heels on the backside of the monument. From there, you'd watch as tiny slivers of light began slicing through the leaves of the lower branches, now rustling slightly, on our stalwart oak. I would pretend that the start of this day was new to me. I was witnessing the earliest dawn of man, as the first sentient being ever to see our rising sun, marveling at the glorious sight.

The light rays were becoming more insistent, and I closed my eyes tightly against their harshness.

Squinting my eyes slowly open again, I found myself transported back to a crumpled and chaotic world, confusion surrounding me. Awakening made me painfully aware of a shrill, brain-piercing screaming. It took me a second to realize the shrieking was coming from between my lips, and when I stopped, the throbbing in my head eased a little.

But the moans I heard weren't from me — those came from somewhere to the front and right of me.

Then, the sound of a heavy-duty engine, maybe a diesel, very close and revving up, interrupted the momentary calm. My stomach felt queasy as the Prius rocked a little. I wanted to sit up but couldn't — the violent collision had crushed the rear door on the driver's side so far inward that I had no room.

As I tried to right myself, my grip kept slipping; I saw that my hand was covered in blood, slashed by the sharp edges of the bent metal and broken glass.

Completely disoriented and feeling nauseated, I lost for a moment my understanding of what was up and what was down — I felt trapped and intensely claustrophobic. It took me several minutes to realize the brightness that woke me wasn't from the car's dome light. It was coming through the smashed door window, now at the top of the Prius, from a halogen fixture mounted on a pole directly above me.

As the ringing in my ears subsided, I began to hear sounds from the street — traffic, the murmur of voices, and sirens approaching.

As I looked toward my new version of "up," I realized both side-curtain airbags had deployed. A gap was growing between them as they deflated, and the crash had blown out the entire rear window of the Prius; I had an escape route.

I touched my head and knew it was bleeding on my right side. Sharp pains were shooting through my hip at regular intervals. My left wrist was sore and had no strength, collapsing under me when I tried to push myself up with it. The sense of being in a dream persisted, and I felt an emotional detachment from anything logic told me was real.

A pair of muscular forearms reached through the opening between the airbags. I raised my hands toward them, and they caught me underneath both arms to pull me out. Two athletic men carried me to the sidewalk and sat me gently on a blanket. It was hard to make out the individual voices. My head was swimming, my temples throbbing with a pounding headache. I did hear someone say through all the muddle, "The ambulance is on its way," and "Is there anything I can do for you, ma'am?"

A sudden wave of panic came over me when I realized I still had that unregistered .38 revolver in my purse. That my brain considered the weapon the utmost priority at that moment should have warned me I wasn't thinking clearly. Still, I tried to stand up, but concerned hands stopped me, and I tottered back to the ground.

"I need my purse; my medications are in it," I fibbed.

"It's pretty smashed up in there," a disembodied voice said, "but I'll see if I can find it — is there anything else you need while I'm looking?"

"Yes, I have two cell phones, mine and my work phone. If you can find them, I would appreciate it *so* much."

I watched as a slender, rangy young man leaned way over through the rear window area and, after rummaging around, pulled out my purse, then one phone, and finally the other. He brought them to me, kneeling and placing my handbag beside me on the sidewalk. Holding one phone out to me, he laid the other on the purse. In my dazed state, the thought came to me — I wanted to kiss him. But I was still bleeding and thought better of it. All I could do instead was say, "Thank you."

He seemed concerned.

"You are most welcome. I hope you're going to be okay…."

"I'll be fine," I replied, though I hadn't convinced myself. "How is the driver?"

"He's in terrible shape, ma'am. He's unconscious. We can see he's breathing, but he's pinned in. The fire department is going to have to get him out. My friends are trying to keep pressure on the places we can see he's bleeding, but he needs to get to a hospital quick."

"What happened? Who hit us? Where's the truck?"

"It was a hit-and-run, ma'am. We were behind you and saw the truck veer off from the side street straight at you. We thought it would hit us, too. After the collision, his engine was smoking, and the radiator sprayed anti-freeze everywhere.

"But he backed up and hauled ass down that other street. Some of the guys from our school followed him down there, but they were on foot and couldn't catch up to him. He only made it a few blocks, ditched the truck in the middle of the road, and took off on foot. My buddies saw a navy Dodge Charger pick him up and drive off; it must have been going ninety miles an hour."

He looked up as more colored lights washed over the scene. "Look, the police, fire department, and ambulances are here. They're telling us we need to move out of the way. They'll take care of you now."

And then the young man was gone, folded into the crowd before I could even ask his name.

"*My God...,*" I said out loud, the thought occurring to me for the first time. My head was still spinning and aching, and I knew it wasn't working quite right, but ... *had somebody just tried to kill me?*

CHAPTER 38

A paramedic kneeled beside me, flashing a small penlight into each eye as he asked where I was experiencing pain.

"I think I sprained my left wrist, and my side and left hip hurt. I hit my head on something."

The street resonated with the chugging of a pump and the squealing of the hydraulics as firefighters worked the jaws of life to free the Uber driver less than fifty feet from us. I worried for Antara, angered that our assailants treated him as nothing more than an inconsequential sacrifice in their attempt on my life. I hoped he would come out of this without suffering more than he already had, and I was concerned for his family. "Is the driver going to be alright?" I asked, raising my voice over the noise of the extraction machinery. The effort amped up the pressure in my aching head.

"Too soon to tell," the EMT replied. "Once they have him out of the vehicle, we'll know more."

The paramedic took my right wrist to get my pulse and wrapped a blood pressure cuff around my upper right arm. "Do you have a headache?"

"Yes … Throbbing. I want to close my eyes and lie down."

"Do you feel nauseous?"

I slowly shook my head no – I had earlier, but it passed.

"How many fingers do you see?"

"Three."

"Are you dizzy or feeling faint?"

"I'm kind of woozy."

"Are you on any medications, like blood thinners or anything for your heart?"

"No."

"Do you have a pacemaker, or have you had stents implanted?"

"No, nothing like that."

After gathering my answers and vital signs, he asked, "Were you wearing a seatbelt?"

"I was," I said, "but I'd just unfastened it so I could get to my cell phone right before the accident."

"I'm as big a proponent of wearing seatbelts as there is. Too many bad things happen when people don't wear them…."

"But…," I protested.

"… but in this case, not having one on probably saved your life," he confided. "I understand a heavy truck hit you dead center where you sat."

"I think so," I said, remembering the enormous shadow before the collision.

"That the Prius wasn't moving forward, and your body was free to move sideways likely helped mitigate some of the energy in the impact."

The thought that a mere stroke of luck had saved me was sobering. "So, it's good I was unfastened, then…," I said.

"But don't tell anyone you heard that from me." He smiled gently. "Your overall odds are still far better with your seatbelt on." He clicked off his penlight. "You've suffered a concussion and need to go to the hospital. The doctors will check you for internal bleeding or injuries."

"I can't…," I started.

"Concussions are tricky. They mess with your judgment. Football players end up with CTE because they think they can go right back into games after suffering one. It's not worth taking the chance. I've applied butterfly bandages to your head wound. But you'll need further attention to manage any scarring; someone should look at that wrist. Is there a hospital you'd prefer we take you to?"

"Look, I appreciate everything you've done, but I can't go to the hospital."

I didn't want to be separated from my purse or have anyone looking through it. "I want to see my regular doctor; she'll provide me with whatever treatment I need."

"From what I can tell, your concussion was serious. You cannot drive or operate any equipment that has the potential to harm you or anyone else."

"I understand — I'll be good," I said.

"I can't give you anything for your headache. You can't take anything yourself because those medicines can increase internal bleeding. They can also mask symptoms of other serious conditions. You can't engage in any strenuous or stressful activity. You need adult supervision for the next seventy-two hours — no exceptions. You really should go to the hospital."

Hospitals are where people go to have their life savings exhausted by corporations and then die, I thought. I recognized feelings about Dad's death were coloring my thinking. And I understood the paramedic was doing his job and might have a point. Still, beyond having an unpermitted weapon concealed in my purse, I had no interest in being admitted to a hospital under my name. Once there, I'd be a stationary target, potentially too drugged to know what was happening to me, much less defend myself.

"Okay, I'll call a friend." I thought of Cathy.

"I can't force you to go to the emergency room," the paramedic said sternly, "but you're not in good shape. If you go anywhere else, it would be against medical advice. You'll have to sign this release form. Enter all your information at the top and sign it at the bottom."

It struck me that, for all his concerns, he thought I was lucid enough to sign a legal document, so I completed the form and handed it over. As the EMT took it, he said, "Let's see if you can stand, but take it slowly and lean on me if you have to."

I gingerly stood up and walked forward and then back a few steps. Aside from a pronounced limp caused by the pain in my left hip and the general soreness in my side, I was mobile again. The paramedic told me to call 911 if I experienced new or increased symptoms. After first advising me again against any medication, he relented, saying I could take Tylenol sparingly for the pain until a doctor could see me. Then he left to help extract the Uber driver.

I wanted to see how Antara was faring, but the firefighters and paramedics weren't allowing anyone to get close. The atmosphere around the scene was tense, and my read of body language told me the driver's situation was dire. I unzipped the top of my purse and tucked both cell phones inside.

Surveying my surroundings, I saw uniformed police officers interviewing crowd members for witness statements. I realized they'd be over to talk to me next. An interview would lead to a paper report stating that I was still alive, with other information I didn't want Strike Response to have. I had to get out of there.

It bothered me immensely that I was abandoning the Uber driver before I knew he'd be okay, but what could I do? "To what hospital will they take him?" I asked the nearest medical tech.

"They'll go to Sharp Memorial Level II trauma center — it's the closest," the paramedic replied. I quickly noted the location to check on Antara's status later.

Moving closer to the crowd, I merged in with it. Through the multitude of people around us, I could see a Metro bus idling in the backed-up traffic, and that seemed to me the safest way out of the area. I began making my way to the bus. My somewhat confused calculation was that they would need a hell of a truck to take out something that big, and I could monitor and assess anyone getting on board after me. If any passenger accosted me, I could make a scene in front of the other riders — and I still had the .38 in my purse.

I kept my seat through the next seven stops until I felt better and confident there wasn't any threat to me on the bus. I got off near a Starbucks, went inside, and sat there for a few minutes. Whatever shock I'd experienced was wearing off, and my thigh and ribs were becoming even sorer. I wanted to lie flat on my back on the bed in my room. But how was I going to get back to my temporary home?

A sudden wave of nausea passed through me as I realized that, but for her dinner date, that would be Cathy out there on the street. It would have been *her* bloodied and broken body that the fire crew would pry from that mass of shattered glass and crumpled metal.

My increasing paranoia didn't yet extend to thinking all unfamiliar Uber drivers were out to get me. I thought about calling another rideshare rather than putting Cathy at risk. But I didn't want to answer questions from company supervisors about the earlier crash if they'd flagged my Uber account. And if Strike Response was monitoring rideshares, I didn't want them to know their attempt to kill me had gone awry.

It was just past nine-thirty. Cathy's dinner date should be over. I checked my burner phone, glad it was still working. I called Cathy, letting her know enough about what had happened so she could decide whether to pick me up.

"Where are you now?" Cathy didn't hesitate, her voice conveying both urgency and concern.

"I hopped on a city bus just to make sure no one followed me, and I ended up at a Starbucks," I said.

"You should be safe until the dust settles," Cathy calculated, "at least until officers file the accident reports or local journalists pick it up from the police blotter. Which Starbucks are you at? I'm coming to get you."

"I'm at the Bancroft exit on I-5."

"Oh, I know it — give me fifteen minutes," Cathy said, and we signed off.

While waiting for Cathy, I called Harry Sanderson's office. His receptionist was working late and put me straight through.

"The Uber I was just riding in got rammed in the side by a construction vehicle right after I left your office," I told Harry. "I'm pretty sure it was no accident. You mentioned that Strike Response was watching your offices, and I wanted to let you know they're doing more than that. I'm just winging it here, but given the attempt was so clumsy, I'm guessing it was a spur-of-the-moment thing they cooked up on the fly."

"That fits their style — but are *you* okay?" Harry was genuinely disturbed by the news.

My ribs were reminding me how sore they were, but I wasn't calling him to complain. "Thanks for asking, but I'm alright; dinged up a little, but I'll survive. I'm not as sure about the driver. Fortune was on my side. I'd unfastened my seatbelt a few moments before, or I'm sure the truck would have crushed me."

"Dammit, Debra Ann, this is on me. If I'd known they were that deeply involved before we met, I'd have gotten together with you away from the office. We knew they'd been hanging around here, but until now, they've been harmless."

"It's not your fault, Harry. They would have gotten to me somehow. It hadn't registered that they'd seriously want to kill me. I won't be that ignorant going forward."

"Strike Response may have posted you to their internal 'be on the lookout' list," Harry replied. "The operative they assigned to my place could have gotten lucky and spotted you going in or out."

"I'm not so sure this is about me explicitly. It doesn't make sense to kill me now. Seaver heard I have letters from Brian, but as far as the doctor would know, they describe only the night Brian witnessed Seaver moving the body. Seaver wouldn't believe that Brian could have told me anything that revealed who beat him to death.

"No, I think I ended up in Strike Force's crosshairs because Darrell Woodson and I began working together."

"OK, but why?"

"Think about it strictly from Seaver's perspective — all of this is about Theresa's money. Woodson was the original reason Seaver couldn't get his hands on the ex-wife's inheritance. Weeks ago, the DA tied up the estate again on Woodson's behalf. When Seaver asks his Magic 8 Ball who's the greatest barrier to him getting that money, it keeps coming up with "Woodson." Seaver may have hired Strike Response to target anyone in Woodson's circle, including your team. If Strike Response is getting more aggressive, coming after me may not be the end of it."

"Hmmm, sounds like I need to be taking my client meetings elsewhere for a while," Harry replied. "Thanks for the heads-up, Debra Ann. I suspect you'll keep going after them, and I won't try to dissuade you. But be careful. And let me know if we can help."

"Thanks, Harry, I'll do that."

By this time, Cathy had arrived. I flagged her down, and she and I headed to my motel room. At my request, when we arrived, she circled the block twice and then made an exploratory pass through the motel parking lot.

Only then did I feel comfortable being left alone.

THE WRITINGS OF
AVRIL MARIA SERENE

CHAPTER 39

It was almost ten-thirty by the time I got back to my room. I left a message with Dr. Merriman's answering service that I'd been in a severe accident and needed an appointment as soon as possible.

The bed was calling out to me. Lying down, I intended to take a brief nap before showering and changing. Instead, the maid vacuuming the hall carpet awakened me at nine-thirty the following morning.

The extra sleep hadn't helped — when I opened my eyes, I discovered I could barely raise my head. All the bones and muscles in my body seemed sore; every movement was painful.

Slowly, I rolled out of bed and stumbled into the shower. Though not a cure-all, the warm water provided welcome relief. I stayed under the soothing spray for as long as I could before it turned me into a head-to-toe raisin.

The doctor's office called back and offered me an appointment at one o'clock. I filled the time by working on a project from Doug Stein's list. But I found it frustrating. I had to push the words to the page because they weren't flowing naturally. Still, I'd imposed a deadline on myself, a habit I developed to ensure the work got done and to keep me from falling into bad habits.

The buzzing of my cell phone alarm was a welcome interruption, notifying me it was time to call Cathy for the drive to Dr. Merriman's office.

Cathy had the car radio on, and we were about halfway to the medical complex when the newscaster announced the death of the Uber driver involved in the hit-and-run yesterday. The anchor's description matched what I knew of Antara — a married father of four driving the rideshare as his second job.

"*Oh, no…,*" My shoulders sagged. An image from such a short time ago flashed to mind: Antara's broad smile as he passed photos of his family over his shoulder to me, so proud of them and himself.

As the news hit home, I felt a surge of guilt. It wasn't just that I'd survived and Antara hadn't; it was that he'd gotten caught up in an attack meant for me and over so little. His family lost their father and husband, and he'd given up his life over a rideshare fare.

Cathy and I rode the rest of the way in silence as I tried to rationalize away my part in Antara's killing. My inner voice reminded me that other people did this to him. I wanted to convince myself that the best thing I could do, maybe the only thing, was to finish what I started and bring this man and his family justice. But the exercise merely traded feelings of inadequacy for some of the guilt. I still felt hollow inside.

<hr>

"Debra Ann, it's nice to see you again," Dr. Merriman said, "but I'm sorry to hear you were in quite an accident."

"Yes, Doctor, but it could have been much worse. I heard over the radio on my way here that the driver of the Uber I was in didn't make it. The people who did this may have been after me. I feel so horrible about putting him in that position. I'm sure this is because of a story I'm writing." As I relayed what had happened to the doctor, I felt the emptiness again in the center of my chest.

"Are you saying this *wasn't* an accident — that it was intentional?" Dr. Merriman asked as she took a blood sample. "It's such a high-risk thing those drivers do."

I could only nod as Dr. Merriman pulled a tiny flashlight out of her breast pocket and quickly scanned my pupils.

"Well, let's see what we need to do to get you fixed up."

Once Dr. Merriman had examined me and determined what services I needed, the radiologist took X-rays, and I underwent a spinal tap to test for any bleeding in the brain. I rested for an hour while the medical staff analyzed the images and fluids, and Dr. Merriman came to see me again.

"I know you're in a lot of pain, but from what I can see so far, everything looks good, considering what happened. I'd file most of the damage under 'very lucky.' It amazes me you weren't more badly injured. You really should have gone to the hospital. The dangers to the human body inherent to a traffic accident where airbags deploy are unimaginable."

"I understand — I hope I never have to apply the lessons learned from this, but if I do, I'll go to the hospital," I promised. *And I hope I won't be carrying a gun without a permit*, I thought to myself.

"Concussions and the onset of shock don't lead to good decision-making. You've suffered a significant impact to your brain, though not as severe as it might have been, given what happened to you. The good news is you seemed to have survived without apparent permanent injuries, although it is a little too soon to say for sure. I'll know more after you undergo a CT scan or an MRI.

"Besides the concussion, you have a couple of badly bruised ribs, a sprained left wrist, several cuts on your scalp, and a deep thigh bruise. The X-rays don't show any structural damage to your hip, but I want to schedule a follow-up in two weeks for another look. I'll fit you with a wrist brace and apply stitches to the lacerations in your head. Then we'll get you a thigh sleeve to use when walking or otherwise active, along with instructions for icing the bruising on your thigh and ribs."

"How long will the pain last?"

"The ribs and thigh bruise will cause you the most pain over the longer term, and you'll be in some discomfort for a month to six weeks. There isn't much I can do to help you with either problem.

"We'll provide antibiotics samples you'll take at home; those will help with any infection. I will also give you a prescription for a painkiller. I must warn you that Tylenol 3 differs from the over-the-counter version; it contains codeine."

"Is codeine addictive? I can't remember."

"Yes. You want to take the tablets sparingly and only as necessary. That said, you'll find the prescription effectively fights the pain. Take it easy over the coming week. No physical work and stay away from anything that causes stress."

"I understand — no pickleball for a while." I smiled in acknowledgment.

I wouldn't share with Dr. Merriman that I'd instead be chasing down the driver of that truck — Antara's killer was going to answer for what they did to him.

CHAPTER 40

Cathy was ferrying me back to my motel room after a trip to the CVS to get Dr. Merriman's prescriptions filled. While there, I'd grabbed a box of Salonpas pain patches and a wrap for my ribs.

Once back on the road, I called Doug Stein for a big favor.

"Hi, Doug," I said as he picked up. "I've got you on speakerphone. I'm with Cathy Andreesen."

"Hi, Cathy, it's been far too long since we last talked. I miss those conversations we used to have over lunch. How have you been?"

"Doug, it's good to hear your voice again. I'm fine, enjoying retirement. But I must admit that the little bit of excitement Debra Ann has brought into my life makes me wish I was still in the game. Let's talk later and see if we can find an excuse to get together."

"Still at the same number?"

"Same phone, same house, same taste for a good Chardonnay, in case you want to stop by," Cathy said, laughing.

"I'll bring a bottle or two, and we can talk shop and the good ol' days. You wouldn't recognize this place — it was so much better when the two of you were here. But I know you didn't call to reminisce…."

"I'm a little banged up," I explained, "and Cathy's driving me home to recuperate, or else we'd be having this conversation over breakfast."

"Wait, 'recuperate?' That can't be good…."

With that, I told Doug about the Uber collision, Antara's death, and what had happened since.

"You warned me about Strike Response, and they're in this up to their eyeballs. The driver of the truck that rammed us was taken from the scene by a navy blue Dodge. I need to call Marci to confirm, but most likely, it was the Strike Response vehicle you looked up for me earlier. I'm pretty sure they were trying to kill me, but they murdered the Uber driver instead."

"Jesus, Debra Ann." Doug's voice revealed he hadn't expected the turn events had taken. "I shouldn't be surprised. I don't know if Strike Response as an organization would have sanctioned such a crude attempt at a hit. However, I've heard rumors of their thugs going rogue and doing things like that for bragging rights within the company. No discipline at all."

"Which brings me to why I'm calling. After your warning, I talked with Harry Sanderson — I didn't realize how well you knew each other — and I did some surfing on the 'Net. There are whispers about Strike Response engaging in nasty business over the years. But otherwise, they've flown totally under the radar. I found their moniker and names of their known associates sprinkled here and there. Still, no one's ever written anything in-depth about them. Would you be willing to help me expose these bastards — maybe get some assistance for Antara's family?"

"Sure, but just so you know," Doug cautioned, "they get away with these things because they know where quite a few influential people keep their dirty laundry. Do you remember when John Lynch, the owner of the *Union-Tribune* at the time, tried to buy the mayor's election in 2012? He wanted to blow Carl DeMaio, the city councilman, past the voters, hoping that with the paper's support, no one would look too hard at him.

"The people who created the brute force side of Strike Response have connections to those two, among others who run San Diego, ties that go back way before then. Rumor says the dirt the company has on them would upend city government. That's why you're not seeing anything about Strike Response from the paper … so long as Strike Response stays local, no one can touch them."

I had to think back to my days at the *Union-Tribune*.

"I remember Lynch's involvement in that race. Lynch had other shady dealings. I recall him putting his massive thumb on the scale to con the public into a new downtown football stadium and convention center — right next to his business partner's hotels, of course. I thought all the paper's staff would walk when they fired Tim Sullivan for not supporting the stadium scam."

"You hadn't been gone from the paper long when Tim passed… helluva sportswriter; lost a great one when he left."

"So many of the good ones quit when they let him go. You couldn't blame them; as reporters, we had to clear every line we were even thinking about writing with management — Lynch didn't want any of his cronies mentioned in a bad light. We couldn't investigate the raging dumpster fire right in our backyard. The same thing's been happening with Bezos at the *Washington Post* for a long time."

"It was booted-out ex-cops and corrupt officers still on the force who provided all the backroom rubber-hosing to back up Lynch," Doug explained. "Their enforcer business was so lucrative they established an armed security company — they needed something legitimate as cover. It eventually merged with a covert operations entity some questionable ex-Feds had put together. They moved their headquarters here and became Strike Response."

As he spoke, the wheels in my head were turning.

"I've got a half-baked idea for an end-around to whatever protection the paper still provides Strike Response. Yesterday's events have slowed me down. I've got eyes on me, and I already have too many things going on with Seaver and Pierce to do a full-blown exposé myself. But you have the resources of the paper behind you, such as they are, and Strike Response's sights aren't set on you yet."

"You've got my full attention. It'd be a great story if there's a way we can tell it."

"So, Antara's death is a murder investigation now. Witnesses at the scene didn't get the plates on that Dodge, but *we* have them. Suppose we come at this sideways — sneak it past Dark as a human-interest story about a hardworking immigrant and family man intentionally killed on the job. I didn't hang around to give the responding officers my name so Dark wouldn't know I was involved. The paper will print it because it makes them look compassionate ahead of the holidays."

"That shouldn't be too hard a sell," Doug mused. "Exactly the kind of soft filler the paper likes these days."

"Then you run a follow-up piece," I continued, "saying that an anonymous source — me — has given you those plate numbers tying that vehicle back to Strike Response."

"Got it. Dark won't be able to bury something like that, having stirred up public interest. And then another follow-on, this time planting the seed that a local journalist investigating serial killings in the area was riding in that Uber. They wish to remain anonymous because of the ongoing threat against their life. That should generate some interest from the local affiliates of the national networks. We'll need to time it so you stay safe since they'll eventually learn who you are."

"Once they find me out, you could add me to the byline — that should get under Dark's skin — and we'll have our launch platform for publishing whatever you turn up on Strike Response. *And* whatever I learn from my Seaver investigation once I confirm he's their client. We can work it out once we get to that point."

"Now, that sounds like a plan!" I could hear the excitement in Doug's voice. "Gigging Dark makes for icing on the cake, but putting Strike Response out of business would be a genuine public service. I'll write up the human-interest piece on Antara and start digging deeper into Strike Response."

"It's great to be doing real work together again, Doug. I'll keep in touch so we can exchange notes."

As I hung up, Cathy looked over at me enviously. "I know you're hurting, but I can see all this is pumping you up. I must admit I'm a little jealous — do let me know if there's anything I can contribute."

Once back in my temporary quarters, I went straight to bed. I tossed and turned through the rest of the afternoon, evening, and night, trying to find a position that didn't aggravate my rib pain.

I gave up trying and watched some late-night TV. I enjoyed Jimmy Fallon's monologue even while learning how much my ribs hurt when I laughed. But that problem was the least of my challenges — until they locked away whoever was trying to kill me, I probably wouldn't be laughing a whole lot.

I finally fell into a deep slumber after taking Tylenol 3s and returning to bed around two-thirty. When I awoke at seven, I felt better than I had the day before. My joints were still stiff and achy, and my thigh and ribs were hurting, but after I got moving, the pain became bearable for longer stretches.

While checking my messages, I saw a text from a number I didn't recognize. It started with "The first step in a process:" followed by a link to a brief news article on the *Union-Tribune's* website, updated yesterday morning. The piece described a police report of an overnight break-in and theft at Strike Response's main office. Sometime before dawn, one hundred weapons and a hundred thousand rounds of ammunition turned up missing. The report listed the value of the stolen property at nearly four hundred thousand dollars — the priciest firearms theft ever reported in the San Diego area.

Authorities were scrambling, canvassing pawn shops, weapon resale outlets, and gun shows, trying to locate the stolen items. Captain Jerrod Jarvis of SDPD had put out a request on local TV for the public's assistance. The article's final paragraph included an odd tidbit: Someone, presumably the thief, had splashed paint stripper on the hoods of Strike Response's vehicles.

A Marilyn Monroe quote closed the text message: "'If I'd observed all the rules, I'd never have got anywhere.'"

The quote told me it was from Harry, but I wasn't sure what to do with the information. *Was Harry trying to tell me that his team had something to do with that break-in?* The unknown number and obscure text might be his way of letting me know that whatever he was into could have severe repercussions, which he wanted to avoid. I took it as Harry's discreet way of telling me not to worry, that he and his crew were on top of things. But to what end, I had *no* clue. He'd have called me directly if he'd been able to tell me more. I made a mental note that if the answer didn't present itself over the next few days, I'd ask Harry as soon as we were in a private setting.

The linked article had Doug Stein's byline, so my fellow reporter already knew about the break-in. Still, I forwarded the message in its entirety to him anyway.

Doug would want to be aware of Harry's interest in Strike Response.

CHAPTER 41

Before I got back in the traces to move my story — *stories?* — along, I needed to take care of some things that had gotten left behind. My first task for this morning was to return to my apartment and retrieve a copy of my health insurance policy. I also wanted to grab a few other items I'd missed when packing to leave the first time.

While recognizing the danger, I gave careful thought to going back. It had been some time since Strike Response had seen any activity at my place, and they'd just tried to kill me. Someone looking at that wrecked Prius wouldn't expect the passenger to be walking around for a while afterward, if ever. If I *were* alive, they wouldn't expect me to re-appear in an apartment they'd been so obviously monitoring, especially this soon after a murder attempt. There was no reason for them to invest billable time watching my place.

Sending someone else to collect my items could put the person helping me in danger, and what happened to Antara weighed heavily on my mind. I couldn't ask Marci because she was on crutches. I wasn't in that much better shape, but I *was* more mobile. Besides, I was in no hurry to hear, "I told you so." There were no other officers I trusted with my personal effects.

I thought about asking Harry if he could loan me some protection. But, given his last message, it seemed he wanted to keep our relationship low-profile. I could be in and out quickly before Strike Response could react to any notification from recording devices they'd planted, and I still had Dad's .38.

I'd debated having Cathy drive me because of Antara's death, but I explained what I wanted to do and why before I asked her. She was entirely on board even after I apprised her of the risks.

"Would you mind driving around the block?" I asked as we approached my apartment complex. "I want to keep both of us safe and ensure we don't have any unwanted onlookers."

Once satisfied that no surprises awaited me in the general vicinity, I made another request. "Can you make a run through the parking lot? I need to see what vehicles are back there. And then, would you pull around to the front of the building to let me out?"

As I opened the door of the Prius, I wanted one more thing.

"Last request, I promise — could you wait while I retrieve some of my things? It won't take me too long."

"No problem. Spend as much time as you think necessary. I'm going to cruise the neighborhood for anything unusual. Keep your throwaway phone on, and I'll call if you need to get out of there."

I tried to hurry as I walked from Cathy's car to my apartment, but my ribs fiercely complained when I walked too fast. My heart leaped into my throat when I got to my apartment door. The handle lock on my front door was latched. But the key turned too smoothly when I twisted it in the deadbolt keyhole — the last person through that door hadn't locked it. Someone had been in my apartment since I was last here.

I had to catch my breath and think, but not before I grabbed the loaded .38 out of my purse. I debated whether I should go in at all. That locked handle suggested whoever was there had left, but an intruder could have set it from the inside to keep anyone from walking in on them — meaning they were still there. Of course, there were more innocent possibilities. Maybe the landlord had to chase down a water leak.

I took two deep breaths, fighting back the pain they caused. Standing to one side beyond the doorway frame, I tried to keep my shaking hand from rattling the keys. Slowly and carefully, I unlocked the handle and turned it with my still-sore left hand, revolver in my right, until the catch released. I crouched down so my head was at doorknob level, holding back the urge to cry out at the stabbing pain in my side.

I opened the door about one-quarter of an inch. Taking another breath, I listened intently for any sounds from the apartment. Hearing nothing, I shoved the door open with my left knee. Both hands now tightly on the revolver, I raised my body to a half-crouch. As I entered, I scooted to the right side of the doorway, lowering myself again. I carefully surveyed what I could see of my apartment, even as I endured another flash of pain.

Oh, please, no, I thought as I looked over what invaders had done to my once tidy and safe abode, simultaneously angry and scared to death. The place was in an absolute shambles. The trespassers had dumped drawer and shelf contents on the floor, left cabinets and drawers open, and tossed furniture cushions about.

I suddenly realized I'd been squatting there, pointing a revolver at an unarmed refrigerator, for several moments as I assessed the mess. Cautiously, trembling in fear, I methodically walked through the bedroom, office, closets, and bath areas. I kept my eyes constantly bouncing from what was in front of my feet so I wouldn't step on anything to the broader view of the hall and bedrooms. Whoever broke in had also torn apart the other spaces. They'd dumped the medicine cabinet contents into the sink and tub and emptied the dresser drawers onto the floor. They'd even taken the clothes in the closet off their hangers and thrown them in piles onto the mattress, now skewed halfway off the bed frame.

In the bedroom I used for my office, the intruders had dumped all of Dad's boxes onto the carpet. They'd rifled through the desk and credenza, but fortunately, I'd taken my laptop, backup hard drives, and flash drives with me when I'd first gone to the motel.

Convinced that I was alone in my apartment now, I collapsed cross-legged onto one of the few bare spots left on the carpet in the living room. Dropping the gun beside me, I cradled my face in both hands. The position amplified my rib pain, and I reacted by sharply inhaling. Utterly defeated and exhausted, I just wanted to sit there and cry.

But the self-pity party would have to be postponed. Cathy was waiting, and I didn't know if Strike Response had left signaling devices that I couldn't see to alert them of my entry. I'd need to take still photos of the apartment's condition with my burner phone. I'd send those to Marci instead of filing an official police report. I didn't want to give my motel address to a random officer whose notes would end up in digital form within the department's databases. The inroads Strike Response operatives might have made into the department and the information they could access still worried me.

Getting myself back together, I carefully rose from the floor, breathing heavily through the pain. I made a complete walkthrough of the place, taking photos and a video using the cell phone. I could review the footage and thoroughly inventory the damage once I returned to the motel room.

The personal papers I'd come for weren't hard to find in all the turmoil. The folders I'd kept them in were on the kitchen table, their contents spread across the surface. I had to assume the intruders had photographed or copied any critical personal and private information. Otherwise, had they taken the papers with them, it would have forced me to replace or cancel accounts and change what information I could, rendering at least some of what they'd copied useless. Once I returned to my hotel room, I would do what I could to make that happen anyway. I haphazardly tossed everything back into the folders to sort out later, placing them near the front door.

Next, I gathered the clothes, shoes, and personal items I wanted into a small carry-on bag, moving slowly to avoid further aggravating my ribs. Though the apartment looked like a tornado had passed through, the good news was that not much appeared severely damaged. My uninvited guests hadn't broken the glass in the picture frames nor slashed the couch cushions or mattress — it didn't seem they were trying to intimidate me or send a message. They'd moved stereo components but didn't harm the units. They'd fully extended the TV from the wall on its mounting arm, but there was no sign the intruders had otherwise tampered with it. Nothing seemed to be missing.

Their sole purpose for breaking in seemed to be information-gathering. They might notice the missing folders I'd taken from the table if they came back. Hopefully, they wouldn't. Regardless, it made no sense to advertise further that I'd been back here. I didn't want them to believe I might have brought anything new to the apartment they'd like to find. I decided not to straighten anything up.

I texted Cathy that I was on my way out. Suitcase and folders in one hand and holding my ribs with the other, I headed out the front door of the complex to her Prius, now waiting at the curb. As we made our way to the motel, we kept a vigilant eye for any sign that someone might be following.

Back in my room, I swallowed two more Tylenol 3s and tucked my belongings away. I texted Marci, attaching pictures of the disarray in my apartment, unsure how well she'd take the news. I also attached the photos of the Dodge Charger, Mustang, and Transit van I'd initially sent to Doug Stein to identify. "Marci, this is what I came home to this morning. I understood what you said about staying out of the Seaver and Pierce murder investigations. Unfortunately, the hoods at Strike Response didn't get the memo. Seaver and Ainsworth likely hired them, and I need to look out for myself. I won't file a police report because I'm living elsewhere for now and don't want my new location in the system. Call me on the burner I'm using for this text if you want the address."

I immediately sent a follow-up text: "BTW, there was a fatal hit-and-run accident at Cabot and Miramar the day before yesterday. I was the passenger in the back seat of that Prius when the truck smashed into it and killed Antara, the Uber driver.

"The Dodge in the photo attached to my last text followed me before it happened. I'm sure it was the same one witnesses saw picking up the driver of that truck after it left the scene. I don't know if that model has an onboard GPS or how much historical data it would store. But if you can get a warrant for it, you may be able to tie it to Antara's murder. If not, there might be traffic cam images to put it at the scene.

"I had to leave - no way to know if anyone following us had mingled with the crowd."

I'd have to clear it with Harry before telling Marci about his agency's GPS tracker.

I texted Doug Stein that someone, likely Strike Response, had tossed my apartment in my absence.

It was time for the last of my housekeeping chores — finding a new motel for my temporary residence. Self-preservation seemed to demand at least some mobility. After an hour of telephone calls interwoven with Web searches, I moved from near the I-5 to just off the I-15, on the opposite side of San Diego. With Cathy providing my transportation and a lot of the labor for carrying things, it didn't take long to set up a home base at the new place. I spent the rest of the late afternoon and evening finishing the writing project I'd been working on, which was now due.

Shortly after supper, the Caller ID on my cell phone showed that Marci was calling.

"I just read in my messages when I got back to work that someone tried to kill you," Marci said, both concern and surprise coming through in her voice.

"Jesus, Debra Ann! *Are you okay?*"

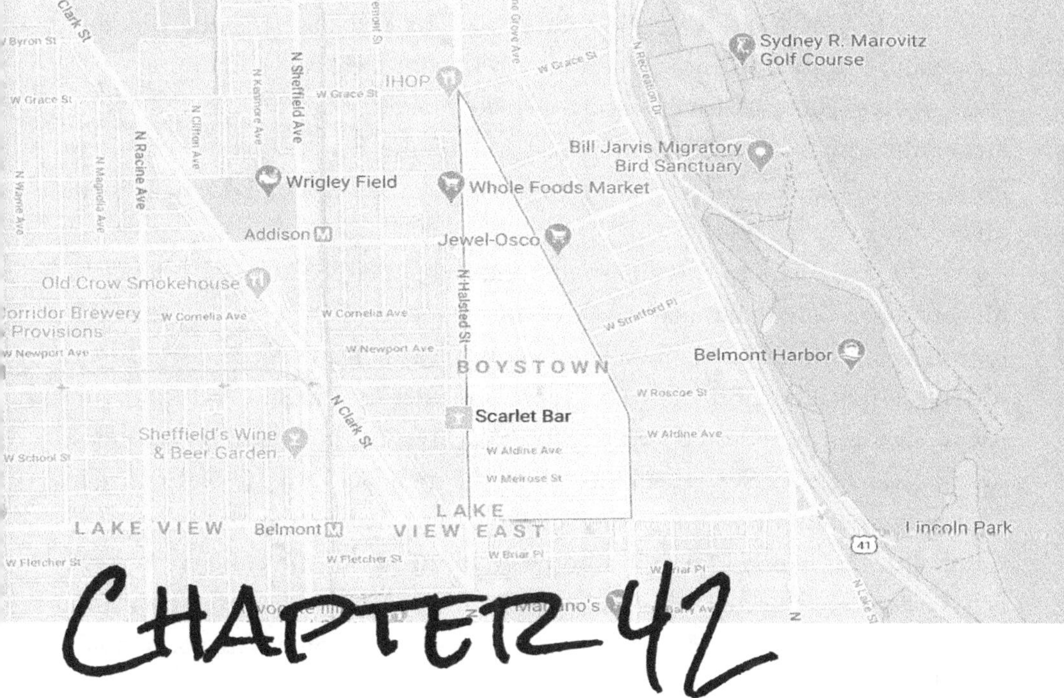

CHAPTER 42

Now that I could hear how upset Marci was at learning of the attempt on my life, I felt guilty for leaving her the information in a text.

"I didn't mean to alarm you with the message I left, but it was nice of you to call back so quickly. Am I okay? It depends how you define 'okay' … but my doctor tells me I'll live."

"Please, Debra Ann — if Strike Response is trying to kill you, this has gotten way out of hand." Marci's tone was insistent. "You need to leave this to the professionals. Whoever is after you won't miss twice. If you force me, I'll have you detained as a material witness."

I paused, unsure where she was coming from. But I gave her the benefit of the doubt. "I know you're just trying to help me stay alive, Marci … but I don't think arresting a reporter will be great for the department's latest public relations push."

"Better a PR shitstorm than me having to attend your funeral," Marci retorted.

It did seem she was still on my side.

"Hey, at least *some* good came out of the day. Just before that happened, I turned up another 'Ricky' who might have had something to do with moving Theresa Seaver's body, a Ricky Mason. They tell me he's a low-level street punk, so I'm unsure where or how he fits in. I'm still checking him out. I wanted to pass you the name in case it might help your investigation." *And mine.*

"God, I hate to encourage you under these circumstances, but 'Ricky Mason' does sound familiar…. Give me a second…. Yes, I logged it. A month ago, I took a call from a late twenties/early thirties male. He claimed to have information on the Brian Pierce murder and mentioned the name Ricky Mason. I transferred him to Homicide, but the guy hung up when the detective answered. We traced the call to the manager of a gay bathhouse in Chicago; the place is called 'Steamworks.' The manager gave his last name as Caminetti. He claimed he didn't know anything about the call and that the cell is a courtesy phone he makes available to his clients. The detective's note says, 'prank call,' so we didn't pursue it. The out-of-town bathhouse angle for a local murder case made it stick in my head."

"Thanks, Marci, that's good to know. Since you're not working that angle, I assume it's okay if I check it out." I presented it as a statement rather than a question.

"Dammit, Debra Ann, stop going around poking bears!" Marci was frustrated, even angry, with me. "Take some time off to get yourself feeling better. And call me before you do anything."

I knew just one person who could relate to the group with the information I needed and had extensive investigative experience. I wanted to talk to Claire, Harry's lead detective, but I made my first call to her boss. I didn't mention the cryptic text I'd gotten that I suspected came from him.

"Harry, I need a little help," I said instead. "But before I go there, I have a delicate question I want to ask."

"You sure I'm the one to ask about anything delicate?" Harry chuckled.

"I'm trying to run down a guy who may frequent bathhouses and seems to know something about the Ricky Mason tied into the Seaver case. I don't have any good connections in that community. I wanted to ask Claire for her advice, but I don't want to offend her by crossing any lines … you know, assuming something I shouldn't. I don't want to disrespect her privacy. Maybe she doesn't want some things — I think you called them 'personal choices' — associated with her job or discussed other than in private."

"I know your intentions are good, Debra Ann, but I don't think Claire would mind. Listen, I'm not the most sensitive guy — I know, 'Tell me it ain't so, Harry!' — and I'm not into all the stuff going on today. So, when Claire first came to me looking for work, I won't lie; it was awkward. But she's not shy about it, loud and proud, and she put it out there for what it was. That made it easier for me to come up to speed. Besides being the best hire I've ever made, I've learned from it. I'm sure she'll help you. I don't think she hits the night scene as much as she used to before the surgery, but she'll know the players and who to go to for information. She's in the office today; should I tell her you're on the line?"

"Harry, thanks again. Talking with you is always educational, to say the least. Yes, if she's got a moment, I'd appreciate chatting with her."

"I can tell you're up to something, Debra Ann. Whatever it is, be careful."

Claire picked up a few moments later. "Good evening, Debra Ann; it's great to talk with you again. Harry tells me you need assistance in an area where I'm uniquely qualified."

"Hi, Claire — to be honest, I'm in a situation where I need some questions answered, but coming off like a bull in a china shop among people I don't know wouldn't be good for anyone."

"In other words, you're an outsider in this 'area,' and if someone did share with you, you couldn't trust anything they said. Am I on the right track?

"You pretty much nailed it," I admitted.

"So, what are we working with here?"

"A month ago, SDPD's tip line gets a call from Steamworks, a gay bathhouse in Chicago. Some guy, thirtyish, claims he has information about Ricky Mason and the Brian Pierce murder. He hangs up before saying anything else; the police blow him off as a crank. But what he led with seems *too* specific, and I wonder if we missed something. Neither Mason nor Pierce would be considered public figures, so if this guy knew them, maybe he's spent some time in San Diego. Assuming he's gay, that narrows things down a little more, and I thought it wouldn't hurt to ask around and see if anyone here might know something."

"I've got friends, and I know people who know people. For something one-off like this, it's better if I did the asking. Someone straight showing up suddenly asking questions about particular individuals associated with a killing won't fly. Give me a couple of days, and I'll get back to you."

"Thanks, Claire, I'll owe you."

"No problem — we'll get together soon and exchange fashion tips," Claire said as she signed off.

True to her word, Claire called me two days later.

"Got some news for you, and you might be on to something," Claire said by way of introduction.

"Wow, that didn't take long." I was surprised at the turnaround.

"You were right about him being local and your boy's popular. He's been a regular on the scene in San Diego for a while until he took off a couple of days after police found Pierce beaten to death. He's a big, good-looking guy, gets along, and knows how to make his friends happy — his name's Mark Christensen.

"I wouldn't have guessed this, but it happens that our wannabe tough guy Ricky Mason is well-known to the same people. But he's a different story altogether. Mason's still in the closet, hitting the bars once a month, trolling for one-night hookups — pretty much a full-of-himself little jerk. The story goes that Mason took Christensen home, and a third man showed up and surprised them in the middle of the night. The street says it was a gender-phobe looking for a fight — the word hasn't gotten out yet about Pierce's letters and the blackmail setup angle.

"Either way, bad things happen to the uninvited guest. Suddenly, Christensen has cash and is in the wind with no notice. He tells friends he's leaving to visit family. However, the smart money says Christensen saw something he wasn't supposed to, and somebody paid him off to go away."

"Christensen could be a material witness, then," I mused. "Sounds like I need to go to Chicago."

"The bathhouse scene in Chi-town can get pretty rough," Claire offered. "And you're going to have the same problem fitting in there as you do here. I can help you out. I know someone — a former Chicago police officer until they outed him and kicked him off the force. His name is Dale Newsome. He knows the Boystown scene well. He can point you in the right direction and keep you safe."

"Boystown?"

Claire explained. "That's what they call the Northalsted neighborhood in East Lakeview where the LGBTQ crowd hangs out. I texted you his number. Call him first, and he'll set you up with decent accommodations. And be sure and let him know I said 'hi.'"

I caught the slightest hint of affection in Claire's voice and sensed some history between them.

Either way, I'd be making my journey before long to the Windy City by air to interview a tall man about time spent with a short blowhard.

THE WRITINGS OF
AVRIL MARIA SERENE

CHAPTER 43

D r. Merriman had warned me not to fly, but several days had passed since the collision — I'd have to take my chances. The only flight with seats available on short notice was the red-eye going out at midnight. I didn't want to disturb Cathy at that hour. So, after quickly packing a carry-on and making a few phone calls, I got in some work before pinging for an Uber and heading to the airport

In the moonless morning's wee hours, the hooded figure of a young man passed on the sidewalk across from the yellow-orange glow of the streetlamp. His eyes followed his long, angular shadow as it darted up from behind his left shoulder onto the freshly mowed lawns of the neighboring homes. It raced ahead and then faded into the darkness as he walked. His slender frame dressed head to toe in black, the man kept his nitrile-gloved hands in his jean pockets, his hoodie drawstring pulled tight, only his eyes visible. Pushing forward steadily with his head down, he glanced neither to the right nor the left. Crossing the railroad tracks, he reached the noise abatement wall on the far side. Suddenly, he made a hard right turn, disappearing into the darkness behind it.

The soles of his shoes were sanded free of any telltale tread and slipped slightly with each step onto the dew just forming upon the grass and weeds. Suddenly, the brightening beams of a vehicle's headlights approached the wall from behind him. Crouching down into the shadow the barrier provided from the streetlight on the other side, he froze until the sedan passed. Once the vehicle was a block away, he resumed his journey.

Slightly bent over, he stealthily crossed the small ditch alongside the wall, then hopped the hurricane fence enclosing the backyard of the nearest residence. Carefully crossing the yard, he avoided the children's toys scattered in his path. Slinging his body over the galvanized bar, he topped the next fence, landing catlike on the lush turf on the other side.

A yard light mounted to the top of a pole three houses to the north dimly lit the area. Slinking to the nearest corner of the modest single-story home before him, he flattened against its brick wall. Kneeling and moving away from the patio, he found the small overhang between the brick and the slab with his fingertips. Following along the joint, he felt the telltale loop of the phone line. He clipped the line with a small set of wire cutters pulled from his righthand pants pocket to prevent outgoing messages or alarm notifications.

Sliding along the wall back to the corner, he stepped softly onto the patio's smooth concrete. Feeling the sliding door's cool glass against his back and shoulder, he reached out with his left hand to test the door handle. It pulled open slightly with a gentle tug. He stepped back, waiting for a sign of any alarm or activity inside the house. His heart was pounding in his chest, like when he was just a kid breaking into his first house. Sneaking up to a home where he knew someone was inside sleeping intensified his nervousness. It was a risk he'd never take under ordinary circumstances, against his every instinct.

Hearing and seeing no response to sliding the door open, he pulled it further ajar, just enough to allow his slim physique to pass. He stepped onto the vinyl flooring of the kitchen, part of the home's layout he'd learned from two previous trips casing the house when it was empty. Pulling a foot-and-a-half length of inch-diameter steel pipe from his jacket, he held it like a baseball bat to feel its heft.

Suddenly, the refrigerator's automatic icemaker churned momentarily, spitting new cubes into its container. The muted clatter made the uninvited guest nearly jump out of his skin. Putting his chin to his chest briefly, he took a deep breath and reminded himself, *You've done this a hundred times before.*

Turning to the right from the kitchen, he knew the hall ended in two bedrooms, one on each side. The occupant used the one to the left as a home office; the visitor's destination was the other. Kneeling on the carpet before the door, the foul odor of stale, sweaty gym socks made his eyes water. Undaunted, he turned the round knob until the latch softly released. Staying low, he quickly duck-walked into the room, closing the door behind him without a sound.

A nightlight from the open bathroom had dimly illuminated the hallway; in this bedroom, only the distant yard light filtering through the closed drapes provided any way to see. He gave himself a moment to let his eyes adjust. Heavy snoring from the bed told him he wasn't alone — all was as planned. Standing up, he slowly tiptoed to the headboard and raised the pipe.

But before he could swing it, a man lying in the bed abruptly sat up, saying, "Mindwingers and gentlemen, we are about to begin our final descent as we begin our approach to Chicago's O'Hare International Airport. On the ground, skies are overcast, and the temperature is fifty-four degrees, with a brisk breeze from the northwest coming off the lake…."

My dream had been so vivid that I was confused and disoriented upon awakening. I guessed that was a side effect of my injuries and the medication I was taking.

But what the hell is a "mindwinger?" I could only shake my head and smile at the craziness my brain conjured up.

THE WRITINGS OF
AVRIL MARIA SERENE

CHAPTER 44

S everal hours of being sedentary had brought the pain and soreness back, and I downed a couple of Tylenol 3s. Once I was moving again, I began feeling much better. As I exited the plane, Dale Newsome was waiting for me, my name prominently displayed on the paper sign he was holding. He was slender, of medium height, with long, dark hair and two weeks of stubble. His circular glasses made him look more like the love child of Johnny Depp and Yoko Ono when they were both very young than a former Chicago cop. Then I had a thought — *undercover* — and that made everything fit.

"Good morning, Debra Ann. I hope you had a pleasant flight. I've put in an open-ended reservation for you at the Villa Toscana — it's in the heart of Boystown, close to everything. It's a Victorian-style bed and breakfast, and your room has a private bath. I think you'll find it clean and safe. I've talked to some friends, and we'll see that you're not disturbed."

"Thank you for picking me up, Dale. That sounds perfect. I hated traveling until Airbnbs came along, and I don't know a better way to take in local culture and color.

"I haven't scoped out a plan as to how I'll find Mr. Christensen. Claire said you might have some ideas for the best places to start."

"Not to worry, you're in capable hands. We might want to begin with the bathhouse. Hopefully, we can match the description of the man and get some idea of his tastes, habits, and maybe companions. But it's a little too early for that yet. So, what say we get you settled into your room and maybe grab breakfast? By that time, things should be stirring in the neighborhood."

"Sounds like a plan," I agreed with a smile.

As I slid into the front passenger seat of Dale's black 335i, I was grateful for having a tour guide, with no worries about trying to figure out driving in a city new to me.

The bed and breakfast Dale had chosen was ideal. Quaint but with considerably more square footage than it appeared from the street, it had been divided into fourteen rooms — many, like mine, with private bathrooms. The owner had furnished them with beautiful Victorian pieces; the flooring fabrics, wallpapers, and wall hangings were lovely and period-appropriate. It would be unfair to say the rooms were small — "cozy" would be more accurate. The best part was the bedding, which was plush and inviting. I struggled to fight off its siren song, wanting to lie down and not get up until around Christmas.

But Dale and breakfast awaited. So, after unpacking my carry-on, splashing my face with water, and refreshing my makeup, I returned downstairs and went outside to where Dale was perusing his cell phone in the car.

After taking our seats at the Kanela Breakfast Club, we chatted, dawdling over Julius Meinl coffee and cinnamon chip pancakes. Both were firsts for me and were well worth the wait. Dale and I exchanged stories about our past lives — *did Claire know her feelings for Dale were reciprocated, even after all the changes?* — until ten-thirty, when we agreed it was time to go to work.

On the way to the Steamworks bathhouse, Dale laid out the ground rules. "Understand that some of their clients aren't out yet. Even for those who are, getting caught with someone other than who they're supposed to be with stirs up jealousies that can turn ugly. The people here are comfortable with me but wouldn't be with you. And who knows, I might have to do some flirting to get the necessary information, which works best if I'm flying solo."

Sometimes, as an investigator, you need to apply your resources wisely. Now seemed like a good time to delegate.

"I understand; I'll stay with the car. Can you text me now and then to let me know how things are going?"

"Absolutely. Here's the keyfob so you can adjust the climate controls to your liking. I'll try to make it quick."

As he entered the bathhouse, I busied myself on my phone, researching the Internet again for anything I could find on Mark Christensen in San Diego or Chicago.

Dale returned shortly, and he'd had more success than I did.

"Our friend Mark is waiting tables at Drew's on Halsted," Dale reported as we pulled away. "He's working the noon rush. We're still early, so hopefully, we can catch him before he gets too busy. From what I understand, he's a big guy with blond, short hair, and pretty easygoing."

"That squares with what Claire told me about him."

"He doesn't sound like someone who'd be tied up in a murder, especially beating someone to death. Maybe that's why he called the San Diego police."

"Looks like we're about to find out," I said as we pulled up to the valet stand.

The cramped but well-appointed lobby was empty as we approached the hostess. "We'd like a table for two in Mark Christensen's section, if possible," Dale asked.

"Certainly. Follow me, please." She led us to a small table near the back of the restaurant. "Will this do?"

"Excellent, thank you," Dale replied as we sat.

The restaurant was mostly empty, but guests were filtering in steadily. Our timing should give us a chance to talk briefly with Christensen.

This time, I took the lead. As Mark leaned in to take our drink orders, I said softly, "Mark, my name is Debra Ann Wynn. I'm a reporter from San

Diego. I need to ask you about a phone call you made to the San Diego Police Department about a month ago."

Mark's posture straightened, and his complexion blanched noticeably. He glanced from side to side and then leaned forward again. "Look, I don't know what you're talking about, but you have no right to come here. This is my *job*."

Dale stepped in. "We apologize for the intrusion, but our schedule is tight. We've been to Steamworks and confirmed your identity. I'm a client there, too — I'm from here, used to be a cop."

"*Fuck*," Mark said, keeping his voice low. "I can't handle cops right now."

"Former," Dale reiterated. "I'm just here to help. You weren't hard to find, Mark. And you don't have a lot of places you can hide that I don't know about. Your best bet is to talk to us before Chicago PD gets wind of this. Just take our drink orders, and we'll work something out when you return."

Appearing shaken, Mark entered our requests into his tablet and turned toward the wait station.

I made eye contact with Dale.

"Are you sure letting him go was the right move? How do you know he won't take a powder out the back door?"

"Mark's submissive." Dale seemed confident with his assessment. Seeing a skeptical look cross my face, he explained. "Trust me, it doesn't have anything to do with size. I'd guess this has bothered him for a while, hence the phone call. Now he knows I'm inside his world; he hasn't many options. He wants to get this off his chest. He'll be back."

But I wondered — *are we getting Mark's cooperation because Dale is the dominant one in this new acquaintanceship?* I decided to let it go; I wasn't sure the answer was any of my business. Whatever Mark's motivations were, Dale's instincts were spot on; several minutes later, Mark came to the table with our drinks.

"Look, I'll talk to you, but you can't tell the police," Mark implored us. "I'm not ready to deal with that shit."

"I'll keep as much of it off the record as possible," I offered, "but you have to know they're going to find out eventually."

"Whatever." Mark's tone betrayed that he was flustered. "But we can't talk here. I'll lose my job. I'm off Thursday; we can do something then."

Not wanting to give him too much time to reconsider, I pushed. "I'm only in town until tomorrow, and it's best for you if I go back to San Diego knowing your side of the story."

Mark looked around the restaurant once more. "I've got another table." Mark's voice showed stress. He cocked his head at another server. "Franco's here; let me see if he'll trade days off."

We gave Mark our entrée orders, and he headed to the kitchen.

"I'll be off tomorrow," Mark told us when he brought our meals. "I can meet you somewhere, maybe ten o'clock?"

"Let's get together at the Chicago Diner," Dale replied. "They don't open till eleven, but it should be pretty quiet midweek if we go early." Turning to me, he said, "It's right up the street, within walking distance."

Mark nodded.

"Can I get you anything else?" he asked, reverting to his server role.

Dale looked at me, and I shook my head.

"No, I think we're good."

I returned to the last few bites of what the menu had listed as "Hickory Roasted Jail Island Salmon." It was excellent and might have been even better had I not just eaten a late breakfast. I'd have given our server a nice tip simply due to the circumstances, but the food and his efforts had earned it.

"I've got some business to tend to this afternoon," Dale announced when we were back in his car. "Okay if I drop you off at your room?"

"Sure; I'll be fine/" I'd begun to feel my hip aching from sitting too long in a chair — my injuries seemed more tolerable when I kept moving. "I'll do the tourist thing and check out the sights. How are the rideshares here?"

"Oh, you won't have any problem getting around," Dale replied, pulling up to my bed and breakfast. "The taxi companies put together a local service called 'Curb' if Lyft and Uber aren't doing it for you. It's the same principle: Download the app and set up an account. I'll be here at ten-thirty tomorrow to pick you up."

"I'm going to take the opportunity to walk off some of that good food."

Chuckling, I stepped out of his car, leaning back in before closing the door. "I appreciate the help today, and I'll see you tomorrow.

"Let's cross our fingers that Mr. Christensen shows and has a story to tell."

CHAPTER 45

After visiting the Museum of Science and Industry, I returned to my room, changing into more comfortable shoes for the "Gangsters and Ghosts" walking tour. When I got back from seeing the sights, I was ready to experience those enticing bed covers. Sinking into the down pillows and comforter was heavenly, and I quickly drifted off to sleep.

The next thing I knew, the alarm was going off; eleven hours had passed in the blink of an eye. Despite the great night's sleep, my movements were stiff as I climbed out of bed. But things were rapidly improving when we arrived at the Chicago Diner.

Dale exuded more confidence than I had in Mark Christensen appearing at the appointed time. Mindful that Mark had bailed out of the phone call that led to us coming here, I was pleasantly surprised when he entered the diner. A polo shirt revealed the big man's muscular biceps and the tattoo sleeves down his arms.

His reluctance to talk to us about Ricky Mason and Brian Pierce was apparent. Still, he seemed determined to see this through, roughly the same approach I have to dental appointments. When we placed our orders, I asked our server if she'd give us some privacy once our food arrived.

Mark was naturally soft-spoken and pleasant even under these circumstances — projecting what Californians might think of as a surfer-dude vibe. I leveraged his eagerness to get this over with as my cue to plunge right in. I started by recapping where things stood.

"I think you know that the police are looking at Ricky Mason as one of two people who beat a man named Brian Pierce to death. Someone dumped his body in an alley two months ago. They have DNA and prints. You've never been in any trouble that we know of, so your biologics aren't in the system. But everyone at this table knows that once they have samples to compare, some of the DNA and prints will match yours."

I knew my message was getting through when Mark drew a deep breath and sighed.

"The police have a voice recording of an individual calling the San Diego police tip line. After being dragged into a bad situation they never expected, decent people sometimes do that as their conscience begins bothering them.

"That's why I'm here. I care about the story, not convictions, so circumstances and the reasons behind things mean something to me. I have no idea how this situation will turn out. My experience tells me that when someone in your position gets their side of the story in front of the public, things go much better for them. That depends on your role in the homicide and how cooperative you are with the authorities when the time comes, but still…."

"And just for the record, Mark, I'm here as a tour guide for Debra Ann," Dale reminded him. "As I mentioned yesterday, I'm not on the force anymore."

Mark spoke quietly, his eyes fixed on the plate before him.

"I hear what you're saying, and it *has* bothered me for a while. I've had time to think about it. I want to go back home, put this behind me, and have a chance for a decent life once I've paid my debt."

I pulled my digital recorder from my purse.

"Tell me, then, in your own words, what happened that night and the next day. I'll record this, but it's for my ears only, so I get the story right."

Mark's eyes darted between mine as though searching for understanding.

"I'll never forget that night for the rest of my life. I've never been involved in violence like that before, ever. I wake up at night remembering what happened. Every moment's burned into my brain."

"How do you know Ricky Mason?"

"I didn't before that night. I mean, I'd seen him around, but we never connected. He had a reputation for sneaking roofies into drinks to get dates. But that night, I'd had too many vodka Red Bulls, and I didn't care. I was at The Loft when he picked me up for a sleepover. I rode in his car and left mine in the lot.

"Ricky talks a big story but can't deliver if you know what I mean, so the best thing about that hookup was falling asleep."

"Both of you?"

"Ricky had crashed by the time I came back from the bathroom, so, yeah. But I'd only slept maybe an hour when I woke up. Someone in a hoodie wearing a facemask was hitting Ricky's side of the bed with a pipe.

Holy crap — that's exactly where my dream on the plane ended! A guy breaking into a house and ready to hit someone in bed with a steel club…. Un-frigging-believable.

I shook it off, returning to reality as Mark continued.

"At first, I thought I was having a nightmare. I just watched as the guy stood there for a second — I guess he wasn't expecting Ricky's head to be *under* the pillow. He reached down with his left hand to pull it off.

"Left hand? Why would you remember that?" Dale asked.

"I used to box. You set your feet differently for a righty than a southpaw."

"What happened next?" I wanted to know who took the lead when they fought back.

"The guy with the pipe hadn't seen me. I pushed off the mattress with my left arm and kind of launched myself over Ricky's legs.

"I got hold of our attacker's left wrist with my right hand before he saw me coming. I was screaming like a banshee.

"He started yelling, 'Son of a bitch!'"

"The pipe was in his right hand, and he tried to swing it at me. I grabbed the covers with my left hand, wrapping my forearm to block the pipe.

"I was bigger and stronger, and I had the momentum.

"With the adrenaline and everything, I had a grip on his left arm like a vise. I pulled on him to get myself across to Ricky's side of the bed, and then I swung my legs around to get my feet on the floor."

"So now you're both standing, facing each other beside the bed," Dale summarized.

"Yes. By now, Ricky was up on his knees on the mattress.

"I shoved the man holding the weapon backward as Ricky grabbed the hand with the pipe.

"Our attacker was staggering back, off balance. The lower section of the bookcase had a lip that stuck out like a little shelf, and his spine caught it squarely at the beltline.

"His shoulders slammed back and crashed through the top portion of the case's glass front. He made a groaning sound."

"You remember this thing pretty clearly," I remarked.

"There hasn't been a night since that I haven't had nightmares. I need to know that he was still alive every step along the way, that what I did wasn't what killed him."

"PTSD," Dale offered. "Some people can't remember; others can't forget."

"At this point, my eyes had adjusted to the light, and it was like everything was happening in slow motion.

"The hoodie guy dropped the pipe.

"His mask had come off — and I could see his face was all twisted up with the pain.

"It hadn't seemed natural when his back arched over that bookcase ledge. He'd messed up something pretty badly. He tried to use his left hand, swinging it behind him to push himself away from the bookcase."

"What was Ricky doing?" Mason didn't seem to be helping much for someone who'd been the original target.

"By this time, Ricky had scrambled out of bed and was on his feet.

"He wouldn't stop yelling 'Motherfucker!' — over and over.

"He bent over and lowered his head to bull-rush the hoodie guy. Ricky caught him under the right armpit with his right shoulder. He was using the attacker's body to shield his face from the broken glass.

"The man was screaming, and I caught him squarely on his jaw with my right fist. His mouth was still open; the blow snapped his neck to the left.

"Ricky and the masked man crashed to the floor in the middle of the broken glass. Drops of blood were splattering everywhere.

"Ricky got up right away to flip on the bedroom light. He found the pipe dropped on the bed.

"Whoever built that thing meant it to do serious harm. I once tried being a plumber's apprentice and recognized it for what it was. He'd made it from stuff you could buy new at Home Depot for forty bucks or from old junk for free. The handle was eight inches of galvanized water pipe threaded at both ends. A pipe cap on one end kept your hand from slipping off. They'd screwed the other end into an adapter; that connected to a longer, thicker pipe with a bigger pipe cap.

"He'd filled the center with sand. Made a club with the perfect weight and balance; it wouldn't break or bend. To get rid of it, all you'd do is take it apart and throw the pieces in the river."

"Do you know where that pipe is now?" Dale asked.

"I think Ricky took it. He thought it was kinda cool. I wouldn't be surprised if he still has it."

"What happened next?" I asked.

"The hoodie guy was on the floor —he'd rolled himself onto his back. I must've broken his jaw — it wasn't lined up with the rest of his face anymore. It was flopping around like he wanted to say something.

"His feet and hands were slipping and sliding when he tried to scoot himself on his back away from me, and he was too far gone to get anywhere. I was hovering over him, timing it up to drop all my weight on the man's chest.

"I pinned him to the carpet with my right knee and pounded him with my fists around the head and neck until he was unconscious. The guy couldn't even lift his hands to fight back.

"The only sound coming from him was a shallow wheezing when he breathed. I figured he was done to where he couldn't hurt anyone, so I stood up and stepped away. My adrenaline was about gone, and my arms were getting tired."

"So, what you're saying is, everything the two of you did to this assailant was in self-defense?" I asked.

"Yeah, I mean, we were sound asleep, and this guy broke into the house and was trying to hit Ricky with a pipe. What were we supposed to do?"

"But your intruder is still alive, right?"

"At that moment? Yes."

"So, what happened to kill him?"

"I thought it was over — we'd call the cops, turn the guy in so they could take him to the hospital, and that would be that. But no, that's not what happened. It was just like Ricky to use a weapon to beat on a defenseless man when he's down — *after* somebody else stepped up to save Ricky's sorry ass.

"All of a sudden, for no reason, Ricky starts screaming in uncontrolled rage.

"He goes down on one knee and raises the pipe above his head. He starts beating the hooded man's face and chest with that steel cylinder.

"I yelled, 'You're going to kill him, Ricky!'

"But Ricky was shouting at the top of his lungs like I'd be the next to get it.

'*Fuck him*, Mark. He ... was ... trying ... to ... kill ... *me!*' — accenting every word with another swing of the pipe."

"He slung blood from the club's end every time he raised it for another strike.

"It landed on the ceiling, the fan, the bed coverings, and the headboard.

"The walls looked like they'd been spray painted red; the carpet was gory, sticky, and wet.

"He didn't stop until he exhausted himself. That thick steel tube got too heavy for him to lift anymore."

"He's just been beating this guy mercilessly, then?" I asked.

"Yeah, Ricky wouldn't quit until he couldn't go any longer."

"Did you do anything else to try to stop him?" Dale's hand was on his chin. The other arm was across his chest, the hand tucked under his elbow.

"No," Mark answered softly, hanging his head as he looked down at his hands, their fingers interlaced on his lap.

Our server had come to check on us, and I could tell she'd overheard something; her eyes were wide, her eyebrows high on her forehead.

"Oh, don't worry," I told her, feigning a laugh. "I'm a playwright, and my friend here is just rehearsing his part in a murder mystery I've written."

"He's a good actor … had me fooled!" Still, she didn't seem entirely convinced. We wouldn't see her again until I gave her a two-finger wave later to summon her.

"I watched that bloody pipe slide out of Ricky's hand onto the floor," Mark continued. "He had no energy left even to grip it.

"His tantrum had covered his entire front with splattered blood, along with most of the area in a circle around the hoodie guy's torso and head. The only bare spot left was where Ricky himself blocked out the little flying drops of blood.

"I had to go into the bathroom and throw up. I was totally screwed. I had no wheels or other clothes. If I called a cab or an Uber, the driver would be another witness placing me there. I knew Ricky would turn on me the minute he got the chance, and I was the bigger man, so who were the police going to think did this?

"Plus, when I was in the bathroom, he called another guy to clean up the mess. Whoever they were, they'd be on Ricky's side, not mine. I thought about just running away. But when we left the bar, I was hammered, and Ricky was driving. I hadn't paid any attention to how we got to his house — no idea where I was."

"Did you hear who Ricky called when you were in the bathroom?" I asked.

"I didn't hear their conversation, but I think he was like a teacher or professor."

"A doctor, maybe?"

"Yeah, could be," Mark replied, a look of concentration on his face. "You know, I think he *was* a doctor."

Why does that not surprise me? I thought.

"When I came back into the bedroom, Ricky and I took a few steps away to stare at the carnage around the side and end of the bed. The hooded man's body was splayed out on its back, just past the foot of the bed. Ricky had bludgeoned his face and chest into a gooey, oozing pulp; the features above his neck were no longer recognizable as human. The blows had caved in his chest; it was now half as thick as it had been.

"I can't keep it out of my mind. No warning, there it is, *boom*, and I'm thinking about the last sensation that dying man would have felt, his lifeblood draining away from him. It was soaking into the light blue carpet; the stain was spreading outward from his shoulders.

"At night, I keep seeing him staring at me like he was when he was trying to talk before Ricky killed him. But in my dream, with his blood running out and his face all gone, his eyes are still in their sockets, and they're looking at me as he's dying, like, *Why did you do this?*"

"Anyway, it was starting to get light. We walked around the neighborhood to see if we could spot any vehicles belonging to the hoodie guy. We didn't find anything, so Ricky said we needed to leave — some people from a place called Strike Back…"

"Strike Response?"

"Yeah, that's it, Strike Response. Anyway, they were coming to clean up. Ricky took me back to my car. He said if I kept my mouth shut, he'd get me enough money to get out of town until things blew over. He handed me fifty thousand dollars cash a few days later, and I came here the next day."

<hr>

The once ruggedly handsome young man's battered and broken shell lay motionless, his soul slipping away as his bodily fluids seeped into the fabric of a stranger's bedroom floor. As his essence wafted skyward, the last letter he'd ever written would escape into the wild, falling to the wet ground some thirty miles away.

Sliding from the ring of iron in which he'd placed it, the slightly curled envelope broke free. It skipped and danced through the sprinklers as they refreshed the manicured, sparkling grassland. Eager to explore its quickly expanding universe, the liberated letter bounced joyfully along on its corners, pushed ahead by the light and playful winds of early morning.

As I awoke from dozing off during my flight home, the dream's metaphor worked just long enough that I opened my eyes to a sense of peace. I'd found comfort in realizing that otherwise evil circumstances had released Brian from an existence that hadn't been happy for him.

But then I caught the flash memory of Mark's face as we left him at that restaurant. I realized that no matter how this went, he'd ruined his life and others for one night of poor decisions and events he couldn't control. A feeling of crushing sadness washed over me — not just for Mark's situation, but for everyone who'd been lost and, especially, for those who loved them at some point in their lives. Mikey, Joe and Letti, Terrence, Darrell, Cassidy and her sisters, Shannon, Lindsay, Antara's wife and children … and yes, me. All this needless sorrow and suffering — *to what end?*

And then came the anger.

James Seaver and Ricky Mason will pay for what they've done. If the police can't get them, I will.

THE WRITINGS OF
AVRIL MARIA SERENE

CHAPTER 46

After my flight landed back in San Diego, I spent the rest of the day catching up on forsaken odd chores and clearing my freelance work for the coming week. The next day was Thursday, and I was up bright and early. At first, I struggled to get out of the motel bed and thought I might have overtaxed myself the day before. But once I was active, I felt closer to normal — until my ribs or thigh spoke up to curb my enthusiasm.

My first task was to repay Marci for telling me of the tipline call that led to my interview with Mark Christensen. I left a message on her office line; this would be official business.

As I scanned my messages with my morning coffee, I saw a text from another unknown number. It read: "Fortune smiles on the brave. The OxyContin and cocaine they found were dumb luck. We had no information the driver was dealing drugs on the side."

A link to another *Union-Tribune* online piece followed, time-stamped yesterday afternoon. The article revealed that the alleged theft of weapons and ammunition from Strike Response's warehouse was now considered insurance fraud, the entire thing staged. Police had learned from an anonymous tipster that the firearms were divided up and secreted in the trunks of the company's fleet of vehicles. Investigators recovered the "missing" guns and ammo; they'd never left the company's property.

In the passenger compartment of one of those, a 2023 Dodge Charger, officers also discovered twenty-five hundred OxyContin pills and a half kilo of cocaine — together, an estimated street value of around ninety thousand dollars. They'd arrested the operative assigned to the vehicle, and charges were pending. The Bureau of Alcohol, Tobacco, Firearms and Explosives (BATFE) revealed that Strike Response had never registered several of the recovered weapons, and many had inaccurate or missing importation records. The agency also discovered illegal post-market auto-firing modifications to those and other firearms.

More text followed the link to the news article. "We used a back channel to send SDPD our GPS tracking data for the Dodge. That data puts it right at the time and location down the street from where the truck driver struck the Uber, and witnesses saw the Dodge picking him up.

"Our sources say the driver is singing the authorities an opera, dropping dimes on everyone. He's turning on anyone involved in the murder of the Uber driver and the cleanup after Julius Cantor's homicide. The operative claims Ainsworth did the neighbor. He's saying Strike Response handled the Pierce body dump at Seaver's request. However, the flipped witness denies the agency had any contact with Pierce's killers. And he insists Strike Response operatives had nothing to do with the execution of Seaver's wife or moving her body."

In the message's closing, I got the Easter egg I was looking for: "'It's the friends you can call up at 4 a.m. that matter.'"

Ahhh, Dietrich — the ending quote confirmed Harry as the sender. I'd been afraid that those pursuing Seaver and Ainsworth for their crimes might lose sight of Brian's and Antara's murders. With Harry's message, I felt an enormous weight lifting from my shoulders. The guilt for unwittingly putting the Uber driver in harm's way hadn't fully subsided; still, knowing that Antara would get justice was comforting.

The newspaper article Harry cited had Doug Stein's byline. Still, I forwarded the text to Doug in case Harry had added something the reporter didn't know.

Tying up Strike Response with investigations into their activities cleared the path for what I wanted to do now that my health and pain tolerance had improved. Running Seaver's girlfriend, Sheryl Jansen, and then Ricky Mason to ground had waited too long already.

But before I could start on either task, Marci returned my earlier call.

"Hi, Marci; thanks for calling me back. I wanted you to know the Chicago bathhouse tip bore fruit. The man who called *is* a material witness to the murder of Brian Pierce. I committed to protecting my source. However, my companion at the time of my interview didn't, and he happens to be a retired Chicago police officer. His name is Dale Newsome. I texted you his contact information. He helped me locate the witness, so he knows everything I know."

"Nice sidestep," Marci said, acknowledging my ethical dance move. "I'm glad you chased the tip down. Shame on the detective who took the call for not following up, but now we can move forward. I'll give your former officer a shoutout."

Having Mark Christensen's situation addressed freed me to go after Sheryl Jansen. She was last known to work at a nail salon, and the best way to get information from a manicurist is to have your nails done. I texted myself a picture of studded nail art I'd worn for a Halloween party last year to show on my phone later. I called Cathy, and again she was available. And knowing I'd be in unfamiliar places and situations, I tucked Dad's old revolver into my purse.

The photo Claire sent me of Jansen was several years old, and I didn't recognize her among those I saw working today as I walked into Color My World. "Does Sheryl Jansen still work here?" I asked the receptionist, a pretty Vietnamese girl. "I don't see her."

"I don't know the name," she replied, "but I've only been here a month. Randi would probably know — she's been here the longest. She's working with a client now. Do you want me to put you on her waiting list?"

"Yes, would you, please?"

"You'll be her next client; it shouldn't be over ten or fifteen minutes at the latest."

"That's great, thank you."

I grabbed one of Randi's cards from the rack in front of the cash register — I'd need her information if she proved helpful.

Once my turn came, I took my seat in the chair. Randi was a big, beautiful black woman with a broad smile, offering all the banter her customers could handle at no extra charge.

"Honestly, I came in looking for Sheryl Jansen — does she still work here?" I snuck the question in during a brief lull as she talked.

"I'm sorry, honey, but that name don't mean nothing to me," Randi said, her brow furrowed.

"She might go by Campbell, Clarke, Dearman…." I didn't get to finish before Randi let out a laugh.

"Oh, you mean Sherri White. We all gave her *such* a hard time - she sure could catch 'em, but she couldn't hold on to 'em. Oh, no, child. That girl doesn't stay anywhere long. She's what my friend Jackie calls 'flighty.'"

"Do you know her well?"

"We was tight when she was here, and I see her around now and then. We're not BFFs, but she gave my daughter the cutest little stuffed bear for her birthday last month. What do you need to see Sherri about?"

Sensing that Randi could tell me what I needed to know, I invested a little in her. I displayed the photo of last year's holiday nails on my cell phone and showed them to Randi. "My girlfriend got these done here last year and told me Sherri did them. I wanted something like them."

"Oh, sweetie, I can do that for you. Look, we can even do better if you let me. You don't want them all the same anymore; things have changed. Now, you want something to be a little different. Maybe set one finger on each hand apart, or they can all have the same colors, but each finger does its own thing. I am an *artist*, girl!" Randi exclaimed with a laugh and the mock pawing of her right hand.

Her confidence was a great sales tool, and I decided I couldn't lose — it was the perfect opportunity to get her to dish on Sherri.

"Do I need to remove my wrist wrap? I had an accident a couple of days ago."

"Oh, no. I can work around it; just keep it on."

She started in and immediately removed any doubt that she knew what she was doing. When she gave me an opportunity during her stream of commentary about everything from the weather to lingerie, I lobbed her a softball question: "Why'd Sherri leave here? It seems like a nice place, and she had you for a friend — how bad could it have been?"

Randi ran with it as she began applying the base coat. "That girl just can't sit still; she's always stirring up trouble. If it's not boyfriends, then it's drugs or money problems. It's something new every day with her."

"My friend told me she's been married four times?"

"Oh, honey, I think it might be a few more than that. I never could figure out what's up with Sherri. Like, check it out. She has this doctor friend. I don't know if he's s'posed to be her boyfriend or what his deal is. Even when she was seeing someone else, he'd still come around. She says he keeps promising he'll pay to fix her teeth, but it ain't happened yet. The man's supposably a doctor, so it's not like he doesn't have the money. And the way he strutted around here, you'd think he was the governor."

Randi passed an air dryer over my fingers.

"Is she working at all, then?"

"She was dancing at a men's club for a while. That much I know for sure. And she got into some trouble there; messed with a married man, and the wife whupped her ass, or so people say."

Randi began applying the hardening clearcoat to my nails.

"I told Sherri to her face, 'You're not as young as you used to be, and you're not in good enough shape to be fighting anyone.'"

Randi had me place my fingers in the ultraviolet nail dryer. "I don't think that girl paid attention to a word I said.

"But the last I heard, she was working over at Broadmoor Nail Techs. She told me she's trying to stay low, keep an honest job, and doesn't want trouble. Something happened around six months ago, and whatever it was, she's afraid it'll come back on her."

Randi's collection of nail studs was awe-inspiring, and it was fascinating to see her designs come to life.

"Huh… wonder what could have spooked her?" I wanted to keep the conversation flowing in that direction.

"She wouldn't tell me exactly, but for quite a while, she'd keep asking if the police came around looking for her. She wanted to move away but couldn't get the money together." Randi paused, her eyebrows knitted with doubt as she applied a layer of clear polish over her work. "Say, you're not from the po-po, are you?"

"Oh, no," I gave her a quick laugh, following it with a little white lie. "I write children's stories for my living." Anything interesting I told her now would likely make it into her chatter later. I didn't want the news getting out in the neighborhood that a reporter came around asking questions about Sheryl.

"My girlfriend needs to know I made an honest effort to find the nail tech she recommended," I added, waggling my nails. "But these are gorgeous — you truly *are* an artist! So, I'll tell her upfront you did them instead, and then she can be jealous." I grinned.

Randi seemed satisfied with my answer as she placed my hands in the UV dryer again. She gave me what I took as her standard spiel about caring for my freshly decorated nails. As she began prepping for her next client, she looked over her shoulder at me with a grin.

"Next time, bring one of your books so I can show my daughter."

I felt a twinge in my gut. There are times when I'm not happy with myself that I have to lie; this was one of those.

CHAPTER 47

Cathy patiently awaited me, and I thanked her as I climbed into the front passenger seat. My side hurt from sitting too long, so I popped two over-the-counter Tylenol, wanting to wean myself off the addictive prescription version. Armed with Randi's information, I had some leads I could check out. As we rode along, I started with the low-hanging fruit — I called Broadmoor Nail Techs to find out if Sheryl Jansen worked there.

The woman picking up the phone didn't recognize "Sheryl Jansen." But like Randi, once I gave her my spiel, the serial use of false names was familiar to her. "Oh, you must mean Shawntelle — yes, she's here."

Someone needs to explain to Sheryl Jansen that being famous for having so many aliases is no less identifying than everyone knowing your real name.

"Thanks, I'm in the neighborhood. I'll drop in and make an appointment with Shawntelle. I need to show her what I want done and see if she can do it."

Cathy drove me to the closest CVS pharmacy, and I asked her to wait for me again. I bought a bottle of nail polish remover, some cotton balls, tissues, and baby wipes. Once back in Cathy's Prius, I had her take me to a fast-food restaurant. Removing Randi's art from my nails in the McDonald's restroom broke my heart. But it made little sense to go into a different nail salon and not need their services. I certainly didn't want Sheryl to recognize Randi's work. If they were still friends, as Randi believed, I'd prefer Randi not tell Sheryl I'd been asking all those questions. For this introduction, *I'd* use an alias, presenting myself as a referral from a past client of Sheryl's. I'd confirm where she worked, see what she now looked like, and check out any challenges I might face. I wasn't about to confront her in the salon over Theresa Seaver's body dump.

Cathy drove me to the Broadmoor salon, and I had her park in a space near the front door. "I'm just getting an appointment to have my nails re-done; maybe ten minutes?" I told her.

"I'm good." Cathy was gracious. "If I'm not in the car when you get done, don't worry — I've just gone to get something to drink or the ladies' room, and I'll be right back."

When I asked the girl at the front desk, she told me Shawntelle wasn't busy and directed me to a station near the back. When I first set eyes on Sheryl, it was immediately apparent that time had not treated her kindly. She was almost unrecognizable from the five-year-old photo Claire provided me.

I never cared for the expression, but the men who worked construction for Dad would have described her as "rode hard and put up wet." She had severe crow's feet around her eyes and crepey skin around her neck and upper chest as if she'd had too much sun in her past life. Her makeup base didn't hide her pockmarks. She kept her lips together when she smiled, but her stained, missing, and jagged teeth were impossible to hide when she spoke. Her face and body had sagged significantly from the old photo.

She reminded me of all those former twenty-something, silicone-chested blondes in La Jolla. Now in their forties, they trolled Match.com for men with 401Ks large enough to support their dates' spending habits. A snippet from Alex Siegel's rendition of "Beauty Fades" sprinted through my mind.

"Hi, Shawntelle; it's so nice to meet you. I'm Angie, Angie Carlson, and I need my nails done for a party. Debbie Armstrong from church said you did a great job for her. Here's a photo of what I'd like to do," I said, purposefully rushing through it and stabbing my cell phone at her with last year's photo of my nails.

"Hi, Angie. It's nice of you to stop by. Oh, beautiful; yes, I can do that. Let me see your hands. Oh, did you recently have a manicure?" Sheryl seemed eager to do the work but a little let down that I didn't need more.

"I have to be honest; I tried to do them myself, and they turned out *so* badly I took it all off so you wouldn't see them," I lied with a shy smile, trying to sound embarrassed.

"Oh, we get that all the time." Sheryl flopped a wrist at me, showing tact and sensitivity I didn't expect. "No problem, we'll fix you right up." She turned away to prepare her station, and I interrupted her.

"I'm sorry, I won't be able to do them right now — I have an Uber waiting for me outside. I just wanted to see if you did work like this and set up an appointment for later."

The tiniest trace of disappointment faded Sheryl's smile ever-so-briefly — I suspected she was hoping for immediate income. After setting an appointment I didn't intend to keep, I returned to the Prius.

As we left the lot, I had Cathy cruise slowly past the shop windows so I could take photos of Sheryl with my cell. I slid down in my seat, capturing only a side angle of her, but it was still better than the photo I came with.

Cathy let me know she'd be entertaining family from out of town over the next few days and needed time this afternoon to prepare. I had her drop me off at a car rental agency. The dark gray Nissan Sentra I leased had little oomph, but it wouldn't stand out. It was small enough that I could park it quickly if I needed to. I wanted more freedom and control than an Uber would provide so that I could follow Sheryl home from work — my next challenge was to find out where she was living.

I returned to the Broadmoor nail studio, mobile and on my own. Driving slowly past the plate glass windows, I could see that I'd lucked out — Sheryl was with a client, still working. I pulled into a nearby parking slot and waited, using the opportunity to down a couple of regular Tylenol.

I watched as Sheryl left the shop by the front door two hours later. She briefly chatted with someone inside as she held the door open, then, turning away, waved goodbye. She walked across the lot to a row of parking spaces next to the street and got into an older-model white Corolla with a badly dented rear bumper. Sheryl pulled out, and I followed her at a safe distance.

After a meandering path to a Taco Bell drive-through and a Walgreens, she ended up in a depressed older neighborhood that inhabitants call "Mount Hope." The center of the impoverished area was a municipal cemetery and its supporting businesses. It had a primarily transitory population. Graffiti promoting gang signs appeared everywhere: on walls, benches, street signs, and sculptures.

Old age, wear and tear, and poor maintenance had taken their toll on many of its homes. Residents had bestrewn overgrown front yards with broken-down vehicles and discarded porcelain bathroom fixtures. They'd littered the backyards with old, filthy mattresses, broken appliances, and garbage bags filled to bursting. Sheryl parked on the curb on L Street and made her way to the side door of a brick residence with fading and chipped white trim, rusted wrought iron, and a neglected lawn.

I parked a few cars behind her Corolla and waited until Sheryl disappeared inside. As pleasant as Sheryl might have seemed at the salon, she associated with stone-cold killers and had helped desecrate at least one body. The woman was dishonest enough to use aliases and had one or more drug dependencies. Sheryl had worked in the seediest places with the sketchiest of customers and had a history as a runner. When uncomfortable with a situation, her first tendency was to take off.

I had the tools for scoping out Sheryl's environment and Dad's .38 to protect myself. I wanted to manipulate her natural tendency to run and turn it to my advantage. Pulling my burner phone from the center console, I silenced the phone's ringer and notifications. I created a speed-dial shortcut for the number from Sheryl's business card. Then, tapping the shortcut's icon to call Sheryl, I hung up as soon as she answered.

For a split second, I considered letting the air out of a tire on Sheryl's car to frustrate her if she tried to leave in it before I wanted her to. But I immediately rejected that idea. I worried she would have no means to escape if exposed to real danger before re-inflating it. With her lifestyle, and in a neighborhood like this, there was too much potential for a serious problem — I'd be responsible for the outcome.

So, with the throwaway cell in my back pocket, my right hand on the revolver in my purse, and my left carrying a peephole reverser, I quietly walked up the metal stairs to the door I'd seen Sheryl entering earlier.

Peering through the reverser into a tiny room with an adjacent small bathroom, I saw Sheryl's back as she was standing, possibly in front of a sink. The floor in the main room was a teak-colored laminate, with no rugs or other floor coverings and no pictures on the wall. The only furniture was a single bed, a brown Formica chest of drawers with a large mirror mounted above it, a small TV standing on the bureau, and a metal folding chair.

A door on the wall opposite this one had a handle with a keyhole in it, not a locking knob, which likely meant Sheryl's room didn't have access to the rest of the house.

She'd have no way out except through the door before me.

THE WRITINGS OF
AVRIL MARIA SERENE

CHAPTER 48

Aware of Sheryl's environment, I put the reverser in my purse, stepped back on the small landing, and knocked on the door. At first, there was no answer.

"Shawntelle, it's Angie. I know you're in there — I need to talk to you. Something happened to your car." I fell back on an old ruse that had worked for me in similar situations.

Sheryl answered through the four-inch crack allowed by the latch chain, looking apprehensive and then confused. "Angie, what are you doing here? What happened to my car?"

"Is your car a black Monte Carlo? I saw someone trying to jack the rims."

"No, I have a white Corolla," Sheryl answered hesitantly.

"Oh, I'm sorry; I thought somebody was stealing from you. I was coming here to talk to you about Doc when I saw what was happening — I thought you'd want to know. May I come in?"

"Doc's not here; what do you want?" Sheryl's eyes narrowed, and her face turned slightly to one side as she backed further away from the opening. Her tone and demeanor showed suspicion, and she was clearly on the defensive.

"Sheryl, Doc wants you dead because you helped him move Mrs. Seaver's body six months ago." I caught the irony in having to lie again to gain her trust. "One of my snitches told me you're here and where you work — too many people know where to find you. I don't think you want to talk about this outside where everyone can hear."

"Go away!" Sheryl exclaimed, pushing the door closed.

"Sheryl, the word on the street is Doc sent Ainsworth to kill you," I called through the door. "The police are closing in on them, and you know too much about Theresa and everything else they've done." I was winging it. "Talk to me, Sheryl, and I'll help you. But you're out of time. Someone's going to call Seaver and tell him where I found you, where you're working, and about your friends. All I have to do is wait for his crew or the police to get here, whoever's first. You'll *have* to come out then."

"*Shit!*" I heard Sheryl scream, and then a few seconds later, "*Get the fuck away from me!*"

"Look, Sheryl, there's no place you can hide. You need my help. That's why I'm here."

After waiting a moment, I added, "I'm not going away, Sheryl. I can camp out by your car for a week if I have to.

"You can't leave without coming through this door.

"And when you decide to come out, I might not be standing here — it could be Ainsworth or Ricky Mason instead. Maybe they'll just shoot you through the door with a silencer. They'd probably do that at night, though, when you sleep."

I wanted to overwhelm Sheryl with things to think about.

"Sure, you could call somebody … but Doc's offering up a lot of money. How do you know they wouldn't be working with him? Or that Doc won't kill them for helping you? Do you want Doc going after Randi's daughter to get to you?"

It took another couple of minutes before I got a reaction. In the meantime, I whistled the *Jeopardy!* theme song to let her know I was still there.

"Who the fuck *are* you? I mean, when you're not lying to people...," Sheryl asked through the closed door, a little calmer but not yet convinced enough to let me in.

"My name is Debra Ann Wynn. I'm an investigative reporter; I do freelance work for the *Union-Tribune* and other papers. You can look me up online and see my picture. I'm just trying to make sure nobody else gets hurt from Doc murdering his wife."

"I'll see if I can find you on the Internet." The reluctance in Sheryl's voice was apparent.

"That's W-Y-N-N," I called out, crossing my fingers that I was making progress.

It was a good sign when she opened the door again a few minutes later, albeit using the latch chain. At least she hadn't shut me out for good.

"Okay, so you're a reporter. Everybody wants something. How do I know you're not here to screw me over?"

"If I wanted to hurt you, I could have just made a scene at the nail salon, and you'd lose your job. Slashed your tires so you couldn't go anywhere. I didn't do any of that — I'm not here to cause you trouble. But you need to be aware Doc and Ainsworth are murdering everyone who knows the true story about his wife.

"I knew three of the people he killed, and I'm trying to stop him from hurting anyone else."

"Who'd Doc off that *you* would know?" Sheryl's voice had softened slightly but was still doubtful. I noticed she didn't question the idea of Doc killing three people.

"The police think Doc had his neighbor shot dead in the poor man's living room. That neighbor was Coach Cantor, my high school basketball coach and Sunday school teacher when I was little."

I showed her the brace on my left wrist.

"And I know people working for Doc killed an Uber driver named Antara when Doc tried to get at me. But before that, Doc was involved in the murder of a man named Brian Pierce."

"I never heard about wasting any 'Antara' or 'Brian'...," Sheryl said hesitantly.

"Brian used to rob places once in a while to make some money. He was in the middle of stealing from that house when Doc, you, and Ricky Mason moved Theresa's body. Brian painted the wall and the carpet to tell Doc he knew what he did to his wife.

"Ricky Mason killed Brian, and the police know the dead man graffitied Doc's place. That gives Doc motive and proves there's a connection. You and Ricky became one big headache for Doc when the police started asking questions and looking for witnesses."

It seemed I was gaining traction as Sheryl showed surprise at what I knew, but again, without denying anything. It was good that she didn't dispute Ricky's last name, indirectly confirming one of my working theories. Now, it was time to get a little creative.

I couldn't know what Doc's sleeping arrangements might be, but Sheryl wouldn't doubt he had at least one other woman. "Doc has a new girlfriend feeding him bad thoughts about you and what you might do. Jealous, just staking out her territory. Doc doesn't want the police to find you before he takes you out of the picture."

"But I didn't do anything to hurt him!" Sheryl's tone was defensive.

"It's not what you did; it's what he *thinks* you'll do. Doc's new lady has him believing you'll rat him out. You know how he gets when he decides someone's disloyal to him."

"Is anybody with you?" A trace of suspicion lingered in Sheryl's voice. She tried to see the surroundings over my shoulder, pressing her face into the gap between the door and frame.

"No, it's just me. And nobody else knows I'm here."

I added another white lie to protect myself from any threat Sheryl might pose once I was alone with her.

"The police have this address and your job, but Ricky Mason's got more blood on his hands, and they want to get him first."

That was good enough for her to buy into my pitch. Sheryl closed the door just enough to remove the latch chain and then stuck her head outside to scout the side of the building, first to the left and then to the right.

"Okay, you can come in. But you can't stay too long. I've got someplace I need to go."

Now I had my opportunity — I knew her priorities would change if I did my job well.

But I didn't realize how much the story she was about to tell would change mine.

THE WRITINGS OF
AVRIL MARIA SERENE

CHAPTER 49

My original goal was to get Sheryl to let me in for an interview. Now, I wanted her to take me into her confidence, so I'd have to reward her for her trust. I needed to be as pleasant as possible without appearing too phony.

"I'm so sorry that I didn't tell you the truth at the salon," I said as I entered her tiny room, "but I didn't want to upset you there."

"I need that job." Sheryl sat on the edge of the bed and offered me the folding chair. My ribs weren't fond of hard-backed seating, but I made sure not to grimace as I sat in it.

"My girlfriend moved in with her boyfriend," Sheryl explained apologetically, "and she's letting me stay here until her lease ends. I'm trying to find a place, but the rents are more than I can afford.

"So, why would Doc try to kill me now?"

"With the police closing in, you're a loose end he can't control. He has nothing on you — you didn't kill anybody or get any money from his wife's inheritance. Maybe he could scare you that you'll go down for desecrating a body. But you're no big-time criminal, and you could make a deal to get out of anything to do with Doc's wife."

"But why *now?*" Sheryl was insistent.

"Did you see the newspaper articles about drugs and a stolen gun insurance scam at Strike Response? It's a private investigations company...."

Sheryl shook her head.

"That's the company Doc hired to clean up after he had Ainsworth murder his neighbor and again when Ricky killed Brian Pierce. The police flipped a contractor at Strike Response. With Doc involved in two known murders, Doc's lawyers can't keep the police from investigating Theresa's death any longer.

"Once they have Ricky in custody, he'll give them the location of the body. And when they lock you up, Doc will think they have a corroborating witness to put him and Ainsworth away.

"Doc's *got* to get rid of you and Ricky before the cops arrest you."

"*Shit.*" I heard a hint of despair creeping into her voice. *Maybe it's registering just how much trouble she's in?*

"If Doc finds out I said anything to anyone, he'll kill me just for *that*." Sheryl's eyes had widened, her eyebrows high and together in fear.

"Sheryl, I'm afraid you're dead if Doc thinks you *might* talk." I leaned forward. "I don't believe it matters to him whether you *have* yet."

I tried a different tack. My instincts told me Sheryl looked to men to define her, to provide for her, and to fix things for her. Her life now reflected the failures and betrayals of that belief system. She'd self-identify as a victim, but her challenges were the results of poor choices she'd made willingly. More troubling, it didn't seem she'd developed any other skills or tools for dealing with adversity. She'd had no backup plan for when her physical beauty would no longer pay her way.

Sheryl's ignorance was no excuse when judging her character. Still, a reasonable observer had to give at least some consideration to the source of her many problems.

"Men see you are attractive, but they can let you down, and Doc is one of those. Look, you have every right to be tired of running, being afraid, being used, and being lied to about things like getting your teeth fixed."

"He keeps promising, but nothing ever happens...." The spoiled child's pout on Sheryl's face would have been comical under different circumstances.

"Now he sees you as a threat, and Doc goes after people he doesn't trust. That's why Theresa and Coach Cantor are dead."

"Ainsworth did Mr. Cantor after Doc asked him to." Sheryl's expression had morphed into that of a sixth grader tattling on someone.

"Ainsworth is the one he'll send to do me. God, I *hate* that son of a bitch. He is always dissing me behind my back, and once he called me 'trailer trash' right in front of Doc." Her face was red, and her upper lip curled slightly. There was anger in her voice.

It's still important to her what Seaver thinks, even after she's told he's going to kill her, I noted with disappointment. But I couldn't say the discovery shocked me.

Sheryl stood up, taking the empty glass from the top of the chest of drawers. She stepped into the bathroom to draw water from the sink faucet.

With Sheryl's mind on Ainsworth and others who might be coming for her, now was my opportunity. As discreetly as possible, I took the burner out of my back pocket, held it next to my hip where Sheryl couldn't see it, and hit the speed-dial icon for her number.

Sheryl went to her purse on the floor next to the bed, turning her back to me as she answered her phone. I immediately hung up and slid the phone under my thigh.

Sheryl pulled the phone away from her ear and looked at the Caller ID. As she did, she turned toward me just enough that I could see she was a little frustrated.

"Spam call, I guess; second one today," Sheryl announced as she returned to her seat.

I wanted to plant a seed.

"Is there anyone who might be trying to trace your location through your phone? I'm told they can find out what cell tower you're close to when you answer."

"I don't think so…," Sheryl replied hesitantly.

When I was just a cub reporter at the *Union-Tribune*, my mentor was Doug Stein. He taught me that sending someone already on edge a hang-up phone call from a number they didn't know is a great but subtle way to dial up the paranoia. Usually, an out-of-view fellow journalist would make those calls, but today, I was adapting.

"Probably nothing, then. We were talking about Ainsworth...," I reminded her.

"If he *is* coming after me, what can I do?" Sheryl's tone reflected both doubt and grudging acceptance of her situation.

I needed to provide her with an alternative.

"We need to get you out in front of this now because if I've found you, anyone else can. Sometimes, the best place to hide is in plain sight. I think that applies here. The cops are hanging all over Doc and Ainsworth. If the police knew where you were, they'd also know if either was making any moves in your direction, and they'd stop them. It truly is that simple."

"So, what are you saying? You want me to try surviving on the streets as a *snitch?* I've seen what happens when people talk to cops. No thanks, I have enough problems."

"Sheryl, you don't understand how the process works. Please hear me out. Think about this — the minute Doc, Ainsworth, and their crew are off the streets, they're not out here chasing you. And Strike Response has a boatload of problems that are way more important to them than you are, right?"

"Maybe. But I've seen Doc get out of everything they've tried to do to him," Sheryl protested. "You don't know this guy. If they *do* lock him up, it won't be for long."

"Sheryl, you've only seen Doc get away with penny-ante stuff, scams, and financial crimes — not a homicide, and certainly not three killings. There's no time limit on murder investigations, so he'd have to hold the police off forever. And multiple murderers? They're such a huge threat to everyone that the system *has* to put them away. I mean for good. And they don't get to come back after that."

"Doc has lawyers...."

"It won't matter. What Doc and Ainsworth did, they did together as part of the same set of crimes. That means they both have to answer for all of them. They'll turn on each other to save themselves. Trust me; they'll never get out of prison."

"But other people will know I talked...." Sheryl was refusing to submit easily.

"No, truly, they won't. In the first place, the police may not even need your testimony. You won't have to go on the stand if the evidence speaks for itself. As we're talking, they're trying to find what they call 'probable cause' to get search warrants for that evidence. Your story helps them get those warrants. The warrants get the police the DNA, fingerprints, bullets, and all these other things to convict Doc and Ainsworth."

It was time to try my ploy again.

"Sheryl, can I ask a favor? My allergics are acting out, and I've run out of tissues — do you have one?"

"Is toilet paper good enough?"

"That'll be fine, thanks."

With that opportunity, I slid out my burner and called her phone again.

After another hang-up, Sheryl was visibly upset as she faced me, punching her screen with her forefinger to return the call. When no one answered, she shook her head and threw her phone back into her purse in frustration.

"Another one? Hmmm, something must be going on...," I said as Sheryl passed me a wad of toilet paper, and I feigned wiping my nose.

Picking up where we left off, Sheryl asked, "Why would I have to go to court? I can tell them at the station what they need to know to get the evidence. I don't want to be where Doc can give me the evil eye while people ask me questions."

"You may not have to testify. We know there's lots of evidence and witnesses whose stories are more important to the case than yours. And honestly, they can't force you to testify if you don't want to. But don't forget, testifying could make you look good to everyone else watching. Maybe they can get you a better job or help you financially and in other ways."

Sheryl shook her head.

"If I just talk to them without getting on the stand to testify, how do they keep it secret that I said anything?"

I could see that telling her story in front of Seaver was the big thing on her mind. She'd only entertain the situations where she didn't testify.

"The police will interview you in a safe, private place. You can have a lawyer there to look out for you. That conversation remains secret between you, the police, and the prosecutor for the case. They might have you talk to the grand jury if they think your part of the story is important enough, and that's secret by law."

"But nobody will know?" Sheryl seemed a little more receptive.

"No. For most people, that's it. Usually, when the DA has a strong case, the murderer doesn't want to get the death penalty, so they make a deal to get out of it. They plead guilty.

"You'd only testify at trial if the defendants don't plead out and if what you say is so significant that they can't make the case without you. That is what they call a 'material witness.'"

"But you already said I was one of those!" Sheryl had immediately become apprehensive again.

"To the moving of the body, yes. But now, the detectives care about the murder, which is a bigger deal. Being a material witness to the actual homicide would make your testimony far more vital to the case.

"But even then, the DA would give you police protection or get you into a safe house. Or they could help you get to some other city, maybe change your name legally, where you'll always be safe."

As soon as the words were out of my mouth, it was clear something I just said had upset Sheryl.

"What do *you* know? I don't care *what* you say; Doc will hunt me down." Sheryl's lower lip was quivering, the pitch and volume of her voice rising as her fear suddenly returned in full force.

"I saw *too much*."

"We can help you, Sheryl." I tried to think of something to reassure her while hiding my frustration that I'd lost the ground I thought I'd gained by breaking through.

"Jesus — you're just not *getting* it!" Sheryl was half-sobbing, half-screaming. "I was *there* that afternoon when Doc killed Theresa.

"*I saw it with my own eyes!*"

CHAPTER 50

oly crap. I hadn't prepared for Sheryl's revelation; it took a moment to absorb its implications.

I'd assumed Theresa's homicide was another one of those in-the-dark-of-night things where a solo attacker waits to ambush the victim. From what I knew of the man, that would have been Seaver's style.

Learning that Sheryl was in the house at the time of the homicide was surprising in its own right. But it would have been too much to expect Sheryl to be *in the same room* when James Seaver killed his wife. And if the police had any idea the murder happened in front of her in real time, they would have interviewed Sheryl long before I arrived on the scene.

How much more of this story had I — *and everyone else* — missed?

"I've never told anyone this before, but I saw Doc kill Theresa," Sheryl repeated, slowly shaking her head as she looked down and hugged a pillow that she'd pulled off the bed. She was still visibly upset but calmer, her tone softer. Her shoulders sagged, and her expression had gone flat.

"It didn't happen the way people think."

I realized that what I heard in her voice wasn't despair as much as the acceptance of defeat — she was giving up the fight.

"You're a material witness to a homicide?" I was incredulous. "Maybe you should tell me the whole thing right from the beginning. I want to record this and give you a copy of the tape. That protects you from someone claiming you said something you didn't. Once I know the entire story, I can help you figure out the best thing for you to do."

"Only if you promise you won't share the recording with anyone."

Pleased that she agreed, I nodded my assent.

The memory installed on my burner phone wasn't enough to record long conversations, so I took my handheld digital recorder out of my purse.

"They can't make me reveal my sources. And I won't let them have anything you give me unless you tell me it's alright with you." I wanted the recording only as source material for what I would write — I had no intention of sharing it with anyone. But I *did* have an ulterior motive. Hundreds of interviews have taught me how helpful recordings are. That's especially true when a subject later gets cold feet and wants to recant or deny something they said. That can happen with someone as malleable as Sheryl seemed to be.

"Okay. So, everybody thinks Doc came up with this fancy master plan to kill Theresa," Sheryl explained, "and that's how she must have died — something clever and well thought-out… What's it called? 'Premeditated?' But it wasn't like that at all."

"He didn't intend to kill her?"

"He *was* planning to get rid of her somehow to collect her inheritance. Eventually. But not that day, and not that way."

"So, what happened was spontaneous, then?"

"Sort of, I guess. Here's how it worked. Doc and I have been tight for a long time, and he used to take great care of me. He'd buy me things, give me gifts, and we'd go out for nice dinners. But mostly, we liked to sleep together, sometimes at his place or maybe mine. Now and then, we'd go to a motel or do it right out in public places. Whenever we wanted — we were seeing and getting married to other people, but Doc and I had a *thing*. I can't explain it."

"Chemistry. Sometimes, there's just no way to account for it."

"Yeah, and besides that, Theresa could be a real bitch sometimes," Sheryl continued. "Okay, maybe all the time. She'd rag at him over the least little thing, and lately, she'd been questioning him about what he was doing with her money."

"They were fighting a lot?" I remembered Darrell Woodson telling me how hard it was to get along with Theresa.

"Nag, nag, nag. All the time. And she was *such* a prude. She didn't want to do any of the stuff Doc likes, and Doc likes lots of things," Sheryl said with a bashful smile.

So do you, I thought as the excitement in Sheryl's voice came through.

"That afternoon, she had to go downtown to talk to the lawyers — she was always having drawn-out fights with her ex. Then she was supposed to go to one of those hoity-toity charity things they kept inviting her to after she got her father's inheritance."

"'Supposed to?' That isn't what happened?"

"It got all messed up. I came over to Doc's place, and Doc and I were screwing around, just having fun like always, and out of the blue, Theresa walked in on us. She must've come from the charity thing — she was dressed to the max, wearing an evening gown that went all the way to the floor and opera gloves up to her armpits."

"I take it you were *in flagrante delicto*, as they say?" I surmised.

"No, we weren't in anything; Doc likes to save the kinky stuff for later when he gets bored — we were just in bed having sex."

I resisted the temptation to roll my eyes, just letting it pass.

"She was screaming at him, saying she'd divorce him, and yelling at us to get out. Doc kept telling her, 'Keep your voice down; the neighbors don't want to hear this,' but she was on a tear, ranting and raving."

"So, what — you were sitting there not doing anything while those two fought?"

"Oh, no, she was cussing me, too." It seemed a little off to me that her demeanor had become matter-of-fact, almost as though she was recounting a shopping trip. "My clothes were on the chair on the other side of the room, and she was between them and me. So, I'm on the bed, and I've got the sheets pulled up around me, but I couldn't do anything. She finally sees my clothes and throws them at me, one thing at a time."

"So, just a lot of yelling and throwing clothes?" I wondered where this was going.

"Doc keeps a golf club leaning up against the armoire over by the window in case somebody tries to break in and he can't get to his gun case. Doc wasn't having any of her shit that day, and he ended her right then and there."

"'Ended her?' You mean, ended her life?" She'd been right earlier; this was nothing like what I assumed might have happened.

"He hit her in the head with the golf club to shut her up, and that was all she wrote."

"Who cleaned up the mess? You? Or Doc?" I wondered how much evidence authorities could find to confirm her story almost six months later.

"There was hardly any blood or anything, just some around her mouth, which was weird, but he must have caught her just right. I think he knocked her out cold while she was still standing because she fell straight back onto the floor without bending or trying to catch herself."

"How do you know she was dead? Maybe he just knocked her out." I knew better from Brian's letters, but I wanted confirmation.

"Doc leaned over, listened for her to breathe, and took her pulse. He said she was dead, and well, he *is* a doctor…. There was blood on her face, and his stupid little dog kept trying to lick it."

"Bubbles?"

"Yeah," Sheryl answered, seeming surprised I knew its name, "so he had me grab one of those reusable plastic shopping bags and put it over her head. He wanted to keep the blood off the carpet and make the dog leave her alone." She paused and shivered. "Worst thing Doc ever asked me to do."

Still, she didn't seem as upset as I thought she might. *Perhaps getting rid of a competitor for Doc's affections wasn't as terrible for her as she'd like me to believe.*

"He was just going to leave her there?"

"No, well, he wanted to cover her up," Sheryl explained, again with little emotion, "but he said we should wait until we had help before we moved her. There was this big oval rug, a fake imported Oriental, under the dining room table downstairs, so he sent me to get that."

"To hide her body? Or to make it easier to slide her corpse around?" Again, I was pretty sure I already knew the answer.

"To hide her. By the time I got back, Doc had found some clear tape and sealed the shopping bag around her neck. So, we rolled her up in the rug.

"I watched him make phone calls to people because he wasn't ready for this. He was making it up as he went, trying to figure out what to do. That prick Ainsworth usually takes care of this stuff for Doc, but he wasn't available — I think he might have been out of town, but I'm not sure."

"Who did he get to help him?" To avoid confirmation bias, I wanted her to provide the name.

"Doc got hold of Ricky Mason and told him to come by after the bars had closed and everyone had gone home. He didn't want anybody out and about seeing them move her body."

Perfect — I had my confirmation.

"So, Theresa's body was still in the bedroom?"

"Yes. Bubbles wouldn't leave that rug alone, so Doc took him downstairs. Bubbles will yip all night if he's away from Doc, so Doc laces his food with Benadryl to get him to shut up. He locked Bubbles in the guest bathroom."

Ahah! So that's *why Brian never mentions a dog in his letters.*

"Doc and I went back to bed. It was funny because it was different. The whole thing with Theresa being dead in the same room got him super-excited, like a rock, if you know what I mean, so we messed around for quite a while. It was like he was free to do whatever he wanted."

"With her dead now, I assume there was no time limit on how long you could stay?"

"Until he told me to go home, yeah. We ordered Chinese delivery, and he played on the computer while I watched TV. We got tired, turned off the lights, and fell asleep."

"So, when did you move Theresa's body?"

"After we slept for maybe a couple of hours, Ricky showed up, driving a van through the alley with the headlights turned off. Doc said to keep the house lights dark and not to make any sounds because he didn't want to draw attention from the neighbors."

"About what time was this?"

"Three, maybe three-thirty."

"In the morning?"

"Yeah. Rolling a dead body around on the floor was hard enough, but I didn't know one was that heavy to lift. It was stiff in places but flopped around; you couldn't get a good grip on it. We had flashlights, but it was mostly dark, making things harder."

"Did you go with them to bury Theresa's remains?" I was hoping she could tell me where that corpse was.

"No. Once we got the wife's body into the van, Ricky and Doc took off. My car was still down the street, where I parked earlier that afternoon — Doc didn't like the neighbors telling Theresa that he had visitors while she was gone."

"That was it? You never got involved in anything else with Theresa's body?"

"Not me, no. I *was* with Doc the night Ricky killed the graffiti guy, but that was different. I didn't have anything to do with it. Ricky beat him up at his place."

"How do you know that?" She'd again caught me off guard.

"Doc and I were in bed when Ricky called him wanting to know what he should do with the dead man."

Excuse me?

CHAPTER 51

Sheryl Jansen was proving herself a fount of unexpected information. That she was a witness to a murder and the desecration of a corpse was one thing. Learning that she was a hearsay witness to the disposal of another was beyond the pale.

"How much of that conversation did you overhear?" I asked.

"I heard Doc's side of it, if that's what you mean," Sheryl replied.

I suppose it would have been too much to hope that Doc would be on speakerphone. But the way this interview had gone, it wouldn't have surprised me.

"So, when did that conversation happen?"

"It was maybe five or six weeks ago, I guess. Two or three months after Doc killed Theresa. When I party, I get messed up with time, but I think that's right."

"Got it. Can you tell me how it went?"

"I was doing speed the day before, so I was crashing. I got up in the middle of the night to go to the bathroom. I wasn't wearing anything, so I was cold, and I went to turn off the little fan on Doc's nightstand. Right then, Doc's cell phone rang, scared me half to death."

"Doc wouldn't answer it, so it stopped. But after a minute, it started up again.

"I'm thinking, '*Oh, come on! Just turn off the stupid phone — I want to sleep.*' But finally, Doc answered it, cussing up a storm even though he was only half-awake. He goes, 'Alexa, turn on the fucking reading light…,' and he's all irritated she couldn't understand him. He was fumbling around, trying to find the pack of cigarettes and his lighter. He wouldn't say anything into the phone until after he lit one."

"Him having the phone turned on pissed me off because I figured once Theresa was out of the picture, there wouldn't be any marriage crap interfering with our romantic life. I was his only girlfriend left, so I thought nobody would interrupt our time together in the evenings. But I should have known. Once he didn't have to answer to Theresa, her kid, or her idiot dog, Doc started doing most of his business after dark.

"But really, there was nothing I could do about it that night; making him mad wouldn't be good for my health. I knew he wasn't paying attention to me anyway, so I rolled my eyes at the back of his head and started filing my nails. I stacked the pillows against the headboard so I could sit in the bed, bouncing around on the mattress so he'd know I was there. At least I wasn't pouting — he always says I do that when I don't get my way."

We're talking about people getting killed, and this is what she thinks matters? Still, showing an attitude about her priorities wouldn't help my interview.

"So, who was the caller?" I tried to move the conversation along.

"The first thing I heard was '*What situation?*' from Doc. He sounded like he wanted to take someone's head off; it sure didn't help his mood any. Then he said, 'Dammit, Ricky! Are you on a disposable?'"

"So, it was Ricky Mason? Or Richard Ainsworth?" I was sure I knew the answer, but I needed absolute clarity.

"Oh, he'd never call Ainsworth 'Ricky'; that's a kid's name." A look of disdain crossed Sheryl's face.

"So, Mason, then…. What else did Doc say?"

"He snapped at Ricky, 'I'll call you back on a secure line,' and then hung up. He reached into the top drawer and grabbed the TracPhone he uses when he doesn't want anyone to know who he's talking to. Ricky Mason's not on his speed dial, and he was trying to remember the number.

"Doc said, 'Okay, Ricky, what have you gotten yourself into that you called me at this hour?' He sounded more awake, but he wasn't any happier."

"Doc didn't say anything for a little bit while he was listening. But you could tell he was frustrated — he does this thing rubbing the top of his head, where he used to have hair, with the hand holding the cigarette.

"'Chrissakes, man, take a Xanax; you're panting into the phone,' Doc said. 'I can't understand a word you're saying. Okay, so the guy broke in, and you killed him. So, what does that have to do with me?'

"Doc was listening again. Now he was off the bed and pacing around in his rumpled boxer shorts and that muscle shirt he likes, the one that doesn't reach all the way over his big stomach. He's always talking tough, but he's really not that scary-looking, at least not at night — more like Homer Simpson.

"Then he said, 'Okay, let me get this straight — he's carrying a blackmail note claiming you and I killed that bitch? You think his big plan was to knock you off to get the cops' attention — and that's what he was doing at your place?'

"Now Doc's stopped pacing, and he's paying super-close attention to whatever Ricky is saying.

"Doc goes, 'And you're saying this is the guy who tagged my walls and carpets and ripped me off? *Fuck*. I was sure Cantor was behind it. That's all right; good riddance — I never liked that black son of a bitch anyway.'

"Did he mean Julius Cantor, your neighbor? The one you said earlier that Doc told Ainsworth to murder?"

"I guess." Sheryl seemed unsure. "I mean, he asked Ainsworth if he would, and then the guy turns up dead. Doc never said nothing to me about doing him. I just know Doc didn't get along with him."

"But you're pretty sure it was Ainsworth, not Doc, who shot Coach Cantor?"

Sheryl raised both shoulders and then dropped them.

"Okay, then what happened?"

"After Doc listened for a minute or two, he said, 'The guy you killed knew way too damned much. What else did you find in his pockets?'

"Then Ricky must have said something, and Doc answered, 'He was a pro, knew what he was doing — nothing to ID him, only the tools he needed.' Then Doc asked, 'How'd you kill him?'

"Doc went quiet again, waiting for the answer.

"After that, it was like Doc was taking control because he wasn't happy about whatever went on. 'Okay,' he says, 'I want Strike Response to deal with this. I don't want you fucking things up any more than they already are, Ricky. Was there anyone with you when this shit went down?'

"Then Doc didn't say anything for a few seconds. But after that, he went off, and I could tell he was pretty mad now. Ricky had left a witness, one that could maybe tie everything back to Doc. He kept banging on Ricky about whether she'd keep her mouth shut.

"Did you hear the witness's name?"

"No, Doc never repeated it. Whatever Ricky said back to him calmed Doc down a little, and now Doc was giving orders. He said Ricky had to tell her she'd be an accessory if anyone went down for this — that if she ran from us, we'd find her wherever she hid. He told Ricky to text him her number and tell her we'd be in touch, that she'd get a nice chunk of change if she played her cards right.

"Then he told Ricky how to get the dead guy's fingerprints, and Ricky sent Doc a picture of them."

"Do you have any idea where that burner phone might be?"

"No, Doc changes them up every couple of weeks. I don't know what he does with the old ones.

"Anyway, whatever Ricky said after that got Doc all wound up again. I guess Ricky wanted to do everything himself. So, Doc's yelling, 'You think I'd trust *you* to fix *your* fuckup? Just leave the prints on the floor next to the dead guy. Strike Response will take them.' Then Doc told them both to get out of there for twenty-four hours, get a motel, and pay cash. I could tell Doc was pissed off by the way he crushed out his cigarette, mashed it so hard he knocked the ashtray on the floor. He made me get a wet towel to mop up the mess and make sure the carpet didn't catch on fire.

"Doc told Ricky that while they were gone, Strike Response would clean it all up and dump the body where the police would find it. He wanted to send a message to anyone working with the stiff."

"Did Doc ever tell you who the fingerprints belonged to?"

"No, he just said if the prints didn't tell them who the guy was, the cops needed to earn their damned paychecks and ID the body. He could get the name from the papers or the Internet. Doc thought the guy's license plates would tell them something about him. But Ricky said they checked the dead man's pockets and didn't find any keys."

"Locating his car would be even better than matching his fingerprints," I mused.

Sheryl nodded. "Doc started off again, a little quieter, '*Fuck*. We don't know where your dead guy parked his ride. In the morning, walk around the neighborhood after everyone's left for work, see if any vehicles look out of place.' Doc said if they got the body's identity before anyone else had it, Strike Response could run down where the guy lived and toss his place for anything tied back to them. If Ricky hadn't found the man's wheels by then, maybe Strike Response would run across something to give up what the guy was driving...."

"...like vehicle paperwork — title, registration, pictures, parking tickets — anything that showed what he was driving, so Doc could get to it before the cops," I finished for her. Several things surprised me this afternoon. The level of detail Sheryl was providing ranked high among them.

"Yeah. It was freaking Doc out that the guy might have left an address, a copy of the note in his pocket, a map, or maybe a cell phone in his car that would tie him to Ricky or Doc."

"Did they ever find the man's transportation?"

"Not that I ever heard about. But that was pretty much it. Doc hung up without saying another word on the phone. After that, he just stared at the wall and, in a little bit, he said, 'Girlfriend, my ass. Ricky's a moron. I don't know if he's the pitcher or the catcher, but if he thinks he's still in the closet and people don't know, he's only kidding himself.'

"'But this other crap keeps coming back around like a bad penny. Christ, I thought Ainsworth had already taken care of that bullshit with the graffiti.'"

"So, Doc was saying he had Ainsworth kill Coach Cantor because he thought his neighbor tagged the inside of Doc's house?"

"That's how I took it, yeah."

"Was there anything else that you remember Doc telling you?"

"No, that's all there was. Doc went into the bathroom to call somebody, but I couldn't hear. Things have cooled off between him and me lately, and he doesn't tell me much anymore. I don't think it's as much fun for him now that we don't have to sneak around. Doc said different times that he'd give me money to help me, but now he keeps saying he can't get any cash out of the inheritance yet. This last month, he hasn't been returning my calls."

I couldn't help but notice the quick segue from the murders to Sheryl's wants and needs.

"When her son reported Theresa missing, and the police came to your home, did they ever interview the two of you separately?"

"No, Doc just told them I worked for him and didn't really know Theresa, and I went along with whatever he said."

My eyes focused off into space, finger to my lips, as I sat on the chair, deep in thought for a moment. My interview with Sheryl revealed much more than I first thought it would. There wasn't any question —the police needed this information sooner rather than later. Someone had to tell Sheryl that only she could deliver it.

"Sheryl, here's the deal. First, there's no doubt about it — you're not just a material witness; you're the *only* eyewitness to Theresa's homicide. And to Doc's involvement in covering up Brian's murder — the guy who painted Doc's walls. If you don't tell them what you know, the police could charge you with being an accessory after the fact. If they wanted to push it, they could charge you as an accomplice to the same murders."

"But I didn't *do* anything!" Sheryl protested, giving me the side-eye as if I was responsible for the news she didn't want to hear.

"There's a thing here in California called the felony murder rule. That means law enforcement can charge and convict you for being a party to a felony where someone gets killed. Even if you never touched the victim or directly harmed them in any way. And moving a murdered body is a felony."

"How can they say *I* killed her? That's not fair!" Sheryl had a pout on her face. I wondered for a second if her emotional development had stopped in adolescence.

"Trust me; you don't want any part of that. Tell the police everything you know as soon as you can. If the authorities decide to charge you with something, they'll get you a lawyer if you can't afford one."

"Yeah, but the ones they give you aren't any good...."

"It won't go like that. What you know can put Doc away, so it's valuable to the prosecutors. You should be able to negotiate your way out of any serious charges *if* you are completely open and honest with them. That's a monster 'if,' Sheryl. You can't be screwing around with it."

Staring down into her lap, Sheryl fidgeted with her nails as she nodded, unwilling to look me in the eye.

"Honestly, Sheryl, you don't have any choices here. Doc knows you're the only witness to the murder — you're nothing more to him now than the threat of a life sentence behind bars, or worse, and he needs you dead."

"He hasn't done anything to me...." Sheryl was still clinging to her belief that Seaver cared for her. As exasperating as that was for me, I couldn't blame her for trying to hang onto what she had; she didn't have much. I had more work to do.

"I *am* surprised he hasn't gotten to you yet — I assume that's because he has too many other fish to fry, and he's trying to stay hidden behind the green curtain. But everything you just told me, he's known for a long time; there is no way he takes the chance you'll get him convicted. Don't take his silence — not returning your calls — to mean he's *not* coming for you. He won't give you a heads up."

Tears appeared at the corner of Sheryl's eyes, and her hands began shaking as panic seemed to set in. If she were ever to pose a threat to me, it would be now, with her basic flight-or-flight instincts kicking in.

"Please, Sheryl. I've been to too many graves already, and I don't want to be bringing flowers to yours."

CHAPTER 52

Like a cornered animal desperate to find an escape, Sheryl's eyes darted back and forth as she tried to absorb her situation and, at the same time, figure a way out of it. I could almost see the thought processes spinning behind her pupils. Feelings she still had for Seaver wrestled with how he'd been treating her recently and the threat she knew he represented to her. What she'd seen of his past behaviors toward people he thought betrayed him had to be in the mix somewhere.

"So, what should I do — go to a police station and turn myself in?" Sheryl finally asked, and I got the odd feeling she was playing for time. I suspected she knew what needed to happen and that *anything* would be better than that. I simply assumed the correct answer to avoid getting hung up on making it acceptable to her.

"I know someone who can help us. I will stay with you as long as you need me to. The police have to take a statement from you. We can have the officers come here, or you can go there … or we can meet them somewhere else."

"I don't want the police here. This place belongs to my girlfriend. She doesn't need any trouble or questions from the landlord or the neighbors. There's a Burger King up on Market — can I meet them there?"

"Absolutely. Let me call my friend. I'll put it on speaker so you know what's happening."

I dialed Marci's work number. The great thing about her desk job was that she usually answered if she was on duty, and my luck was still running true. She picked up on the third ring.

"Hi, Marci, this is Debra Ann. Just so you know, I'm calling you about official business, and I've got someone else with me — you're on speakerphone," I said in my at-the-office voice.

"Hi, Debra Ann." Marci sounded slightly concerned. "Is this about Mark Christensen and the Brian Pierce case? You should know Chicago PD dragged their heels interviewing Christensen, and by the time they got around to it, he was in the wind. All we've got for the moment is hearsay from Dale Newsome, and it's not enough to pick up Ricky Mason."

Dammit — one step forward and two steps back. I'd had doubts several times that Mark would see it through, but once I'd recorded the interview, I thought he was locked in.

"That's not good..., but that's not what I'm calling you about."

"Are you okay? Are you reporting a crime?"

"No, I'm fine, thanks for worrying about me. I'm helping a material witness to a different homicide come forward. But, as luck would have it, she can also help with the Pierce murder."

"Oh, Debra Ann … this isn't about the Seaver missing-person case, is it?" Marci didn't hide the frustration in her voice. "I thought we had an understanding,"

"We did, Marci. But someone forgot to tell Seaver's goons that our understanding didn't include them trying to kill me. Or trashing my apartment and copying my private papers."

"I got your messages. That's a discussion we'll have to have at another time. So, tell me about your witness." Marci seemed resigned to the situation.

"I'm sitting here with Shawntelle Whitman. You have her in the system as Sheryl Jansen."

"The name sounds familiar, but I can't place it…."

"Sheryl Jansen was one of James Seaver's associates when Theresa Seaver's son reported her missing. A detective interviewed her early on but without considering her or her circumstances. They knew their principal suspect in a potential homicide was a bully. You'd think the investigators would realize that witnesses around him might feel — wait, what's the word? Oh yeah, *'bullied.' That's* something we should discuss."

"You should tread a little more lightly, Debra Ann. The department had to shelve any follow-up interviews by senior detectives. That's because Seaver's lawyer sent a cease-and-desist letter. What does Shawntelle offer to change anything?" Marci sounded like she was going to need convincing.

"I've interviewed Shawntelle on the record at some length, and it's pretty clear she's an eyewitness to the homicide of Theresa Seaver."

"Wait, you said *eyewitness?*" *Now,* I had Marci's full attention.

"She wants to make a statement and will need protection once she does. Shawntelle was in the room when James Seaver killed Theresa with a golf club. She was in the house throughout the rest of that day and into the next until Seaver and Ricky Mason drove away with the body in a van. Seaver is aware Shawntelle's the only living witness to the killing, and there are clear indications he doesn't trust her anymore. She also overheard Seaver's side of the conversation when Ricky Mason called him to clean up Brian Pierce's homicide."

"How the hell did we miss all *that?*" Marci sounded genuinely surprised. "We've been treading water for a year because we couldn't come up with a witness to contradict Seaver's stories."

"Shawntelle was James Seaver's friend on the side during his marriage. He needed to keep her out of the limelight, and he finessed a sympathetic detective into thinking Shawntelle wasn't involved. No one interviewed her separately and apart from him. At that point, it was just a missing-person case, not that big of a deal yet."

"*Jesus Christ*, witness interviewing 101," Marci groused, now seeming to grasp the situation. "Still, there might be a silver lining. The fact the police have not talked to her apart from him may have kept her alive; Seaver wouldn't have to worry about what she might have said. But I take your point. We need to get her to safety. The bodies are piling up around Seaver and his cronies."

"Do you think you can get someone from Homicide to record her statement and see that she's cared for?" Marci worked for Major Case, not Homicide, but I knew she had great relationships within both squads.

"Lt. Greg Roe's in the precinct, working on his reports, and I think he's available. He's a solid detective." Marci's tone was noticeably softer and more personal. She seemed no longer in the mood to scold me. "You've met him. He's good in these situations, and he knows the Seaver case. Give me a few minutes, but stay on the line. Does that work for you?"

While I couldn't say I knew him well, I had interacted with Roe at several crime scenes over my years with the *Union-Tribune*. He was one of the better detectives — bright, hard-working, and articulate.

"He'd be the right guy, no doubt. There's a Burger King off Market's westbound lane, just east of Thirty-Sixth Street. It would be great if he could meet us there. We'll hang tight until you come back on the line." I hoped I sounded as appreciative of her help as I was.

After a few minutes, Marci returned. "Lt. Roe can meet you at the Market Street Burger King in thirty minutes. Shawntelle will have to explain everything in her own words to him. He can get her protection for tonight until the department can make other arrangements."

"Good. I'll talk to you later, Marci. And thanks; you've been great." It was gratifying to learn she wasn't one to hold a grudge.

"You're welcome, but it *is* my job. Debra Ann, just be careful; that's all I ask. And, please, *do* call me once the officers have provided for Ms. Jansen's immediate needs." She sounded genuinely concerned, yet another sign she'd put aside any hard feelings between us.

Our challenge now was getting Sheryl protected so she could tell her story to the people who needed to hear it — *before* James Seaver or any of his thugs could get to us.

CHAPTER 53

Sheryl rode with me to the Burger King — James Seaver would know her car, but not my rental. If possible, we needed to avoid any of Seaver's crew seeing the two of us together. Lt. Roe pulled into the Burger King lot in an unmarked unit at the appointed time. He was now in his early forties, and his waist and hairline had moved in different directions since I'd last seen him. I motioned him over to our table as he entered the restaurant.

"Good afternoon, Ms. Wynn; I look forward to working together again. I'm sorry to see that you've injured a wing there," Roe said as we shook hands, his eyes flicking down to my wrist wrap, "but otherwise, you're looking well."

"I appreciate your help, Lieutenant. I'm glad it was you who came. Let me introduce you to Shawntelle Whitman, better known to the department as Sheryl Jansen. She was present when James Seaver killed his wife Theresa almost a year ago."

"Hello, Shawntelle … or would you prefer Sheryl?" Roe offered his hand, his manner professional but cordial.

"You can call me Sheryl — my birth name," she responded timidly.

"Thanks, Sheryl; it's nice to meet you. I understand you've been through some pretty trying times, and you want to share what you know of a homicide in the Seaver household. Is that right?"

"Yes, I was there when it happened." Her voice was quiet. Roe gave me a nod, signifying he needed time alone with Sheryl to take her affidavit.

"Sheryl, Lt. Roe will walk you through your statement now. Let me get something to drink — I'll be in the booth back there if you need me." I pointed to an empty table across the seating area.

Roe got down to business as I was leaving. With Sheryl occupied, I made another quick call to Marci.

"Hi, Marci. Lt. Roe is here talking to Sheryl Jansen; he's got things well in hand. But I need a favor. I'd like you to send a uniformed officer in a marked squad car to Broadmoor Nail Techs and have them make a big deal about needing to talk to Shawntelle or Sheryl Jansen. That's it."

"Ah, I get it. You want anybody else looking for Ms. Jansen to believe we don't have her yet."

"That, and should she be thinking about bailing out of serving as a witness, I want her to know her exit routes are closed off if she tries to go back to the nail shop. Maybe Mark Christensen going on the run has me spooked, but it doesn't hurt to cover our bases."

"Makes sense, doesn't cost much, and it hedges our bets," Marci agreed. "I'll send Munro and Roberts — they're not big on subtle."

I ordered a soda and returned to the main seating area. Although I kept my distance, it wasn't hard to hear most of what the detective and Sheryl were saying to each other in the small room. Roe went through Sheryl's identifying information. He gathered some background context, fleshing out how she related to the Seaver and Ainsworth cases. Sheryl then repeated to him everything she'd told me. In response to the lieutenant's questions, she added specific details that made her rendition of the events even more relevant. As much as you can be of someone you just met, I was proud of Sheryl for keeping to the straight and narrow.

My role had transitioned to providing moral support for her. Once Roe had finished taking Sheryl's declaration of fact and she'd signed off on it, Roe waved me back to their table. His businesslike expression told me he'd found Sheryl's story convincing. Roe had some questions for me about how I'd located Sheryl. I related to him the path I'd followed. I had to reveal that she'd been way more accessible than was healthy for her, considering that people out there wanted to do her harm.

He turned back to Sheryl. His voice was subdued and showed concern. "Sheryl, from what you've told me, you're in grave danger from James Seaver and Richard Ainsworth. I'm particularly concerned about Strike Response. I think they may well be the bigger problem right now. They might feel like they have nothing more to lose. We've got sworn statements from one of their operatives in custody that they've already tried to kill Ms. Wynn."

Sheryl's eyes widened, and she looked at me in surprise. Though I'd meant to tell her how well I understood the threat to her, circumstances had gotten away from us, and I hadn't.

"We need to get you to a safe house tonight," Roe continued, turning slightly to face me. "Ms. Wynn, can you take her back to her place to get her personal effects and some clothes? I want to avoid the obvious presence of officers or anyone else strange to the neighborhood. I'll follow you, but I'll be hanging back. There's a Chevron station about three miles straight east of here on Market Street. It's busy — plenty of activity we can blend into — and it's open and well-lit; easier for us to monitor the environment. Meet us there. We'll have unmarked units in the parking lot for backup. That'll be the safest place to move Sheryl from your car to mine."

I nodded in agreement.

"Sheryl, once you have your things, Ms. Wynn will bring you to the gas station." Roe returned his attention to her. "By then, I'll have arranged a safe location for you tonight, and you can ride with me from the Chevron. We can work out everything else later, but we'll keep you from harm."

Sheryl bobbed her head in acknowledgment. I think she wanted to land somewhere safe where she could collect herself. I could see in her eyes that events had overwhelmed her; her facial expression had gone blank.

Sheryl and I left the restaurant in my rental, with Roe not far behind. She remained quiet. I'd noticed earlier that Sheryl's lips moved when reading, and now I could see she did the same when having an internal debate with herself. That tell warned me Sheryl might try to rabbit. I would need to watch her and calm her fears whenever I could.

"Okay, we're here," I said as I pulled up to the curb outside Sheryl's place. "Let's get your things as quickly as we can."

"I can do it by myself; just wait for me." Sheryl was suddenly more alert — it hit me that she was setting up her escape.

"No, we need to go in together." I played dumb while intentionally foiling her plans. "Someone could be in your room, waiting. And even if they're not, I want to keep us safe while you're doing your packing." I moved my purse so she could see the butt of Dad's .38 through the unzipped opening.

Sheryl's shoulders sagged as she realized her hastily made plan wouldn't work. Scanning the area as we went, we hurried to her door, and she unlocked it, my right hand on the revolver still hidden in my bag. Fortunately, no one was there. Sheryl pulled an empty suitcase from under the bed and began packing. She seemed committed to her deal now and a little more at ease — I was probably more concerned about James Seaver or his hired goons dropping by than she was.

Once she'd gathered the clothing and toiletries she wanted to bring, I made a thorough visual sweep of the surroundings, and we lugged everything to the car. I felt tremendous relief as we pulled away from the curb.

For her part, Sheryl seemed to be looking forward rather than back.

She started peppering me with questions about her new temporary residence, questions I couldn't answer. I deferred to Roe, knowing I was setting him up to get an earful. It didn't take long to get her to the lieutenant's vehicle. Arriving without incident, Sheryl and I said our goodbyes.

"I'll check in on you regularly, and Lt. Roe will take good care of you. It's been great spending time together. I only wish it could have been under better circumstances. You've got my card and burner number, so call me if you need me."

"I'm sorry you can't stay, but I really, really appreciate all your help." Sheryl cocked her head at me. "Maybe Angie Carlson will let me do her nails sometime?"

Touché — I had to smile a little at that. "She will, I promise! Do take care of yourself until then."

There was a touch of sadness on her face as we parted. The two of us were from different worlds, but I felt she'd become a friend over the short time we'd talked. I honestly wanted the best for her, whatever she assumed that meant. It made me genuinely happy that she was safe. I was glad, too, that, at least as far as Sheryl was concerned, I'd done the right things for the right reasons.

There was one more task left to do. Though I'd satisfied my professional responsibilities, I needed to fulfill my obligation to Dad and his request for my help. As things now stood, that meant seeking closure for the death of Brian Pierce — "Bubba" — the author of the graveyard letters Dad had found.

But first, I checked my phone messages — Marci had left one and Doug Stein another.

"You'll be happy to know a warrant for James Seaver's arrest was issued this morning," Marci's recording said. "The apprehension team is gearing up as I speak. On another front, one of our snitches tells us Richard Ainsworth jumped bail and fled the jurisdiction, headed east, trying to buy himself some time. Hit me up when you get a chance."

Doug's message simply asked for a callback. When I phoned him, he opened the conversation with a three-word offer I couldn't refuse.

"IHOP at ten?"

CHAPTER 54

The morning dawned cool and cloudy, and I awoke in good spirits. My body felt better every day that passed, and I planned to do without Tylenol 3 if I could. I needed unmasked clarity. I'd keep my rental car for at least one more day, thinking it unlikely that anyone had yet tied me to that vehicle. That meant I was now driving myself around, and though I hadn't felt impaired, the codeine in my prescription probably wasn't good for that. Or so it said right on the label.

Given my intention to confront Ricky Mason at some point over the next few days, I debated whether I should carry the .38 with me. The revolver was too bulky, and its shape too obvious to hide anywhere in my clothing. The weather didn't justify a coat or sweater. Carrying the weapon in my purse meant fumbling for it in an emergency unless I kept a hand on it. That would be the opposite of clandestine, especially when approaching a known criminal with a heightened awareness of those things. And if they separated me somehow from my purse, I'd be handing an adversary the instrument of my demise. After a fierce debate with myself, I decided not to carry the handgun. Instead, I tucked it into the car's glove compartment in case I later changed my mind.

Doug Stein's invitation to brunch allowed me to catch up with his work investigating Strike Response, and he was curious how my Seaver investigation was going. Through all our years working side-by-side at the paper, we'd kept secret from the rest of the world our shared guilty pleasure: IHOP cheese blintzes. Status updates were a perfect excuse to indulge ourselves today.

We ordered, and I told Doug about running into Harry Sanderson. "Chasing down information on James Seaver and his cohorts was the first time I'd met Harry — he's quite the old soul and quotations guru. He sent me two articles you wrote about the Strike Response warehouse thefts that proved to be frauds." I poured coffee for both of us from the pot on the table. "I've watched right and wrong take a lot of different forms through all of this, and Harry is teaching me to recognize nuances I've never considered. That whole incident with the weapons disappearing and awkwardly reappearing seems awfully convenient. And I couldn't help but notice that Harry didn't miss a beat letting me know about it.

"The man insinuated that the two of you go back a ways. I got the idea there's some interesting history between you."

"Harry Sanderson? Oh, yeah." Doug's face sported a wicked grin. "His name keeps popping up here and there in all of this. Harry and I have been tearing the place up together for thirty years — I could tell you some stories, but as the old CIA joke goes, then I'd have to kill you." Doug snorted, the twisted smile still on his face.

"Oh, I'm sure." I shook my head. "Until he told me, I didn't realize you knew each other — *that alone* is a scary thought!"

"Back in the day, more than a few bottles of good Scotch were sacrificed in chasing down some crazy stories together. I can't imagine anyone I'd want fighting by my side more or dating my daughter less."

"I've been too busy running down witnesses in my cases to keep up with your other Strike Response articles." I wanted to get back on track. "What's been going on?"

"Strike Response was in some ways as powerful as the mob, and not all that long ago. But those days are gone. I'd like to take the credit for that myself. But with these latest incidents, you started me on a good path. Law enforcement's been playing it straight for once, and I think our mutual friend's been giving us a boost from behind the scenes. And while Strike Response is still dangerous, especially now that they're wounded, they can't seem to stop shooting themselves in the foot. Once Strike Response began their downhill slide, they crumpled fast."

"How so?"

"The authorities have launched several investigations. I've got to give them their due: they were already working on some of these things before Strike Response killed Antara. They convened a grand jury. It's churning out indictments, and I understand plenty more are coming.

"Those have severely damaged Strike Response's business opportunities, profits, and the careers of past and present employees. Pending prosecutions for insurance fraud, federal weapons charges, and revelations from operatives about their practices have taken their toll. The grand jury's proceedings may be secret, but the indictments are public now. Much of the source material for those indictments is in print and preserved for the ages — past trial transcripts and witness statements, civil depositions, police interrogations, et cetera."

"Has any of that helped Antara's murder investigation?"

"A cartage company had reported the truck stolen — the vehicle that rammed you in the Uber and killed Antara. I learned the company was a Strike Response client during a union-busting conflict. Law enforcement's seen an advance copy of my piece, so they know of the relationship.

"The trucking company's trying to get ahead of the coming lawsuits. You might want to climb aboard that train, Debra Ann — I know you don't need the money, but you could always donate it to a good cause. The company should pay for what they did."

"I'll give it some consideration." I smiled. *It wouldn't hurt anything to ask Bill Hanniquet his opinion.*

"The cartage firm did offer a settlement to Antara's heirs," Doug continued, "which should enable the family's move into a larger home."

I felt a wave of grim satisfaction, but it fell short. "Was that it? There were a lot of people involved...."

"There have been other repercussions," Doug replied. "The Strike Response operative who drove into you and killed the driver is looking at a life sentence. Charges are pending for a few others, lesser crimes related to Antara's death. You know how these things go, though — only contractors and low-level employees would serve any actual time. Strike Response has fired two management team members, so there's that. On the surface, it looked like that would be the extent of it."

"'On the surface?'"

"Meaningful justice may have arrived on a different bus altogether," Doug replied wryly. "Some people, me included, believe that the original Strike Response warehouse break-in — the event that inspired those false reports of stolen weapons and ammunition — was at least partially a diversion. We think the actual goal was to breach Strike Response servers and, at the same time, access their paper files. Others theorize a brilliant hacker working independently hit those hard drives, and the timing was purely coincidental.

"But *somebody* broke into Strike Response's offices. They took tens of thousands of confidential documents from their computers and file cabinets."

I sat back in my chair as the server brought our blintzes.

"Harry's shown me that correcting inequities is something we can sometimes achieve without a formal process. I'm certain it's purely happenstance that Claire's become a partner in Harry's agency. And that he seems to be grooming her to take over the business eventually. *Surely,* he wouldn't reward her for helping him color outside the lines."

I was trying not to laugh at my own overtly disingenuous observations.

"Oh, of course … lots of co-inky-dinks." Smiling broadly, Doug took a moment to enjoy the thought before resuming his account.

"Either way, by the time the first Strike Response employee realized the document theft, the damage had spread too far to contain. Legitimate after-the-fact activity had overwritten the deleted space on those same servers. There was no way to recover the originals or identify the offending transactions. No one could tell the rightful day-to-day modifications of a file and its permissions from whatever the hacker might have done. And too many hands had been in those file cabinets since to investigate the heist properly."

"This part of the story I *do* know something about. Batches of those documents have begun turning up all over the Internet in regular releases."

"And that's proved devastating to Strike Response," Doug added. "A half-dozen of my articles were about the company's downfall. The depth and breadth of the crimes in which Strike Response has engaged as a regular part of their business are astounding. Federal, state, and county prosecutors have started investigations, made arrests, and even gotten a couple of guilty pleas by going after more than one hundred upper management and staff. All based on information from those exposed documents."

"So, that's why they folded so quickly…," I murmured.

"The revelations demolished Strike Response's reputation for discretion and trustworthiness overnight," Doug added. "Activity in their parking lot's been nothing but process servers, lawyers, and law enforcement coming and going. The company closed its sales offices last Thursday. They made it all of maybe a week after the day several websites published the first tranche of documents they received from that anonymous source."

It seemed Doug was being a little too modest.

"I don't think that happens if there isn't parallel support in mainstream media," I noted. "You have a knack for making an impact, even as sad as the paper's gotten. It would have been a powerful one-two punch with the Internet follow-up."

Doug had a wide grin.

"I like to think of myself as a humble guy. But for this one, I'm going to accept the high praise. Very few of the pieces I've written in the last few years have been more satisfying, personally or professionally, than the ones I've written about Strike Response. Again, thanks for the story idea and the help.

"By the way, since we've tossed around some of our impressions around the warehouse weapon relocations … any thoughts as to who might have staged the theft of those Strike Response documents?"

I gave Doug a conspiratorial wink.

"I've developed a theory, an idea I'll share with nobody but you…. Like everyone else, I was curious when those records started appearing on the Web. During some deep dives researching those stolen documents, I would, now and then, find an Easter egg — an oddly pithy phrase, sentence, or paragraph springing from an obscure page among those published in each of the batches. I can't get over the feeling that someone had explicitly dropped those additions into the documents for me to see.

"Until I read them, I hadn't fully realized how remarkably quotable Marlene Dietrich had been."

Doug grinned, and we both clammed up, given that further discussion might require us to investigate our suspicions professionally.

"Okay, your turn," Doug said, changing topics. "What's been going on with James Seaver and his crew?"

The waitress came around to check how we were doing and exchanged our pot of coffee for a fresh one. After she'd left us, I told Doug everything he didn't already know about my interviews with Darrell Woodson, Harry and Claire, Mark Christensen, and Sheryl Jansen. As I recounted those events, my cell phone buzzed on the table to notify me of an incoming text message.

When I finished telling him all the details, I snuck a look at my messages app.

"Now *that's* perfect timing." I had to laugh. "Marci Robbins just texted me that the officers picked Seaver up yesterday afternoon without incident. She says now that Ainsworth is conveniently in the wind, Seaver's throwing him under the bus for everything."

"Probably to be expected," Doug acknowledged. "Both Ainsworth flying the coop *and* Seaver taking advantage of the opportunity. But Ainsworth's a pro — he should know that modern technology will make it much harder for him to escape.

"I suppose thirty-odd years of the Internet can't trump 2,500 centuries of human evolution, that 'fight or flight' thing. It seems criminals always want to run and never think they'll get caught."

I smiled in agreement as I finished reading Marci's text.

"Oh, and get this," I relayed. "Marci was in the courtroom for Seaver's arraignment. She writes that he cursed the judge and lunged at him during pretrial motions. The bailiffs had to clear the courtroom. That stunt won't help Seaver's cause at all."

"How much do the prosecutors have against Seaver?" Doug refilled his coffee from the pot left on the table.

"I called a friend in the DA's office this morning before I came here. There are still some big holes, but then again, they're just getting started. Prosecutors have the damage done to the golf club. There's Theresa's doctor's report and Sheryl's statement. They've got testimony from current and former Strike Response contractors and operatives. Along with the evidence and information from Darrell Woodson."

"And Brian's letters, I presume. Pretty overwhelming," Doug acknowledged.

"At first, the DA worried he wouldn't be able to get those into evidence — hearsay and all that, no opportunity for the defense to question a dead witness. But Seaver opened the door for them months ago. He'd filed a police report about someone vandalizing the inside of his house with graffiti. Now, he's trying to use the graffiti to create reasonable doubt, claiming that someone else was involved, setting him up as the fall guy. That allows the DA to use Brian's letters explaining what happened that night to refute Seaver's claims."

"Good. Any indications where Theresa Seaver's body might be?"

"That's the biggest of a couple of challenges they're up against. They don't have Theresa's corpse or forensic evidence of a murder. They have the presumed murder weapon from Sheryl Jansen's statement. But the lab couldn't get blood, hair, or tissue from the golf club for DNA purposes. It does, however, have Seaver's prints and damage consistent with being used the way Sheryl recounted it.

"There *is* some additional support for Sheryl's statement. Theresa's medical records show treatment for an arterial wall weakness in the back of her brain — her doctor describes it as an unruptured cerebral aneurysm. It was severe, but her physician elected to treat it with blood pressure medications and monitor her with regular MRIs. He testified a blow like the one Sheryl described could easily have ruptured that aneurism, and the results would have been as she testified.

"Theresa would have dropped to the floor like a rock."

"It sounds like you've got more than enough to add you to the byline." Doug nodded. "We need to get the first installment written — I assume we'll start with an introduction to the general story and then get into Seaver's background."

"I've already written up the draft." I grinned as I handed Doug a flash drive. "Make any edits you feel are necessary; I don't need to see them before publication. Let me have your markups when you finish, though. If anything that gets dropped out becomes relevant as the story develops, I can add it back through one of the later pieces."

I was in mid-sentence when suddenly I realized I had a *big* problem.

I'd been so wrapped up in our conversation that the implications of Marci's text message describing James Seaver's arrest and Doug's observations about Ainsworth were only now hitting home.

"What's wrong?" Concern showed on Doug's face. "You look like you just sat on a tack…."

"Oh, *crap*. Doug, I think I might have screwed up." I tossed my credit card on the table. "When the news of Seaver's arrest gets out on the street, Ricky Mason will run.

"I have to go."

CHAPTER 55

To find Ricky Mason, I'd first need to drive to his address and check out what I'd be up against. My options and opportunities would ride on whether he was there, who might be with him, and how he'd react to seeing me. My first foray into his domain needed to be during the bright light of day so I could see clearly. I wanted to bolster my ability to protect and defend myself.

As I approached the address Claire had provided, I saw Mason's old blue Civic in the drive with its hatch open. And there was the diminutive Mason, carrying a large box in one hand and a duffle bag in the other. He crossed the yard quickly to place the cardboard container in the open hatch and the bag in the front passenger seat.

I pulled up on the opposite side of the street just as he hurried back into the house. I could see from my vantage point that he'd already stuffed the Honda to the gills. It was apparent Mason was flying the coop and would soon be on his way.

My pulse began pounding at the sheer stupidity of what I was about to do. The choices left to me were to alert someone who couldn't *possibly* make it here in time or to handle the situation head-on by myself. The only acceptable compromise was to reduce the risk somewhat. I'd let my one reliable police contact know what was happening, hoping Marci would send a backup. But, given our previous talks, I wasn't sure she wanted to help me again with problems I was about to create for myself.

Still, I punched the speed dial I'd set up for her on my burner phone, worried the call would go straight to voicemail, and I'd never know when or if she'd gotten my message. I was happy to hear Marci's voice answering live.

"Hi, Marci, this is Debra Ann — I'm on my burner, so no Caller ID."

"Oh, Debra Ann, I was just thinking about you." Marci sounded upbeat.

"Thanks for your text about arresting James Seaver." I began. "It's good to know, and it explains what's going on over here. Look, I'm sorry if this comes off as rude, but I have a situation, and time's run out. I know I don't have the right to ask, but I was hoping you'd help me out one more time…. I'm across the street from Ricky Mason's house at 13482 Elm Bluff, the one described in Brian Pierce's letters. I'm guessing Mason knows they've arrested Seaver. He's packing his car in a rush, and it looks like he's getting ready to flee the jurisdiction. I'm going to stall him."

"Dammit, Debra Ann, you can't be pulling this kind of crap!" Marci exclaimed, now almost screaming at me through the phone.

"You're going to get yourself killed. Get away from that man's property — right now! You don't need to do this; we'll get him. You *promised* me you'd leave it alone! Christ, that was for *your* benefit, to keep you out of this kind of trouble."

"Look, I get it, Marci," I pleaded. "I know I have no credibility with the department, but you *must* believe in me. Please send a squad car. I'll slow him down as long as possible, but he'll feel cornered, and there's no telling what he might do. Please, Marci. I have to go."

I hung up without getting assurance that she'd send anyone.

Mason had come out of his front door again with an armload of loose clothes and was locking the door behind him.

If I was going to intercept him, I needed to do it now.

I pulled the rental across the end of his driveway, blocking the Civic so it couldn't take off. With a short, red-brick wall running the length of one side of the drive and tall hedges on the other, I'd effectively trapped the Honda in place.

Jumping out of the rental car, I left it running with the driver's door swung wide open as I scooted around the back bumper.

I trotted at a half-run into the yard until I was close enough to Mason to converse without yelling.

By this time, the man had tossed the clothing on top of the duffel bag in the front passenger seat of the Civic. He'd closed that door and had both hands on the hatch lid, getting ready to slam it shut.

He twisted his head and shoulders toward my car, realizing the Civic had no pathway out of the drive. His head turned back slowly as his gaze followed me around my vehicle. Eyes creased, he slowly looked me up and down as I approached.

Mason appeared to be biting the inside of his cheek, sizing me up, trying to assess who I was and what I was up to.

"Ricky, I'm Debra Ann Wynn," I said through heavy breathing — the dash over the last twenty yards was causing stabbing pain outside my left lung.

"I'm a journalist working on the Brian Pierce homicide. I have some questions I need to ask you."

"I know who the hell you are," Mason snarled. "You've been making trouble for everybody just because Doc Seaver's wife split.

"I'm not talking to you! Get off my lawn, get your damned car out of my way, and leave me alone."

"Ricky, I'm not going away."

I stopped about eight feet from him, lying to slow him down.

"Even if I did, there were a lot of reporters trying to beat me here, and you're going to have to answer some questions no matter what I do.

"Your best bet is to handle this like a grownup and tell your story how you want it told before the rest of it hits the news."

"You're on my property, lady! If you don't leave, I have every right to throw you out of here — there's nothing says I have to be gentle about it."

Suddenly shooting his right foot forward, Mason quickly closed the distance, lunging and raising his arms as if intending to attack me.

His unexpected move startled me, but I tried not to show it and held my ground. He stopped short, his eyes darting toward the street.

Dropping his arms, he glared at me, now just two feet between us.

"What, you don't want the police to deal with your trespasser, Ricky? Here, let me call 911 and help you out."

Pulling my burner phone out of my purse, I saw why he'd abandoned his attack — three area residents had gathered on the sidewalk on the opposite side of the street and were looking our way.

Another walking a dog stopped at the yard next to us to listen in.

I took advantage.

"You and I both know your DNA and fingerprints will match the ones they pulled off Brian Pierce. You know, the man you beat to death and left in the alley."

My adrenaline was pumping more than I wanted to let on.

"You won't do anything that gets you into even more trouble out where all your neighbors can see you. And I'm not leaving until I get some answers."

I saw the gears turning in his head as Mason tried to calculate his next move.

I'd limited his options with his vehicle hemmed in and mine attracting attention from onlookers. My not-quite-parallel parking with my driver's door open into the traffic lane drew irritated stares from passing vehicles.

Mason turned away to slam the hatch closed, then rushed towards me as I raised my forearms in self-defense.

I couldn't back up fast enough to keep him from grabbing my elbow with his right hand and taking my phone with his left.

"Stop it; you're hurting me!" I protested loudly and tried to resist, but my sore ribs were having none of it.

"Fine, you want to talk? You get five minutes," Mason said, steering me toward the house and staying slightly behind me, "but that's it, and then you're out of here. You *feel* me?"

I knew talking wasn't what Ricky had in mind.

I wanted to scream, but I realized Ricky could make his escape in my still-running rental.

I'd have to hope that he wouldn't do anything violent with the neighbors looking in, and there was always the possibility one might call 911.

"I hear you loud and clear; you don't have to push." I tried to pull my elbow out of his grip as he took out his keys.

Mason didn't respond as he unlocked the front door to the house. He looked furtively back at the street and then pushed the door open.

He shoved me inside as I yelped in pain.

Stumbling, I nearly fell over the coffee table.

I realized I was now in deep trouble inside his house, with no one else able to see what was happening.

Quickly composing myself, I tried to regain at least some control.

"What I need from you is to confirm where you, Doc Seaver, and his girlfriend dumped Theresa's body," I said with as much authority as I could muster.

I was still facing away from him, with my hands on the coffee table where I'd caught myself from falling.

I tried to get my ribs to cooperate in pushing myself back upright. "My sources tell me the police have located it, and if you give it up before they announce it, you might have some leverage for a plea deal."

I may have fibbed a little, but I needed to focus his attention on the bigger picture now that he had me cornered.

"Screw you, lady," Mason bellowed as he threw my TracFone at the wall, its shattered remnants scattering across the carpet.

"You don't know what the *fuck* you're talking about!"

AVRIL MARIA SERENE

Chapter 56

Even if I'd brought the revolver, I wouldn't have had the slightest chance of fighting Ricky Mason off.

I hadn't seen the sheath on his left hip because of the angle he'd been standing in the yard. Mason pulled a hunting knife from it with his free hand. He was on me immediately, with the blade at my throat, his right hand clamped firmly to the hair at the nape of my neck. He kicked backward with his right shoe to slam the front door closed.

"So, what do you have to say for yourself *now*, bitch?" he hissed into my ear, standing behind me. "You think you can poke your nose into everyone's business, and it won't *cost* you?"

"Listen, Ricky, I called the police before I came. They're on the way. They know you beat Brian Pierce to death and left him in the alley. A witness saw you helping Seaver get rid of his wife's body. The detectives think you might have helped him kill his neighbor."

"There you go again, bitch — you don't have a fucking clue. I don't know anything about any damned neighbor. I don't believe a word you say.

"You're freelance, which means nobody will hire you for a decent job. And without the paper, who's going to back you? I didn't see anybody coming to your rescue when we tapped your Uber — did *you*? No, you sure the fuck didn't."

I wanted to respond but thought better of the idea, the knife's sharp edge pressing against my throat.

"No one gives a shit about your little crusade to make Doc look bad. You and your fucking made-up stories. Doc could have had you killed any time he wanted. I'm gonna hand him your rotting corpse as his birthday present."

Amid my panic and confusion came sudden coherence — I needed to gain control of myself and these circumstances, or I wouldn't survive.

"But first, you're gonna tell me who you've been talking to and what you think you know. And then, if anyone ever finds all your little bits and pieces, you can join your mommy, daddy, and baby brother feeding worms under that tree. You can spend all eternity explaining to them the screwups that got you there."

Okay, he wants to talk. I have a little time.

But I couldn't think what to do. On the one hand, Mason came off as if he'd watched too many gangster movies, showing off for the benefit of a camera that wasn't there. On the other, Mason *had* beaten a man to death, albeit with help.

Bottom line: He had a knife at my throat and knew way more about me than he should. All I could do was cooperate and hope for the right opportunity.

In the meantime, Mason had twisted the back of my hair into a ponytail, using it to drag me about the living room. As I tried to keep pace while off-balance and stumbling backward, he kept the blade pressed to my neck, moving it just long enough to cut the cord off a lamp or stereo component with his free hand while using his foot to steady the appliance. I assumed he meant to tie me up; that thought was comforting because it told me he wasn't planning to kill me right away.

Mason suddenly froze, tilting his head as if listening for something.

"Goddammit. What's that?"

Yanking me into the living room's corner, Mason used two fingers to separate the slats of the blinds in front of the big picture window, bobbing up and down as he peered out.

"Fuck!"

Suddenly, an explosive *WHAMM!* The front door, torn from its hinges, slammed into the wall.

The loud, crisp snapping of cracking wood. Splinters, dust, and drywall flying madly about. Bright filtered shafts of sunlight knifing through everything.

Then, through the noise and confusion, a stomping of boots and clattering of equipment.

Barked commands filled the air as three camouflaged men in riot gear charged through the opening, one side of the doorframe now dangling out in space.

From the rear of the house, I could hear the shattering of glass, military footwear pounding on the deck, and furniture screeching across the flooring.

I screamed as Mason cursed, pulling my posterior against him as he backed into the corner behind us.

Then, through a pass-through opening between the kitchen and the living room, my eyes caught the kitchen's sliding door bursting inward.

Millions of tiny tempered glass particles cascaded onto the dining table and vinyl floor.

Torn from its track, the aluminum frame for the patio door clattered against the cabinetry, scudding into the corner at a rakish angle.

I could hear the cleated boots of two burly men in green fatigues as they entered at a half-crouch, armed with assault rifles. Their footfalls went quiet as they paused in the kitchen's passageway to the living room, their weapons trained on Mason and me.

Two more men emerged from the back bedrooms, lining up in the hallway that branched off the living room. Placing their fingers alongside the triggers, they pointed their rifles toward the carpet at a 45-degree angle.

Pinned into the corner, Mason cowered behind me, trying to hide his more compact body behind mine, using me as a shield.

"Back off!" he screamed. "I'll slit this bitch's throat ear-to-ear, so help me, God!"

Mason's head darted back and forth between the three closest officers. He alternated between jabbing the blade toward the officers to punctuate his words and bringing the knife back to my throat.

My eyes had begun watering from the fine, acrid powder floating around us, clogging my nostrils and clouding my vision. Still, I noticed the SWAT team members in front of me placing a fingertip on the earpiece in their left ear. They'd listen intently, and then I heard each in their turn quietly say, "Understood, Lieutenant." It was apparent they were receiving specific instructions. But about what? The situation seemed a stalemate, my life in extreme peril.

And then, much to my surprise, hobbling cautiously through what remained of the front door, came Sgt. Marci Robbins, wearing her walking boot and leaning on crutches. Though my circumstances hadn't yet changed, I felt immense relief.

As she made direct eye contact with me, the first words out of Marci's mouth made no sense. "Nice shoes," she said, as casually and in the same tone of voice she might have used if we were discussing a passerby's outfit over coffee at an outdoor café.

Having limited style options, given what I had to work with back at the motel room, I was wearing the shoes I fondly called my "clodhoppers." They were a pair of sturdy and comfortable pumps with clunky one-inch block heels. But in what alternate universe was Marci living that the clothing I had on mattered?

"What is your *problem*, bitch?" Mason yelled, apparently thinking Marci directed the comment at him. "Nobody gives a damn about my fucking Adidas!"

"I'm sorry; I didn't mean to offend you, Ricky." Marci's voice was calm and collected. "My pain medication sometimes interferes with my thought processes. I am the hostage negotiator they've assigned to this situation. I am Sergeant Liz Franc, but everyone calls me 'Duck' or sometimes 'Lefty' — you can call me Liz, or you can call me Franc, or then again, you can call me Duck or Lefty; it doesn't matter. I always tell my husband, 'I'm *your* Lefty.'"

Now I knew what she wanted me to do and why my shoes mattered.

"What do you want me to call you? Ricky? Mr. Mason?" Marci asked.

"Fuck you, I don't give a rat's ass about anybody's damned name," Mason ranted. "I want you and these Nazis out of here, *now!*"

He swung the knife away from my throat to brandish it at Marci.

Timing it up perfectly, I slammed the heel of my left foot as hard as I could on top of his left tennis shoe.

Mason howled in pain, releasing his grip on my hair.

As I dove to my left, I heard two enormous bangs made louder by the relatively small space.

Turning, I saw Mason, his eyes shut, face crumpled in pain.

He slowly slid down the wall, leaving a bloody smear. His collapse exposed the hole in the wall where a bullet had passed through his chest near his upper right lung.

His knees hit the floor with a thump; he moaned as he weakly tried to get up. Crawling forward a few feet on his hands and knees, he dropped with a whimper onto his face.

I spun my head around to see the rounds had come from Marci, her service weapon still held straight out from her body in both hands, pointing at Mason. One crutch was under her arm, leaning against her, and the other had fallen to the floor.

A SWAT officer kicked away the knife on the carpet, handcuffed Mason's hands behind him, and rolled him onto his back. One of the SWAT team members announced loudly, "Offender neutralized, stand down. Repeat — offender neutralized. Stand down." Another officer called into his shoulder mike, "Lieutenant, we're going to need the paramedics, front room."

Stunned by the sudden events, I sat open-mouthed on the floor beneath the picture window.

A patrol officer helped me to my feet and then escorted me to the outside porch in the backyard. After running his hand over it to check for splinters, he sat me on the lid of a long wooden box, old and handmade, likely intended for storing firewood or gardening implements. The box sat on the concrete at the right side of the opening once occupied by the patio door.

A paramedic began checking me out.

As other officers were stringing crime scene tape, the SWAT tactical unit began packing to leave the premises. Patrol officers, detectives, and the forensics team were replacing them.

Several minutes passed before I spotted Marci through the wall's opening, gingerly limping over to check on me.

"Nothing wrong with your thought processes that *I* could see," I said with a relieved grin as we hugged.

"There must have been *something* badly amiss — if I were in my right mind, I would've left you to wriggle *yourself* out of the can of worms you opened." Marci gave me a sideways grin as she sat beside me, leaning her crutches against the stucco wall.

"There was a moment right after you hung up on our last call that I seriously wondered why I wanted to help you."

"Sorry I made that decision so hard...," I said meekly, eyes on a pebble a few inches past my toes.

"And then talking the lieutenant into trying the Lisfranc thing wasn't as easy as you might think. One strongly worded comment was that you might be too clueless to understand what we needed you to do. But the lieutenant talked me out of what I'd just said, and I took it back."

"Okay, I deserved that one." I playfully swiped at her shoulder. It amazed me how lightened my mood had become, something like a sugar high.

"But you'll never be able to take back the humongous relief and gratitude I felt when I saw your face at that door."

"Thanks, but seeing you still standing was a damned fine sight. We had to fly blind coming in. No time to set up." Marci tilted her head, giving me a "what the hell were you thinking?" look.

"A roller coaster ride for a few seconds there." I shook my head, my eyebrows arched, my eyes wide open.

"I *did* wonder if you'd lost your marbles when you complimented my shoes. By the way, how'd you get two shots off before the SWAT team fired?"

"Oh, nobody wanted me going into a hostage scenario unarmed." Marci showed me her right crutch. "So, the boys wire-tied my holster to the outside of the hand grip — what do you think?"

"No points for style, but obviously, it worked." I had to chuckle. "Give them my compliments."

Things behind us were quieting down into a steady murmur of workaday voices, and I thought I heard something that didn't belong.

"Do you hear that? Some kind of a hissing noise; comes and goes...."

"Maybe SWAT broke a water pipe on their way in?" Marci concentrated, trying to pick up the sound.

It seemed close to us, and Marci and I glanced around, looking for any signs of a water leak on the ground or coming out of the walls.

I was about to write it off as nerves or overstimulation when I heard it again.

"I hear it, too," Marci said with a slight frown.

"I don't smell anything." I tried to imagine what would cause it. "But it's hard to tell with the gunshot residue and all the filthy dishes Mason had piled up in the sink and on the counter. SWAT knocked them all over the floor when they crashed through."

"Mason was getting ready to flee." Marci's look was now worried. "You think he's asshole enough he'd intentionally rupture a gas line, maybe to burn the place down after he was gone?"

Looking at one another, we suddenly realized that's *exactly* what somebody like Mason might do.

Scanning the area near us for gas pipes or flexible hosing, we saw nothing. Then it occurred to me we might be sitting on the problem.

"Marci, I think it's coming from inside this box." I stood to help Marci up, passing her the crutches.

With her standing behind me, I lifted the plywood lid of the old box. As the light pierced its darkness, I could barely make out what was inside.

My screaming was so loud it froze everyone in their tracks.

THE WRITINGS OF
AVRIL MARIA SERENE

CHAPTER 57

My hands went to the side of my face as I began shrieking, letting the lid slam shut. Jumping backward, I nearly knocked Marci off her feet. As Marci caught me, her left crutch jammed itself into a crack at an angle, keeping both of us upright.

"My God, Debra Ann, what did you see?"

"It's Mark Christensen. I think he's *dead!*"

I took a deep breath. Lifting the lid together, we saw what had startled me — a man's eyes staring back at us, both wide open but unseeing, from a face spattered with grime and gore. He wore a blue tank top saturated in dried blood. Several small pools of bright-red bodily fluids oozed from slashes through the clothing on his chest, stomach, and thighs, with a thick puddle of dark crimson drying underneath him. A slow wheezing was escaping from between his lips.

"I need a team of paramedics at the back door, *stat!*" Marci yelled into the patio door opening. "I've got a victim down, multiple stab wounds, bleeding out!"

We stepped back to clear space for the paramedics and their equipment.

"Marci, that's the hotline tipster from Chicago — I interviewed him. I swear he was looking straight through me…. I'm sorry for losing it. My God — I've seen and reported some terrible things, but this is the first time I've ever discovered a body. Or come across one I wasn't expecting.

"*Jesus*, all that blood… I can't believe he's still breathing."

"He's pretty far gone." Marci pursed her lips. "The paramedics have some serious work to do to save him."

"What in the world is he doing back here?" I wondered out loud. "And why would he be anywhere near Ricky Mason?"

Marci and I stood for several moments, watching the paramedics work feverishly to stem the bleeding.

"Whatever he was thinking, he's paid a steep price," Marci observed.

"They're going to need his medical history," I said. "Let me make sure they at least have his name."

I walked over to a paramedic standing apart from the others. She was busily entering information into an iPad, and I gave her Mark's identity. I explained that I didn't know much about him — that he had friends in San Diego and spent the last several months in Chicago. I gave her Dale Newsome's contact information as a source who might know or could find out if and where Mark had received medical treatment in Chicago.

The paramedics were swarming the wooden box, knocking down the sides of it with a fire axe so they could get the man out without having to lift him. Two paramedics rushed through the patio door opening, carrying a collapsible gurney. Once they had him safely out of the box and the gurney raised on its wheels, a scramble followed to get his significant wounds identified, the blood flow slowed, and low-titer O-positive blood into his system. Once they'd done what they could, they hand-carried the gurney through the rough yard and around the house to the ambulance waiting in the front.

Marci and I watched in hopeful silence, and as the paramedics left, one stepped over to where we were so he could fill us in.

"I thought you might want an update. We can see seven significant wounds; we may find others once we get the patient into the trauma room.

He's in rough shape. Our biggest challenge is that he's in no condition to tell us anything. Still, I think he's got a chance if they can get him into surgery in time. The fact that he's a larger man may help, but he'd have been a goner if he'd spent another fifteen minutes in that box."

Marci hobbled over to the nearest uniformed police officer.

"Which of the detectives has the crime scene?"

"Lt. Roe took the lead. He's been working the Brian Pierce homicide, and he's back at the ambulance with the suspect," the officer replied, jabbing a thumb toward the front door of the residence.

"Would you take him a message for me? He may already know this, but make him aware that Mark Christensen is the victim the paramedics just put in the other ambulance. Christensen is a material witness who was present at the beating death of Brian Pierce — he's an admitted participant. Our investigators thought he was in Chicago and were trying to locate him there. Thank you, officer."

"My pleasure, Sergeant," the officer said as he returned to the living room on his way to the first ambulance.

"Okay, Debra Ann, this is an active crime scene," Marci announced once she'd returned. "Let's get out of their way."

We walked together in silence around the side of the house, stopping as we neared the sidewalk.

Marci filled me in on what to expect.

"You'll need to stay outside the crime scene tape. A detective will be around to get your statement once they take care of this new victim. Hopefully, it will be Lt. Roe, but it's no big deal; tell them exactly what happened. They'll refer you to the victim's services unit for counseling and follow-up support. You've seen how this works with other witnesses, so you know the drill."

"Got it," I said with a nod.

"I'm going to be unavailable. As soon as Internal Affairs and my union rep get here, I'll have to surrender my weapon and give a statement for the shooting review board."

"Will you get into trouble for shooting him?" Now, I was concerned for Marci.

"Oh, no — who knows, I might get a commendation." It was apparent Marci wasn't worried. "They like it when everyone comes out alive. It's just standard procedure any time an officer discharges their weapon."

"Oh, thank God. I'd feel terrible if you got punished for coming to my rescue." Perhaps my emotions were elevated by everything that had just happened — still, a tear came to my eye.

"About that, Debra Ann… Look, we don't always agree on everything. But we are friends. I am *so* sorry for giving you a hard time when you called today.

"When I saw he had that knife at your throat, I thought we could lose you. If I'd let that happen, I could never live with myself. I'm here to serve the public, even the hard-headed, stubborn ones, but more than that, you mean a lot to me. I'd never want you to think I'd let you down for any reason."

Now Marci's eyes were wet.

"I've kind of figured that out, Marci — *damn*, girl, you brought an *army*!"

Marci and I hugged tightly for quite a while, our respite from everything happening around us. I'd been *so* proud of my independence as a contrarian outsider, something I could get away with when I still had Dad's emotional support. But with that as my focus, I'd completely lost sight of my underlying need for acceptance. I'd finally found it in Marci and wanted to immerse myself entirely in that moment.

But the surrounding events were sweeping us along. I swiped my tears outward from under my eyes with my forefingers and clasped Marci's shoulders with both hands as she leaned against me, crutch sliding away.

"I am sorry that I am so pigheaded," I said through sniffles as I held her. "I don't mean to make it so hard for everyone. You're always there for me, and your friendship helps me get back on the right path when I wander too far off."

"Thanks for taking it that way." I could see gratitude in Marci's eyes, which seemed ironically backward, considering what she'd just done for me.

"But all other things aside, I *do* have to hand it to you," Marci added as she accepted the retrieved crutch from me. "Your instincts were spot on this time, and I was wrong. That man in the box has a chance because of what you did today."

"Glad you think my coming to confront Mason had a positive outcome." I realized now was a good time to be candid. "But honestly, I was just as surprised as you were that Mason had another victim in the backyard. You kept him and me alive by swooping in with the cavalry when you did.

"Under those circumstances, a SWAT officer might have killed Mason where he stood. So, if you want to count the bad guy, three people are among the living right now because of you. On behalf of everyone still here, thank you for being one damned fine police officer...."

I paused, unable to stop a broad smile.

"... oh, yeah, and for taking your training at the shooting range seriously.

"There might have been a split second there when I wondered how long it had been since you last qualified."

THE WRITINGS OF
AVRIL MARIA SERENE

CHAPTER 58

ONE YEAR LATER

Though shot twice at close range with high-powered police rounds in the right lung and abdomen, Ricky Mason would recover from his injuries. After a week in the hospital, authorities remanded him to San Diego County's jail facilities. He made the journey in a walking boot for the broken bones in his foot, courtesy of yours truly. Soon after, medical professionals released Mason to incarceration with the jail's general population.

Marci obtained permission for me to visit Mark Christensen in the hospital. He was undergoing follow-up surgery after emergency operations saved his life a year ago. I went to see how he was doing, but I also wanted answers to questions that puzzled me from when they took him out of that wooden box.

Mark had propped himself up on pillows, one leg cuffed to his hospital bed, an immobilization brace strapped across his chest and abdomen to support his neck, shoulder, and right arm. His left hand was tucked behind his head like he'd been watching television. A police officer sat outside his door, absorbed in a movie on his cell phone.

I approached Mark from his left side and stood at the bed's safety rail.

"Hello, Mark, it's good to see you again."

"I'm sorry I couldn't arrange better accommodations for your visit," he replied, raising his shackled foot. "But the alternative would have been much worse. They tell me I owe you my gratitude for discovering me in that box and saving my life."

"One of many surprises that day. I'm glad you survived. I admit I had doubts when I saw you lying there. How are you doing? Have they given you a long-term prognosis?"

"You'd have to ask the judge about my future." Mark's smile was lopsided. "But I assume you meant health-wise. The stabbing severed a bundle of nerves in my right shoulder. I don't have any control of my elbow, arm, hands, or fingers on that side. They're trying to get everything stabilized."

Mark patted his shoulder brace with the fingers of his left hand.

"They're talking nerve transplants to bridge the damage, but I'm not sure the prison's health plan will spring for it. But I'm adjusting. As you might have heard, I have bigger problems."

"I don't understand why you ran from Chicago. You seemed ready to make things right when we left you at the diner. If you'd cooperated, given the self-defense aspects of your involvement in the death, there was a decent chance you wouldn't have gotten much prison time, mostly probation. Brian Pierce's letters made it clear he came to kill one of you and set you up to take the blame for other crimes. Why take off — especially, why come back to San Diego and Ricky Mason?"

"After you left that day, I couldn't sleep thinking about being in jail. I'm not cut out for that. Look, I've been a big guy all my life. People always want to take me on to show how tough they are. I've had to learn that I'm not much of a fighter.

"And I'm claustrophobic as hell. If losing all that blood didn't end me, being helpless and trapped in that box would have. Jail cells aren't that big of an improvement.

"Plus, I wanted to return to San Diego, where my friends are. Chicago's no place to spend the winter."

"But why reach out to Ricky Mason?" I was still perplexed.

"I wanted Ricky to know I was back, so seeing me wouldn't surprise him; otherwise, he might think I pulled a fast one after taking his money. And he's the only person I knew who'd have access to the resources I needed to stay out of sight —he might know a good lawyer. If I told him you were onto us, maybe he'd take the warning as a favor and reciprocate. It was the only leverage I had.

"Jesus, I never thought he'd try to kill me. C'mon, I was twice his size, and we'd slept together. He promised me more money if I came to his place, but he was on me with that knife as soon as I stepped through his door. I never saw it coming."

"I've seen for myself how fast he is with it." I let out a sigh. "It's too bad you'll have to do more time than you would have. But you've never been in trouble before. If your lawyer does his job well, you'll have a chance to put a decent life together on the other side. Let me know if I can do anything to make things easier. In the meantime, I'll keep my fingers crossed for you."

"Thanks, Debra Ann, for coming to see me." Mark seemed sincere yet resigned to his fate. "And for everything you've done trying to help."

Marci and I went out for lunch later that day. I'd asked her to be my source for the installment wrapping up the series of articles Doug and I had written. I wanted to chronicle the completion of the Seaver and Pierce investigations and the results of the prosecutions. I already knew much of it but hadn't yet buttoned up the ending for my readers.

Marci dove right in once I'd turned on my recorder. "Flipping the Strike Response operative on the weapons, insurance fraud, and drug charges gave us much of what we needed to fill in the gaps in these cases, including Coach Cantor's."

"By the way, say 'hi' for me to your friend Harry; I see he's been keeping himself busy." Marci winked.

Until then, I didn't realize she knew of Harry or his involvement, but apparently, she thought well of him — I'd have to ask her more over our next lunch.

"He's *quite* the interesting character," I replied, equally coy, "but it seems he doesn't always put things back where he finds them." *That* drew a grin from Marci.

"We learned Strike Response did the body dump and cleanup at Mason's residence after Brian Pierce's homicide," she continued. "They made it challenging for the forensics team. There was a strong smell of bleach throughout the bedroom and bathroom; the carpet and pad were brand new. The bleach rendered the blood in the cracks between the bedroom floorboards under the padding beyond use to us."

"Unfortunate, but from what I know, Strike Response has had lots of practice."

"It wasn't all bad. The signs they left doing their work told us where Strike Response had cleaned up. So we knew that the violence occurred in that bedroom and where to concentrate our efforts. And we found glass slivers from the bookcase front in those cracks where the blood would have been. Their refractive index matched shards embedded in the body. We discovered tiny, uncompromised drops of Pierce's blood on the underside of the bed frame rail and the edges of the ceiling fan blades.

"And Strike Response missed other things. We located a stamp pad in a desk drawer in the other bedroom, and the ink matched what we pulled off Pierce's fingertips."

"So, forensically, you had what you needed for trial despite the cleanup?"

"For our purposes, yes. As expected, Mason's prints and DNA matched a set found on Pierce. Evidence recovered in the alley where they dumped his body didn't tell us which of the two prints and DNA contributors delivered the blow that resulted in death. But, as you know, it doesn't matter in California."

"Here, multiple parties to a murder involving another felony are equally guilty."

"But it gets better." Marci was on a roll. "While we were gathering evidence against him, supposed tough guy Ricky Mason may have set the world's record for the least elapsed time to flip. He was terrified of incarceration. Trying to play a hardcore banger with his small stature doesn't work out well in a place where everyone else is bigger and badder."

"When we faced off in his front yard, it surprised me he's no taller than I am."

"That, his attitude of superiority, and his mouth do not a likable combination make," Marci noted. "After the first few nights, he was on his knees begging the jailers to let him talk to the district attorney for a plea deal."

"Now *that's* a visual I wish someone had filmed." Granted, smirking at the image in my head was mean-spirited, but that knife at my throat had earned me the privilege.

"His statements, along with the evidentiary material from his house and vehicle, ended up supporting three cases: Seaver, Pierce, and the new one for the attempted murder of Mark Christensen."

"Let's get into the Seaver case, then," I suggested.

"Mason gave James Seaver up for moving Theresa's body — the first words out of his mouth sitting across from the DA. The dump site location he gave us was empty; he claimed someone must've moved the body afterward. We did find a sex worker's corpse a few yards from where Mason sent us. The killer wrapped her in the plastic sheeting painters use — too much cross-contamination on it to be helpful, likely used and discarded before being re-purposed. The probable cause of death was blunt-force trauma in the back of the head, and she'd broken her leg perimortem. We couldn't make enough of a connection to Seaver or Mason for the DA to file additional charges — he didn't want to muddy up his other cases."

"Assuming Seaver *did* bury Theresa's remains there before moving them, he must have something to do with that other corpse," I mused. "Serial killers tend to use a favorite dump site over and over...."

Marci nodded.

"Mason denied involvement in Theresa's homicide or the murder of Julius Cantor. Mason did confess to taking part in Pierce's beating death, but it took some work. He initially blamed Mark Christensen for murdering Pierce.

"Mason claimed he met Christensen at a straight bar and that the killing happened in his living room. We knew the last portion of that wasn't true. We assume by relocating the incident to the living room, he was trying to take the male-on-male sexual component out of it."

"I imagine he finds it difficult to reconcile the hard-ass image he tries to project with who he truly is," I offered. "It's a little reassuring to know Christensen has a conscience. And Christensen is an out gay man whose story makes much more sense than Mason's. Too bad Christensen didn't stay in Chicago — he wouldn't have ended up in that box nearly bleeding to death."

"Exactly," Marci agreed. "The DA was inclined to go lighter on Christensen because he seems more of a standup guy, though a little late to the game with the honesty. Christensen didn't get a free pass — they'll keep him locked up a while longer. Still, with time served, a few added months of incarceration, and probation, he can build a better life if he behaves from here on out.

"Mason went a different path and screwed himself," Marci continued. "As the evidence came in and we learned Sheryl Jansen's and Christensen's stories, it became obvious Mason had lied. That violated his plea agreement. We no longer needed Mason's testimony against Seaver once Jansen came forward. So, the DA threw the book at Mason for all of it: the desecration of Theresa Seaver's body, Brian Pierce's murder, your abduction, and the attempted murder of Mark Christensen."

"Brian *will* get some justice after all." I mustered a sad smile. *As for Dad, he can rest easily, knowing that his last mission is finally complete.*

Just a few days later, Doug Stein and I got together to put the concluding installment of our series to bed. We met at a picnic table in one of our local parks to enjoy the sunshine. The Court had sentenced James Seaver the day before, and that was the first thing on Doug's mind.

"Executions may be on hold in California, but the law still allows lethal injection as punishment, should Federal courts ever release the stay. I wish the DA had gone for it in the Seaver case," Doug said.

"I'm sure that's part of why Seaver took the deal before the jury came in," I replied. "The death penalty had him shook. It wasn't much of a deal — three consecutive life sentences without the possibility of parole. That won't keep him out of the courts, though. He's got dozens of civil suits to defend — private citizens and federal and state authorities trying to recover funds from his frauds and illegal enterprises."

"You said that was 'part' of it – what did you mean?"

"The assistant DA and I were out in the hall talking afterward. Seaver had this little dachshund he was hung up on, called it 'Bubbles,' kind of a strange relationship… anyway, the ADA told me the dog died as the judge was giving the jury its instructions. She says Seaver completely freaked and took it as a bad omen. Right after, he asked if the deal was still on the table. You think you have someone figured out, but you can never be sure."

"True… A shame no one's found Theresa's body." Doug's expression was contemplative as he changed topics.

"Won't help Seaver, though." I didn't hide my disdain for the man. "He'd have been better off to give it up. Once he allocuted to the plea deal, the court granted a formal finding of Theresa Seaver's death to make it legal.

"There's a twist of cosmic justice to it — her official passing did Seaver no good. Theresa made Seaver sign a prenup before marrying him to protect the inheritance she was expecting. He signed it to convince her of his proclaimed interest in her rather than her future wealth. I'm guessing James Seaver was counting on his manipulative skills to get from her whatever he wanted after their vows."

"He shot himself in the foot…," Doug murmured.

"Worse for him," I continued, "the state barred him from profiting through his crimes. That meant the proceeds from several life insurance policies went to Theresa's son, Terrence Martin. And Theresa had never revised her will from when she and Darrell Woodson were still married — therefore, no mention of Seaver. Its provisions split her estate between Darrell and Terrence."

"How much money did she have? I mean, *really?*"

"Her old man had a ton of money," I answered. "This area's first billionaire family, some say, and she and Terrence were the only heirs…. But I don't think we'll ever know, honestly. Only small parts of that estate, assets she kept in the United States, were visible. Most of her wealth was in offshore accounts and tax havens, some of that likely Seaver's idea."

"With her estate tangled up in Seaver's crap, you'd think all kinds of people would be after her money. After all, her holdings represent the deepest pockets," Doug speculated.

"I heard the parties to the civil suits against Seaver were digging in," I replied, "along with the IRS and law enforcement authorities. They searched for and monitored any accounts they could find that benefitted Seaver. But at least so far, lawyers have kept them from touching anything that belonged to Theresa's estate. That prenup's holding its own, and they have no claims against her specifically."

"Theresa had *serious* issues," Doug observed, "but she seems to have gotten smarter as she went along. It's too bad she ran out of time."

"Makes you wonder what might have been," I agreed, swatting at a fly. "But from a karma perspective, it's hard to top what happened with that mall property. Theresa had regained the controlling interest, so Darrell inherited that as well. The judge awarded him the remaining ownership when Darrell sued Seaver in civil court."

"For all his murders, scams, and bullying," Doug summarized, "Seaver came up empty-handed. Perfect. So, what happened to the other players?"

"Six months after Seaver's arrest, Texas Rangers detained Richard Ainsworth in Houston. California extradited him, and they've tried and convicted him for three homicides. There was Seaver's neighbor, Julius Cantor, of course, and two prior homicides linked ballistically to the rounds found in Coach's body. Ainsworth received the death penalty for Coach's murder and life sentences without parole in the other two killings."

"Good triumphs all 'round," Doug said.

"Some shining moments stood out to me, and Terrence Martin gets the golden statuette. He did one of the most amazing things I've ever witnessed a teenager do. The kid gave up half of the money he received without prompting once the judge declared his mother legally dead.

"He sent most of what he donated to Antara's family, and the rest went to Coach's estate… the two most innocent of James Seaver's victims."

"It's surprising how positive things can come out of ugliness." Doug turned sideways on the wooden bench, leaning on his elbow.

"Terrence is an interesting young man." I let my eyes follow two kids with a soccer ball. "I went out to see my parents a couple of weekends ago. I spent a moment at Brian's family's grave to pay my respects. There was an unsealed envelope in the vase holder, which reminded me how all this started for Dad. I shouldn't have, but I just had to peek inside."

"What did you find?"

"A brand-new invisible ink pen, a spare battery, and an unsigned note that read, 'Brian — you might need this if you don't have one where you're at.'

"The preprinted front of the envelope had a return address in the corner — The Casbah."

"Interesting, indeed...," Doug murmured.

"I realized then and there that the rest of this had made me too damned cynical. I hadn't been able to shake the feeling Terrence was overdoing the generosity — like he was trying to atone for something. That envelope reminded me he's just a teenager; *none* of this was his responsibility."

"You shouldn't be beating yourself up, Debra Ann. You've written several quality in-depth pieces this past year related to the murders of Theresa Seaver and Brian Pierce and the aftermaths. Six during the trials, and this one will make five after the convictions."

"Thanks, Doug." I paused in thought. "Still, I'm more pleased to see it end than happy with how this story turned out. And it's not just the pointless murders. I still wake up at night with questions.

"I guess only James Seaver will ever know the answers, and he's not talking."

CHAPTER 59

SIX YEARS LATER

The display on my cell phone read "Unidentified," as the ring tone added to the commotion. I was running late already. My husband and I were frantic this morning. We were trying to get Tommy and Sarah their lunches and backpacks before the school bus and daycare van arrived, all while coercing the dogs into the backyard and away from the kids and the food.

"You can take it, honey; I got this handled," Paul called out from the kitchen.

I stepped into the bedroom we used for a home office.

"Is this Debra Ann Wynn?" the throaty voice on the other end asked.

"Before I was married, yes. What can I do for you?"

"Well, Debra Ann, I've been a fan of your writing for a long time as I've followed your fascinating career. I have a story I know you'll want to hear, and I can't think of anyone else qualified to report it."

"I'm flattered, but… I'm sorry, I didn't catch your name…." *And I don't have time for this* raced across my mind.

"I didn't give it, Debra Ann," the disembodied voice replied. "I *will* say I've become rather expert on quality reporting — the media has written about me extensively. But you'll know who I am soon enough."

"Look, I don't want to be rude, but...." I pulled the phone away from my ear to punch the disconnect button.

"It concerns two murders you don't know about and one that wasn't," the voice intoned, not seeming too concerned about me hanging up. "You're being given a chance to get it right this time. Or not — your choice. But you'll want to do your job, Debra Ann. Meet me in the main lobby of the Hotel Del at ten."

"How do I know...." I started to ask, but the line was dead. *They'd* hung up on *me*.

I started an independent news bureau four years ago. I'd thought about doing it sooner after Dad opened up my options with the money he'd left me, but there were too many things going on then.

Honestly, running a business had never appealed to me for many reasons. For one, I hadn't inherited that greed gene modern capitalism requires for success. In my mind, I would picture the allele representing mercenary sleaze just slip-sliding out of my DNA chain because it's so greasy. However, I'm pretty sure that's not how it works in reality.

Most things I valued in life weren't quantifiable in dollars and cents: love, laughter, friends, and family, to name a few. Sure, I get that some people spend their entire lives using perceived, contrived, or stolen advantage to take more from other people than they give back. I understand that they call the unearned gain 'profit' — which, as it happens, also perfectly describes the proceeds from a gangbanger robbing a liquor store. But I'd always wanted my life to stand for something less transactional. And it was hard to respect business leaders who displayed the same narcissism and sociopathy I saw among the criminals that I investigated every day.

The old saw goes that you don't get to choose them, but I've always been grateful for my parents. They'd raised me never to allow myself to become so weak and insecure that I needed to scam things from other people — the plain-spoken description of what modern advertising does — to affirm my identity. I preferred honesty in some form. Given my skills and aptitudes, that meant getting my hands dirty chasing a story. I'd earn any kudos that came my way through the benefits my readers derived from my work. I'd follow the paths of my father, who built quality structures, and my mother, who nursed patients back to health, to show my worth.

For all of that, I've never been good at predicting my life's direction. Doug Stein, however, had read the tea leaves well. He'd been awarded the MBA he earned by attending classes part-time during his last several years at the *Union-Tribune*. By the time the paper let Doug go, we'd spent many a cup of coffee discussing his belief that we could build an honorable business the old-school way.

He'd convinced me we could focus on providing much-needed, high-value pool reporting and investigative services accessible online, trusting the rewards for our efforts would come organically. Doug would become my indispensable right hand, managing our business affairs while dabbling in editing and writing as time allowed. That permitted me to guide our reporters and story development while taking the lead on interesting, breaking, or critical pieces.

Things were a little rough at the start. However, after a few lean years, our formula began working beyond our wildest expectations. We'd migrated from local pieces to national and, occasionally, international articles.

Claire now ran Harry Sanderson's detective agency. My bureau contracted the liberated Harry and the small crew he supervised to do deeper investigations for us. The private detective called it his "semi-retirement," but Harry worked as hard as anyone. The man seemed happier out in the field, away from business worries, though he kept things at the office entertaining.

Marci had gotten her gold detective's shield and had proved an excellent investigator. We'd remained close, but she could no longer be a confidential source in her new role. Still, we lunched regularly — Marci would fill me in on the department's doings, keeping me abreast of the more compelling cases as they came along. When publishing a story would help with one of her investigations, she knew I'd be there to push things along for her.

My husband Paul was now a supervisory physical scientist in the forensics lab for the FBI's San Diego division. After several years with California's Bureau of Forensic Services, he'd landed the coveted new role, and ours was a good life. We'd built a new home in Carmel Mountain after we'd married. Tommy was born three weeks after our vows, and Sarah came along almost four years later. Both were happy, healthy, and bright kids with curious minds and stubborn streaks as wide as their shoulders. Paul and I wouldn't have had it any other way.

Cathy Andreesen passed away almost six years ago after a long bout with pneumonia following treatment for a stroke. We gave Sarah "Cathy" as her middle name when she was born.

In the meantime, I'd written my first book, a compilation of short stories fictionalized from my experiences. It sold well, and I worked on the follow-up whenever I could find off moments.

The thought that I didn't have time for mind games wasn't merely reactive; reality can be harsh. Still, the anonymous caller's comment about having been the subject of "extensive" writing was cryptic. *A celebrity, trying to avoid the paparazzi, perhaps?* I didn't recognize the voice, though they may have altered it. But California was full of stars in a variety of orbits. And every day, there were mysterious goings-on among them, some undoubtedly illegal, up to and including disappearances and deaths. Yet, something about the caller and what they'd said seemed… *personal.*

Not knowing the whole story bugged me, and I talked myself into playing along. I made phone calls to rearrange my schedule, leaning on Doug to keep things rolling. An hour later, I sat under an elegant chandelier in a deeply tufted, green velvet center seat at the restored main lobby of the Hotel del Coronado. I may have known the iconic San Diego landmark well, but I had no idea what to expect from this meeting.

A tall, slender man in a black uniform suit, crisp white shirt, and black cap with a patent leather bill approached me from the entrance. His British accent was unmistakable as he leaned over and made his request.

"I've been asked to come and collect you for your appointment. Would you care to follow me, please?"

I dutifully gathered my belongings, trailing a few feet behind. *I was right about the celebrity thing. This guy's right out of central casting.*

As he opened the stretch limo's rear door, I saw just one occupant, wearing a tan raincoat and seated near the opposite window. They seemed vaguely familiar despite the floppy hat and oversized sunglasses. Though the idea did flash through my mind that I might be looking at the reincarnation of Truman Capote, that wasn't it. The small dog lying in their lap was graying, and the stiffness of its movements suggested it was suffering the afflictions of old age.

It wasn't until my host spoke that I realized she was an older woman.

"Would you care for some gum?" she asked as I took my seat catty-cornered from her, offering a stick from a pack with a foreign brand I didn't recognize.

I politely declined, and she made a show of selecting a stick for herself, then began chewing it as the limo started moving. She pressed the button to raise the privacy partition between us and the driver.

"No matter, I have a little gift for you."

Chewing furiously, she opened the purse beside her, pulling out a sandwich-sized zippered baggie. She took her gum out of her mouth with a forefinger and thumb and dropped it into the little plastic pouch.

"In the event you should have any questions." She winked as she zipped it closed. She then opened the fastener on a large manila envelope she pulled from behind her purse and dropped the baggie into it. After refastening the clasp, she handed the envelope to me.

She's likely harmless, I thought, *but no doubt an eccentric old gal.* The meeting so far would qualify as one of the strangest introductions I'd experienced in my journalistic career.

"You can test it later," she offered, removing her hat and sunglasses.

It took a moment.

After all, I'd never met the woman in person; the only photos I'd seen were almost eight years old. The appearance of a female of a certain age can change radically over so much time.

But there she sat, right before me, apparently feisty — and very much alive.

"You're ... *Theresa Seaver?*"

I was too stunned to think of anything more clever to say.

"That was once my name, yes," she replied. "The great thing about international travel is that new identities are readily available if you have the money. And it's not like I'm wanted for any crimes or have a history of such behaviors.

"But you can call me Margorie McCall. Do you know your Irish legends, Debra Ann?"

"'Lived once, died twice.' Yes, I've heard the story."

I had to give Theresa, now Margorie, credit for her sense of the theatrical.

"And this must be Bentley," I said, smiling at the little dog. Suddenly, an awareness struck me: *what a fool I'd been.*

"Ah, you've spoken to Terrence. After my son, Bentley is my pride and joy," Margorie nodded, looking down as she petted him tenderly between his ears.

Terrence knew, I thought, as I tried to keep the realization from showing in my expression. I'd rather believe he found out *after* that night at the Casbah, but either way, he let me go on wasting my time trying to nail his mother's presumed killer. *Terrence knew when she came to get her dog, if not before, and he said nothing to me.* It never occurred to me that Terrence would be complicit in a scam. It was hard to admit I was so far off my game back then.

"I'm confused… Darrell and Terrence both told me that you didn't like traveling." I was genuinely perplexed — I could no longer trust Terrence, but Darrell wouldn't have had any reason to lie.

"Of course not." Margorie gave me a sly smile. "Not when someone else is making me do it. But going where I want when I want and doing *what* I want is a lot of fun!"

That explains that.

"I promised you a story of two murders you didn't know." Margorie's expression had turned serious. "The homicide that never happened should be obvious. The envelope's contents will provide all the verification you'll need. Are you ready to hear it?"

"Of course; may I record this?"

"You may." She waited as I pulled my digital voice recorder out of my purse.

"Ready," I announced. "Where do we start?"

"You may recall there was a point before my presumed death," Margorie began, "when Doc had completely screwed up my financial affairs — so much so that I was facing criminal charges from the District Attorney. Not to mention a litany of coming civil suits, all the results of Doc trying to get at my inheritance from my father."

"I do. One theory at the time was that you'd run off, but there were witnesses to the moving of what we assumed was your body...."

"Oh, there was a body. Just not mine." Giving out a wry little laugh, Margorie seemed to change subjects. "Don't you just hate it when certain men assume their gender makes them smarter than you?"

"I know the feeling."

"I'll bet you do. Vulnerable is not necessarily stupid. Anyway, no one was more surprised than Doc when I called the weasel out and told him unless he got me out of the jam he created, I'd cut him off, money and all. So, he came up with the only one of his schemes that ever worked as conceived. The plan was to grab a working girl off the streets and kill her in a way that her injuries would be above the neck. He had to kill two; the first broke her leg as she fell. We kept the good one in the fridge until the night we did the deed. Doc arranged for two witnesses, both known to be flakey, but who'd support the tale we wanted them to tell."

"Ricky Mason and Doc's girlfriend, Sheryl?"

"The wannabe thug and the speed freak nail-tech-slash-stripper." Margorie snorted. "What a pair. We knew neither of those two could keep a secret, and it would be just a matter of time before one of them talked about my murder. So, after we heated the hooker's skin with a hair dryer and sprayed some air freshener around to keep down the smell, we put a plastic bag over her head. We rolled her under the bed, dressed in copies of the same clothes I'd wear to my charity function."

"I'm beginning to understand where this is going...."

"Doc calls up his skank," Margorie continued. "Cat's away; time for the mice to play. I stage my little scene, breaking in on them; Doc swings the golf club — the idiot nearly hit me. I bite my little ampule of theatrical blood before I drop to the floor. Doc checks my pulse and announces I'm dead. He tells the tart to put a shopping bag over my head and then sends her downstairs to get the big rug under the dining room table. She's not physically strong, so we know it'll take her a while. We roll our working girl out from under the bed and exchange the shopping bag over her head for mine. I sneak into the bedroom across the hall and hide in the closet."

"Sheryl Jansen didn't strike me as all that observant. That probably helped the ruse...."

"Absolutely. I almost coughed when I bit the ampule, but the meth addict didn't notice. The hardest part was not laughing or gagging when Doc's wiener dog..."

"Bubbles?"

"I see you've done your homework." Margorie seemed impressed. "Yes, Bubbles. He kept trying to lick the fake blood off my face, and what was so disgusting was he'd just come from under the bed licking that dead hooker all over — his breath was horrible.

"Anyway, Doc makes a big show of taping the bag around the streetwalker's neck to keep it from coming off and then rolling her up in the rug. Doc closes the door, and he and his slut-puppy start banging bones, which gives me a chance to make my escape. I left my car on the street in front of the house so passersby would think I was still there. Doc had stashed his a few blocks down, and I took it to the airport, flying out under my new identity."

"So, at this point, you *are* bouncing around Europe...."

"Yes. Eventually, you do *your* thing, which makes everyone pretty sure I'm dead. No one's looking for me. The DA has to dismiss the charges against me. I'm free to party on the money my father left me in all those offshore accounts. But that wasn't the fun part."

"Sounds like a laugh riot so far." I chose, for the moment, not to confront Margorie as an accessory to the murders of the two working girls. "Considering the circumstances you were facing before you did all that."

"Oh, no, *ma chèrie*." Margorie had a wicked grin on her face. "The good part was sticking it to that asshole, Doc."

THE WRITINGS OF
AVRIL MARIA SERENE

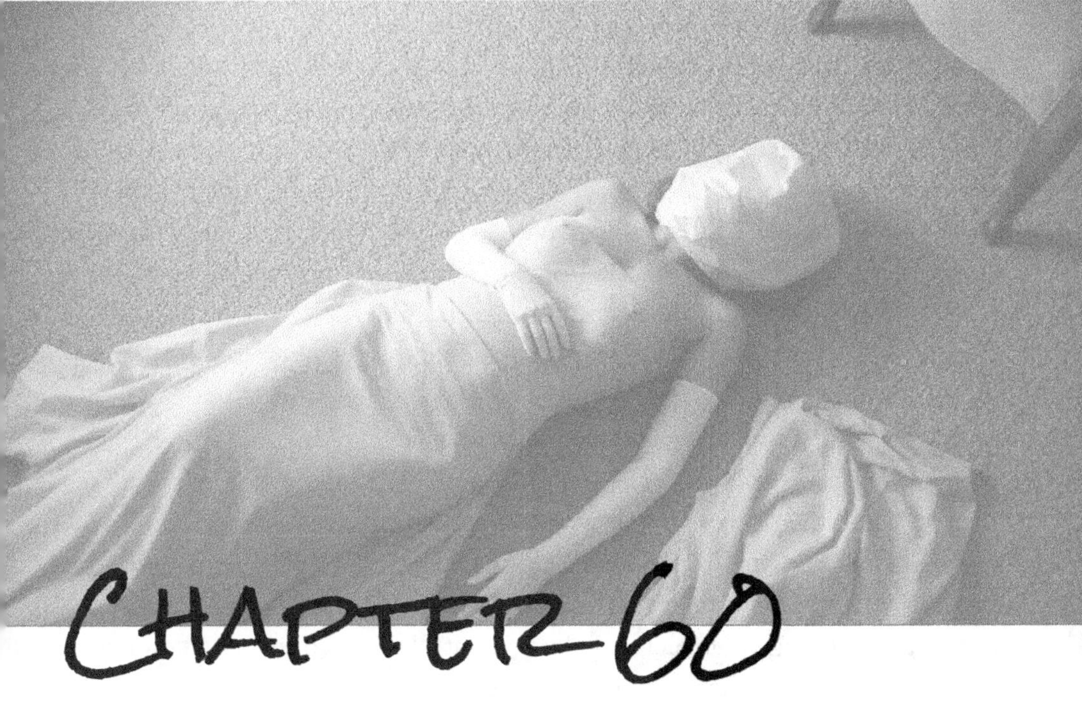

CHAPTER 60

Since first learning how much she knew about his activities, I'd often wondered why James Seaver hadn't killed Sheryl Jansen. He had a reputation for being quick to eliminate anyone he saw posing any danger to him. Or why he hadn't worked around the reliable Ainsworth's travel schedule to have the professional kill and bury Theresa. For that matter, why had Seaver let Ricky Mason live after the man had screwed up and killed Brian Pierce, doing so in front of a witness?

Genius, in a twisted way: Seaver needed bystanders under his control who could pass a polygraph attesting to Theresa's "death" and burial. But they had to be too undependable in the eyes of a competent DA to withstand defense cross-examination in a criminal court.

I had to admit — at least to myself — that it impressed me they'd pulled this off. And, if there was more to this story, I couldn't wait to hear it.

"Doc's an arrogant prick," Margorie said matter-of-factly, "and he doesn't see anyone he thinks inferior as a threat."

"That comes across loud and clear." I hadn't forgotten the conversation in the hallway outside my apartment.

"He took it for granted he'd get a deal from me in exchange for his help out of the mess *he created*." Margorie had a derisive smile on her face. "Doc expected me to give him any signatures he'd need on legal documents and access to enough money to close out all the scams he had in play. He made two mistakes: Doc should have gotten my signatures first. And he should never have just trusted me for the money."

"What made him think you'd give it to him?"

"I 'accidentally' left my online banking app open on my laptop screen, showing a big balance I had in one of my accounts. I gave Doc the account and routing numbers but told him he couldn't have the online password until I was 'dead.' The idiot bought it."

"He thought he had you wrapped around his little finger...."

"His screwup," Margorie acknowledged. "I don't know why he thought he'd still have his hooks in me once I was in the wind. But on the morning of the staged homicide, I cleaned out all the accounts he knew about and sent the money offshore. But it gets better."

"How so?"

"He told me the police couldn't arrest him. Their witnesses would be too weak. They had no remains, they couldn't find physical evidence of a murder that never actually happened, and he had good lawyers. He thought so long as I stayed elsewhere, he could put all the blame for his other problems on his now-dead wife … *me*."

"Sloughing the nasty parts off onto other people — the approach he takes to everything," I mused.

"Then, if there was too much heat," Margorie continued, "and it looked like he *was* going down for my murder, I was supposed to pop up and say, 'Hey, just kidding, here I am, guys!' The cops would look like fools. Doc could play the harassed victim. We'd expose the unreliable witnesses for what they were, and I'd play the ditzy heiress having a field day on my dead daddy's bankroll."

"If Darrell's recounting was accurate, it wouldn't have been your first resurrection. And Seaver could fix everything else by throwing around more of *your* money."

"*Of course.*" Margorie's voice dripped with sarcasm. "So, when your guy with the letters…"

"Brian Pierce," I interjected.

"Yes, the one in the house the night we moved the body," Margorie confirmed. "When he turned up as a third witness to dumping the body, and then that shit-for-brains Ricky Mason killed him, Doc freaked out. He demanded I come back home. *Demanded!* Oh, and he'd be *so gracious* as to forgive me for writing the multimillion-dollar bounced check — like he was doing me this huge favor. What an *ass!*"

"The arrogant prick thing. And wouldn't you still have the fraud charge Doc set you up for hanging over your head?"

"Exactly. I wish I'd told Doc on a Zoom call where I could have seen his expression, but I worried it would be too easy to record or trace. Still, I could imagine Doc's jaw dropping to the floor when I told him I was staying right where I was. And, wait for it… that I'd recorded him killing the two prostitutes out by the Navy base and kept the videos in a safe deposit box. I informed the mastermind that I'd had the second hooker's remains moved, and he'd never find them. Without those, he had nothing to show the authorities if he wanted to change his story about me being dead. But *me*? I could reveal that corpse's location any time it suited me.

"If he so much as breathed a word about me being alive to anyone, he might get out of killing me, but he'd go down for two more homicides."

Margorie pressed the button to lower the privacy partition and then tapped on the partition's frame to get the driver's attention.

"Edward, take us back to the Hotel Del so we can drop Debra Ann off."

Raising the privacy partition again, Margorie made it clear our conversation was over.

Still, before our discussion ended, I needed an answer to one final question.

"I'm still struggling to understand why in the world Doc would have agreed to subject himself to suspicions of murder — that just seems extreme."

"That's because you didn't have the privilege of watching Doc's eyes turn into saucers when he found out exactly how much my father had left me in the will. If he'd have been one of Pavlov's dogs, you could have filled a swimming pool with the slobber."

"That part I get. But even so, why set himself up for murder?"

"I had him over a barrel. The only way he'd get access to any of my accounts was on my terms, and he knew it. I told him the idea of having me run off to Europe again was pure crap, and I wasn't having it. No way was I going to spend the rest of my days looking over my shoulder as INTERPOL's trying to find me, like happened the last time. Whatever he came up with, my role — in *any* of it — had to be finished, and for good. The only way I'd even *think* about letting him have any money was if he came up with a way to make that happen — and one that made sense to me.

"And I'm sure having a bird in hand was motivating him. Doc needed the money in a hurry, and there I sat, willing to give it to him. *If….*

"Knowing him, Doc probably figured that once he had a boatload of cash, he'd wave it in front of people to make any problems he'd created in the meantime disappear."

Margorie's tone and demeanor changed as we neared Hotel Del.

"Don't try to find me. I won't have any name you'd recognize or be in the same place when you go looking. The gum will give you DNA to prove who I am, but there's no chain of custody, so the authorities can't use it as evidence. The same goes for your audio recording."

Margorie pointed at the manila envelope I was hugging.

"I've given you the locations of the two hookers' bodies and the proof of their murder."

"Proof in what form?" I was curious how solid it might be.

"You'll see. Look, those girls didn't deserve what happened to them," she continued, "and if I could take it all back, I would.

"I promised you on the phone that you'd choose whether you want to set things right for them and how you'll do it. But I think you know there's a cost."

With that, the limo stopped, and Edward opened the door to let me out. I glanced back at Margorie, in sunglasses and floppy hat again, unsure what to say.

And so, I said nothing, walking to the curb silently and standing there deep in thought as Edward closed the door, climbed into the driver's seat, and slowly drove the limo away.

CHAPTER 61

The moment I arrived home, I ripped the manila envelope open. What I found in it immediately took me back over seven years — two pages of blank lined white paper and a USB flash drive.

I assumed the blank paper was not, in fact, empty, taking it as Margorie's homage of sorts to Brian Pierce's letters. But before I tried to scrounge up a black light, I wanted to see what was on the thumb drive.

I found two high-definition video files on the drive, both filmed in the green glow generated by a night-vision movie camera. They revealed James Seaver killing both of the working girls, one in an alley and the other behind the tree line of a park. There were enough details in the videos that law enforcement could determine their precise locations.

Years ago, I'd buried Dad's black light and scanning rig in a box deep in a storage unit. I didn't know what shape they were in, so I decided ordering the black light overnight from Amazon made more sense.

When the lamp arrived the next day, the kids' afternoon sitter held it in position for me as I snapped readable cell phone images of the exposed pages of Margorie's letter.

Her message started with an explanation of sorts for the invisible ink:

> I thought you might appreciate the twist, ending this adventure as you started it.

She followed that with GPS coordinates for the buried remains of the two sex workers, providing detailed descriptions of the locations. The authorities knew about the first hooker's body but not its connection to Seaver. After not finding any remains where Ricky Mason claimed he'd helped bury Theresa, they searched the surrounding area further, discovering the unexpected corpse.

If it existed, the second body — the woman allegedly killed and used as a stand-in for Theresa — could upset years of investigations. It would affect all the work that had gone into prosecuting and convicting Seaver and his cronies. I wasn't about to open Pandora's box until I was absolutely sure there was a corpse that matched the story Margorie had told me.

Complicating all this was that Sheryl Jansen, a key witness against James Seaver and the only one present when he swung that golf club at Theresa, had died. She'd relapsed in her fight against addiction, finally succumbing to an overdose two years ago.

I had a pretty good idea of what we needed to do, but I wanted Paul to chime in before I took it much further. The first step was to copy the digital audio I recorded from my interview with Margorie onto a flash drive. I added the camera images of the two pages she'd included in the manila envelope and the night-vision videos she provided. The next day was a Saturday, and the kids were heading off to their first summer day camp. I hit Paul up after breakfast as I got them ready to go.

"Paul, I'm going to drop off Tommy and Sarah at the 'Y,' and then I've got to meet with Harry on the Edgerton story. I should be back in a couple of hours. But I need a serious favor. You know Thursday when I met a source at the Hotel Del?"

"Sure… I thought maybe the chef served you some bad romescada — you've been quiet since," Paul's smile was hesitant as he caught the serious look on my face.

"Let's just say I ran into a ghost from the past, and I'm going to need your help; maybe your strong back, too." I handed him the new thumb drive. "Would you mind looking at this if you can find the time? It'll explain everything. Maybe we could talk about it later tonight?"

"It's a lazy day for me, so sure — drive safely and give my regards to Harry...," Paul said, and we kissed our goodbyes.

When I returned home, Paul greeted me at the front door. "Wow," he exclaimed. "I didn't see *that* coming…. If you're ready for a conversation, I'm all yours."

"Can't wait. It's been in the back of my mind all day. Let me drop Harry's notes on my desk and grab a Diet Coke — we can talk in the living room."

After we'd settled into our favorite spots on the couch, I handed Paul the baggie with Margorie's chewing gum.

"A gift? Oh, you shouldn't have," he joked. "I assume this is a DNA sample from Margorie proving she's Theresa? Do you want me to have it tested?"

"Not yet. Could you hold on to it for me and keep it from degrading? The techs keep logs of DNA testing, and if it *is* Theresa's, I don't think either of us wants to be associated with it until we've decided what we're going to do."

"Got it. I'll preserve this but under lock and key."

"Theresa knew enough about me to realize I'm married to the best forensics scientist in California." I smiled at Paul. "I don't think she'd give me the sample if she weren't who she claimed to be. She's a *lot* sharper than I gave her credit for."

We briefly discussed the video contents of the thumb drive. But we were at a point where we both knew they didn't matter as much as deciding what to do about them.

"This information alone will hurt so many people, Paul. It hands Seaver all the new reasonable doubt he needs to throw out at least his conviction on Theresa's death. That Theresa's alive and the claims she made, even if they turned out to be total BS, are enough to reopen that case."

"Not only for Theresa's murder," Paul agreed, "but every case for which any connection to Theresa's death or movement of her body was part of the presumed motive. That would be true for Seaver, Mason, possibly Christensen, and some Strike Response operatives — maybe, though more indirectly, Ainsworth."

"The streetwalker murder videos would make up for some of the harm to Seaver's prosecution. Theresa's case would go away, but he'd face two homicides to replace hers."

"Those fresh charges by themselves shouldn't affect the cases against Seaver's partners in crime," Paul added. "But if they can't find Theresa-slash-Margorie-slash-whatever and get her on the stand, I'm worried there's not enough to convict Seaver. I'm not sure the forensics from the sex worker's bodies will be strong enough. Seaver not only buried one of them nearly eight years ago but, if Margorie is believable, someone re-buried her later."

"If Margorie's claims are bogus and there is no second woman's body at the location she describes, the hurt this causes is all for naught. It could even be an intentional ploy by Theresa to help Seaver. I'd rather destroy everything Margorie gave me than fall victim to a Seaver scam again."

"I can't go on the record about any potential obstruction of justice," Paul said with a sideways grin. "Maybe you're wearing a wire." His expression then turned serious again. "If the Theresa stand-in's body *is* there, it creates an even bigger set of problems, but those we can address once they present themselves."

I balled up and then relaxed my fists. "I'm not comfortable giving the authorities any of this until I know that corpse is, or isn't, where Margorie says. Call it a reporter's duty to confirm her story, if nothing else. I want to go to that location and find out. I'm not talking about digging up the body. All I want to do is the bare minimum necessary to say 'yea' or 'nay' that someone likely buried human remains at that spot."

"A cadaver dog or ground-penetrating radar would do the job," Paul offered, "but I can't access either without explaining my need to a handler or a tech. I can't think of one we could trust to keep things quiet if that's the path we decide to take."

We looked at one another for a moment.

"Field trip, then?" Paul arched his eyebrows.

"Field trip."

I called the nanny to see if she'd work on Sunday. While we waited for her to arrive, Paul commandeered the driveway to pressure-wash the spade, rake, garden trowel, and other tools we'd take. "We don't want to contaminate the scene," he told me, ever the forensics professional.

He'd already made a morning run to the FBI offices, loading our Bronco EV with various forensic devices and equipment. Paul had gotten bunny suits for both of us, masks, gloves, shoe covers, cleaning brushes, and an evidence sifter box. There were evidence bags, a high-resolution camera, and a collection of crime-scene evidence scales to use when taking photos. He'd even brought a portable gas sniffer/chromatograph. The specialized machine detected the gasses given off by a decaying corpse.

Once we were ready to go, I punched into the Bronco's GPS the address off the service road that Google Maps showed as closest to the presumed burial site.

The location Margorie had given us was a few hundred feet from what was more of an open space between the trees than a road. We'd landed in an undeveloped wooded area of northern San Diego County. We reached a small clearing after picking our way through the trees, shrubs, and underbrush. Paul got down on all fours, his head turned sideways, looking across the space at grass-top level. "If buried remains aren't treated or encased in something durable," he explained, "the surface above the body eventually sinks a little as it decays. The shape of the depression is roughly the same as the decomposed organic matter's was originally."

"And we have a strong candidate...." He pointed at an area about a dozen yards north of us.

I hadn't realized how hot a forensic bunny suit could get until I donned mine and turned a few spadefuls of earth. It didn't bother Paul, who alternated between digging and taking photos of our progress.

But I'd be the lucky one on this day, though "luck" didn't feel like the appropriate term. I caught the tip of my spade on what I thought was a root. As I put my weight on the end of the handle for leverage to free it, a chunk of earth roughly the size of a football suddenly popped out of the ground.

And there it was — rotting and discolored, but without a doubt, the fringed and rounded edge of a thick rug with an Oriental design. Paul slid over and captured the GPS coordinates with his cell phone, taking several photos with the scales to show the comparative dimensions.

We both took a dozen steps back, unzipping the hoods of our jumpsuits and taking off our masks and gloves.

For me, as an investigator, there's always that little rush that builds in the moments you are closing in on a truth. Then comes an immense sense of victory, followed by an extended period when you can take satisfaction from your accomplishments.

But as I reached for Paul's hand, I became immediately aware that those feelings wouldn't last very long today. Already, I felt intense sorrow for all the victims and the many innocents whose suffering would only get worse because of that chunk of material poking up from the ground.

First and foremost, our discovery wouldn't return a single homicide victim to life.

Worse, Seaver and his henchmen would get new trials and appeals but likely would never have to face Theresa Seaver's or Sheryl Jansen's testimony. Sheryl's death from self-administered illicit drugs would undermine her recorded statements. The prosecution's original challenge, proving Theresa was dead, would turn into a classic Catch-22 situation. If they couldn't find Theresa — and I had my doubts — their case would instead have to rely on defending against the same woman being alive. Terrence would face a criminal investigation and likely charges for his role in helping Theresa hide.

There would be severe collateral damage, especially, and maybe rightfully, to investigators in law enforcement who did such poor work on the original cases. The careers of good people would be affected, some thrown under the bus, some perhaps ended, and reputations would suffer. That could include mine, although hopefully, the public would spare me the worst of it. I'd only been a messenger; still, that wouldn't stop some people from taking shots at me.

Paul and I bowed our heads and said a little prayer over the grave.

We had no real choice but to correct a wrongful conviction and prosecute the killer of the poor woman whose remains were before us. I pulled my cell phone from my hip pocket, tapping the third icon on my contacts list.

"Hi, Marci," I began, my tone somber. "Do you remember back when we thought we had James Seaver's murder of Theresa solved?"

"*Thought?*" Apprehension was suddenly apparent in Marci's voice. "Oh no, please...."

"You'll want to take a second look. And you'll need to send a forensic team to my location. There's another body."

I raised my eyes heavenward for a moment.

While Marci might not be happy with me, Dad would have understood.

THE WRITINGS OF
AVRIL MARIA SERENE

Did you enjoy reading *Six Degrees from Killing Brian*? Would you be willing to leave a review?

Honest reviews from you and others who have read my work help me write the kinds of books you will enjoy. I write to earn kudos from my readers, and your comments keep me on the right track – I appreciate your input more than you know. Your reviews also help new readers find quality books they will like. Please follow this link to leave your review:

https://www.amazon.com/review/create-review/?ie=UTF8&channel=glance-detail&asin=B0F2FWJJ48

Thank you,

Avril Maria Serene

THE WRITINGS OF
AVRIL MARIA SERENE

Look for these Debra Ann Wynn Mystery series books, arriving shortly: